CHIMERA

Praise for the Parasitology series

"An incredible, disturbingly plausible tale of
what happens to a world where medical treatments
have minds of their own" *io9 com*

"*Parasite* is believable, disturbing and only the beginning . . .
The realistic plot, coupled with interspersed events of hostility
from the infected, make for a suspense-ridden read" *SciFiNow*

"A creepy spine-tingler of a medical thriller" Charles Stross

"Interesting, morally ambiguous characters and some
genuinely unexpected plot developments . . . lives up
to its intriguing premise" *The List*

"Existing in a unique space somewhere between medical
thriller, psychological science fiction and body horror,
Parasite is a properly chilling read" *Eloquent Page*

"A riveting near-future medical thriller that reads like
the genetically engineered love child of Robin Cook
and Michael Crichton" John Joseph Adams

"*Para*   *nday Sport*

D0257049

BY MIRA GRANT

CHIMERA

PARASITOLOGY VOLUME 3

MIRA GRANT

orbit

www.orbitbooks.net

ORBIT

First published in Great Britain in 2015 by Orbit

13 5 7 9 10 8 6 4 2

Copyright © 2015 by Seanan McGuire

The moral right of the author has been asserted.

A CIP catalogue record for this book
is available from the British Library.

ISBN 978-0-356-50705-7

Printed and bound by CPI Group (UK) Ltd, Croydon, CR0 4YY

Papers used by Orbit are from well-managed forests
and other responsible sources.

MIX
Paper from
responsible sources
FSC® C104740

Orbit
An imprint of
Little, Brown Book Group
Carmelite House
50 Victoria Embankment
London EC4Y 0DZ

An Hachette UK Company
www.hachette.co.uk

www.orbitbooks.net

This book is dedicated to Theodora Hope Buchanan.

You saved me in Montreal. Someday I'll return the favor.
But probably not in Montreal.

INTERLUDE 0: ADAPTATION

If you ask the questions, best be sure you want to know.

—SIMONE KIMBERLEY,
DON'T GO OUT ALONE

This isn't what I wanted. Please believe me.
This isn't what I wanted at all.

COLONEL ALFRED MITCHELL, U3AMRIID

December 18, 2027: Time stamp 08:04.

[The recording quality is low, filled with static and choppy artifacts left over from the transcription process. Portions of the file have either not been uploaded or have been overwritten by some error in the codec. The lab in the picture is clearly mobile, clearly in a state of constant flux: Every piece of equipment is on a rolling stand of some sort. Some machines are supported by hospital gurneys. People rush by in the background, making no effort to turn away or conceal their faces. By this point in the outbreak, there is no longer any reason for them to fear having their identities revealed.]

MALE VOICE: We're recording.

[A woman in a wheelchair rolls into the center of the shot. She is blonde and abnormally pale, as if she has not seen the sun in some time. Dark circles surround her blue eyes, speaking of sleepless nights and long hours spent poring over data. She wears no makeup. Her hair has not been styled. A small whiteboard rests in her lap, covered in a string of apparently random letters and numbers. She holds it carefully, keeping the whole thing visible to the camera.]

DR. CALE: My name is Dr. Shanti Cale. If you are seeing this, you know who I am. I am either your creator or I am the cause of your empire's final dissolution. Either way, I am sorry. I did what I did because I thought I was making the world better. Maybe, in the long run, history will decide that I was in the right. But right here, right now, it's difficult to see that as anything other than a pretty dream in a world that isn't very forgiving of such things.

[Dr. Cale looks down at the whiteboard, and then back up at the camera. She smiles. It's a sad expression, tangled with old ghosts and unforgiving realities.]

DR. CALE: At the end of this introduction, the video feed will switch to a compressed data format. The data encryption code that I am currently showing you will allow you to extract and analyze this week's findings. Unencrypted, I will say this: The specimens recovered from the San Francisco, Sacramento, and Oakland reservoirs have all shown genetic similarities to the worm originally encoded for chimera Subject nine-A, code name "Persephone." Because of Persephone's unique ability to bond with her host without causing severe neurological damage, I recommend you stick to bottled water for the foreseeable future. All of you, I mean. I haven't been able to fully analyze these new worms. They may pose a danger to preexisting chimera whose integration was accomplished through less natural methods.

[Her smile twists, turning almost vicious.]

DR. CALE: Hear that, Sherman? You may have just fucked yourself. Putting her into the water supply probably seemed like a brilliant idea. It may have paid the wanted dividends initially, but you may well have created a bigger problem for us all down the line. You may have doomed the very people you were trying to protect. I know how that feels. Like mother, like son.

[Her smile fades entirely.]

DR. CALE: My next message is for Colonel Alfred Mitchell, of the United States Army Medical Research Institute of Infectious Diseases, or whoever may have taken his place. I know you are attempting to track and monitor my people. We are taking precautions to remain off your radar. You will not find us. You will not recover us. But you have someone of mine. You know who I am referring to. We are prepared to offer you a trade. Proof of life, and proof that she has not been harmed, and I will provide encrypted copies of my research on the modified *D. symbogenesis* organism. Return her to us, intact, and I will provide unencrypted copies of my research.

[Dr. Cale is calm, almost serene, despite her obvious physical exhaustion.]

DR. CALE: I have been accused of being a traitor to the human race because I refused to take sides when my children began turning against their creators. Me, who made them, not Dr. Steven Banks, who altered them recklessly and without concern for what his changes might mean. Not Dr. Richard Jablonsky, who died knowing what he had unleashed, without contacting the authorities or sharing his knowledge with the world. Me. Just me, alone. Well, fine. If you want me to be a traitor to the human race, then I will be. I will gather my children close, and I will see them through this storm. Return my daughter to me, and I will help you fight the chimera who think more of themselves than they do of humanity. Keep her, and I'll let you burn.

[Her smile returns, terrible and thin as the blade of a razor.]

DR. CALE: My name is Dr. Shanti Cale. I am the traitor you have ordered me to be, and I am a better monster than you deserve. The broken doors are open. You will never make it home.

[The picture goes briefly to a negative image, static chewing at the edges of the screen. Then it is completely gone, replaced by a several-megabyte flood of data. This onslaught of encoded information continues for ninety seconds before the visual feed abruptly terminates. The audio continues for a few seconds more, then ends.]

[End report.]

December 3, 2027: Time stamp 23:57.

This is not the point of no return.

The point of no return is a philosophical construct, an idea that looks beautiful on paper or in a computer model, but which cannot hold up under the bearing strain of reality. The point of no return is reached in a thousand places at the same time, a thousand little fractal iterations all coming together and collapsing until the center cannot hold. It's chaos theory given flesh, and it can't be stopped.

I wasn't there when the center failed to hold, but I understand why it meant as much as it did. This is not the point of no return. But it is the only point that matters.

Claudia Anderson was dying.

The people who had custody of her body didn't know her name, and wouldn't have cared if they'd been told. They didn't know that she'd been top of her class at Berkeley, that she'd been a competitive chess player since she was eleven years old, or that she had liked to attend comic book conventions wearing costumes that she had made herself in the privacy of her rent-controlled condo's spare room. None of that mattered anymore. In a way, none of it had really mattered since she signed her NDAs and employment forms in SymboGen's HR office, starting her life down the path that would inevitably place her here, lying motionless, attached to as many machines as they could jam into her veins, slipping farther and farther away.

The people who worked to save her didn't know her name, because it wasn't hers anymore: Claudia Anderson was dying, but in a very real way Claudia Anderson was already dead. They worked tirelessly to save a girl named "Anna," a girl who looked at the world with eyes that were both new and old, innocent and educated beyond her brief weeks in the body she had tried to claim as her own. Anna had shoved Claudia to the edges of her own mind, and then she had shoved more, until everything that had been Claudia had toppled off the cliff into nothingness. All that remained was her body, an empty shell that had become a haunted house in the hands of its new owner.

Claudia Anderson was dead and alive at the same time, falling ever farther, falling too far to make it home.

She had no hospital to sustain her, no gleaming modern facility where miracles could be performed and the course of nature could be reversed. Her bed was a narrow cot being wheeled through endless halls, with a medical team that worked to save her even as they worked to save themselves. She could never have been their first priority, and if she had still been capable of anything as complicated as gratitude, she would have been grateful. Death had been held in abeyance for too long. It was time to go.

Inside Claudia Anderson's skull, a war was being waged.

Rather than recognizing the *D. symbogenesis* tapeworm as an ally, the body was responding to it as what it actually was: an invader, an intruder designed to disrupt the natural course of things. Immune responses were mustered, and Claudia's temperature had been spiking steadily for hours as her body sought to repel the invasion. Unable to understand what was happening, the implant—Anna—reacted by burrowing deeper into the tissues around her, damaging them irreparably in the process. It was a chain reaction too far gone to be stopped, no matter how hard the attending medical professionals worked.

Maybe if they had been able to stop running. Maybe if they had had access to a better hospital. The world was built on a scaffold of "maybe," and it was crumbling down around their ears, leaving them standing on ground that had never been capable of supporting their weight.

"Dr. Cale, we're losing her."

"I need an epi!"

"I'm not getting a response."

"We can't find a pulse."

"Call it."

The time of death was shortly after midnight on December 4, 2027. Claudia Anderson would not be mourned.

Neither would Anna.

STAGE 0: MUTATION

Destroy your files before you leave your office. Deletion is not sufficient. Destroy the computer. Shred and burn the paper records. Leave nothing behind. It's over.

—FINAL SYMBOGEN INTERNAL MEMO

Is there a point when all this will start being fair?

—SAL MITCHELL

We are receiving reports of infection in individuals who had been previously confirmed free of the SymboGen implants (see attached personnel screening report), and have already completed a full course of preventative antiparasitics. As our doctors have tested these drugs, and found them fully effective against D. symbogenesis *in both egg and cyst form, we must assume that the worms are finding their way into our people through some other mechanism. I do not know what this mechanism may be. My troops do not know what this mechanism may be.*

We need help. We need support. We need more bodies on the ground. We are on the verge of losing the San Francisco Bay Area. If this is a location you are prepared to surrender to the enemy, pull us out. If it's not, give us the support that we need and deserve, as representatives of both your armed forces and your medical community.

Don't just leave us here to die.

—MESSAGE FROM COLONEL ALFRED MITCHELL, USAMRIID, TRANSMITTED TO THE WHITE HOUSE ON DECEMBER 3, 2027

I let her go.

On some level, I must have known what she was planning to do. She's always been conflicted. Human or parasite; good

*little girl or independent adult woman; Sal or Sally. I walked
with her right into the physical representation of that conflict,
and when it offered her the chance to save everyone by giving
up herself, I expected her not to take it. I thought she'd be...*

*I don't know whether I thought she'd be stronger, or
whether I thought she'd be weaker. I don't really know anything anymore, except that she's gone, and I have no idea
how we're going to get her back.*

God, Sal, I'm sorry.

—FROM THE NOTES OF DR. NATHAN KIM, NOVEMBER 2027

Chapter 1

NOVEMBER 2027

They kept me inside an unused office for an hour while Colonel Mitchell and Dr. Banks went over what had happened at Dr. Cale's lab. Three soldiers with USAMRIID patches on their shoulders stood over me, guns in their hands and eyes narrowed with justified suspicion. I looked calmly back at them, trying to pretend that my hands weren't cuffed behind my back, that my boyfriend and my allies and my dog weren't being escorted across San Francisco by soldiers who had no reason to let them live. Colonel Mitchell was never going to let me go. If his people wanted to shoot my friends in the head and leave them among the sleepwalkers and the deceased, what was going to stop them? Not me. And certainly not the ghost of Sally Mitchell.

It was starting to occur to me that I would never know if he broke his word and killed them all. I had nothing left to bargain with.

One of the men made eye contact with me. It may have been an accident, but it still happened. I seized the moment, offering him a small, strained smile. I've always looked young for my age—Sally left me with an excellent bone structure to call my own, and when people searched my eyes for experience, they didn't usually find it, since technically I'm only about eight years old. Hopefully he would read my smile as shy, the sort of thing he might receive from any human prisoner under the same conditions.

He paled, and turned his face away when he realized I was looking at him. I let my smile die. These men either already knew who—and what—I really was or they knew me as their superior officer's daughter, and hence dangerous in a whole different way. I was a mission objective to them, nothing more and nothing less. As long as they brought me back alive, they would win.

Keeping my face neutral, I looked around the office for what must have been the hundredth time. It was small, corporate, and virtually pristine. The only personal touches were a Disneyland snow globe on one corner of the desk and a picture frame next to the computer. The frame faced away from me; if it held anything other than the blank paper from the frame store, I would never know. I felt a strong, irrational urge to ask them to turn that picture around, to let me see, but I didn't say anything. It was going to be one more unsolved little mystery in a world that was full of them, and had been since the day I made my "miraculous recovery" in the hospital, coming back to life after the doctors had already pronounced me dead.

Only I wasn't the one who'd been pronounced dead. I wasn't the one who'd suffered a massive seizure while driving and steered my car into a bus. I wasn't the one who'd concealed important facts about my own medical history in order to protect my father, whose military career depended upon him not being revealed as a secret epileptic. All those things had been done to and by Sally Mitchell, the human girl whose body I now called my own. I had earned it. I was the one who put her brain back together, however instinctually, creating something that I could use to sustain the body she had left behind. I was the one who had to clean up her messes. Including this one.

My name is Sal. I was born in a lab in the basement of the SymboGen building, where geneticists who thought they were being clever combined a little bit of this, a little bit of that, and a whole lot of terrible idea to make a tailored "biological implant" for Sally Mitchell, one that would naturally secrete the antiseizure medication she needed kept off the books and outside of the public eye. I was placed in her body when I was still an egg smaller than the head of a pin, hatching in the hot warm dark of her digestive tract and growing to maturity there. I hadn't known what I was or where I came from, because those were concepts that didn't matter to a tapeworm—and all pretty language and marketing nonsense aside, that's what I was. A tapeworm, a member of the genetically engineered species *Diphyllobothrium symbogenesis*, designed to improve and promote human health, human well-being, human welfare.

What my creators didn't bank on was the fact that all living things will seek to improve their own circumstances, and for me—for all the worms like me—that meant taking control of our own lives. I had been migrating through Sally's body at the time of the accident, which is how I was able to survive the gross physical damage to her abdomen that had crushed at least part of my own long, threadlike body. While she was hooked to life-support systems and her parents were exploring other options, I was working my way through the bones at the back of her skull, following an instinct I didn't understand until I was able to connect myself to her brain. Normally, that was where things would have gone wrong. Very few worms, even ones as carefully designed as I was, can fully integrate with their human hosts. But I was made to prevent seizures, and I integrated with minimal physiological issues. For all intents and purposes, I *became* Sally Mitchell the first time that I ordered her body to open its eyes.

For literally years, that's what I believed I was. I thought I was a human girl suffering from traumatic amnesia, and not a tapeworm wearing a human body like a fancy dress. I let Sally's parents and Sally's doctors and Sally's therapists try to make me into someone I had never been and had no real interest in being. Nothing any of them had to tell me about her made her seem like an appealing person to transform myself into, but still, I tried. I tried for their sakes, and because they said they loved me, and I believed them. How could I have done any different?

They were my family. They were all I had. That's what I'd thought for a long, long time, and now that I was finally starting to understand what they'd really been to me—what they had done to me, all in the name of trying to bring Sally back—I was right back in their hands.

Or at least, I was right back in the hands of Sally's father, Colonel Mitchell, and since he was the only member of the Mitchell family who had ever given signs of understanding what was going on with me, that didn't make me feel any better. His wife, Sally's mother, hadn't known, I was sure of that, and I was almost as sure that his other daughter, Joyce, hadn't known either. She would have told her mother. She would have told *me*. Instead, she had told me how much nicer I'd become since my accident, and how happy she was that we were finally friends, instead of just people who happened to be related.

No. Joyce couldn't have known. But Colonel Mitchell had known from the beginning that I wasn't his daughter. He had looked into the eyes of an alien creature, of a chimera born from the union of tapeworm and human, and he had decided that the appropriate thing to do was try to brainwash it into becoming human after all. Brainwash *me* into becoming human after all.

And now I was his, to do with as he pleased. That had been the cost of saving Nathan, Fishy, and Beverly...and as I remembered the looks on their faces when I turned away from them, I realized I wasn't sorry. I had lived the first six years of my life going along the path of least resistance and letting other people make my decisions for me. I'd been allowing my tapeworm nature to dictate my decisions. I was a tailored symbiont; I existed to be led. But I was here because I had stood up and said I would go if my friends could be set free...and that was an impulse from the human side of me, wasn't it? That was me struggling to become a person who *acts*, a person who controls her own fate.

I needed to be that person now. Because the person I had always been wasn't going to cut it anymore.

The men who had been assigned to watch me snapped to attention as the office door swung open. Colonel Mitchell stood framed in the doorway, holding his hands folded behind his back.

"Who opened the door?" I blurted, before I could think better of it.

Colonel Mitchell blinked at me. "That's your first question? Not 'What happens next' or 'Where are we going' or 'Did your friends make it back to their transport,' but 'Who opened the door'?"

"You could lie to me if I asked you any of those questions, but the big thing right now is yes, who opened the door? You can't have moved your hands that fast. You'd have to be a wizard, and there's no such thing as wizards."

"That's not what you said when you were a little girl," he

said, stepping into the room. Another soldier stepped in right behind him, answering my original question. Colonel Mitchell ignored him. All his attention was on me, even though it didn't feel like he was looking at me at all. He was seeing Sally. Poor, dead, long-buried Sally.

"You checked the mailbox for your Hogwarts letter every day for an entire year," he continued. He walked toward me as he spoke, one hand dipping into his pocket. "You were so sure that your owl was coming, and you told me over and over about how you were going to be the greatest witch of your generation. Do you remember which House you hoped to be Sorted into?"

"I don't know what you're talking about," I said. I was supposed to be keeping up the pretense of being Sally Mitchell, somehow returned from the grave and reclaiming ownership of her own body. That didn't mean that I could somehow recall family trivia and jokes that she had shared with her father long before I arrived on the scene. "We always lived in the same house."

If Colonel Mitchell was disappointed by my answer, he didn't show it. "I'll see about finding you copies of the Harry Potter books," he said, moving behind me and taking hold of my wrists. I stiffened, but he was just undoing my handcuffs. They hadn't been tight enough to hurt. There was still a feeling of glorious freedom as they fell away. "I know you've had trouble with dyslexia since your accident, but they're available in audiobook form. You can listen to them, and then we can talk again."

I bit my lip to keep myself from laughing. The world was crumbling outside the building where we stood. People were dying by the thousands, maybe by the millions; cities were being deserted, and the two sides of my heritage—the humans and the tapeworms—were destroying each other at an unspeakable pace. The human tendency to focus on the inconsequential to avoid focusing on the traumas at hand could be completely ridiculous at times. It was a habit I'd picked up from the humans who'd raised me, but that didn't mean I really understood it.

The slow, constant beating of the drums in my ears reminded me to stay on guard, no matter how amused I was. They were my compass through a world that seemed determined to destroy me, and they weren't going to allow me to relax. Not one bit.

"Okay," I said, keeping my voice meek and low. He seemed to be in good spirits; whatever Dr. Banks had said to him, it hadn't been enough to make him lose his temper. I decided to risk another question. "*Did* my friends make it back to their transport okay?"

He paused before walking in front of me, a solemn expression on his face and my newly removed handcuffs dangling from one hand. He held them up like they were a reminder that I needed to stay mindful of my position and the limitations it entailed. "I have no idea whether your friends made it back to their starting point, and to be honest, I don't care. A group of my people escorted them into the streets, and maintained visual contact until they were approximately one mile from this location. Then my people came back here. The goals of this mission were to retrieve you and to harvest certain essential data from Dr. Cale's research before she moved again. Both these things have been accomplished."

I frowned. "How did you get that data? We didn't give Dr. Banks anything. Dr. Cale had him under guard from the time he stepped into the building. She even took his hard drive away, and we're sure he didn't have any tracers or trackers, or—"

Colonel Mitchell was looking at me oddly. The soldiers who shared the room with us weren't looking at me at all. I stopped talking. I was showing too much interest in the people I had allowed to leave me behind. That sort of thing would indicate that I wasn't as committed to being his daughter as I was claiming to be.

"I just, I talked to him, but I was still pretending, you know?" I made my eyes as big as I could, trying to sell the part. "To be Sal, and to think that they were on my side, not on the side of the parasites. So I know how thoroughly they searched him."

"They didn't search him for wireless sniffers, or for download signals," said Colonel Mitchell. "If they had, they might have found out how much of their data he was copying. But that's none of your concern. I'm glad to see that you can still care about people, even if you're caring about the wrong ones. No matter. That will change soon enough. Gentlemen, prepare her for transport." Then he turned, and walked back toward the door.

He took the handcuffs with him, which meant I could put my hands up to ward the soldiers away when they started closing on me. Their faces were grim masks, efficient and cold. "No, please," I said, not knowing what they were about to do, but knowing that whatever it was, I wasn't going to enjoy it— not when they were looking at me like that.

I was so focused on the ones in front of me that I never saw the one who slipped behind me with the Taser. Electricity arced through my body, stunning and scrambling everything, and then I hit the floor, and if the pain continued, I didn't know about it anymore.

Everything was warm and dark and perfect. The drums hammered ceaselessly away in the background, and I felt like I was floating on a hot tide of weightlessness and peace. Everything would be perfect forever if the world could just stay exactly the way it was, filled with comforting darkness and the sound of drums.

Only no. Everything *wasn't* perfect, because while I was

warm and I was dark, this wasn't the hot warm dark: this wasn't the comforting sea that had buoyed me up since before I knew what it was to be a person. This was something different, and "different" was another word for "dangerous," especially now that things were changing again, now that I was back in the hands of people who would use me for their own ends and not allow me to be who and what I really was. Dr. Cale was a scary woman, and the things she wanted weren't always things it was safe or reasonable to want, but she'd never tried to force me to be anything other than myself, whatever that was. She wasn't safe. She was safer than this.

With comprehension came the return of consciousness, and with the return of consciousness came the slowly growing awareness of my body, coming back to me an inch at a time, like the power being turned on in an office building. It wasn't the worst comparison. The connections between me and the body that had been Sally Mitchell were strong, built by science and reinforced by biology, but they weren't as natural as a human brain's connection to its own body. Sometimes things were slower than they were supposed to be. I'd attributed that to my accident, right up until I learned that it was really a case of mind over matter—my mind, Sally's abandoned matter.

When enough of the power had come back on, I opened my eyes and blinked up at a dark, oddly shaped ceiling. There were lights there, uncovered bulbs that were so bright they hurt, yet somehow didn't manage to illuminate most of what was around them. It was a senseless design. I didn't understand it, and so I closed my eyes again, willing myself to return to the weightlessness and the dark.

Something nudged me in the ribs. "You dead, girl? Or worse, you turning into one of those *things*? We'll kill you before you can hurt any of us, so don't you even think about jumping up and going for our throats."

"I don't think you can reason with monsters, Paul," said a

female voice. It was farther away than the first voice; wherever we were, it was large enough to include things like "distance," even if there wasn't all that much of it. "If she's going to rip your throat out, she's going to do it no matter how much you kick her. Hell, maybe she's going to do it *because* you kicked her. I'd go for your throat if you kept prodding me with your filthy-ass foot."

"Shut up," said the man. The nudge to my ribs was repeated. Based on what the woman had said, he was nudging me with his foot. I tried to decide whether I cared, or whether caring would be too much work. Part of me still felt like I was floating, disconnected from myself.

I'd never been hit with a Taser before. I decided I never wanted to be hit with one ever again. The electricity had been enough to disrupt me in ways that were terrifying and invasive at the same time, and I wasn't sure how long it would be before I felt like myself again. Too long. Even one minute would be too long.

"Look, lady, we don't actually think they'd throw you in here with us if you were getting sick or some such shit, but we'd really, really appreciate it if you'd do something to indicate that you're not actually a mindless killing machine getting ready to feast on our tasty flesh, okay? It's the polite thing to do."

"Don't lecture the semiconscious woman on how to be polite," said the woman.

"Shut up, Carrie," said the man.

My jaw seemed to be working again. I opened and closed my mouth a few times, reacquainting myself with the motion, before I took the deepest breath my chest could contain and forced it out, resulting in a thin squeaking sound, like a bike tire in need of air. That didn't seem like enough, so I did it again, squeaking with a bit more vehemence.

"The zombies moan, she's squeaking, she's fine," said the woman.

"They're not zombies," said Paul. "Zombies exist in movies and in Haitian folklore. They don't wander around the streets of San Francisco attacking people." I tensed, expecting another prod to my ribs. It didn't come. Instead, a hand was slipped gently under my shoulder while another gripped my wrist, tugging me into a sitting position. "Poor kid's been zapped."

"Those soldiers are animals," said the woman—Carrie, Paul had called her Carrie. Both of them had names. There was something comforting about realizing that, like they had just become real people. And since they were talking to me like I was a real person, that meant their reality was transitive: They existed, and so did I.

Electric shocks were definitely bad for me, if this was how they left me feeling. I moved my jaw again, trying to tell them my name, and succeeded only in making another squeaking sound. My eyes were still closed. I willed them to open. To my sublime relief, they did, and I found myself looking at a skinny woman with bright green hair, folded in on herself like a piece of origami as she sat on the long bench that ran the length of the wall behind her. No, it wasn't a wall: We were moving. The feeling of weightlessness was coming from the vibrations that passed up through the floor.

As soon as I recognized why I felt so comfortably weightless, the feeling stopped. Sometimes awareness had its downside.

The woman tilted her head, looking me thoughtfully up and down before she said, "Clean, looks well fed, decent haircut… where did they find you, honey? Were you in a closed-off survivor's alcove? Why the hell did you leave?"

"There could be a lot of explanations," said Paul. "Don't pressure her. Hey, I know you can't talk yet, but do you think you could stand if I helped you? I want to get you off the floor. There's no telling when they're going to throw somebody else in here, and I don't want them to land on top of you."

We were in a truck. This was a covered truck, like the ones

the Army used for troop movements. I'd been in one of them once before, shortly after my accident, when they were in the process of transferring all my care over to SymboGen. Colonel Mitchell—who had been insisting I call him "Dad" back then, a habit that I probably needed to get back into if I wanted him to believe I was really his daughter returned from the dead, and not the genetically engineered tapeworm that had stolen her body—had commandeered one of the trucks from the USA-MRIID base to move me and the machines that were dedicated to monitoring my health over to SymboGen's San Francisco office.

I had been younger then; I hadn't possessed language yet, or fully grasped the complexities of what my newly human mind kept trying to tell me. But I'd been integrating faster than a human child, building on all the work Sally Mitchell had already done to grow neurons and form connections, and my recall of those early days never faded the way a human infant's recall does. I remembered looking at the walls and finding them soothingly dark in comparison to the white ones at the hospital. I remembered wanting the light to go away. And I remembered Colonel Mitchell holding my hand, telling me it was going to be all right, that they were going to find a solution, that I was going to come back to him just as good as new.

He hadn't really talked to me that way after the move. I wondered whether that was when he'd learnt about who—what—I was, and that his daughter was never coming back to him. But that thought just conjured more questions. He *knew* I was a tapeworm. He *knew* I had shoved Sally out of her own mind, assuming that she'd been left to push aside: The accident had been bad enough, and the brain damage had been severe enough, that it was entirely possible she had been gone before I even managed to squirm through the remnants of her skull.

If he knew those things, why was he asking me to pretend she could have come back?

With Paul's arms supporting me and pulling when my balance threatened to give way, I was able to climb shakily to my feet and be moved, one halting step at a time, to the waiting bench. By the time we finished the process, I was feeling more like I actually lived inside my own body. I moved my jaw again. This time, what came out was a croaky but distinct "Thank you."

"It's no problem." Paul let go of my arm and retreated to sit down next to Carrie, who unfolded herself just enough to hook one foot under his leg and place one elbow on his shoulder. It seemed less possessive than it was simply a means of seeking comfort in a bad situation, the way the dogs would sometimes pile together when there was a rainstorm. A mammalian instinct, written through the DNA all the way to the masters of the world.

I wondered whether I would have learnt to offer comfort that way, given enough time, given the luxury of learning things on my own and not learning things for the sake of emulating the dead. I liked to snuggle with Nathan, but it was never a matter of comforting him: It was all about comforting myself. It was a way of being close, of allowing for the part of me that was always going to be a little unhappy in wide-open spaces. I was a mammal and I wasn't a mammal, all at the same time. I still didn't know what was natural for me and what was learned, and maybe I never would.

"They picked us up down by the ballpark," said Carrie, mistaking my contemplation for personal interest. "It was stupid. We should never have left the office, but we were running low on bottled water, and Paul remembered that the coaches kept a supply for the players. We both figured we'd be able to get in and get out without anyone noticing us."

"We didn't count on an Army sweep happening in the same area," said Paul wryly. "It didn't make any sense. They'd cleaned out all the major hot spots last week. We should have been totally fine."

My heart sank. It made *perfect* sense, because the ballpark was only a few blocks away from the Ferry Building. We had made land there. We had stirred up the sleepwalkers there. If anything was going to trigger a response from the military, it was the arrival of an unauthorized vessel from the other side of the Bay. These people had been caught in a dragnet that I helped trigger, and nothing was going to save them now.

"Do you know where they're taking us?" My voice still sounded rusty, like part of me was still remembering how to talk.

"A quarantine facility first, so they can triple-check us for signs of infection," said Paul. "After that..." His expression turned grim. He glanced to Carrie before leaning over and placing a kiss gently on her forehead. She started to cry, burying her face against his shoulder. He looked back to me, and said, much more quietly, "They're going to take us to the Pleasanton encampment. They're going to put us with all the other 'survivors' of this little science experiment, and fuck us if we don't like that idea."

I frowned. "Why don't you like that idea?" Being under USAMRIID's control didn't sit well with me for a lot of reasons, but those reasons were entirely my own. Paul and Carrie seemed like reasonable people. I couldn't imagine they had the same sorts of issues with my—with Sally's—father.

To my surprise, Paul's expression faded slowly into one of pure pity. Carrie buried her face deeper into his shoulder, like she was trying to keep herself from needing to face me. "You mean...you don't know about Pleasanton?"

"I've heard the Pleasanton facility mentioned a few times.

I understand not wanting to be locked up, but the sleepwalkers are dangerous. Isn't it a good thing not to have them in the same place?" The sleepwalkers were even dangerous to me. I had scars on one wrist, and a whole lot of nightmares, from my encounters with them.

My encounters with the other chimera—Sherman in particular—had left me with even more nightmares. Sherman thought he knew what was best for me, and didn't see a need to let me have a vote. He had performed surgery on me without my consent, removing samples of my core. He could have killed me. He hadn't hesitated. So I guess species wasn't as big a deal as I tried to make it out to be.

"The Pleasanton 'facility,' as you put it, doesn't exist. We're going to an encampment. Do you understand the difference?"

I did, a bit. A facility was large and clean and filled with chrome surfaces and clean glass windows. SymboGen was a facility. Even the candy factory that had served as Dr. Cale's temporary home was a facility, albeit a more sugar-soaked one than was necessarily normal. An encampment...I wasn't completely sure what that was, but it sounded bad. "Not really," I admitted.

"They fenced off half the neighborhoods in the city," said Carrie, rolling her face slowly toward me, so that she could watch me as she spoke. She was crying, and her tears drew mascara trails down her cheeks, like she was trying to outline her own bones. "Then they went in and cleaned the sleepwalkers out. House by house. I know a woman who managed to escape, before they reinforced the fences. She said that the Army men removed the bodies, but they didn't really make any effort to clean up the bloodstains. They're putting people in houses that still have bloodstains on the walls."

"Oh," I said blankly. I didn't share the normal human aversion for the bodily secretions of others. All living things were just a combination of fluid and rigid structures. Everything bled; everything defecated. I didn't want to play in sewage, and I was as sensitive to foul smells as anyone with a human olfactory system, but blood generally dried dark and mostly scentless. It shouldn't have been an issue. Not in a rational world.

But humans didn't live in a rational world, did they? Not really. I was human enough not to live in a rational world any more than they did. I just sometimes faked it a little better, because I'd been faking it for my entire life.

Carrie appeared to take my confusion for concern, because she said, "They swear everything's been cleaned to within a 'reasonable standard,' and that no one's going to get sick from being in those houses, but it's not the houses that people need to worry about. It's the other people!"

"They're sleeping upwards of twelve adults to a single-family home. The only way you get more space is if you have children or disabled adults: Then you'll be put in private apartments in what used to be the bad part of town," said Paul grimly.

"Pleasanton has a bad part of town?" The question sounded incredibly naive. I still wanted to know the answer. Pleasanton was one of those places that had always struck me as being as innocuous as its name: sleepy and suburban and filled with malls and car dealerships and families, not close enough to San Francisco to really be subjected to population crush, not far enough away to be suffering from a bad economy. Maybe it wasn't a perfect place to live, but it had always looked that way from a distance.

"The slightly less good part of town," amended Paul. "It's the bad part of town now."

"Everything is the bad part of town now," said Carrie.

"I don't understand," I said. "Aren't you safer there, with people who you know aren't infected?"

"Those things will just kill you," said Paul. "It's an awful way to die, but that's all that happens. You change or you die. Humans are worse. Humans are terrifying."

"Humans will hurt you because they want what you have, not because it's their instinct," said Carrie. "We should have stayed hidden. We should have stayed safe. We knew how to survive where we were. Here…here, we don't know anything." She buried her face in Paul's shoulder again, and none of us said anything. It felt like there was nothing left for us to say.

Break the mirror; it tells lies.
Learn to live in your disguise.
Everything is changing now, it's too late to go back.
Caterpillar child of mine,
This was always life's design,
Here at last you'll find the things you can't afford to
    lack.

The broken doors are ready, you are very nearly home.
My darling child, be careful now, and don't go out
    alone.

—FROM *DON'T GO OUT ALONE*, BY SIMONE KIMBERLEY,
PUBLISHED 2006 BY LIGHTHOUSE PRESS.
CURRENTLY OUT OF PRINT.

*I don't know why I keep pretending this book is going to be
published someday. "Dr. Cale, the woman who betrayed the
human race, tells all in her explosive memoir." That's not
exactly something that's going to fly off store shelves: not
unless we're talking about 300 pages of "I'm sorry, I'm sorry,
I'm so sorry" over and over again, and as I discussed earlier in
this volume, I am not sorry. I've never been sorry. I've said
it—Lord, have I said it—but I've never meant it. That just*

isn't how I'm made. When my parents combined the genetic material that would become Surrey Kim, they included genes for brilliance, for ambition, for curiosity... but they forgot to include the genes that would have taught me regret. What's done is done. We live with it, and we move on.

What's done is done. I have learned to live with it. Now is the time when we move on, and when we ask the world, "Well? What's next?" Because there has to be a form of equilibrium somewhere on the horizon: There has to be at point at which the systems currently in motion find a way to rest. There has to be.

—FROM *CAN OF WORMS: THE AUTOBIOGRAPHY OF SHANTI CALE, PHD.* AS YET UNPUBLISHED.

Chapter 2

NOVEMBER 2027

We stopped three times during our drive. Each time, the back of the truck was pulled open by a group of grim-faced men in uniform, who would then proceed to throw more passengers into the vehicle with as much compassion as the people at the animal shelter where I used to work showed to the sacks of dog food. They added one passenger at our first stop; three at our second; and finally seven people at our third, including a woman who was wrapped almost completely around a toddler, limbs rigid, like she was forcing her body to act as a human cage. Of the eleven people who were thrown into the truck, only the toddler hadn't been hit with a Taser. She sat on the bench, crying huge, silent tears while the rest of us helped her mother uncurl and shake herself back into the moment.

None of the people who had been thrown in with us shared

my slow recovery from the shock. They weren't *happy*—I don't think anyone could be *happy* about getting zapped with that much raw voltage—but they sat up quickly, getting their bearings back. One of the men threw up in the corner of the truck before slinking guiltily back to sit beside the woman and the toddler. Most of them were crying. No one looked happy to be there.

One by one, the newcomers revealed how they'd been caught. Looting a supermarket that still had an active alarm system. Running from a pack of sleepwalkers in a public park. Trying to find a CVS that had children's cold medicine on the shelves. That last was the young woman with the toddler. She glanced guiltily at the child as she spoke, as if she was questioning the wisdom of trading freedom for cold medication.

None of them had any possessions beyond the clothes on their backs, not even the little girl, which seemed odd to me. When I saw children that age, they almost always seemed to have a doll or a toy truck or stuffed bear. This little girl had nothing, and she clung to the woman she was with like she was afraid that even this last scrap of comfort would be taken away from her.

"No one's managed to escape in weeks," moaned one of the men, closing his eyes as he slumped against the wall of the truck. "They've shored up the fences and increased the patrols. There's no way anyone is getting out of there once they go in."

"So we escape from the quarantine facility," said Paul stoutly. "I'm sure it's possible."

"Oh, it's possible," said the first man. "Some lady escaped from the quarantine facility months ago, and killed almost a dozen men getting to the exit. They have instructions at the quarantine facility now. They start with 'shoot,' and they end with 'to kill.'"

I managed not to squirm, even though I knew I was probably the woman he was talking about. I had been held in a quarantine facility the first time USAMRIID had captured me. Sherman had somehow managed to infiltrate the team that transported me to the facility, and hadn't even waited a day before he'd come for me. He'd come with a full team. One of them, Ronnie, had been dealing with some anger issues. He was the one who had killed those soldiers. Not me, even though they'd died so that Sherman could have me all to himself.

At the time, I'd been grateful for the rescue. I'd even stayed grateful once I was aware of the lives it had cost—at least for a while. Sherman had a way of stomping the gratitude out of people.

It wasn't a surprise that Sherman had been able to infiltrate USAMRIID: In some ways, it would have been more of a surprise if he hadn't. Sherman Lewis was a man with a talent for getting into places where he wasn't needed, wanted, or allowed to be. He'd started when he got into the skull of the body he inhabited. Like me, Sherman was a chimera. Unlike me, he couldn't access the hot warm dark, and he hadn't been able to take his body unassisted; he had been Dr. Cale's second surgical protégé, following on the heels of my eldest brother and her first successful chimera, Adam. Sherman had been intended to show her that the process was stable and dependable and could be repeated. He'd shown all those things.

He'd also been the first one to show her that her children could be—would be—disloyal. He'd left her lab immediately after Sally Mitchell's accident and had been waiting for me at SymboGen when my head finally cleared. I'd known Sherman for literally years before I'd become aware of my own nature. He'd been my friend and my guide through a world that was bigger and more complicated than it had any right to be. I'd always felt safe in his presence, like Sherman of all people would always understand what I was dealing with, and better, like he would be able to explain it all to me. He *got* me in a way that very few people ever could. Finding out the real reasons why had been, in some ways, a greater betrayal than finding out that I wasn't human. He'd known all along that I was his sister in petri dish and production line, and he'd never said a word. Not until it was profitable for him.

Sherman was playing a very long game, and the necessary conditions for victory involved the destruction of mankind and the replacement of their rule with his own. Dr. Cale wasn't going to let him do that. Neither, if I could help it, was I.

The conversation in the truck was continuing, growing more urgent by the minute. "What about the transfer point?" demanded the woman with the toddler. "They have to move us from the truck to the quarantine, right? We can run then. We can just break away and run."

"Bang fucking bang, Gloria," said one of the men she'd been captured with.

She shot him a poisonous glare. "Not in front of the kid," she snapped.

The little girl wasn't originally hers, then. That explained the differences in their appearance—the child was at least three shades darker than the woman, which could have been a matter of paternity, adoption, or recessive genes, but was more likely, under the circumstances, to mean the woman was taking care of a child whose parents had been killed. Or who had started killing. SymboGen implants were cleared for all humans, all ages, genders, and weights. There was a good chance the little girl had an implant. I watched her across the truck, looking for signs that her eyes were coming unfocused or going cold. I wished I had a dog. They could accurately predict when someone was about to go sleepwalker—something that neither humans nor chimera could do.

USAMRIID wasn't using dogs. I wondered why not, and whether they had even realized how useful dogs could be when it came to catching the early stages of a tapeworm takeover of their host body. I decided just as quickly that I wasn't going to tell them. If they were really reacting to all outbreaks and escape attempts with deadly force, regardless of the situation, I didn't want to give them any more ammunition than I absolutely had to. Dogs could be used to capture more humans, and ferret out more sleepwalkers who weren't hurting anyone. And I didn't trust them to take *care* of their dogs. I wasn't going to be responsible for opening a new avenue of animal abuse.

And none of that mattered. They had me now. One way or another, I was going to wind up giving them a lot of ammunition. The only question was whether I was going to answer their questions honestly, giving them ammunition that could actually be used, or whether I was going to start lying to them.

"She doesn't care if I cuss," said the man. "Her own mom tried to chew her face off and left her stuck with the babysitter. A few swear words aren't going to fuck up her world any worse than it already is."

The little girl moaned and buried her face against the woman's—Gloria's—shoulder. It was a human sound, filled with confusion and pain, rather than the hollow hunger of the sleepwalkers. Most of the people around us still flinched, and more than a few of them glared at the man, like he was solely responsible for their growing sensitivity to such things.

"Don't look at me like that," he said, settling against the truck wall. "The world is fucked up. We did that. We broke it because we were too lazy to take our allergy meds and monitor our own health. All I'm doing is trying to stay alive in the pieces that remain."

"Fuck you," said Carrie dully.

"Please," said Gloria. "Please, not in front of the kid. Please."

Her quiet plea was enough to silence the others. The truck drove on, and we rode in silence, each of us sinking down into the pits of our own thoughts. The drums hammered in my ears, providing me with some small comfort. I only wished that I could believe the humans around me had something similar. But they didn't, and I didn't have any way to help them, and so we just rode on.

I don't know how long the drive took. There were no clocks in the truck, and if anyone had a cell phone that was still keeping time, they weren't pulling it out. The cell networks were down. The phones were glorified wristwatches now. That didn't mean the soldiers who'd sedated my fellow passengers would have let them keep their things. The absence of the little girl's expected security object was the best indicator I could find that anything people had been carrying had been cast aside. Less to sterilize, I guess.

Our first sign that things were about to change came when the truck screeched to a sudden stop, sending some of the passengers rocking forward while others gripped the bench seats and stayed exactly where they were.

"Are we there?" whispered Carrie. "Are we at the quarantine?"

Paul, who held her, said nothing.

There was a clattering from the back of the truck, near the doors. All of us, from the oldest to the youngest, pulled instinctively away, pushing ourselves together in our need to escape from that terribly mundane sound. Then the doors swung open, and what looked like an entire platoon of soldiers was standing there. Some held guns that seemed too big for their arms. Others held cattle prods, their active ends sparking and crackling in the evening air.

The sun was almost down. Or maybe it was almost up: this could just as easily be morning. I realized I had no idea how long I'd been unconscious after Colonel Mitchell had me electrocuted. Maybe I'd lost hours. Maybe I'd lost days.

And maybe these men were here to take even more away

from me. Most of them looked young, their faces gaunt and their eyes haunted with specters I couldn't even imagine. All of them looked grim, like they had given up hope of anything but this world, this place and time.

"Everyone out of the truck," commanded one of the men. His voice broke in the middle of the sentence. Based on that and the acne that was scrawled red and raw across his face, he was barely out of his teens, going through a delayed and possibly painful puberty. I hadn't even realized it was possible to enlist that young...and maybe it wasn't. There were always going to be people willing to trade a place in a cage for a gun and somebody they could point it at.

No one moved.

Another soldier stepped forward. This one was carrying a cattle prod. The sight of it made us all shrink back just a little bit farther. "My name is Sergeant Hinton. Will Sally Mitchell please come with me?"

No one moved.

Looking annoyed now, Sergeant Hinton said, "Sally Mitchell, we know you are present in this vehicle. We have confirmed your name on the manifest. If you do not present yourself, we will be forced to take steps to subdue the entire area before locating you. You won't enjoy that. I won't enjoy that. Some of my men may enjoy that. I'd rather not know. So if Sally Mitchell would please get *her damn ass up* and come out, of her own free fucking will, I would very much appreciate it."

Those cattle prods seemed enormous. They loomed in my field of vision like the answer to a question I had neither asked nor particularly wanted to have answered. Slowly, I pushed myself off the bench seat and walked on shaking legs to the mouth of the truck. The muzzles of the guns and the sparking ends of the cattle prods tracked me with every step I took. The people who had been my fellow passengers until only a few moments before—travelers on the same terrible journey that I was involuntarily taking—recoiled as I passed them, eyeing me with all the suspicion they had previously reserved for the men with the guns.

I wanted to protest, to tell them I was the same person I had been for the whole journey. I didn't say anything. I just stopped at the lip of the truck and said, without looking back, "I'm Sally Mitchell, sir."

"Excellent." Sergeant Hinton turned away from me. "Private? Secure the prisoner."

I didn't have time to dodge before the cattle prod hit me in the small of the back, and everything dropped away again.

This time when I woke up, it was to a hose pointed straight at my face, dousing me in lukewarm water. My scalp felt like it was on fire. As I sputtered and squinted and tried to move away, I realized there was someone holding my hair. They were holding me *up* by my hair. My hands were cuffed behind my back again, my clothes were gone, and the rough floor of the room around me dug into my knees, hard and sharp and painful. I screamed, or tried to; the water flowed into my mouth, reducing the sound to a pained gurgle.

"Stop the water!" shouted a female voice. Blessedly, someone listened: The water stopped.

I spat out as much water as I could before I took a shaky breath. More water promptly found its way into my lungs. I began to cough, and the hand that was holding my hair let go, dropping me to the wet floor. I couldn't catch myself with my hands cuffed behind me. I fell face-first onto the rough concrete, still coughing, unable to catch my breath.

Sounding almost bored, the same female voice spoke again: "Roll her onto her side. If she dies, we'll catch hell from the Colonel."

"Yes, Sarge," said the man behind me. Hands gripped my shoulder, rolling me onto my side. I kept coughing, but less fiercely now. The hands released my shoulder and thumped me soundly on the back. I retched, water boiling up from the back of my throat and spilling down my chin in a thin, vomitus stream.

After that, I could breathe, if still not terribly well. My throat was as raw as my knees. My entire body felt loose, like the slightest disturbance could jar me out of it for good. I wasn't sure what it was about the electric shocks that did that to me, but one thing was for sure: I didn't want to experience that again.

I tried to lift my head, to see either the person who was physically abusing me or the owner of the voice commanding it, but the muscles in my neck refused to obey. I was as helpless as a day-old kitten, without the benefit of fur to keep me warm or a loving shelter staff to keep me safe. All I had was this place, this room, and I didn't feel like either of the people who were in it had my best interests at heart.

There was a loud sigh. "Larsen, get her on her feet," commanded the woman. "We can't take her to the quarantine drop looking like this."

"We shouldn't be taking her to the quarantine drop at all," said the man. He slid his hands under my arms and hauled me to my feet, leaving my head to loll limply against my chest. He was fully clothed: As he lifted me, I could feel the zips and buckles of his tactical gear against my skin. Why would anyone wear full body armor into a shower with a defenseless girl who could barely move her own head?

"Your opinion on the subject has been noted, Private," said the woman.

I struggled again to lift my head. This time, I managed to shift it just enough to let me see the person who was giving the orders. She was tall, thickly built, and wearing the same tactical gear as the man behind me. She was also scowling at me, an expression of unadulterated loathing on her face.

"You going to give me an opinion too, kid?" she demanded.

I didn't feel up to speaking. I wasn't sure my mouth would have obeyed me if I'd tried. So I didn't say anything. I just hung there, helpless in the arms of the man behind me, and wished death upon her with all my parasitic heart.

"Good," she said, and stepped closer. "Colonel Mitchell wants you brought to the lab. It's our responsibility to get you cleaned up and ready for him. But here's the thing. Some of us? We know what you did. We know who you've been working for. We know why you're his Hail Mary, and we're not going to tell him not to use you, but we're not going to help you fuck us over a second time. You got me? You traitorous little whore, you got me?!"

She was screaming by the end, and I realized, finally, what I'd done to earn myself this kind of treatment: to make them hate me so.

They didn't know about Sherman. They didn't know about Ronnie and his clever knives, or Kristoph, the bruiser who never spoke but could probably have crushed a man's skull in his bare hands if he had ever wanted to. As far as they were concerned, I had found a way to escape from their quarantine facility all by myself, and I had killed a bunch of people on my way out. People they worked with, knew, probably even liked. It was no wonder they hated me. If anything, it was a wonder they hadn't arranged for my "accidental" death on the way from SymboGen to wherever we were now.

The woman nodded, looking satisfied. "Good. You got me." Then, with no more warning that a slight tensing of her shoulders, she drove a fist into my stomach so hard that it knocked what little air I had out of me. I gasped, bile rising in my throat, and she stepped back just in time to avoid getting splattered by the thin stream of vomit as I upchucked on the floor in front of me.

"I should make you eat that," she said in an almost genial tone. "Instead, I'm going to be merciful, because I want you to remember that it can go one of two ways from here. It can go hard, or it can go easy. Now, let me be clear, you're not going to enjoy either option. Both of them are going to suck for you, and you deserve it. But that doesn't mean you wouldn't be smart if you chose the easy way."

I wheezed, trying to suck in enough breath to let me speak. My lungs didn't seem to be cooperating. I realized that I didn't care. She could punch me as much as she wanted. She could break my ribs and smash my fingers and I would be fine with that, as long as she didn't hit me with another electrical shock. I still felt like the world was out of joint and not quite working. The first shock had been the worst thing I'd ever experienced, and the fact that I didn't have better words for the feeling of electricity running through my body was a testament to how shaken I was. The second shock had been even worse. Two in one day had been almost more than I could stand. A third shock...

I was genuinely afraid that a third shock would kill me.

"I'm going to take that as agreement. Just to be sure, let's check." She stepped neatly forward and drove her fist into my stomach again. I didn't throw up this time. I just sagged limply against Private Larsen, and wondered whether this was ever going to end.

My response seemed to be what the woman had been hoping for. She smiled, and there was murder in her eyes. "Excellent. Now here's how it's going to go. You've been cleaned, and you've been sterilized. We took blood while you were out, and that's heading off to the doctors, so that we can be sure you're not bringing anything nasty into our kennels. That's all that happened. Do you understand? No one hit you. That would be entirely inappropriate, and we don't allow things like that here. No one would dream of laying a finger on Colonel Mitchell's little girl, even if she were a traitorous bitch who'd killed several of our own. If you think those things happened, you're wrong. Nod if you understand me."

Slowly, laboriously, I forced my chin to rise just enough to let me drop it back down against my chest. Even that much movement exhausted me, leaving me temporarily grateful for the arms that held me away from the cold, damp floor. Private Larsen might mean me nothing but ill. Honestly, I didn't care, as long as he didn't drop me again.

"Good girl," said the woman. "Private, take her to her clothes. Dress her yourself if you have to. Her father expects her within the hour."

"Yes, Sarge," said Private Larsen. He hoisted me higher, with a rough "Come on," and started walking toward the door on the far side of the room. My feet dragged against the floor, leaving layers of skin behind. My toes, raw and abraded, ached and stung. The sensation was centering, reminding me of the existence of my extremities. Remembering them meant remembering all the things between them and my brain, and bit by bit, I felt my arms and legs begin to come back online. I twitched my toes and straightened my fingers, confirming that they belonged to me. Everything responded like it was supposed to—a little slow, maybe, but it was still there, and it was still mine. Right now, that was good enough.

I let myself remain limp as Private Larsen dragged me through the doorway and into a small changing room. The longer they wanted to underestimate me, the better. More and more, I was coming to realize that not all action was good, and not all inaction was passivity. Sometimes the bravest thing I could do was refuse to move.

He dumped me onto a bench, knocking the air out of me yet

again. That was starting to become a habit. I moaned when the wood bit into the bruises that were forming on my stomach, but I didn't move, not then, not when he removed the cuffs from my hands, and not when he scooped up an armload of fabric and dumped it unceremoniously on my back.

"Put these on," he said. "I'll be right outside the door when you're finished."

I couldn't resist the urge to lift my head and blink at him, confused.

He smiled. I finally recognized him: He was the boy with the acne from outside the truck when we had first arrived, the one who'd been holding a gun too big for his frame. He didn't have that gun now. Somehow, that didn't make him look any less terrifying.

"I'm not helping you," he said. "If you take too long, I'll tell the Colonel you weren't willing to come out of the dressing room. I don't know where you've been all this time, and I don't care. Your little terrorist summer camp is over. It's time to come back to the real world. And I'm not worried about leaving you alone. What's the worst that you can do? Hang yourself with a pair of sweatpants? If you wanted to do that, you'd be doing the rest of us a favor. Feel free to take yourself out of the way before somebody else has to." He pitched his voice lower as he spoke, keeping it from cracking again. It was obvious that he was trying to be tough. I couldn't even hold his words against him. He sounded too much like his Sergeant, a woman who believed that she had every reason to hate me.

Then he turned and swaggered out of the room, slamming the door behind himself, and I was alone.

Even with my muscles back under my control, it took me too long to sit up. It felt like my body was arguing with itself, unsure of the order in which things were meant to be done. I tried to ride out the fight, not taking sides. My muscles and tendons and bones had come to me pre-used and already well aware of their capabilities. I was happy to work with them, to exercise them and feed them the things they needed to grow, but that didn't mean I needed to inject conscious thought on a system that had always worked perfectly well without me.

As I finished sitting up, I realized there was another advantage to letting my body set the pace. There was no way I wasn't being monitored right now. I turned my head slowly, scanning the top of the walls, and was rewarded halfway around the room when I spotted a small, boxy protrusion that had nothing to do with the shape of the room itself. There was no light to give it away, but I knew a camera when I saw one. I forced my eyes to keep traveling, not letting them know that I had spotted their surveillance device. The longer they kept underestimating me, the better.

My hands shook as I dressed myself: plain white panties, sweatpants, a sports bra with no underwire, and a loose blue cotton top that looked more like a doctor's scrubs than anything from my own closet. The tennis shoes had Velcro straps, and they were still almost too much for me. I was all too aware of the industrial nature of the clothing that had been chosen for me. There were no drawstrings or internal supports that I could pull out and use for weapons. If not for the USAMRIID logo on the thigh of the sweatpants, I could just as easily have been getting dressed for prison.

My wet hair was drying in corkscrew curls and tangles that would take me hours with a brush to work out. I pulled my fingers through it once, wincing as they snagged on the solidifying knots, before I turned and walked to the waiting door.

Private Larsen was waiting outside. He looked me once up and down, sneered, "You can't even make yourself presentable, can you?" and grabbed my arm, pulling me with him as he started down the narrow concrete hall and toward another, waiting door.

I didn't fight. Passivity was the best weapon I had at this point, and if they'd been intending to kill me, they would have done it in the shower, when it could have been most easily written off as an accident. No, whatever USAMRIID and Sally's father intended for me, it required I remain among the living for at least a while longer. I wasn't happy. My feet were scraped and sore, and I could feel the bruises forming on my stomach, making every breath an ordeal. But I wasn't going to give them the satisfaction of seeing how scared I was, or give anyone an excuse to hit me again.

Private Larsen didn't look happy when we reached the door. I was willing to bet he'd been hoping for resistance on my part. "This is where I leave you," he said, and opened the door, shoving me roughly through. I stumbled, barely keeping my balance, and looked up only when a hand clamped down on my shoulder.

"What took you so long?" asked Sergeant Hinton. He directed a flat look at the door which was swinging closed behind me. "Did you encounter any trouble getting cleaned up?"

This was a moment of decision. I could tell the truth, and hope he would believe me even when everything told me that he wouldn't, or I could cleave to the story I'd been given—the one that bought me access to an "easy way" that came with bruises and vomiting in the shower, but might get me through to the other side with my lungs still inside of my body. "I felt sick," I said. "I don't like being shocked. Please stop shocking me."

"It's an interesting thing about electroshock therapy," he said, removing his hand from my shoulder and motioning for me to follow him down the hall. "We were using it on some of the early victims, back when we thought we were dealing with a purely psychological problem. We found that it incapacitated them as well as it did unaffected individuals—maybe even better, since the worms that have taken them over depend on the electrical activity of the brain to function. Some of them never regained control of the bodies they'd stolen. We could see them thrashing on the MRI, and when we opened the skulls of those individuals, the parasites were incredibly agitated. But they weren't in charge anymore. We started using Tasers for crowd control immediately."

"Can't…can't normal people be hurt, too? There was a little girl in the truck with me." I had to struggle to keep the horror from my voice. He was talking about creatures like me becoming prisoners in their own stolen bodies, unable to move or communicate—trapped. I didn't know how much sleepwalkers were capable of coherent thought. No one knew that, not even Dr. Cale, and she had created them, even if it had been an accident.

If electric shocks could strand sleepwalkers, they could do the same to chimera. The only difference between us was the precision of our connection to our human hosts. The idea of being lost like that…

I'd been frightened before, and I was sure I'd be frightened again. Before that moment, I hadn't really understood what it was to be terrified.

"Some people have died, yes, but there are always casualties during times of war." There was something almost gentle about Sergeant Hinton's tone, like he was trying to make me understand a complicated fact of life. "We can't afford to look at winning and losing in terms of single bodies anymore. We have to look at the bigger picture."

I didn't say anything. There was nothing I could say. The drums were hammering in my ears, screaming danger, screaming that I needed to run away as fast and as far as I possibly could. It was a pity there was nowhere for me to go.

The hall we were walking along was all industrial linoleum and plain concrete walls, making me suspect that we were back at the Oakland Coliseum. As a building, it had been originally designed to hold sporting events and concerts by bands big enough to number their fans in the millions—the sort of place that was literally visible from space when it turned all the lights on. As a government asset, it was massive, self-contained, and capable of generating the bulk of its own power needs even under normal circumstances. The only thing more tailor-made for this sort of large containment-and-quarantine situation would have been a teaching hospital, and most of those had been overrun during the early days of the crisis. This was the best thing the government was going to get, and they weren't going to let it go without a fight.

I wondered if they'd been able to get the bloodstains out of the concrete in the loading dock where Ronnie had done the bulk of his delicate, brutal work. I somehow didn't think it would have been appropriate for me to ask.

Sergeant Hinton steered me along the hall with the calm assurance of a man who simply couldn't believe I would try to run away from him. It wasn't even a matter of my being his prisoner, although I absolutely was: Any attempts to flee would have resulted in my death or incapacitation, while he'd have been able to go along like nothing had happened. Would Colonel Mitchell be pissed? My gut told me "yes," even as my head tried to argue that he'd be relieved to have me out of the picture. Somehow, he'd been able to keep his people from real-izing I was anything other than an ungrateful daughter who ran away to be with her boyfriend and his bioterrorist mother. They thought I was also a mass murderer, but that was some-how less important than the fact that they believed I was a human being. If I died in transit, he would never have to tell them the truth.

Then again, if they kept electrocuting me, they'd figure out I wasn't a normal human girl sooner or later. Normal human girls don't react to Tasers by losing all use of their bodies. Of all my many tells, that was the one that suddenly seemed to be the most dangerous.

We stopped outside a plain wooden door that looked like it would lead to an office or backstage area. Sergeant Hinton gave me a frank up-and-down appraisal before he said, "Colonel Mitchell is the ranking officer at this facility. I recognize that he's your father, but we will not tolerate insubordination at this time. It's bad for morale. I'm sure you can see why, under the circumstances, morale has become extremely important."

"Yes, sir," I said. My voice was squeakier than I liked, the fear bleeding through and making itself plain.

Sergeant Hinton seemed to like that. His chest visibly puffed at the sound of my small, frightened voice, and he smiled— the sort of friendly, painted smile that men had been using on me my entire life, always when they thought they could control me. "Good. This will be easier for you if you understand. Answer any questions he asks you. Answer them politely and completely, and remember, there are different levels of quarantine. We can make this easy on you. You might even enjoy your new life with us. It's only temporary, until we can get this country back under control. But if you make things difficult for us, we can respond in kind."

The memory of the unnamed sergeant burying her fist in my stomach rose unbidden to my mind's eye. I couldn't tell him about her. For all that I knew, he was already aware and was waiting to see whether I would tattle. I swallowed, standing straighter, and said, "I understand, sir."

"Good. Now I hope you don't harbor any loyalty for the people who helped you break out of here—assuming you didn't break out on your own. You're going to be telling us everything eventually. Unless you'd like to begin telling me everything now?"

I shook my head silently.

"I didn't think so." He opened the door, holding it wide for me to go through. It was clear just by looking at him that he had no interest in hearing what I had to say; my opinion was worse than useless here, it was unwanted and surplus to requirements. I still wasn't sure what my part in this little drama was supposed to be, aside from prisoner of war and punching bag, but I had the grim feeling that I was about to find out. I looked at him for a moment, worrying my lip between my teeth, and then I turned, and I stepped through the empty eye of the doorframe.

The room on the other side was small, and had been outfitted according to the USAMRIID standards for patient care. Everything except for the workstations was covered in plastic, and a sheet of clear plastic bisected the area, which explained my initial impression of smallness: It had been a medium-sized room before the structural changes began.

Curtains were pulled on the inside of the plastic wall, blocking whatever was on the other side from view. Colonel Mitchell was standing in front of that wall, talking quietly with a man in a lab coat. The sight of it made me feel briefly homesick for Dr. Cale and her lab, until the man turned slightly and I saw the USAMRIID logo on his shoulder. I was a long way from home. I might never get to go home again.

"Sally," said Colonel Mitchell. He smiled warmly, and it seemed like the expression actually reached his eyes. "How was your trip here?"

What would Sally do? Sal would have done as she was told: As Sal, I had been taught to follow orders and follow directions and keep my head down as much as possible. But Sally, who had come before me, had been a lot more demanding. Colonel Mitchell had me here because he thought I had somehow transformed back into her, like her pushiness had been enough to let her dig her way out of the grave and reassert control of the body that she had abandoned. He didn't want Sal. He wanted Sally.

I was here to give him what he wanted. I crossed my arms, managing not to wince as the motion tugged at the bruises on my stomach, and glared at him. He blinked. I smiled as angrily as I could, showing all my teeth in the process.

"Is there a *reason* I was loaded into the back of a gross old truck with a bunch of filthy strangers your men harvested off the street?" I demanded. I forced myself to keep showing my teeth as I spoke, even as every instinct I had reminded me— loudly—that it was a sign of aggression, an invitation for the person I was looking at to take offense and attack me. Showing teeth was anathema to every chimera I'd ever met, even Sherman and Tansy. Sherman could fake it when he had to, when he was trying to pass for human, and that was what I clung to now. If Sherman could do it, so could I.

Colonel Mitchell blinked. He might have wanted Sally back, but he'd still been expecting passivity and agreement: That was obvious, even as he started to smile again, more earnestly this time. "Some of my men didn't like the idea of you riding with us when you hadn't gone through decontamination and been properly examined. I didn't like doing that to you, sweetheart, but it was important for their peace of mind. You understand, don't you?"

"Understand that you let a bunch of gun-monkeys tell you to throw your oldest daughter into the grossest truck I've been in for like, months? Oh, sure, I get that. Is there a reason you let them practice their electroshock on me? Because that shit *hurts*."

His smile died like a switch had been flipped, leaving an expression of total neutrality behind. "You are not a member of USAMRIID, Sally. You're not here as a guest, either. You're here because you've been flagged as potentially useful personnel, and because I was willing to vouch for you. That means you get treated like any civilian, at least until you've proven yourself to us. If you want to be handled with more respect, you'll earn it."

I cocked my head. "Got it." He wanted to believe I was Sally—whether because he didn't fully understand the science behind the SymboGen implants or because he was delusional, I didn't know—and yet he was still too much of a rationalist to have fully convinced himself that it was possible. That was almost reassuring. The Colonel Mitchell I knew was a man who would lie to his family, who would strive to convince an alien stranger that she was his daughter, but he wasn't a fool. And only a fool would have believed that I was really Sally Mitchell without some very good reason.

"Then here's your first chance to earn it." He looked to the man in the lab coat, giving a very small nod, and said, "Open it."

The man nodded in return before crossing to a simple, almost primitive pulley that had been set up in the corner. He tugged the cord, and the curtain on the other side of the plastic wall swung open, revealing a small figure on a plain white surgical cot. I gasped, one hand coming up to cover my mouth without my consciously deciding to do so.

It was an adult woman: She only looked small because of the machines around her, strangling her in wires and cords, dwarfing her with their vastness. There were machines I recognized from my own time in the hospital, machines to monitor her vitals and clean her blood and keep her breathing at all costs. Her head had been shaved, and her scalp gleamed like an eggshell in the pale overhead light, seeming impossibly fragile. Her eyelashes were bruises against the curvature of her cheeks. A breathing mask covered her mouth and nose, a tube that looked obscenely like an oversized tapeworm extending downward to the floor.

"Joyce," I whispered through my fingers.

"So you remember your sister," said Colonel Mitchell. He turned back to face me. "We tried the antiparasitic drugs your terrorist boyfriend suggested. They were successful: We were able to stop the implant from entering her brain."

I dropped my hand. "What? It didn't break through?" Joyce had been diagnosed as entering the early stages of sleepwalker sickness, using a test developed by SymboGen's own scientists. The test showed parasitic growth throughout the muscle tissue, and I had always assumed that the growth was tied to the presence of the implant in the brain…but that didn't make sense, did it? *D. symbogenesis* was a chimeric organism, cobbled together from multiple sources that could never have combined in nature. One of them, *Toxoplasma gondii*, allowed the parasite to spread tendrils through the rest of the body, even the muscular tissue, although I didn't understand why, or what benefit that had. Those tendrils didn't feed the main body of the implant, and they were left to wither and atrophy when integration was complete. So why would they only be triggered by penetration of the brain?

Still, the best test we had for early infection depended on those tendrils, since they showed that the implant had begun acting outside the narrow, human-friendly guidelines supposedly built into its genetic code. When I'd given the SymboGen early-detection test to USAMRIID, they had promptly flagged Joyce as among the afflicted. I hadn't known what I was then: I hadn't known about the chimera, or that the implants had the potential to be thinking creatures in their own right. All I'd known was that my sister was sick, and that I had the potential to help her be well again.

"No," said Colonel Mitchell. "It made it as far as her superior vena cava before we were able to finish the antiparasitics and surgically remove it from her body. It cut off blood flow to her brain for more than eight minutes, Sally. That's long enough that most people would have called her dead. Some people did.

Not me." His eyes searched my face like they were looking for the missing piece of a puzzle—the thing to make this all fit together. "Because you were without oxygen for as long, if not longer, and you came back. You woke up."

I stared at him. I came back because I was safe from the impact that would have crushed me if I had still been coiled in Sally Mitchell's abdomen. In a real way, I didn't "come back" at all. I had never existed before Sally vacated her brain and left it ripe for me to take as my own.

"I…" I said.

"I know that in your case, the SymboGen parasite *did* break through the skull, and was able to enter your brainpan," he said without pause. The man in the lab coat blanched, whirling around to eye me warily. I couldn't blame him. "It may even have done you a favor, by keeping brain activity present while you recovered. We should be able to remove it now that it's done its work, of course, and we'll do that after you've helped us with Joyce."

"*What*?" I felt like I was yelling. My voice was barely a whisper.

His eyes were hard as he looked at me. Had they always been that hard? It was difficult to say. "You're going to help me save your sister, and then I'm going to cut that worm out of your head. Even if you've never given a damn about anything else in your life, you loved her. So save her."

"What is *she* doing here?"

The voice was querulous and thin, so different from the warm, maternal tone that I was used to that hearing it was like a blow. This was the voice that had nursed me through my few bouts with food poisoning and flu, that had helped me with my physical therapy and reeducation. And there was nothing in it now but loathing. Slowly, I turned, and looked into the eyes of the woman who had, once upon a time, believed herself to be my mother.

Mom recoiled when I looked at her, but she didn't budge

from her place in the doorway, placing herself firmly between me and any hope that I might be able to escape from whatever perverse idea of "justice" had come into her head. She glared at me, and all hope of reconciliation died. Her voice had been cold. Her eyes were arctic. Nothing could live on those cruel and frozen shores, and nothing in me would ever want to. The last time I'd seen her, she had still believed I was her daughter. Somewhere between my then and now, she had learnt what I really was: There was no question of that. I'd even been expecting it, on some level. It was only rational.

What I hadn't been expecting was how much it would hurt to have someone who had always been a nurturing figure in my life suddenly look at me like I was worth less than the dirt beneath her heel.

She was thinner than she'd been the last time I'd seen her, with deep lines around her mouth and eyes etched by both hunger and fear. I remembered what she'd been like on the rare occasions that I had been sick. She'd been the one who sat next to my bed and read me the "childhood favorites" that I was hearing for the first time; she'd been the one who brought me soup and toast and told me it was going to be okay. Most of my early memories of the good side of humanity came from her.

Everything was different now. I was still coming to terms with *how* different.

"Gail, please." Colonel Mitchell took a step forward. I would have needed to be blind to miss the way he put himself slightly between us, like he was preparing to block a physical assault. But was he expecting me to go for her, or her to come after me?

"Don't you 'Gail, please' me," snapped Mo—snapped *Gail*, her eyes narrowing as she shifted the full focus of her hatred onto her husband. "What is *she* doing here? What is *it* doing here?"

"I made some arrangements to have her located and retrieved," said Colonel Mitchell. He slanted a warning glance in my direction, and I realized, in a sudden moment of blinding clarity, that he was telling me not to mention Dr. Banks or the situation at SymboGen. Maybe Mo—maybe Gail didn't know that her husband was still working with the man who had unleashed the implants on an unsuspecting world, and he didn't want this to be the way that she found out.

"Why would you do that, Alfred?" She sounded less angry than hurt this time. I wasn't foolish enough to take that as a sign that we were suddenly on the same side. As much as it broke my heart, I was never going to be on the same side as her again. "Why would you bring that—that *thing* here, when our daughter is lying in that bed, dying? What possible reason could you have for doing this to me?"

"She may be able to help us bring Joyce back." His tone was calm, reasonable, and filled with the sort of false hope that brings no joy, only more pain down the line. I turned to stare at him. He really thought this was something I could do: that I could somehow awaken their Sleeping Beauty and bring her back to them the same as she'd been before she went away.

Gail turned, slowly, to stare at me. "Really?" she asked. It wasn't clear whether she was talking to me or him. Then she reoriented her body, angling it toward me, and repeated, "*Really*? This...this *monster* is going to bring our daughter back?"

"She already did," said Colonel Mitchell. "Sally's still in there. She's fighting her way back to the surface."

Gail's hand struck him across the cheek so fast that he didn't have time to pull away. He stared at her. She snarled at him.

"You think I don't know my daughter?" she demanded. "You think I don't know the way she stands, the way she holds her head, the way she *breathes*? That *thing* is not my Sally! Sally is dead, and you're dancing on her grave!"

"I was in your house for six years, and you never thought there was anything wrong with me." The words were out before I stopped to consider what they confirmed: that I wasn't Sally, and that I was never going to be Sally again. That Sally was dead.

Gail Mitchell didn't say anything. She just lunged for me, her hands out and hooked like claws as she dove for my eyes. I fell back, making a startled mewling sound, and stopped only when my shoulders bumped against the plastic wall between us and Joyce. Colonel Mitchell appeared behind his wife, grabbing her around the waist and stopping her before she could get to me. She kicked and struggled against him, clawing at the air, still trying to reach me. She was making a high-pitched keening noise that shouldn't have been able to come from a human throat. It was animal and cold, and absolutely as terrifying as the moans of the sleepwalkers or the screams of the wounded.

"Get her out of here!" barked Colonel Mitchell. Two men rushed through the open door, taking hold of Gail's shoulders, and pulled her, still struggling, out of the room.

For a moment, everything was silence. Colonel Mitchell turned his eyes on me, and oh, they were so cold.

"Your mother has not been well," he said solemnly. "Losing you hurt her deeply. Losing Joyce on top of that... I'm sure you can understand why it's so important we get your sister to wake up. I'm also sure you can understand why you can't stay here with me. Your mother simply doesn't understand that you're not the enemy, and that you're really her child."

"Wh-where are you going to send me?" My voice quavered. I hated it. I didn't want to sound weak in front of this man, who held my future in his hands, and wasn't afraid to start squeezing.

He smiled broadly, showing all his teeth. I had to fight not to recoil. "To our Pleasanton facility, of course. We could put you in isolation, but that wouldn't help you understand the situation. Pleasanton will do that. Pleasanton will open your eyes. You'll be safe there, and you can think about how you can best help us. It's all up to you, Sally. Everything that happens next is up to you."

It's done.

Kristoph reported back this morning, and Ronnie wasn't with him. He had all of Ronnie's knives, and he refused to give them to me when I tried to reclaim them. He just looked at me sadly and clutched them to his chest like they represented some sort of connection to his missing friend. For someone so intelligent, Kristoph certainly behaves like a fool sometimes. If he weren't useful as he is, I would have him cracked open and reassembled in a body that came with fewer inbuilt neurological issues.

But I won't allow frustration to dull my moment of triumph. It's done, and by the time the humans realize the war is lost, it'll be too late for them to even raise their hands against me. Welcome to the new age. The Age of Men is done.

—FROM THE NOTES OF SHERMAN LEWIS (SUBJECT VIII,
ITERATION III), NOVEMBER 2027

One of the gardeners collapsed today. He was showing the classic signs of implant overgrowth, and he died within the hour. Examination of the body confirmed my initial diagnosis: There were parasitic threads twisted throughout his muscle tissue and digestive system, and the implant itself was located in the superior vena cava, which seems to be a favored spot of migrating D. symbogenesis.

Analysis of the worm showed that it was SymboGen stock, but had not been tailored for the man in question: His response was part immune and part tissue mismatch. Questions of black market purchase might have arisen had this happened some months ago, but the man had already been tested repeatedly for the presence of an implant and had come up clean. We must now ask ourselves how he came to be infected with a worm that was not designed for him, that was not present at his last checkup.

The body is currently undergoing sectioning and staining for a more thorough examination. More information as it becomes available.

—FROM THE PRIVATE NOTES OF DR. STEVEN BANKS,
DECEMBER 11, 2027

Chapter 3

DECEMBER 2027

Someone was screaming on the street outside my window. They had been screaming for more than an hour, and no one inside the house had been able to work up the courage to go out and try to make them stop. The last time one of us had gone out to make someone stop screaming while people were trying to sleep, it had ended in gunfire, and we'd suddenly found ourselves with more room in the house. That should have seemed like a gift—there were eighteen of us crammed into a three-bedroom home that had been designed for a single nuclear family, not a jumbled alliance of refugees—but instead, it had come with a whole new dose of fear, resentment, and anger, all mingled with our grief. USAMRIID didn't allow any space to go unused for very long; their unofficial motto here in the quarantine facility was "Waste not, want not," and there were always people looking to change housing. But the sort of people who needed to approach strangers to find a place to live were generally not the sort of people any of us wanted to share a home with.

It was possible to get drugs inside the quarantine zone. USAMRIID's soldiers thought they'd cleaned the place out, but people were clever about where they hid things, and the junkies and hustlers were forever finding joints taped to the back of toilet tanks or tabs of Ecstasy hidden in bottles of aspirin. I guess where there's a need, there's a way. I tried not to judge, but we'd already had two people removed from our block due to overdose after the need to escape overrode whatever sense of self-preservation that they might have once possessed.

Getting into the quarantine zone required no qualifications beyond "alive" and "not infected with a SymboGen implant"— and I was living proof that the second qualification could be gotten around, if you knew the right people and were disturbed enough to think this was a good place to be. It wasn't an entirely bad place. There were people like Paul and Carrie. I'd liked them when I met them on the truck, and after living with them for a week and a half, I trusted them as much as I was capable of trusting outside of Dr. Cale's lab. But there were also people like John, who'd been squatting in the house when USAMRIID dropped us off and told us that this was our home now. He'd tried to do…things…to several of the women who were living with us, until Paul threatened to stab him. He'd been brave when faced with unarmed women. He wasn't so brave when up against Paul, who was a foot taller and thirty pounds heavier. John had run, vanishing into the fenced-off streets of Pleasanton.

There were good people in the quarantine zone, but they were in the minority. There were killers in here. There were thieves. There were people whose minds had snapped under the pressure of what was happening to the world, dropping them into endless spirals of panic and despair. They needed professional help, therapy, and oversight, but what they got was a quarter or less of a bedroom in someone else's home, with a bunch of strangers sleeping around them and claiming to be friends. It was no wonder that some people started screaming and never stopped.

It was more of a wonder that the rest of us were so quiet.

Something smashed outside. The screaming finally stopped. I resisted the urge to move to the window and look out. Having a window wasn't a privilege. It was a burden at best, and a punishment at worst. The USAMRIID teams that had prepared this area for us had taken down all the curtains and blinds in open houses, citing the need to have a clean line of sight if something happened—and we all understood that "something" was code for "a sleepwalker outbreak." The people who slept in window-less rooms, or on the other side of rooms like mine, could hang blankets and give themselves the illusion of privacy. Not me. I got the pleasure of sharing my life with anyone who wanted to stand on the opposite sidewalk and look up, and when things went wrong, I was one of the people who were expected to man the window and keep everyone else up-to-date. The only good thing about it was airflow, but most days, none of us were brave enough to open the windows. We didn't want to attract attention.

Inside the Pleasanton quarantine facility, attracting attention from the all-too-human monsters surrounding us was death. Maybe not immediately, maybe not even overnight, but soon enough that none of us were willing to take the risk.

There was a sound behind me. I turned to find Carrie standing in the doorway, twisting a dishrag in her hands like it had done something to personally offend her. She had lost weight since arriving in Pleasanton, and her hair was growing out, revealing brown roots under the artificial green of her hair. It was a small thing, but it seemed indicative of the tragedy unfolding around us. People were going to bed hungry and afraid; the

water ran red with rust sometimes, like we were expected to
bathe ourselves in blood; the government that was supposed to
protect us had turned against us, just like the genetically engineered tapeworms that were supposed to protect humanity had
turned against their creators; and Carrie couldn't re-dye her
hair.

Maybe that was the most human thing about me. Even in
the depths of tragedy, I could find the smallest things to seize
upon.

"What's wrong?" I asked.

Carrie shook her head. The motion was tight and controlled,
designed to make her look as inoffensive as possible. She had
started shaking her head like that sometime in the past week,
and I didn't even think she knew that she was doing it. It was
just another small piece of protective coloration, and unless she
held to it religiously, she wasn't going to survive in here. None
of us were.

"Paul hasn't come back yet."

I blinked at her for a moment, absorbing the meaning behind
her words. They were so simple, with no room for ambiguity,
no hidden meanings or concealed intent. Here, in this glorified
cage, I had finally met people who spoke like parasites: quick
and brief and uncomplicated. I could have thrived in an environment like this one, if it hadn't come with such a terrible cost.

"Oh," I said finally.

We all took turns leaving the house and going out into the
streets to scavenge for the things we needed. There were food
trucks twice a day, and USAMRIID doctors who came around
to dispense medicines and check on the sick or wounded, but
they didn't provide many of the basic necessities of life, considering them "frivolous" or otherwise low-priority. Sani-
tary supplies for the women. Toys for the children. Condoms
and birth control for the people who had depended on their
implants for contraception, and who couldn't fight the primate

urge to seek comfort in the arms of their own species. I had walked in on Paul and Carrie several times, some by accident, others out of sheer curiosity. I had never seen people having sex before. When I slept with Nathan, I was always too much in the moment to observe. In those moments, I was a mammal like any other, and my origins didn't matter in the least.

They fucked with their eyes closed and tears running down their cheeks, and they clung to each other like the world was ending. Paul had opened his eyes once and seen me standing there, watching them. He hadn't said anything. He'd just looked at me, sorrow and understanding in his eyes, until I'd been forced to turn away.

I hadn't walked in on them since then.

"What time did he leave?"

"Just after breakfast," said Carrie. "Gloria's little girl was crying again. He thought he'd seen some Otter Pops in one of the convenience stores. Most adults won't eat them—they don't register as food—and he said he'd try to pick them up while he was out. That was hours ago."

The little girl didn't have a name. The woman who had found her, Gloria, had tried name after name on the child, looking for something she would respond to. The rest of us had done the same, dredging up names from our past that we thought were pretty, but that weren't attached to losses so bright and recent that hearing those names over and over again would hurt. The child had refused them all. Somewhere out there was her real name, and until we found it, she wasn't going to let us call her anything. She still treated Gloria as her primary caretaker. The rest of us were acceptable substitutes, when necessary.

I'd never spent much time around human children before. Puppies and kittens, yes; infants and toddlers, no. It was refreshingly similar, and confoundingly different at the same time. We all catered to her every whim. She was our tiny queen, and if she had wanted Otter Pops—whatever those were—then of course Paul would have volunteered to get them for her.

"Oh," I said again. Then, with a slow, almost morbid dread gathering in my stomach, I asked, "Why are you telling me this?"

Carrie just looked at me for a moment, and her expression was so oddly similar to the one Paul had worn when I watched them making love that it was all I could do not to turn my face away, cheeks burning with conditioned shame. I didn't want to be as human as I was. The people who had created me had made sure I didn't have a choice.

"The soldiers treat you different because of who you are," she said finally. "You try to pretend they don't, and we try to let you, because we have to live with you. Things are hard enough here without us being at war against ourselves. But they won't shoot you if they find you in the wrong part of the camp. They might even give you a ride home."

I didn't say anything. She was telling the truth: There was nothing I could do to change that. The fact that they would kick the living crap out of me before giving me a ride really didn't matter.

"Please, Sal. I don't know what your deal is, and right now, I don't care. I just want Paul back."

"You could go yourself." The words were cruel before they were spoken, and they were crueler when they hung in the air between us, impossible to take back or ignore.

"I could," Carrie agreed. "But I wouldn't make it three streets before something happened, and you know it. The patrols will come to your defense. I've seen it."

She was right. Colonel Mitchell was happy to keep me with the general population for now—pacifying his wife and reminding me of my place at the same time, until I was willing to be a good little girl and play by his rules—but he wasn't going to let me get killed. Not while there was still a chance, however small, that I could be used to call Joyce back from the void where she existed now. So he set extra patrols on the streets around the house that had been assigned to me, and he made sure people were there to monitor my activities on the rare occasions when I dared to venture outside. I was probably the safest person in the Pleasanton quarantine zone, and I didn't want it. I didn't want the responsibility that was implied by Carrie's face, or the burdens of being able to walk without fear of my fellow inmates. I didn't want to be afraid of the soldiers who were supposedly protecting me. I didn't want any of this.

And what I wanted didn't matter. Maybe it never had. "We could go together," I said, one last desperate bid for something other than what she was asking me to do. I realized resentfully that she had never actually *asked*. She hadn't needed to. All she'd needed to do was stand there and look at me, and allow my guilt to fill in the rest.

"I don't want to leave the house," said Carrie. Her voice was meek, especially compared to that of the angry, anxious girl who had arrived here with me. Bit by bit, this place was wearing her away, reducing her to the bones of herself. I wondered if she liked who she saw when she looked in the mirror. "Paul might come back. I should be here when he comes back. I don't want him to be scared because I'm not here."

That answer made sense, and I knew it was a lie, just as surely as she did. Paul wouldn't be scared if he came back and Carrie was gone: He would assume she'd gone looking for him, or that she'd gone to get something else we needed, especially if I was gone too. She just didn't want to go outside, where the world might take notice of her. Then again, why should she? The last time she'd gone outside of her own free will, she'd been seized and thrown into the back of a truck, and her world had changed forever. I sighed heavily, trying to keep my frustration from showing in my face. I didn't do a very good job, I knew, but the effort seemed better than nothing.

"All right," I said. "I'll go."

Carrie smiled. "I knew you would," she said, and the worst thing was, she had known—and she hadn't been wrong.

Pleasanton was located in the deep East Bay, a sleepy suburban community that served both Livermore and San Francisco, feeding commuters into the tech and science industries thriving across the Bay Area. There had always been people who lived and worked at home, of course, but most of them had been keeping the city infrastructure functional, and when the sleepwalkers had overrun Pleasanton during the early days of the outbreaks, those people—and the infrastructure—had been among the first to fall. According to every soldier who'd been willing to give me the time of day, the selection of Pleasanton for the quarantine facility had been as much a matter of efficiency as anything else. By the time USAMRIID rode in with their tanks and their guns, there hadn't been much of anybody left to fight them.

I closed the door of our assigned home behind me as I stepped out onto the porch, breathing in the chilly December air, and for a moment, I was grateful to be exactly where I was. Everything smelled like rain, and the grass on the lawns around me was patchy and brown, where it hadn't been churned into a muddy froth by passing feet. California winters are gentle compared to most of the rest of the country. If our quarantine zone had been almost anywhere else, I would have been standing in snow outside a house where the electricity was intermittent and the hot water didn't always work.

Not for the first time, it struck me that the rest of the country was probably in real, serious trouble, and that if this crisis didn't either pass or come to a head soon, a lot more humans were going to die for reasons having nothing to do with the sleepwalkers. The sleepwalkers were going to be dying too, if they hadn't already started. Their minds might be parasitic, but their bodies were mammalian, soft and warm and susceptible to frostbite and the weather. They'd freeze before they ever understood what was happening to them.

I took a deep breath and stepped down off the porch. The world didn't end. I took another step forward.

The screamer was gone, leaving the sidewalks empty on either side of the street, but I could feel the eyes watching me from the windows. I inhaled instinctively, looking for traces of sleepwalker pheromones. I didn't find any, but that didn't necessarily mean anything: I still didn't fully understand my connection to the cousins, and I'd only been beginning to develop my ability to detect them, when things had gone to hell and I'd wound up in USAMRIID custody. They could be all around me, standing just slightly downwind, and I would never know.

This was supposed to be a secure quarantine zone. I was safe. I had to be safe.

I took another step, and just like that, I was walking, moving with quick, anxious purpose down the walkway to the sidewalk, and then down the sidewalk toward the part of town where Paul had been heading. I caught movement out of the corner of my eye as I passed the windows, and I did my best not to turn toward them. The people who were hiding inside didn't want me to see them, and I was willing to respect that. They had so little left to call their own; the least I could do was allow them to keep what remained of their tattered privacy. I walked faster, and then I was jogging, enjoying the open sidewalk and the smooth, untroubled stretch of my legs. I was still getting stronger. It had started when Sherman had held me captive, and it had continued since then. It was like learning the provenance of my body had finally made it acceptable for me to turn it into something new, something other than the soft, untested thing that Sally had deeded to me. This was *my* body now, and it was going to do what *I* needed it to do. And what I needed it to do was run.

My feet slammed down against the pavement as I continued to pick up speed, and each impact was like a door closing somewhere behind me. I might never find my way out of here; I might never make it home to Nathan and Adam and the rest of my family. The broken doors were still open for me—they would always be open for me—but passing through them required the freedom to reach them, and that wasn't something I had right now. I could run for the rest of my life, however long or short that was, and never reach the place I wanted to be.

But that didn't mean I couldn't do some good. I was a chimera in a nest of humans, and I had been created to improve their lives. Maybe not like this, maybe not with eyes and hands and the freedom to make my own decisions, and yet I still felt like maybe they needed me. We didn't create humanity, after all. My parasitic ancestors had been perfectly happy for thousands of years. They had never woken up and thought *we need to create a whole new species to make sure that we're okay.* It was hard not to look at the humans, with all their advantages and strengths, and feel just a little bit sorry for them. They were so *bad* at living in their own world.

Take Carrie, for example. She'd been fine when she felt like she was in control of things. I wasn't sure how she'd managed to avoid receiving a SymboGen implant, although I suspected it had something to do with her diet—I'd never seen her voluntarily eat animal proteins, not even cheese or eggs. If she was vegan, the idea of swallowing another living thing would have been anathema to her. Or maybe she had an allergy. SymboGen had been working on reducing the protein tags of the implants when everything went wrong, since there was a very small percentage of the population who couldn't handle the waste products we naturally generated. People whose immune systems reacted poorly to the implants had been viewed with pity for years, since they couldn't take the easy route to health that had been promised to the rest of humanity. It was sort of ironic now, since those people might make up the bulk of the survivors.

She'd been fine when she was in control, and now she was falling apart, and it wasn't fair to focus on her to the exclusion of all others, because *everyone* was falling apart in their own ways, even the nameless little girl. Her refusal to accept an identity that wasn't exactly right was a sign that she wasn't coping any better than the adults around her. She just had a better chance of doing it eventually as her memories of the world before the apocalypse dropped away and were replaced by memories of a world where this was normal.

There was something about that thought that was sad and hopeful at the same time. She would find a new name; she would find a new family; she would grow up thinking of the human race as scared and endangered, but ultimately enduring. Assuming, again, that they *could* endure, and that she'd get to grow up at all, rather than winding up in the hands of someone like Sherman, who would look into those wide, trusting eyes and think that the space behind them was the perfect incubator for a daughter of his own. One who would never need to forget her name, one whose family would never leave her.

I honestly didn't know whether or not that would be a kinder ending for her than the blasted, frightened world I was envisioning, and so I kept running, trying to outrace my own thoughts, trying to find the place where I could sink down into the dark and let the drums become the backbeat of the world.

I was so focused on what I was doing, on where I was going, that I didn't notice when I ran out of our residential neighborhood and into one of the narrow bands of strip malls and commercial establishments that ringed every set of houses. Pleasanton was designed to keep people home and happy when they weren't at work, and that meant no one had to go too far before they reached a grocery store. The sidewalk hadn't changed, so I kept on running, letting my feet take me where I needed to go. I didn't see the men lurking behind the battered old Dumpster until I was almost on top of them. A hand grabbed my arm and yanked me roughly off balance, pulling me into the shadows between the Dumpster and the wall.

A second, even rougher hand was clapped over my mouth, cutting off sound and air at the same time. I didn't have time to scream. Then the four of them were surrounding me, moving in until I could smell the sweat and desperation baking off of their skins like sour perfume.

"What are you doing on our turf, little girl?" asked one of the men. He was shorter than the others, but held himself with the sort of confidence that left no doubt as to his status in the group: he was their leader, and he wasn't going to take any shit from anyone, least of all from me. "Don't you know that you're not supposed to be here?"

I didn't squirm. I didn't fight. I didn't bite the hand that held me in place. I just stood perfectly still and glared daggers at the man responsible for my current situation.

He smirked. "Ah, you did know, you just hoped we wouldn't notice. Aaron, let her go. I want to hear what she has to say for herself."

The hand was removed from my mouth. The other hands were not removed from my arms. The man made a gesture with his hand, indicating that it was time for me to speak. I continued to glare, and resisted the urge to spit until the taste of unwashed hand was no longer lingering in my mouth.

"I knew no such thing," I said. "This is public space. We're allowed to search the local stores for supplies that may have been overlooked." It was a terrible policy, and I had to assume that USAMRIID had put it in place because they'd run out of places to stow the looters. Better to just make it legal than to keep arresting people you couldn't hold.

"That may be what the Army says, but they're the ones keeping us locked up in here," said the man. "Standing up to them is the American way. This is unconstitutional, and when it comes out what's been done to us, people like me and my boys are going to be heroes, while people like you are going to be collaborators."

I looked at him blankly, my glare giving way to confusion. "I don't understand what all those words mean," I said. "Not in that order, anyway."

The short man sneered. "They mean that if you have anything valuable on you, you'll give it to us now, and we'll let you go on your way. No harm, no foul, no punishment for failure to understand the rules. You look like pretty new meat, and we try to be forgiving of ignorance in circumstances like yours."

"I've been here a few weeks," I said. "I don't have anything valuable."

"Then you won't mind if we search you," said the man, and lunged forward, shoving his hand into the pocket of my coat. I squirmed as best I could against the man who was holding me in place, trying to fight my way free, but it was no use: My captor was bigger than me, and his grip was strong.

The short man stepped back again, holding a few crumpled slips of paper in his hand. He held them up, brandishing them triumphantly, and demanded, "Did you really think you could hide these from me? You come into my territory, you refuse to pay the toll, and then you try to hide your ration slips?"

"I didn't try to hide anything," I said. "They were in my coat pocket. They're not that valuable. I only had them in case I ran into a distribution truck—we have a little kid living with us, and sometimes the trucks have chocolate bars, if you have a little kid."

The faces of the three visible men changed, going from scowling intimidation to slow comprehension. I realized my mistake too late to take it back. Ration slips were supposed to be precious: most people only got so many per week. You could get a small number of additional slips if you had a child under the age of ten living with you, since little kids don't understand rationing as well as adults do—not that most of the adults I'd encountered since reaching Pleasanton really seemed to understand rationing. They were forever running out of basic supplies, and blaming it on the people who operated the trucks instead of blaming it on their own appetites.

If I didn't think ration slips were precious, that implied I was somehow not experiencing scarcity like the rest of them were. And *that* implied… "I knew I recognized you. You're the Colonel's girl, aren't you?" asked the short man. "The one who did something to piss off her daddy and wound up getting herself banished to the hinterlands with the rest of us expendables. Oh, don't look so surprised, princess. Everybody knows about you. You're supposed to be off-limits, you know. I guess your father wants you punished, but not *too* punished. What are you learning here? Humility? Good behavior? You're sure as fuck not learning how to be hungry."

"Boss, she's got two egg slips here," said one of the other men as he looked through the crumpled rations that had been thrust into his hands. "A dozen each."

Greed and rage warred for ownership of the first man's face. In the end, greed won. "Daddy takes care of his little girl, doesn't he? Where do you live, sweetheart? We'll walk you home, check your cupboards for anything that's going wanting, and then let you go on your merry way."

"Or you could let her go right now, and we might not have to shoot you," said a voice to the side. I turned my head, struggling against the man who still held me, and saw three men in USAMRIID uniforms, two holding guns and the third holding a cattle prod, standing about ten feet away. The sight of the cattle prod was enough to make my stomach drop and the muscles in my legs go weak, like the electricity would somehow jump the distance between us and shock me out of myself.

The man didn't let me go. The shorter man stepped to the side, as if he was trying to block me from view. "This is a private matter," he said.

The man at the head of the patrol looked genuinely surprised. "You're going to fight me on this?" he asked. "You're really going to stand there, with your hands on an innocent woman, and fight me on this?"

"It's a private matter," the man replied.

"All right," said the soldier, and fired.

The report was small, more of a cough than a bang. The short man looked surprised. Then he looked down at his shirt, where a red stain had appeared on the left side of his chest. He looked up again, mouth moving silently. Then, finally, he fell, hitting the pavement with the grace of a sack of wet oatmeal. He didn't move after that.

The soldier calmly worked the bolt on his rifle and turned to look at the three men who were still clustered around me. The one whose hands were on my arms had tightened his grip at the sound of the gunshot, and was now holding me so hard that it was going to leave bruises. Bruises on top of bruises.

"Do the rest of you want to argue with me?" asked the soldier. The man let go of my arms, shoving me toward the patrol as he did, so that I stumbled forward and fouled any possible shot. The three of them turned and bolted away into the strip mall before I managed to catch myself and spin around to watch them go.

For a moment, the only sounds I heard were their footsteps, pounding hard against the pavement. Then a hand touched my elbow. I jumped, whipping around again, and found myself staring at the lead soldier. He looked back, expression unreadable under the lip of his helmet. When he spoke, he didn't show his teeth. I appreciated that more than I could say.

"You shouldn't be this far from your assigned quarters, Miss Mitchell," he said. He spoke more politely than most of the soldiers did when they addressed me, which meant he was probably new, assigned to the quarantine zone when other bases and detachments began collapsing. He didn't know what I'd supposedly done, or if he did know, he didn't believe it. I was such a little thing, after all, and so quiet when I wasn't trying to accomplish anything. There was no way I could have killed half a dozen trained soldiers.

I hadn't. A man named Ronnie did all that, and he did it wearing the body of a prepubescent girl. Mind over matter is what chimera are all about, and Ronnie's mind never met a challenge it wasn't willing to stick a knife into.

"One of the people who's been assigned to the house where I live is missing," I said. The drums were in my ears again, soothing me, chasing the tremors from my voice. Mind over matter. Don't let it get to you. "His wife asked me to go look for him, and I figured it couldn't hurt anything."

The soldier looked meaningfully in the direction my attackers had run before looking back to me and saying, "It could have hurt you. It could have hurt you very badly. You know your father values your safety. He doesn't like it when you wander too far afield."

The temptation to ask why, if he valued my safety so much, I was out in the general population with the looters and the addicts and the people driven insane by grief was strong. I swallowed it down, one more bitter pill for the pharmacy growing inside of me, and said, "That's why my housemate asked me to go. She figured that if there was a problem, the patrols would step in and keep me from getting myself too messed up. She's a smart enough lady to know that she wouldn't get the same treatment."

The soldier looked uncomfortable at my accusation. "It would still be best if you returned to your home. Report your missing housemate to your region's patrol, and they'll be able to keep an eye out for him."

Sally. If they knew who I was, then they knew that I was supposed to be Sally: pushy and brassy and capable of demanding whatever it was that I thought I deserved to have. I narrowed my eyes, folding my arms across my breasts, and said, "Oh, because *that's* going to be a slam-dunk. You'll totally divert manpower to finding one refugee in this whole mess. No. I will not go back to the house. Not unless you make me."

"I could," said the soldier. "I am authorized to do whatever is necessary to keep things peaceful within the compound."

"We're allowed to move around," I countered. "I don't know if you people are going to hit the point where you strap us all to beds 'for our own protection,' but we're not there yet, and we're allowed to move around. If Daddy doesn't like me acting like any other member of the quarantined population, he should be keeping me in the big house with my sister."

The soldier looked even more uncomfortable at that. Discussing the personal choices of his commanding officer was apparently not high on his list of things to do. Doing it in the middle of the street, where we could easily attract attention, was probably even less ideal. "Miss, please. It would be a great favor to me if you would return to your home. You have my personal word that I will go looking for your missing housemate. I won't even make you talk to your local patrol."

Weariness washed over me. I had been here before, multiple times since arriving in the quarantine zone and being pushed out of the USAMRIID quarters into general population. Half the soldiers thought I was a murderess, and would treat me with kid gloves when they thought they might be seen—kid gloves that concealed lead pipes and brass knuckles the second no one else was watching. The bruises on my stomach never quite faded, and I was pretty sure at least one of my ribs was cracked if not dislocated, based on the way it kept digging into my side when I breathed. I didn't complain. Who would have listened to me? Colonel Mitchell might have, if he hadn't been so concerned about the daughter he thought he still had, the daughter he was using me to try and save.

The other half of the soldiers thought I was a babe in the woods, an innocent bystander who was being damaged by the fight between the Colonel and his wife. Everyone knew she wouldn't let me stay in the quarters that had been reserved for the commanding officer's family. If she hadn't been able to make it out of the San Francisco area when the sleepwalkers started attacking, I wouldn't have been in with the general population. I would have been sleeping on clean sheets in a room with dependable air-conditioning and my own toilet, just like all the other pampered civilians who had been pulled in by their military families. The quarters they had at USAMRIID's temporary headquarters inside the Coliseum were nowhere near as nice as our own rooms, back in our own homes, but compared to the rest of the quarantine zone, they were a palace.

"Of course you won't make me talk to my local patrol, because you don't want me to have a way to follow up with you," I said. "I'll go home like a good little girl and you'll pretend you're actually looking for Paul when you're really just pretending that none of this ever happened, right? Oh, maybe you'll track down the looters and shoot them or something, because you don't want it to become totally unlivable in here, but do you think I'm stupid? I need to find him. So how about we do this. How about you come with me, and that way I'm not wandering around unprotected, and you don't have to tell my father that you lost track of me?"

One of the other soldiers coughed, trying to use the sound to conceal his laughter. I relaxed marginally. At least two of the five men currently holding guns were on my side—or if not on my side, they weren't actively hostile toward me. These days, that was the equivalent of a ringing endorsement. If they were laughing, they weren't punching me in the gut.

"You really think that's going to happen?" asked the soldier.

"I think you have a gun, but I have my father, which means I have the bigger stick," I said. It was oddly refreshing to pretend to be Sally. She didn't care if she pissed people off: She just wanted to get what she wanted. I don't think I would have enjoyed being her all the time, but as a mask that I could slip on when I needed to, she was remarkably useful. "So come on. How about you tell me your name, we all make nice, and you and your people come with me to find my missing guy?"

"We're supposed to be patrolling this area," said the soldier. "And I'm Lieutenant Robinson. Do you want introductions to the rest of my men, or will that suffice?"

"Only if they feel like giving me their names," I said. "You're supposed to be patrolling to find people who are misbehaving, or who need help. You found people who were misbehaving when you found me. Now it's time to help me find people who need help. Come on. You didn't enlist because you wanted everyone to hate you. You did it to serve your country and defend your fellow citizens, right? Paul's a fellow citizen. Defend him by bringing him home."

"She's got you there," said one of the other soldiers. Lieutenant Robinson twisted enough to shoot a glare at the man, who grinned unrepentantly. He showed his teeth in the process, and it was all I could do not to flinch. That was the flip side of pretending to be Sally: The harder I tried to fake humanity, the more some parts of it seemed to crumble, becoming virtually impossible to maintain. My distaste for the primate habit of baring fangs in amusement or greeting was one of those crumbling pieces.

"If we accompany you, will you report this to your father?" asked Lieutenant Robinson, turning back to me.

"Only the part where you and your men heroically rescued me from my own stupidity, at great risk to yourselves but with no damage to property or loss of life," I replied without hesitation. I had been doing this for weeks now, and I had always been a fast learner. "I won't tell him you deviated from your patrol route unless you tell me to."

Lieutenant Robinson looked at me carefully, apparently weighing the pros of having me give his men a ringing endorsement against the cons of that endorsement coming from my lips. Finally, with reluctance clear on his face, he nodded. "All right," he said. "Let's go find your missing man."

Walking through Pleasanton with five armed men surrounding me was very different from running through it on my own. The streets were as deserted as they had ever been, but no figures lingered in the windows, and when we passed an open door, no shapes lurked behind it. There were no more looters, just the signs of their passing—broken windows and debris on the sidewalks. A brightly colored chip wrapper blew past, looking almost obscene against the beaten-down gray of everything else.

"You people have done a number on this place," muttered one of the soldiers. My nervousness meant my dyslexia wasn't allowing me to read the name tags on their chests, and none of them had volunteered their names. They were willing to rise or fall with their commanding officer, and not be fingered individually. I could respect that, even as it made me faintly uncomfortable. They could do anything, and I wouldn't know who to point to when my father asked me what had happened.

Then again, what good would pointing at them do? Unless

I took it all the way to Colonel Mitchell, nothing I said would carry any weight with the people around me. I was somewhere between a prisoner and a pet, and there was no immediately visible way for me to change that. The quarantine zone was too well defended for an escape to be possible, unless something went dramatically wrong.

I turned to the soldier, eyes narrowed, and asked, "Would you have done any differently? If you hadn't been enlisted when this all went to hell, would you be sitting quietly in your assigned room, not touching anything, not getting worried or upset or depressed or *anything*, because the people in charge told you not to? Because that doesn't seem human to me. I thought the whole point of this was showing that humanity can win. Breaking things is human. It's stupid and dangerous and irresponsible, but it's *human*." I had learned that early, from the doctors around me, and from Joyce's tales of Sally, who had been a champion breaker of things.

Maybe that was going to prove to be the real difference between humanity and their tapeworm children. We didn't feel the deep-seated need to break the world just so that it would remember our existence.

The soldier I had challenged looked at me uncomfortably for a moment before he looked away, going back to watching the houses and storefronts around us. Lieutenant Robinson didn't say anything. Either he thought the man had deserved my anger, or he just didn't feel like getting involved. It didn't really matter.

"We're getting close to where Carrie said he was going," I said. I was going to keep talking, but I couldn't. The wind had shifted, and when I breathed in, parts of my brain that had nothing to do with Sally Mitchell, and everything to do with the tapeworm that was my true body, activated. *Sleepwalker present*, they said, interpreting the pheromone signals on the wind with ease. *Sleepwalker waking*.

I stopped in the middle of the sidewalk, nearly tripping over my own feet in the process. I hadn't been able to read the pheromones put off by my sleepwalker cousins nearly that clearly the last time I had tried, but I'd been getting there, hadn't I? Maybe exposure followed by isolation had always been the answer. Maybe that was all I'd needed to really figure out what I could do.

The patrol kept going for another few feet, unaware of the danger I was suddenly detecting. They stopped when they realized I wasn't moving, all five of them turning back to look at me with varying expressions of confusion or annoyance.

"Well?" asked Lieutenant Robinson.

I couldn't tell him. There was no possible way for me to explain what I was detecting in the air, because it wasn't a human trait I was manifesting, and they didn't know I was a chimera. If I told them, if I unmasked myself, I was going to find myself with a bullet between the eyes before the Lieutenant could think through the implications of shooting the Colonel's daughter and order his men to stand down. That was human nature rearing its ugly head again: Break what you can't control; destroy what you can't understand.

I still loved humanity, but the more time I spent as their prisoner, the more I began to understand why Sherman had decided they had to be overthrown. And that terrified me, because as much as I feared becoming Sally in earnest—becoming a human girl with a medical problem, and not a chimera at all—I feared becoming a monster even more.

"We should go this way," I said, hoping they wouldn't hear the strain in my voice. I *wanted* to tell them to turn around and run, to keep them from getting too close to the sleepwalker who was putting this pheromone tag into the air. The sleepwalker was more my species than the human soldiers, after all, and it deserved time to come completely into itself. But if it was a sleepwalker and not a chimera—if it was mindless and

damaged and acting only on instinct, I couldn't let it go undis-
covered inside a compound filled with trapped and frightened
people.

Walking the line between the species I was and the species I
was pretending to be wasn't getting any easier with practice. If
anything, it was just getting more complicated.

"What makes you say that?" asked Lieutenant Robinson.
There was a faint warning note in his voice. He didn't like me
taking control of his men, and while I couldn't blame him for
that, I couldn't take the time to soothe his ego, either. Not with
the pheromone tags getting stronger.

They were increasing so fast that it felt like the sleepwalker
was coming closer to us, but even as I thought that, I knew that
it was wrong. The sleepwalker wasn't moving. The tags were
remaining at the same level, they were just becoming *more*.
More plentiful, more consistent, more steadily drifting in my
direction. I took a step back, beckoning for the others to follow
me. "Because I think Carrie said the convenience store he was
going to was in this direction," I said. There were enough convenience stores in the area that I knew there would be one in
whatever direction we went. "That's all."

My voice broke on the last word as things fell into place,
and horror overwhelmed my ability to remain calm—just for
a moment, but that was long enough that I was sure the Lieutenant would see the dismay and agony in my expression. The
pheromone tags weren't getting stronger because the sleepwalker was moving toward us.

They were getting stronger because the sleepwalker was in
the process of taking over its human host.

"If you say so," said the Lieutenant, frowning as he looked
at my face. "You heard the lady, men; we're following Miss
Mitchell. Now, lead the way."

I nodded tightly, not quite trusting myself to speak anymore,
before I turned and started moving upwind.

It was easier now that I had a trail to follow, and also harder, because I knew what I was going to find at the end: I knew I was bringing a team of armed men to execute someone who was in the process of becoming my cousin. And I knew I didn't have a choice.

The smell was strong enough to make the drums start hammering in my ears like a beacon, or a warning—I was walking into familiar danger, and I knew there wasn't any other way, even as I knew that whatever waited up ahead was going to break my heart. Then we turned the corner, moving into the narrow alley between two buildings, and I realized that I hadn't known anything. I had been as ignorant as the men who followed me, and I was going to pay for my blind assumptions.

Paul was huddled against the wall, his arms wrapped around his stomach like he was trying to hold his insides in place, shaking uncontrollably. The tremors seemed to start at the core of his body and radiate outward, sending his legs jittering and knocking his head against the wall.

"Is he having a seizure?" asked one of the soldiers.

"Paul!" I said, and ran forward, dropping to my knees next to my housemate—next to my friend, although that friendship was a strained and stunted thing, kept small and fragile by the circumstances under which we had come to know one another. Maybe it could have been more, in a different world, in a different time.

But in a different world, in a different time, I would never have existed at all.

Paul's eyes flicked toward me, his mouth working soundlessly as he struggled against the tremors that were still rocking his body. It wasn't the mindless grasping of the sleepwalkers, not yet: Paul was still in there, fighting for control. I couldn't have said how I knew, just that it was the truth…and that he was going to lose. He had already lost, and all he could do now was struggle against the inevitable.

"I'm here, Paul, I'm here," I said, putting my hands on his arm. The drums in my ears pounded even louder, and for the first time, I wished that whatever genetic quirk had allowed me to become the person I was now had come with Sherman's gifts, and not my own. I was the only chimera I knew of who could access the hot warm dark at will, sinking down into the peace and safety of my original home. Sherman could use a host's original biology against it, soothing and smoothing out the body's systems until the chimera or sleepwalker fell into a trance, letting him tell them what to do. It didn't always work on sleepwalkers—most of them were too damaged—but Paul wasn't that far gone yet. It might have worked on him, and then he wouldn't have needed to be aware of what was going to happen next.

"S-Sally?" Even getting my name out seemed like an impossible effort. Paul's eyes flicked from me to the patrol, jittering as badly as the rest of his body, before he focused back in on me. "W-what's happening to me? Why can't I move?"

"Sir, we have a situation in the N-sector. Civilian down, apparent epileptic seizure. How do you want us to proceed?" Lieutenant Robinson didn't raise his voice. He didn't have to. His words, and the faint hiss of his radio as he called in the emergency, were more than loud enough to get the point across.

I twisted to look back at him, and said, "This is my friend. This is the friend I was looking for. He's sick. This isn't a situation, he's just sick." The lies came out smooth and easy, like I'd been intending to tell them all along. Paul was sick, all right, but his sickness was going to become a situation very soon. The original personality would die, subsumed by the parasite now working its way into his brain, and we would be left with a hungry, unthinking predator that knew only that it needed to feed. Some sleepwalkers were more capable of planning and strategy than others—some of them might even have a chance at recovering some higher brain functions, if they managed to stay alive long enough—but none of that mattered when compared with the danger Paul would soon present.

And this was wrong, this was *all wrong*. He shouldn't have been able to speak by the time he reached this stage. Something was different. Maybe he was going to be a chimera. I knew how unlikely that was, and I knew that he was going to die. None of the odds were on his side. Nothing about this situation was on his side.

My loyalties were too divided, and I couldn't change that. But I could shield him for now. I could keep them from shooting him while he would still be able to see the muzzle of the gun swinging toward him. If I was careful, I might even be able to do it without giving myself away.

I wasn't sure I knew how to be careful.

"Not s-s-s-sick," stammered Paul, looking increasingly frustrated as the sibilance of "sick" tried to escape him. He made an effort to sit up. The shaking got worse, and he slumped against the wall, twitching and trembling. "Don't know what's w-w-wrong with me."

Lieutenant Robinson's radio squawked. I couldn't make out the words buried in the static. I was too far away, and too focused on holding on to Paul, who felt like he was going to shake himself into pieces. But I heard Lieutenant Robinson's reply.

"As I said, sir, he appears to be having a seizure. Slurred speech, tremors, inability to stand or move. One of his housemates is here: Colonel Mitchell's daughter."

The radio squawked again. There was an ominous pause, during which I heard the click of safeties being released.

"Miss Mitchell, please move away from your housemate." Lieutenant Robinson's voice was suddenly flat, devoid of all inflection or emotion. I twisted to look at him again. It wasn't a surprise to see that all the guns were pointed toward me—

or more accurately, toward Paul, who was continuing to shake and jitter.

I shifted positions, trying to put more of my body between them and Paul without being obvious about what I was doing. The pheromone tags were continuing to get stronger. It would all be over soon. "Why? He's sick. Why are you pointing guns at him when he's just sick? Guns don't make sick people better!" I didn't have to work to add the panicked whine to my voice. It came entirely on its own.

"He's sick, yes," said Lieutenant Robinson. "We cannot offer medical assistance with you between us and him. Please move away from your housemate."

"That doesn't look like medical assistance," I said, pulling one hand away from Paul in order to indicate the guns. "That looks like you're going to shoot him."

"We're going to do everything we can to help."

Paul moaned.

Lieutenant Robinson stiffened, his posture changing to something more closed and military. "Move away from the target! That is an order!"

I didn't comment on how Paul had just gone from being my housemate to being "the target." I didn't need to. I just turned back to him, and watched the last of the clarity slip out of his eyes, replaced by incomprehension and hunger. So much hunger. In the span of a second, Paul went from a man who didn't know what was happening to him but was willing to fight against it to an appetite big enough to eat the world. His jaw dropped, tension going out of it. He moaned again.

"Paul?" I whispered.

He lunged for me.

I scrambled backward as quickly as I could, nearly tumbling over myself as I moved out of range of his teeth. Some sleep-walkers experienced a period of disorientation or even unconsciousness when they took over their human hosts, hence the name, which had been coined following the earliest outbreaks. Others had a more violent response, and went straight to trying to do what they did best: eating. Paul was apparently one of the lucky ones.

A hand grabbed my arm, yanking me farther back, and then the sound of gunfire consumed the world. Paul didn't have a chance. He didn't seem to notice, though: He just kept advancing, even as the bullets struck his body, reaching for me with hands that could never hold enough to feel full.

When the damage became too much for him, he fell, and he didn't move again. The smell of gunpowder and blood filled the alley, wiping away the pheromones that had betrayed Paul's position in the first place. I twisted to find Lieutenant Robinson holding my arm. He didn't let go.

"That's two you owe me," he said. "Your father wants to see you now."

Under the circumstances, there was nothing I could do but nod meekly and let him take me.

We have a problem, and I don't know what we're going to do to solve it.

I've moved my technicians and interns to bottled water for now: I have teams scouring every big box store and grocery outlet in a twenty-mile radius for more. It's not going to last forever, and we don't have a purification system set up for the tap water. The tap water! We let ourselves become too trusting as a species, and this is what that sort of thing gets you. It gets you tapeworms in your drinking glass, and a battleground inside your body.

Even Adam has to avoid the faucet. I'm still trying to culture these eggs, and I don't know whether they'd attempt to take him over. His integration with his host is solid, but that doesn't mean he's prepared for that sort of internal war.

Thank God we caught this before we lost anyone. As it stands, we've burned through a lot of antiparasitics, some of which had to be administered more aggressively than I like, and people are scared. People have a reason to be.

Of all the things I thought to be afraid of, I never thought to be frightened of the water.

—FROM THE NOTES OF DR. SHANTI CALE,
DECEMBER 2027

Mom is terrified. She tries to hide it, but she's not good at concealing her emotions: She never has been. Maybe that's why she's always worked so hard not to have them. Her fear is spreading to the rest of the staff. She's going to start losing control of them soon, and that can't be allowed to happen. We need them. We need their work to continue. And honestly, they're safer here than they would be anywhere else.

We're still looking for Sal. There have been a few unsubstantiated reports that she's been taken to the Pleasanton exclusion zone, but that place is a roach motel—the uninfected check in, and they don't check out. If we still had Tansy up and functional, we could mount a rescue organization and get her back in a heartbeat. As it stands, we have no tactical leader, and Tansy...

Tansy is complicated. But her heart is still beating. There's still hope.

Hope is all we have left.

—FROM THE NOTES OF DR. NATHAN KIM, DECEMBER 2027

Chapter 4

DECEMBER 2027

The room was small and gray, with a large mirror on one wall that was probably a window for the people standing on the other side. The table in the middle of the room came with two chairs, both bolted to the floor. I was seated in the chair that faced the mirror, giving me an unwanted view of my hollow cheeks and greasy hair. I looked like I'd just run through ten miles of hell and had another thousand miles to go.

I *felt* like I'd just run through ten miles of hell. The trip from Pleasanton to Oakland had been spent huddled in a corner of the truck, praying that the men who'd brought me here wouldn't start hitting me again. There had been sirens outside when we were close to the quarantine fence, but after that? Silence. The absolute, unbroken silence of a wounded, uncomprehending world.

I might have been all right if I'd been allowed to stay with

Lieutenant Robinson and his squad, but they had been called away as soon as we reached the main building, and their replacements had been neither friendly nor gentle with me. Why should they have been gentle with me? I was a killer in their eyes, after all. The bruises they'd left on my arms were already starting to blossom, and would continue to grow for days. My only solace was that we'd been in public the whole time. They hadn't been able to do anything worse than grip me too tightly as they dragged me through the halls and threw me into the waiting chair.

I held myself as close to perfectly still as I could manage, keeping my eyes on the mirror that wasn't a mirror. In an odd way, this little room, with its lack of decoration or ornamentation, was a relief. There was nothing here that could hurt me, although I was sure there was something that could hurt me on the other side of that "mirror." Everything was contained and clearly defined, and I felt like I could breathe for the first time in weeks.

Maybe best of all, I wasn't back at the little house we'd been assigned, trying to tell Carrie why Paul wasn't coming back. She wouldn't understand. *I* didn't understand. Paul had been checked out as clean before he was allowed to enter the quarantine zone—all the civilians had. The only reason I hadn't been checked was Colonel Mitchell, and he wouldn't have pulled those strings for anybody else. So how had Paul, who should have been safe, wound up with a SymboGen implant burrowing its way into his brain?

The doorknob turned. I tensed, eyes darting toward the sound, and tried to cling to the drums beating behind my ears as I waited to see what would happen next. I didn't have to wait for long. The door swung inward, and Colonel Mitchell walked into the room, his long face set in a mask of grim seriousness.

He glanced in my direction as he walked to the table's remaining chair, but that was all. He didn't greet me or acknowledge my existence in any other way: just a flicker of the eyes before he sat. He was carrying a thick manila folder under one arm. Once he was settled, he placed it on the table squarely between us, turned so that I could see the label. I had to squint and struggle for several minutes to get the words to swim into clarity. Even then, they twisted and rearranged themselves, leaving me guessing at their meaning.

PLEASANTON PROJECT: SPONTANEOUS INFECTION STATISTICS

Colonel Mitchell didn't say anything as I struggled to read, so neither did I, not even once I was fairly sure I understood the words. We just sat there, both looking at the folder, until I realized I would have to be the one to break the silence. He couldn't do this forever, but if I tried to make him, I was going to get him angry, and I didn't want to deal with that. Sometimes the only way to win is to look like you're losing.

"What is this?" I asked, looking up. As always, I searched his face for some sign that he knew who I was, that he was willing to treat me as me, and not as a surrogate for his lost little girl. As always, I didn't find it—but I didn't find the affection he usually reserved for her, either. All I found was cold, military appraisal.

"It's a report," he said. "Open it."

I squirmed. "You know I have reading issues."

"No, *Sally*, you don't," he said, and his voice was even colder than his face. "Your reading issues came on after your accident, and I don't expect them to have continued."

"My reading issues were the result of physical brain damage," I snapped. "You can't just wish them away because they're inconvenient. Sorry if that's a problem, but it's a biological reality. I'm dyslexic, I'm always going to be dyslexic, and if you want me to know what's in this report, you're going to have to read it to me."

Colonel Mitchell reached out and flipped the report around so that it was turned toward him. He opened the cover with a quick, angry motion, and read, " 'The first case was reported at zero eight hundred on December second, and involved Private Kelly, age twenty-three, Army Reserve. Private Kelly had been given a clean bill of health by USAMRIID doctors, and had completed two full courses of prophylactic antiparasitics to ensure that no eggs or cysts remained in her tissue.' Do you know what eggs and cysts are, Sally?"

"Eggs are eggs, and cysts are infant tapeworms that have gone into a sort of dormant state because conditions aren't right for them," I said.

Colonel Mitchell nodded. His eyes were still so cold. The drums pounded ever harder in my ears, never quite making it difficult to hear but always making it impossible to forget that I was in danger. I was not safe here, no matter how it may have seemed before he came into the room. I was never going to be safe here.

"In the case of the SymboGen implants, they were created to be territorial. We thought they were also asexual, but that turns out not to be true," he said.

I kept my mouth shut. Tapeworms weren't asexual: They were hermaphroditic, capable of reproduction even if they never encountered another member of their own species. The tapeworms created by SymboGen were supposed to have been sterile. The tapeworms created by SymboGen were supposed to have been a lot of things.

"When one of those worms spits out a bunch of eggs, they either lie dormant in the body, waiting for the original to die, or they hatch, realize they can't take out the competition, and encyst themselves somewhere in their host's brain or muscle tissue," said Colonel Mitchell. He was still watching me with those cold, cold eyes, clearly waiting for me to offer some sort of a useful response. I didn't have one. "We've cleared up to eighty cysts out of a single subject. That was eighty little time bombs, all ticking away, waiting for their opportunity to explode."

I still didn't say anything. I knew about the life cycle of the implants: Dr. Cale had explained it to me when she was telling me how she protected her staff. As a chimera, I didn't need to worry about cysts. Even if there were some hidden in my muscles or organs, none of them would hatch as long as I lived in Sally's skull. The pheromone changes I'd caused when I took over would make sure of that. It was connected to the parasitic overgrowth that caused the "tendrils" of tissue that black lights revealed on the bodies of the sleepwalkers, and while I didn't fully understand the science behind it, I knew enough not to have any questions.

Colonel Mitchell's eyes narrowed. "If Private Kelly had no eggs or cysts in her body, and had already consumed a sufficient quantity of antiparasitic drugs, how did she get sick?"

"Did she get sick?" I asked. "You didn't say that. You just said 'the first case.' I didn't want to assume."

"Yes, she got sick." He flipped to another part of the folder, turned it back around, and shoved it toward me. "She got very, very sick."

I knew that if I didn't look, I would be punished. I knew I didn't want to see.

I looked.

The folder was open to a pair of glossy pictures, both large and clear enough that it was impossible not to see details. Private Kelly was a young woman of what looked like Vietnamese descent—or had been, anyway. In the first of the two pictures, she was strapped to a bed, her eyes rolled back in her head, her mouth open in a gesture that I knew all too well. She had broken two of her teeth, and blood covered everything. In the second picture, she was dead. Her skin had taken on a waxy sheen, and her eyes were clouded, staring into nothingness. The blood had dried around her mouth in a thick layer that looked almost like jam, as long as I didn't think about it too hard.

Colonel Mitchell reached out and turned the page, revealing two more pictures, these of a young man. His first picture was similar to Private Kelly's. His second showed him with a bullet hole between his eyes.

"Shall I keep going?" asked Colonel Mitchell.

"Please don't," I whispered.

"Four people under my command have succumbed to the parasites in the last twenty-four hours," he said. Mercifully, he closed the folder as he spoke. I shivered, forcing myself to remain otherwise still. "That's in addition to six civilians—seven now, including your friend. Why do you think that's happening?"

"I don't know."

"What do you think is causing this?"

"I don't know."

"Don't lie to me!" He swept the folder off the table as he spoke, sending it crashing to the floor. I squeaked and fell back in my chair, but he wasn't done. He stood, slamming his hands against the table, and leaned forward until his nose was only a foot or so from mine. "You ran off with that crazy bitch Cale, you were in her *lab*, you have to know what she was doing!"

"Dr. Cale wasn't doing anything like this!" I wailed. "She created the implants, but she didn't distribute them, she didn't modify them to contain unsafe levels of human DNA! That was all SymboGen! Ask Dr. Banks if you want to know what's happening!"

"*You're lying!*"

"I'm not!" I jumped to my feet, stumbling around the chair to get away from him, from the sight of his eyes and the whiteness of his teeth, which showed every time he yelled at me. "Dr. Banks is the one who modified the implants, not Dr. Cale! If they're doing something they shouldn't be able to do, blame him! It's his fault!"

It was all his fault. Even my existence was his fault. That man—that horrible, hateful man—was my father as much as Colonel Mitchell was. Each of them had contributed to one half of me.

"Dr. Banks has been nothing but cooperative since this crisis began," said Colonel Mitchell. He didn't sit down, but he wasn't yelling anymore, either. "He has provided research material and raw data that has proven exceedingly helpful in preserving civilian lives."

"He modified the implants from their original design. He added more human DNA than they were supposed to contain. And he didn't listen to Dr. Cale when she told him what he was doing was dangerous," I countered. "He *knew* the sleepwalkers were a risk. SymboGen was covering this up for months before it got too big. God, Daddy, when did you start believing his lies? You used to know what kind of man he was!"

"Yes. He's the kind of man who offered medical care to my daughter when she needed it, and the kind of man who has provided us with supplies of antiparasitics far in excess of what we had on hand," said Colonel Mitchell. My calling him "Daddy" didn't seem to have changed a thing. "He's not a good man, Sally. I'm not foolish enough to think he is. His bottom line has always been his first priority. But when the cards were down, he stepped up and helped us. What did your precious Dr. Cale do? She ran and hid. She took data that could have helped us, and she kept it to herself."

"You knew where she was all along," I said. "Dr. Banks even said so, when you sent him to us with his science project. Why are you mad at her when you could have gone and collected her any time you wanted to?"

"Because she hid," said Colonel Mitchell. "She hid, and she started sending her research out to anyone who wanted to use it—including the enemy. Why didn't we take her? Because we knew she wouldn't work for us. She made that perfectly clear in her videos. But we still needed her *working*. We needed her trying to find a solution to this problem, and that meant monitoring but not touching. And now we've lost her."

"What?" The word came out softer than I had intended, strangled by terror and hope, which were not easy bedfellows. "What do you mean you've..." Nathan was with Dr. Cale. My dogs were with Dr. Cale. *Adam* was with Dr. Cale. My entire family, my real family, they were all with her.

"We've lost all contact with her lab," he said. "The satellites are still up there, they're still beaming down data, but we have fewer analysts every day. I don't know if you've noticed, Sally, but we're fighting for the future of the human race out there, and we're losing. Now your Dr. Cale may have doomed us all."

"You can't think she did this!"

"I can't think she didn't! Have you *seen* the videos she's released so far? She openly states that she doesn't know whether to side with the humans or the worms! She's a traitor to her own species."

I stared at him. Then, gathering as much courage as I could find, I drew myself up to my full height and said, "If Dr. Cale is a traitor to her species, so am I. I don't know anything about why people are getting sick. I wouldn't have led that patrol to Paul if I'd known he was getting sick, I would have gone by myself and tried to make sure he didn't suffer. He didn't deserve to suffer. I haven't got anything to tell you. But I have bruises on my arms from where your people grabbed me, and I don't want to be here anymore."

Colonel Mitchell paused, visibly thrown off of whatever he had been about to say. "What?"

"Look." I rolled up the sleeve of my sweater until the fingermarks on my arm became visible. The newest ones hadn't quite brightened yet, but that didn't matter; there were plenty of older bruises to take up the slack. I looked like a child's art project, all yellow and purple and black.

"Look," I said again, letting go of my sleeve and pulling up the bottom of my sweater, showing him the deep purple bruises on my stomach. "I think I have a broken rib, too, maybe, but I can't show you that. My chest doesn't come open."

"Lieutenant Robinson told me about the men who'd been harassing you when you were first located. If they—"

"You're not listening. I guess that's not new." I dropped my sweater and just looked at him, wondering when things had changed so profoundly, and so permanently. He had been the man who hung the stars, once, and I'd been his little girl, struggling to live up to a ghost, willing to do anything to make him happy with me. Now I was a monster in his eyes, and he was a monster in mine, keeping me captive when all I really wanted was to run back to my family—my real family, the one that didn't say, "Pretend to be something you're not, and we'll pretend that you're worthy of being loved."

"All these bruises, the ones you saw and the ones I didn't show you, they all came from *your* men, because they think I'm the one who killed all those soldiers when Sherman and his people broke me out of here." I wasn't protecting Dr. Cale, because there was nothing to protect: She had been packing to move when I left the lab with Nathan and the others, and I had no way of finding her if she didn't want to be found.

I wasn't protecting Sherman, because I hated him.

Colonel Mitchell stared at me for a moment before shaking his head and saying, "You must be mistaken. The soldiers under my command know that you're my daughter. They would never lay hands on you."

"The soldiers under your command know you won't let me stay in the family quarters with your wife. They know that you have me out in the general population, where there's no way you can possibly monitor me twenty-four hours a day. They know that you only have me here because you're trying to save Joyce." Her name was ashes in my mouth. I still loved her. Out of everyone in my family, she was the one who'd never turned against me, so of course she was the one who had been targeted by the cousins for conversion, because since when has the universe been fair?

Colonel Mitchell didn't say anything, and so I continued for the both of us. "They did this. You never told them I didn't orchestrate my own escape, and they did this. They're going to *keep* doing it, too, until the day you either cure Joyce or give up on her, and then they're going to do something worse...and you're going to let them, aren't you? You're going to stop pretending you care about me, and you're going to let them."

"Sally, please. Don't be unreasonable."

"Don't call me 'Sally,'" I spat. He recoiled. There was something almost childishly shocked in his expression, like that had been the last thing he'd expected from me. "My name is *Sal*. My name has always been Sal, and you *know* that, none of the things you've done here will change that, and I don't want to play this game anymore. Your people are hurting me while you look the other way. You're letting your wife—"

"Your mother," he interrupted.

"Oh, my mother, right. You realize that makes this worse, not better, don't you? If she's your wife, then she's saying, 'I won't let the monster that took my daughter's body as her own be in the safe place where I am.' But if she's my mother, she's saying that about her *own little girl*. One of us has to be the monster here, Colonel! Is it her, or is it me? Pick carefully, because you can't redeem us both!"

He took a deep breath, visibly steadying himself, before he

said, "Sally, I can understand why you're upset, and I assure you that the men who hurt you will be disciplined. This sort of behavior is not befitting either USAMRIID or the United States Army, and I won't stand for it. I'm not going to punish you for telling me lies about yourself, or about your mother, because I should have done more to protect you. For that, I am sincerely sorry."

I stared at him. "You're sorry? That's what you have to say? You're sorry?" More and more, I was coming to realize that the human brain was capable of some amazing, illogical things. Fishy—an employee of Dr. Cale's— had convinced himself that reality was a video game rather than live with the knowledge that his wife was dead. Dr. Banks had somehow managed to convince himself that he wasn't a traitor to his own species. For a long time, I had convinced myself that I was human, even with all the evidence in the world staring me in the face, telling me that I was wrong. And now, despite all the evidence in the world, Colonel Mitchell was trying to convince himself, again, that I was still his daughter on anything more than a genetic level.

"I should have been more careful with you," he said. "I was trying to teach you a lesson, and I was wrong. You won't be going back to the general population. These spontaneous infections...whatever's causing them, I can't afford to risk you being affected."

"But you said it was affecting your soldiers too," I said. The drums were pounding harder now, spurred by the terror of staying in a building filled with people who hated me. The only one who didn't was Joyce, and she was in a coma she was never going to wake up from. "Why am I any safer in here than I would be out there?"

"Because here, we can keep you in isolation," said Colonel Banks. "We can make sure nothing touches you, and you can focus on your purpose here. You can help me save your sister."

"Nothing's going to save her," I said quietly. "I wish you could see that."

"You had best hope something does," he replied. "That's what's going to save you, too." He turned and walked back to the door, leaving me alone in the little room with the mirrored wall, and the pages of his report scattered across the floor like so many fallen leaves.

There was no clock in the little room. There were few clocks left anywhere, and most of them were keeping their own time at this point, refusing to synchronize. Things were falling apart, one piece at a time, and telling prisoners how long they'd been locked away probably wasn't high on the priority list.

I walked circles around the room for a while, trying to let the exercise both stabilize and soothe me. When my legs got tired, I gathered up the pages of Colonel Mitchell's report, careful not to look at the pictures, and put them back in the folder. I placed the folder itself on the table, where I wouldn't step on it by mistake. Maybe my little effort at housecleaning would convince them that I was trying to play by their rules, and they would be kinder to me—or at least more inclined to treat me like I genuinely belonged.

There was nothing else to do in this isolated little room, and I didn't dare try the door. Either it was locked or it was a trap, and whatever waited on the other side wasn't going to be kind, or gentle, or care how many bruises it left. I retreated to the corner and sat, pulling my knees to my chest and wrapping my arms around my legs before doing what I had wanted to do since being put in here. I released my hold on the world of human sights and human senses and sank down, down, down into the hot warm dark, where nothing was going to hurt or trouble me again.

It was difficult to describe the hot warm dark in words. Nathan could never wrap his head around the idea that it was hot and warm at the same time, that the two things were different states that could coexist without difficulty. There was no color there, because I had no eyes when I was there, but it was still a kind, red world, even when everything was washed away by blackness. Those contradictions didn't seem contradictory at all. Not when I was there.

I moved through the hot warm dark, and time fell away, leaving me in an eternal, peaceful *now*. "Moved" wasn't the right word; I knew I wasn't moving. There wasn't room inside the cathedral of Sally's skull for me to do anything but sleep. Still, some part of me remembered what it had been to move through her body, free and twisting like a ribbon in the tissues of her flesh, and that was the part that ruled when I was in the hot warm dark.

As I moved, I tried to think. It was becoming increasingly clear that I needed to find a way out of here—I should have tried to find it the minute I was taken. The electrical prods the soldiers used as nonlethal prisoner control had frightened me so badly that I'd stopped moving forward, choosing instead to stay where I was and wait for the situation to change around me. Well, the situation had changed. I needed to go.

The quarantine zone was protected by fences and patrols. If there were weak spots in the fences, no one I knew was talking about them, and while there was a black market inside the fence, it seemed to be entirely based on selling things that had been scavenged from homes and businesses. I hadn't heard anything, from anyone, about goods coming in from the outside. It was possible that my position as the Colonel's daughter meant that no one wanted to talk to me, but I doubted it. Carrie, Paul, and the rest of my housemates had accepted me as one of their own. If they'd known anything, I would have known it too.

Trucks left from the Coliseum and entered the quarantine zone daily, carrying soldiers who swept the surrounding areas for survivors and supplies that were starting to run low inside the fence. It was government-sanctioned looting, and it might represent my best chance of getting out of here. If I could somehow get onto one of those trucks...

...which would be packed full of soldiers with guns and cattle prods. Soldiers who could legitimately claim that they hadn't realized who I was before they shot me, or even worse, shocked me. The thought of dying was sad and scary. I wanted to make it back to my family. I didn't want to die without them knowing what had happened to me. The thought of being shocked again was *terrifying*. Death was an end. Electrocution could leave me stranded and still aware in Sally's body, but unable to control it ever again. No. The trucks weren't the answer.

Unless I could steal one.

The thought was shocking enough to pull me out of the dark and back into the bright, sterile light of the interrogation room. My eyes snapped open, the enormity of the idea sinking in. I could steal one. Not without help—I didn't know how to drive—but there were people here who could help me. There was Carrie. She wanted out as badly as I did, and she was going to want out even more now that Paul was gone. The spontaneous infections would lend an element of randomness to the situation, but if I could get her brought here...

They wouldn't be keeping us in quarantine if they didn't want to keep as many people alive as possible. I stood, walking over to the mirror. "Hey," I said, raising my voice to make sure that it would be audible to the speakers I knew had to be present. "Hey, is someone there? I just remembered something. The man who got sick, his name was Paul. His wife, Carrie, is back at the house. And she wasn't feeling good this morning, either."

I'm sorry, Carrie, I thought. Her boyfriend, lover, whatever he actually was to her was dead, and she might not even know it yet, depending on how quickly the patrol had removed me from the area. Paul was dead, and now I was having her yanked out of her home and thrown into isolation, and for what? So I could steal a truck and have someone to drive it for me?

I was sorry, but that didn't change the necessity of what I was doing. I needed a truck. I needed a driver. Who better to serve than the widow of a man who'd just been executed in cold blood by USAMRIID's soldiers?

There was a clicking sound from somewhere above me, and a female voice said, "Thank you for the information. Please step away from the door."

With dawning horror, I recognized the speaker as the woman from the shower, the nameless sergeant who'd threatened to make me eat my own vomit after she punched me in the stomach. I stepped backward, stopping only when my thighs hit the side of the table hard enough to add another bruise to my growing collection. The drums in my ears pounded harder than ever, almost dizzying me with their volume. She hated me. She hated me, and Colonel Mitchell was gone, and I didn't know how she was planning to subdue me, I didn't know, she could do anything—

The door opened, and there she was, terrible in her uniform, a cattle prod in her hands. There were two more soldiers behind her, but I couldn't focus on them: All my attention was claimed by the terrible thing she was holding.

"Seems someone told the Colonel there was some question about how you'd been handled by his people," she said in a low, dangerous tone. "Seems he's concerned about how many bruises you've managed to pick up bumbling around out there. We pointed out that Pleasanton is a pretty dangerous place, but he was dubious. Seems like he wants to believe his precious little princess. So we're going to have to be extra careful with you from now on."

"I won't resist," I said quickly. "Look, I'm not resisting. I'm not running I'm not fighting I'm not doing anything at all. Please. You don't have to shock me. I'll go willingly."

"Oh, I know you will," she said, and smiled. "But no one's looking just now, and you're already denying us so much of our fun. You've got to admit that wasn't very nice. Means we'll have to be a little more creative."

"Please don—"

My words were cut off when the end of the cattle prod slammed into my stomach. Everything was static and pain, and then everything was gone.

The hot warm dark had become a haven since I had become a human, but there was a time when it had been my prison: when it had sketched out the boundaries of my existence, confining me to the spaces inside another's body and refusing to allow me anything beyond the scraps she saw fit to throw my way. I hadn't known resentment then, hadn't understood what it was to yearn for what you couldn't have; all I'd known had been survival, and some deep-coded impulse in my genetic code that had ordered me to swim up, out of the darkness, into the light.

Since the first time I had opened Sally's eyes, I had regarded the hot warm dark as my special, secret place. Even Sherman had admitted what a strange thing it was that I could go back there at will—for most chimera, once they came out of the dark, its doors were closed to them forever after. I was a lucky girl.

And now I was trapped.

I moved through the hot warm dark like I was running from the monster in a horror movie, knowing the illusion of motion was just that—an illusion—but unable to make myself stop. I didn't know whether Sally's eyes were closed or whether the electricity had somehow managed to break the connection between me and her optic nerves, and the fact that I kept thinking of my body as *her* body told me just how cut off I was, how far removed I suddenly was from the existence that should have been my own.

Please, I moaned, and there was no sound, because I had no lips, or mouth, or throat. Was this what it had been like for Tansy when Dr. Banks split her skull open and started severing the connections that bound her to the body she controlled? Had she thrashed in nothingness, reaching frantically for any sign that her existence still had weight or purpose? She'd always been a little neuro-atypical, but most of that had been a consequence of the body she was in, which had suffered some damage before Tansy took it over. Had she felt her sanity melting away in the isolation, when what should have become a privilege became a prison?

Please. This time my moan was a whimper, and it was just as quiet as it had been before.

I stopped trying to move through the hot warm dark and sank deeper, letting go of the motive force that had driven me to seek a way through, a way out. It was over. I had lost. I had taken this body when it hadn't been mine, and now, finally, it had been taken away from me. I was going to die here. I might as well have been dead already.

Wait.

I had *taken* this body. I had been completely unaware of what I was and what I was doing, but instinct had been enough to let me make the connections between Sally Mitchell's abandoned brain and my own boneless form. Her brain tissue and my body were essentially the same, when you really looked at them. They were both quivering tubes of protein, folded back on themselves dozens, even hundreds of times, until they formed something functional.

I had claimed ownership of this body when I couldn't think, couldn't make choices for myself, couldn't do anything but follow the instincts that had been unwittingly built into me by the scientists who designed my genetic code. Even sleepwalkers could manage to do it, and the damage they did in the process was all a consequence of getting *into* the brain. I was already there. I had made myself a comfortable bed, and the tissue had folded itself around me, accepting me as a part of itself. I couldn't damage anything if I was careful.

Where was the hot warm dark? The hot warm dark was in my memory, and in my original body, the one I had forgotten for so very, terribly long. It was in the smooth white flesh and flower-shaped head of a tapeworm, sheltered in the delicate folds of a human brain.

Tapeworms didn't have eyes: I couldn't open them, couldn't do anything to make myself more aware of my environment. But I could accept myself. Bit by bit, I let go of the idea of myself as a human being, as a bipedal creature with hands and arms and eyes and teeth. Instead, I thought of myself as long and fine and ribbonlike, designed for dark places, created to survive no matter what. I thought of myself as I had once been without thinking about it, as the creature that had hatched from an egg created in a SymboGen lab.

Part of me still wanted to regard my origins as shameful, but why should I? Everything started from an egg, even human children. There was nothing wrong with the way I was born. I was alive now, and that was what mattered. I was alive, and I was going to stay that way, no matter what the consequences— no matter what the costs.

The hot warm dark seemed to fade around me, replaced by a new kind of awareness, like the world had contracted still further and somehow become bigger at the same time, maybe because I had become so unbelievably much smaller. The world was black now, not red, but the heat, the warmth, the reality of the hot warm remained. This was where I had begun.

So begin again, I thought fiercely. I felt myself *twitch*, a squamous, slick feeling that had little to do with the kind of motion that had become so familiar to me since the day I woke up in Sally Mitchell's hospital bed. But this was me, too, and I needed to accept that, or I was never getting out of here.

Begin again, I thought, and the twitch repeated itself, my body responding to my commands without bothering to take the time to explain what it was doing—and that was all right, really, because I was so divorced from my original form that I couldn't have understood if I'd tried to tell myself. There wasn't time for that. There was only time to hope that this would work, that I had found the way out after all.

All I had to do was open my eyes.

All I had to do was open my eyes.

All I had to do—

I opened my eyes.

I was once again lying on a cold concrete floor. There was a vent set into the ceiling high above me. Plastic billowed down from it, belling out to form an umbrella shape. The quarantine bubbles. When I'd been taken by USAMRIID the first time, the time that Sherman came to break me out, they had placed me in a quarantine bubble for study before they decided what to do with me. There had been dozens of other bubbles visible from mine; they must have cycled the entire current population of Pleasanton through this facility.

I was so busy thinking about what the plastic meant that it took me a few seconds to realize I could see the plastic. My eyes were working again. I focused on the rest of my body, looking for the places where my limbs diverged from the mass of my torso and hips. Finding my fingers shouldn't have required an effort, but it did; they were slightly numb, like they had gone to sleep and weren't quite ready to get out of bed yet.

Too bad, I thought, and forced them to move, bending each of them in turn until I was sure that they were all present and accounted for. The numbness had faded by the time I finished. I turned my hands over, pressing them against the cold floor until my palms felt fully responsive. Then I pushed, and slowly, laboriously, worked my way into a sitting position.

"You're alive." The voice was dull, uninflected.

I turned slowly, still trying to wake up my sluggish muscles, and found myself looking at Carrie. She was sitting on the bubble's single narrow cot, still wearing her coat over her slightly grimy sweater and jeans. Tears had drawn tracks through the dirt on her cheeks. I hadn't realized how filthy she'd become until seeing her here, in a sterile environment.

"Did they hurt you?" I asked. There were no traces of sleepwalker pheromones in the air; Carrie was still unaffected by whatever was causing the spontaneous infections among the quarantine subjects and Colonel Mitchell's men. That was a good thing. Sleepwalkers couldn't drive.

I was sorry for the thought as soon as I had it. There was being practical, and then there was being inhumane. I didn't want to allow the first to make me become the second.

"They shoved me around, but they didn't hurt me," said Carrie. A tear ran down her cheek, drawing another line through the dirt. "Is it true what they said? About Paul? Did he really become one of those... those things?"

"Carrie, I'm sorry." I gathered my limbs, pushing myself away from the floor again until I was standing, unsteady as a newborn puppy. I felt like *I* was a little numb, a little distanced from myself. That would pass with time... or, if it was the cost of reconnecting with my original body, it wouldn't. It had still been worth it, to claw my way back up out of the dark, to find my way back to a world where there was light, and motion, and the chance that I could still find a way home.

She looked at me for a moment, lower lip wobbling like she was trying to keep her feelings inside and failing, one escaping tear at a time. "How is that even possible?" she asked. "He was clean. We were both clean. The Army made sure of that before they locked us up. He *can't* have become one of those things."

"But he did," I said. I risked a step forward, toward the bed.

It felt clunky, disconnected, and I nearly fell when my foot hit the floor bent wrong. I managed to turn it into a stumble, and took another step. "I'm so sorry. He was already almost gone when I found him."

"I should've gone with you," she whispered, and ducked her head, bracing her chin against her chest. "I shouldn't have let you go alone. He deserved...you shouldn't have been...I should have gone with you. I should have been there for him."

"I don't think he would have wanted you to see him like that," I said. I took another step forward before allowing myself to half fall onto the bed. Carrie blinked at my impact, but she didn't move away. She still didn't know about me. That was for the best, for both of us. "Paul was almost gone when I found him, and it would have taken longer for the two of us to get there, if we'd been traveling together. Just remember him. Remember why you loved him. And be glad you didn't have to see."

Carrie shook her head. "Maybe it wasn't Paul."

"It was."

"Maybe it wasn't!" The sheer force of her denial raised her voice, and the gently curved walls of our bubble bounced it back at us, making it seem loud enough to fill the whole world. Carrie came out of her curl and turned to me, her eyes blazing with the need to make me *see*, to make me *understand*. "Maybe it was somebody else, there are lots of people in the quarantine zone, and it could have been somebody *else*, somebody who just looked....looked sort of like him, enough like him to fool you but not enough to fool me. He could still be out there!"

"Carrie..."

"All those *things* look alike, they're all hungry and snarling, how could you be sure? How could you really know that it was him? Maybe it wasn't."

"I knew it was him because he wasn't all the way gone when we found him," I said. The memories were fresh and raw. I felt even worse for him now than I had then. How quickly had the cousin burrowing into his brain wiped away human consciousness? Had Paul become a passenger in his own body, trapped the way I had been? "He spoke to me, Carrie. He knew who I was. And then he was just gone."

"Before the bastards shot him?"

Nothing I could say was going to ease her pain, and so I said nothing at all. I just nodded, watching her eyes for some sign that she understood me, that she was following what I had to say.

Carrie's eyes filled with fresh tears. "God," she said. "*God.*" She punched the bed with both hands, slamming them down so hard that I worried, briefly, that she had broken a finger. That might make it more difficult for her to drive. "He died, and I wasn't there. I sent a stranger. And now I'm in here. Why am I in here?"

"Didn't they tell you?" I asked anxiously.

Her laugh was short and bitter, the laughter of a woman who had given up on hoping for the best from the world and was now resigned to expecting nothing but the worst. "Since when have these assholes been in the business of telling us anything, Sal? A bunch of men in camo showed up on the doorstep, grabbed me, informed the rest of the house that they'd be getting three new roommates, and dragged me back to their truck. We were halfway here before they told me Paul was dead. How is any of this happening? This can't be the real world. It just can't be."

"I'm sorry." It was a useless comment, and I wasn't fully sure what I meant by it. I hadn't created this world. I hadn't created the cousins. But I could apologize for all of it, and if that was what Carrie needed me to do, I was going to do it. "I'm so, so sorry."

"They wouldn't even let me see his body." She dragged the heel of her hand across her cheek, smearing the grime. "We used to joke about what we wanted to have done with our bodies after we died. Paul wanted to go to the Body Farm and help the FBI study the effects of exposure on the human body. He thought it would be great to just hang out in the government facility, rotting. And now I g-guess he got his wish…"

That seemed to be the last straw. Carrie buried her face in her hands and sobbed, curling in on herself like she could shut out the rest of the world. I pulled back, not touching her. She needed to come through this on her own. If she seemed to be rendered insensate by her grief, I could find another driver. I wasn't sure where, or how, but I would do it if that was what I had to do.

It might be better that way, honestly. Carrie was emotionally compromised, and I didn't know if I could trust her to get me out of here. She was also the only person I currently had access to. Sometimes you have to work with the materials at hand.

"I'm sorry." I patted her, awkwardly, on the back before leaning as close as I could and whispering in her ear, "I told them you were sick too, so they'd get you out of the quarantine zone. I need your help."

"What?" She whipped around to face me. Her eyes were so wide that I could see rings of white all the way around her irises, making her look almost cartoony. "But I'm not—"

I motioned frantically for her to shush. She stopped herself mid-sentence, and just stared at me.

I leaned forward, getting close to her ear once again, and murmured, "I know you're not. The question is, do they know? Or did they put you in here with me to find out what would happen?" Even if Colonel Mitchell had been able to successfully convince himself that I was Sally—and I still didn't know whether that was the case; he'd played a long game before, and he could have been doing it again. He knew I had a tapeworm inside my skull. Since I'd seen Joyce, there had been no more talk of surgery or making an effort to remove my implant. I was incredibly grateful for that, since removing the implant would have killed me instantly, but...

They *had* to know that sleepwalkers were triggered by the presence of other sleepwalkers. Implants that had integrated put off very different pheromone tags than implants that were still quiescent, and those tags seemed to carry a sort of... instruction manual for taking over a host. We still didn't know whether chimera had the same effect. Dr. Cale didn't know. We didn't release the pheromones that triggered migration in sleepwalkers, but that didn't mean we weren't releasing other coded messages, silent, secret instructions for the cousins to follow. Maybe I hadn't said "convert," but I could have said "wake up."

Had Paul gotten sick faster than he normally would have because he was sharing a house with me? I couldn't deny the possibility. So had they put Carrie in my bubble to see whether proximity would make her get sick faster? What kind of game were they playing here?

Carrie shot me a horrified look before whispering back, "What do you mean, 'What would happen'?"

I could tell her, or I could keep my secret a little longer. I didn't like lying to her, not when I was about to try to convince her to drive me out of here, but telling her the truth could very easily result in her panicking and refusing to help me at all. I took a breath and answered, "The Colonel's wife hates me. She says I'm not really her daughter. If you're supposed to be getting sick, why would they lock me up with you, unless it was to see if you'd kill me?"

"That's stupid," she said, louder than I liked. She pulled away. "Why would anyone do that?"

"Why would anyone do any of this?" We were probably being monitored. I moved closer again, trying to use my hair as a veil to hide the motion of my lips. "Things were bad when they put us in here, and you know they've just gotten worse since then. Haven't you noticed that there aren't any new soldiers around? There's no backup coming. There's no support. Of course they're going to start getting desperate, and doing whatever they can for data."

"But you're his *daughter*."

"I'm his little traitor. And you're the wife of a man who got sick when he shouldn't have been able to. We're both expendable in our own ways." I wasn't quite lying, not yet, but I was bending and eluding the truth, shaping it into my own creation. The thought made me feel nauseous, and set the drums pounding harder still in my ears. I didn't want to be a liar. Sherman and Dr. Banks and my father, they were liars, and they weren't the people I wanted to become.

"We have to get out of here," said Carrie.

I had been trying to lead her to this conclusion. I restrained myself to a small nod as I agreed, "We do."

"But how?"

That was where my plan fell apart. I had expected them to lock me and Carrie in a room, not in one of the quarantine bubbles. I sat up straighter and looked around. When Sherman had broken me out of here, he'd used a chemical compound to melt the plastic. I didn't have that. There were no seams or openings, apart from the place where the bubble joined up with the vent; I had to assume that when the soldiers came to feed us or move us, they'd open the bubble in the same way.

I didn't have a knife. I didn't even have an underwire in my bra—and even if I had, using it would have assumed that we weren't being watched somehow, and that the soldiers wouldn't show up the second I started trying to puncture the plastic. We were in a completely exposed situation, with no weapons, no way to take the tactical advantage, and no combat training.

Well. *I* didn't have any combat training. "Do you know how to fight?" I asked.

"Not really? I took a few years of self-defense in college. I can mostly handle myself in a fight, as long as running away is an option."

I nodded slowly. "All right," I said. "Here's what we're going to do…"

Kristoph died today.

Symptoms appeared in his host body shortly after three o'clock in the afternoon. It started with tremors in his hands and loss of fine motor control, and progressed rapidly to full-body convulsions, followed by a loss of consciousness and a systemic shutdown that we were unable to stop, despite the best efforts of everyone in the facility.

Following the cessation of vital signs, we opened his host's skull to extract Kristoph and prepare him for transplantation. We found a nest of tapeworms where the host's brain tissue should have been. Several of them were wound around Kristoph's body, and had successfully strangled it, rendering it inert. Attempts were made to resuscitate the lead segment. All were unsuccessful.

Eggs have been harvested from Kristoph's remains, and will be cultured shortly. Analysis of the invading worms is now under way.

—FROM THE NOTES OF SHERMAN LEWIS (SUBJECT VIII, ITERATION III), DECEMBER 2027

Solve the puzzle, take your time,
Spurn the reason, shift the rhyme,

*Let the labyrinth guide you through the darkness to the
    dawn.
Children's games can break your heart,
We all have to play our part.
Know this world will grieve you when it wakes to find
    you gone.*

*The broken doors will open for we sinners who atone.
My darling boy, be careful now, and don't go out alone.*

—FROM *DON'T GO OUT ALONE*, BY SIMONE KIMBERLEY,
PUBLISHED 2006 BY LIGHTHOUSE PRESS.
CURRENTLY OUT OF PRINT.

Chapter 5

DECEMBER 2027

Carrie seized and spasmed on the floor like she was dying, arching her back until she lifted her hips and the backs of her thighs into the air. She formed a brief, perfect arch before collapsing back down and starting to thrash again.

I wanted to admire her muscular control, but this wasn't the time. Instead, I stood on the cot, shrinking back against the bubble wall, and screamed as loudly as I could.

It was almost a relief, after weeks of keeping quiet, to let my voice out, to hear it echoing off the plastic walls and bouncing back down from the vent above me. Carrie continued to take up as much of the floor as she possibly could, jackknifing her body and flailing her arms, and I kept on screaming until the sound of running feet interposed itself beneath my wails.

As soon as the soldiers were in view, I pointed at Carrie and turned my screams to wails, saying, "She's sick! She's sick! I told them she was sick and now she's sick and she's in here with me *what are you waiting for*?!"

As I'd hoped, the thought that I could be hurt by their inaction actually slowed them down. Not enough so that Colonel Mitchell would be able to say that they hadn't responded, no, but enough to let me be taught the error of my ways. They weren't running anymore. They were approaching calmly, and their expressions broadcast nothing but anticipation for what was about to happen.

I screamed. Carrie thrashed. Then, with a horrible rasping gurgle that made me want to applaud her acting skills, she went still, her head lolling to the side and her wide-open eyes staring blankly off into space. If I hadn't known better, I would have thought that she had actually succeeded in thrashing herself to death.

"Oh, God," I moaned, pushing myself harder against the wall of the bubble. It bent and distorted under me, but it didn't break: it had been made too well for the weight of one small woman to rupture it. That didn't matter. I was putting pressure on the membrane, and that was the important thing.

Stay still, Carrie, I thought, and Carrie didn't move, and for one horrible moment, neither did the soldiers. Did they know? Had we somehow given ourselves away? Did they have monitors that told them whether we lived or died, convenient medical spies built into the bubble's walls and feeding back our vital data? I couldn't put it past them, but I couldn't quite believe it, either. The people here at USAMRIID were so perfectly, beautifully human, and being human meant being arrogant, in some ways: It meant believing that you knew better than anyone else ever possibly could. They wouldn't expect something like this. Not from us. Not from anyone.

"Miss Mitchell, stay where you are," said the figure at the front of the formation—and while I couldn't make out her face in the shadows of her helmet, I recognized the voice of the woman from the shower, the nameless sergeant who'd been so gleeful about causing me pain. Knowing it was her made what we were about to do less difficult. I didn't care if her career went up in flames because I got away.

I shrank back against the bubble, stretching it more, putting more pressure on the whole structure. She pulled a spray can from her belt, shaking it briskly before she traced a fizzing line down the front of the plastic dome. It was supposed to dissolve the membrane cleanly, allowing the soldiers to come inside. It was also supposed to be applied to a bubble that was not under pressure.

The front of the bubble exploded as it finally found a way to vent off some of the tension I had created. It wasn't a reaction with any heat behind it, but it was enough to send chunks of fizzing, dissolving plastic everywhere, covering the soldiers in thin chunks of bubbling membrane. The soldiers screamed, and I realized, to my horror and delight that the stuff they'd sprayed on the bubble to dissolve it was also eating the plastic parts of their uniforms and guns. Once again, humanity had decided to make use of something that couldn't be controlled, and now they were paying the price.

"Come on!" I jumped down from the cot and grabbed Carrie's hand, hauling her to her feet before I rushed for the opening. The lead soldiers were clawing at the fizzing plastic that stuck to their faces and chests, paying virtually no attention to us.

And the woman at the head of the formation had dropped her cattle prod.

I didn't think: I just did. I let go of Carrie's hand and dove for the cattle prod while the soldiers were still scraping at the plastic, not yet reacting to the fact that two of their tractable, controlled prisoners were making an escape. The line of it fit perfectly into my palm, and I began swinging.

Surprise was the main thing we had going for us: surprise,

and the expectation of fear. We were supposed to be paralyzed with terror at the idea of the sleepwalker contagion, so beaten down by what we'd been through that we would offer no resistance. That wasn't the case with either one of us, so when we moved against the soldiers, they weren't ready. The cattle prod hit the nameless sergeant in the throat. She went down flopping and choking. The other soldiers finally seemed to realize that they had a problem on their hands, apart from the plastic-eating chemicals that were chewing holes in their armor. I kept swinging the cattle prod. They went for their guns.

So did Carrie.

She grabbed the sidearm from the fallen sergeant, who was still thrashing, her own seizure much more believable than Carrie's. The soldiers who had managed to get their guns out turned them on Carrie, and I slammed my cattle prod into whatever exposed skin I could find, sending them tumbling to the floor. Some of them had probably been recruited after things started going bad, and had never been trained for situations like this one. The others might have the training, but weren't used to enemies who could think. Too much time spent fighting the sleepwalkers had left them, if not soft, then at least slower than they should have been for situations like this one.

In the end, the only gunshots were Carrie's. Two of them, both small and muffled in the vastness of the room where we'd been quartered. The men she'd shot looked almost surprised before they fell, like this wasn't the way things were supposed to go. Carrie clicked back the hammer, ready to fire again. There was no one to fire at. All the soldiers were either down or already writhing on the floor.

I hated the cattle prod. I hated the weight of it and the poisonous future that it represented. But I knew better than to think that I could be trusted with a firearm, and so I kept my hand locked tight around the hard black shaft as I gestured for Carrie to follow me. "Come on!" I shouted again, in case she didn't understand the gesture. Then I bent, grabbed the access card off the nearest soldier, and ran for the door.

Sherman had freed me the last time I'd been kept here. I knew the way out. I knew where the loading dock was. If there were still vehicles kept there, then it might be our salvation. If not...

If not, at least we had weapons now. I ran, and Carrie ran after me, and we listened for the alarm that would mean we had been discovered as we fled toward the distant, impossible promise of freedom.

We emerged from the umbilical into an empty control room, the monitors scrolling images of the facility. Most of the rooms they showed were empty or severely understaffed. USAMRIID was running out of people. That should have been reassuring—it meant we were so much more likely to escape—but it was really just chilling. If this facility was meant to be the last stronghold of the humans of the Bay Area, and it was this understaffed, what did that say about the rest of the world?

There wasn't time for us to stop or dwell: We were getting out. I kept going, trusting Carrie to follow me, and we emerged into the shadows of the loading-dock garage. It was colder here; the air was unfiltered, filled with the smell of a burning world. Ash, mold, and the distant promise of rain all flooded in through the open doors. I glanced around automatically, checking for sentries, and found none. Instead, my eyes seized on a small patch of darkened concrete, special only in its incongruity. A man had died there, bleeding out after Ronnie slit his throat, just like two men had died for us to get this far. Maybe more, if I'd shocked some of the others too hard.

How many people had died in the quarantine zone? How

many sleepwalkers, how many infant chimera who were only struggling to stay alive? It wasn't me who had made this an us-against-them battle, and now that it was, the only side I cared about was the one that left me free and still alive.

There was a rack of neatly labeled keys on the far side of the garage. I started toward it, motioning for Carrie to follow. "Come on. We need to find something that you know how to drive."

"You electrocuted those soldiers." Her voice quavered. The enormity of what we'd just done was beginning to catch up with her.

I didn't have time for a crisis of conscience—either mine or hers. "Yes, and you shot two of them. Now, find something that you can drive. We need to get out of here before the ones who aren't dead recover and send people looking for us."

Assume three minutes to run from the bubble to here. Assume five minutes for the effects of the electrocution to wear off and leave our former captors capable of calling for help; that was about how long it had taken for the people who'd been tossed into the truck that carried me to Pleasanton in the first place to recover. And it was all just a guess. They could have bounced back in under a minute. I had no way of knowing, and every second we spent was a second we couldn't afford to lose.

Carrie could be upset about what she'd done *after*. After we were out of here, after we were free and clear, after I had decided what came next. What we were doing now would guarantee there *was* an after. Because until we got our butts into a vehicle, that was far from certain.

"I can—I can drive a stick or an automatic. I don't think I could drive a tank."

"I think they'd notice if we stole a tank." The labels on the keys writhed and spun, becoming utterly impossible to read. I was too amped up, the adrenaline racing through my veins until there was no chance I'd be able to calm myself down and fight through my dyslexia. "Pick one of these, and let's go."

Carrie stood there for a few more precious seconds, her eyes skipping from label to label until I wanted to scream, grab the first set of keys that came to hand, and haul her away. I forced myself to remain calm until she reached out and selected a set, jiggling it in her palm for two seconds more before she turned to me. "This one," she said.

"Where is it?"

"Slot fifteen."

"Great. Let's go."

The alarms were starting to scream when we emerged from the loading dock and into the watery light of the early evening. We ran side by side, her carrying keys and a stolen pistol, me carrying a cattle prod and a mountain of guilt. I had to get out of here. That much was certain. Sally's mother was never going to accept me as her child, and Colonel Mitchell was playing some long, terrible game that I didn't understand. He knew I wasn't Sally, he *knew* it, but he kept on pretending. Why? I couldn't force it to make sense.

There was nothing here for me. Dr. Cale might have been able to help Joyce, but she was never going to get the chance; my biological sister would remain here, on life support, waiting for the day her father finally pulled the plug. All we could ever have saved was her body, anyway, and her mother's reaction to me made it clear that donating Joyce to a chimera in need of a host would never have been acceptable to her.

And it still felt like I was running away from yet another family, no matter how dysfunctional: like all I ever did was run from one family after another. The Mitchells, when I chose Dr. Cale; Dr. Cale and Nathan, when I allowed Dr. Banks to sell me back to USAMRIID. The list was short, but even one entry was too long, considering how short my life thus far had been.

"That one," said Carrie, pointing to an SUV. I ran after her, throwing myself into the passenger seat as soon as she unlocked the doors. The alarm was still ringing behind us. Hopefully, they wouldn't think to lock down the motor pool until we were clear.

You're not afraid of cars, I told myself sternly. *That's a fear that belongs to somebody else. That's a fear that belongs to Sally. The people who gave it to you, they were trying to turn you into her. So they gave you her accident, and they gave you her fear. You don't have to keep it anymore.*

I knew that was true. It didn't stop the cold worm of terror from unfolding in my stomach as the engine rumbled into life. My fingers fumbled with the seat belt, clicking it home, struggling to make sure it was tight and secure. I already wanted to throw up.

"There's something you should know," I said, in a strangled voice.

"What?"

"I'm scared of cars."

Carrie shot me a flat you-must-be-kidding look, brows furrowed above wide eyes. "You're telling me this now, and not before you got me to go along with your genius plan? What the fuck am I supposed to do, Sal, drive twenty miles below the speed limit while the army chases us?"

Carrie still thought we were going back to San Francisco. Carrie still thought she could have normalcy again, or something so close to normalcy as to make it easier for her to mourn her husband. Carrie was wrong, and I couldn't tell her that, or she might refuse to take me where I actually needed to go.

Not that I knew where that was. "No, you're supposed to floor it," I said. "Drive like your life depends on it, because it does. But I'm going to try meditating so I don't freak out, because that wouldn't help the situation. So if I start breathing shallowly, please don't get upset." *If I go down into the hot warm dark, where you can't reach me, please don't put a bullet in my head.*

Carrie shook her head. "This is unbelievable," she said, reversing out of the parking space. "This is *fucking* unbelievable. Hold on." And then she hit the gas like the hammer of the gods, and we were rocketing away from the motor pool at the sort of speed that made my mouth go dry and my heart start slamming against my ribs.

Soldiers were emerging from the building behind us, waving their arms like that was somehow going to make Carrie stop the vehicle. She paid them no attention. Her eyes were on the road, her hands were on the wheel, and her foot was on the gas, pressing down with all the force that she could find. All her anger, all her grief, was sublimated into some of the most aggressive driving I had ever experienced.

I didn't grip the dashboard or put my hands over my eyes: I couldn't move. All I could do was sit there, ramrod straight and terrified, as Carrie wove around the men who were now diving into our path, her fingers locked so tight that they had gone white at the knuckles, and accelerated toward the distant fence.

When USAMRIID had seized the Oakland Coliseum for use as their new base of operations, they had made many changes. They had created rooms where there were none, they had set up full medical facilities, and for all I knew, they had installed the two-way mirror in the room where Colonel Mitchell had interrogated me. But they'd done all those things inside. They still thought of themselves as the biggest dogs at the dog park, and they hadn't taken extensive precautions around the outside of the building. As long as their electrified fences were keeping the sleepwalkers out, they had seen no need to take any further steps.

Carrie showed the error of their ways when she veered sharply to the left and went crashing straight through the chain link, punching a hole the size of our stolen SUV in the fence. More alarms started to sound, these loud enough to be audible through the closed windows, adding a whole new layer of terror to my already terrible situation. I tried to force my eyes to close. They didn't obey.

"They're following us!" Carrie shouted.

That got me to move. I glanced at the rearview mirror before twisting to look in the side mirror. Two Jeeps were on the road far behind us. There was, as yet, no air pursuit; if they had any helicopters, they hadn't been prepped to send them out. That didn't mean they weren't going to appear in a few minutes, but we had a chance.

"Go faster," I said, even though it was the last thing I wanted, even though it felt like my lungs were being squeezed by a vast, external hand.

Carrie looked like she wanted to protest. In the end, she said nothing: merely slammed her foot down even harder, until the SUV was moving at a speed that made every inch of me ache with the need for stillness. I forced myself to keep breathing, trying to come up with some scenario that didn't end in USAMRIID catching up with us and taking us back.

We'd managed to escape them this time, but things were different now. We were killers now. We were never going to get a chance like this again.

The freeways were a clogged disaster, choked with the abandoned cars of people who'd been attacked or who had completed their own transformation into sleepwalkers. The surface streets were somewhat better, which I had to assume was a function of USAMRIID's presence: They had been clearing the streets to make it easier for them to get around as they transported people back and forth, as they went on supply runs.

The sun was going down, but it was still bright enough to see—for now. A sign flashed past, miraculously legible in its familiarity, and I knew what we had to do. "Follow the signs!"

I exclaimed, almost shouting in my excitement and my terror. "Go to Jack London Square!"

"What?"

"Jack London Square!"

"You're a crazy person! I stole a car and ran away with a crazy person!" Carrie hauled hard on the wheel as she was yelling at me. It felt like the SUV lifted up onto two wheels when she took the turn, but she didn't slam us into anything, and she didn't flip the car, so I had to call that a victory. My standards were definitely dropping.

"There's a ferry landing there!" I had seen it a few times, when my fam—when Colonel Mitchell and his wife had taken me and Joyce to see free concerts at the attached plaza. It was a shopping area, filled with little stores and big chains. It had probably fallen fast when the sleepwalkers began to wake and hunt. They might still be there, depending on how tactically important USAMRIID considered the place. They didn't matter.

What mattered was the water.

Jack London Square was built entirely along the waterfront. There were canoe and kayak rental stations, and most days, the water was calm enough that it was safe to risk falling out of your boat and going for an impromptu swim. The plaza management had always been very strict about enforcing their "No Swimming" policies, but I really didn't think the Posted signs were going to be a big deal anymore. Something about the collapse of local government told me that no one was going to stop us.

"They're gaining!" snapped Carrie.

"Keep driving," I replied.

Some of the surface streets were narrow, clogged with cars and other obstacles that forced Carrie to reduce speed or risk flipping us over. The setting sun didn't help, casting the world around us deeper into shadow with each passing second. Our followers had less speed to lose, and were making up ground. We didn't need to have that much of a lead; we just needed to have enough to get us to the waterfront before they did.

"You better have a plan!"

"*Keep driving!*"

Carrie swore and slammed down on the gas again, sending us swerving around a tipped-over UPS truck. I took a deep breath, fighting down the urge to scream or vomit. My terror wasn't more manageable than usual: It was just tempered by the knowledge that this was the only way. If we didn't beat the soldiers to Jack London Square, we weren't going to escape, and all this would have been for nothing.

I refused to let it have been for nothing. No matter what I had to do, no matter what I had to pay, I was going to reach the broken doors. I was going home.

The signs for Jack London Square were becoming more frequent as we drove, even if it was getting harder to see them. There should have been more. Some of them had probably been destroyed during the sleepwalker uprising in Oakland. Even with as little attention as I was currently capable of paying to things outside my own head, I could see the signs of the conflict written on the buildings around us in burn marks and blood splatter, which had dried brown and terrible across the storefronts and brightly colored murals. Nathan and I used to visit Oakland to look at the graffiti, which was beautiful and transformative in a way that was difficult to put into words, turning a cold urban landscape into something as virile and alive as any forest or human body. Now those graffiti artists were gone, and their works had been profaned by blood and worse. It made me want to weep for them—and while that might have been an overreaction, it was an overreaction born of my brain trying to protect me from the speed of transit, and I welcomed it.

"Almost there!" shouted Carrie. "Now what?"

"Head for the water!"

She took her eyes off the road ahead to stare at me, shocked into carelessness. "Excuse me but *what*?"

"Can you swim?" That was a wrinkle I hadn't considered when I was putting together my hasty escape plan. If Carrie couldn't swim…

"Are you *insane*?!"

"Good, I can swim too!" I gestured toward the blue sheet of the water, which was drawing closer by the second. Then I unfastened my seat belt. The SUV's internal sensors promptly started beeping, sending ants marching across my every nerve. Even the car knew that what I was doing was dangerous and stupid. So why was I doing it?

Because I wanted to live. The most important reason of them all. "Undo your belt and open your door before we go off the edge!" I swallowed my fear and reached for my door handle, popping it just slightly out of true. "The water pressure won't let us open them once we hit, so this is important! You're going to have to jump before the SUV hits the water!"

"What the fuck is wrong with you?!" Carrie's face was white with fear, but she was still driving toward the water. She didn't see another way either.

That helped. If we both thought this was the only option, then we would live or die together, but we would do it knowing that at least we had tried. "When we hit, swim as hard as you can away from the car, before it drags you down. Find something to hide under, and stay out of—"

The edge of the waterfront dropped out from under our wheels like a rug being pulled away, and we were sailing into the air, soaring out in a wide arc defined by our speed and the dragging pull of gravity. We were dancing with physics, and it was a beautiful, terrible thing.

I can't do this, I thought, and *I have to do this*, I thought, and I shoved my door open wide and launched myself into the open air bare seconds before gravity won and yanked the SUV down into the blue. I didn't see whether Carrie did the same; I was too busy slamming into the water and fighting to keep my breath inside my body. Human lungs need air, and that meant I needed air, and then the descent of the car was pulling me down, down, down into the dark, and so I swam as hard as I could, the taste of salt water on my lips and the shocking cold of the Pacific creeping fast into my bones.

This is not how I die, I thought, and swam in the direction where I remembered the shore. I was trying to keep my entire body submerged. The inexorable pull of the sinking SUV helped; I couldn't have bobbed to the surface if I'd tried.

My hands were empty. The cattle prod had been lost when the car went down. That was a pity—it would have been nice to have some sort of weapon—but it was also a relief. I wasn't sure I could have used that thing against one of the cousins. Better a bullet to the head than an eternity consigned to nothingness, floating in your own body and unable to do anything to make it respond to your commands ever again. And besides, it would only have slowed me down. When survival was the only goal, everything else could fall by the wayside.

My empty palm slapped against something splintery and wet. I couldn't see, but I knew that the waterfront was supported by wooden pilings, and so I gripped the thing and pulled myself upward, trying to take it slowly, even as my lungs burned and ached with the need for oxygen. If I wasn't under the dock…

I emerged into shadow, with the hard wooden slope of the waterfront above my head and a water-stained concrete wall in front of me, marking the line where the actual soil had been shored up against erosion. I was shivering uncontrollably, and it was all I could do to force myself to breathe out slowly, releasing the old air from my lungs, and pull in an equally slow breath. I wanted to hyperventilate, running all the oxygen in the world through my body, but I didn't dare. Even with the water sloshing and crashing around me, the sound might be audible to the soldiers I knew were even now spreading through the square.

There was no sign of Carrie.

That didn't have to mean anything bad. She could have swum in the other direction, or she could be somewhere else under the dock, clinging to a pillar and concealed by shadow. But it was hard not to look at the empty ocean and feel like she was gone forever, one more sacrifice to my endless need to be free. *I'm sorry,* I thought. I didn't say it out loud. Getting myself caught because I was sorry that she might have been lost wasn't going to do either one of us any good.

A flashlight beam played across the water just beyond the dock. I drew farther back against my pillar, trying to move so that I wouldn't be visible if someone decided to peer over the edge. The disturbance caused by our sinking SUV was gone, leaving the water as smooth and unblemished as it had ever been. As long as they focused their attention there, on that patch of waves, and didn't look any further...

My teeth were starting to chatter. I tried to force them to stop. *I am in control of my own body,* I thought fiercely. *I am not going to freeze.*

All the positive thinking in the world wasn't going to change the reality of my situation. I was mostly submerged in extremely cold water, and if I didn't move soon, hypothermia was going to set in. I was already losing feeling in my fingers and toes, and my limbs were becoming sluggish, resistant to my commands. The urge to sink down into the hot warm dark until the danger had passed was seductive, and would be fatal if I gave in. Down in the dark, I wouldn't know what was happening to my body. I would just float, formless and untroubled, until the water filled my lungs and I sank into darkness forever. That wouldn't get me home...although on some level, the thought of dying in the sea, where no one, not Sherman and not USAMRIID, could use my body for their own ends, was tempting. I wanted to live. I wanted to make it home. I wanted to see how this was going to end.

A hand touched my shoulder. I swallowed my scream as I whipped around, legs thrashing in the water, and found myself looking into Carrie's tired, white-cheeked face. She had a cut above her left eye. It was bleeding copiously, looking black in the absence of light beneath the dock.

I reached out without saying a word, grabbing her arm and pulling her toward me. She nodded in understanding and wrapped herself around me while I hooked one arm around the pillar, the two of us using each other to conserve body heat while we waited for the danger to pass.

Almost as an afterthought, I pulled us behind the pillar. None too soon: a light hit the back wall seconds later, playing over the stone as the person who held it looked for some sign as to where we had gone. Carrie and I locked eyes, and said nothing. The sound of the water would muffle our breathing. As long as we could hold on and keep ourselves alive, we could still get out of this.

Someone in the distance shouted something. The light was withdrawn. We stayed where we were. Carrie's lips were turning blue, and the chattering of her teeth was a thin, constant counterpart to the chattering of my own. We were freezing to death an inch at a time, and if we waited much longer, we weren't going to make it out of here.

I started counting to one hundred, trying to pause long enough between numbers that I could be sure each represented at least a second. When I reached the end of my count without any further lights or shouts from above, I gave Carrie a shake, trying to get her to open her eyes. When had she closed them? I wasn't entirely sure. She was still holding on to me, which made me think that she wasn't dead yet, just limp with cold and exhaustion. I shook her again.

Carrie opened her eyes.

I offered her the most encouraging smile I could muster before gesturing toward the distant slice of fading daylight that represented the way out. Carrie's eyes widened and she shook her head in violent negation, pointing down the line of the waterfront. I frowned. Didn't she understand how dangerous it was for us to stay in the water? Even if the tide didn't come in, even if there were no sharks or other predators, we were running out of time. I gestured again toward the daylight.

This time, when Carrie shook her head, she also pulled away from me, and began swimming down the line of the waterfront. I hesitated before following her. Yes, there was a chance that she was about to get us both killed, but she had trusted me when I told her to drive into the water. I was going to trust her now, for as long as I had left.

We swam maybe twenty yards, resting against the pillars when the cold sapped too much of our strength and left us flailing in the water. A dark rectangle appeared a yard or so above the waterline on the gray concrete slope of the wall. Carrie swam for it, and I followed her. The cold had seeped so deeply into my bones that I couldn't feel my feet or lower legs at all; it was like I ended at the knee, truncated cleanly and coldly by some unseen hand. As long as I could thrash hard enough to keep myself afloat, I was going to keep swimming, and I was going to keep surviving. Survival had become the only thing that mattered.

There it was: that was the thing we all had in common. "We all want to stay alive," I said, horrified by the slur in my voice. The cold had its claws deeper into me than I thought.

"What?" Carrie's voice was as strained and slurred as mine was. I wasn't the only one feeling the cold.

"Nothing," I said, and swam closer to the rectangle. It was a door, incongruous and out of place as…well, as we were, two women struggling to stay alive in the bitter waters running in from the Pacific. "Can you get it open?"

"Boost me."

Carrie's command dumbfounded me for a moment. There was nothing to boost her *with*. And then I realized what the answer would inevitably be. There was no use in arguing. It wouldn't change the laws of physics or the reality of our situation; it wouldn't create a ladder or give us another convenient way out. The only way for me to work toward my own survival was to prioritize hers.

"All right," I said. I swam to the wall, putting my hands flat against the concrete. I could see them dimly through the gloom, like pale starfish. Then Carrie's hands were on my shoulders, using them to push herself up. I barely had time to take a breath before her weight shoved me underwater, down into the dark.

It all comes down to survival, I thought, shutting my eyes against the sting of the salt water and trying to resist the siren song of the hot warm dark, which was offering me its sweet, fatal escape. If I went into the dark, I wouldn't survive. That much was certain, even as everything I had screamed for me to give in and go under. The hot warm dark would be kinder than this oceanic chill, which wound its way into my bones and threatened to devour me whole.

It was about survival. Everything, from the very beginning, had been about survival. The human race wanted to survive, so they created the implants to make it easier for them to thrive. The implants wanted to survive, so they became resistant to the antiparasitic drugs, they learned to lay eggs and form cysts even though they had supposedly been engineered away from those behaviors, and when none of that worked, the implants learned to take over their hosts. But that still didn't work, not always, so they learned how to take over their hosts *better*. They learned how to become chimera.

If one implant in ten could successfully take over, and one in a hundred, or a thousand, of those successful takeovers resulted in a chimera, that was still better than nothing. That was still survival. But not for the humans, which was why their fight to survive had changed forms, becoming open war against the creatures they had created. We were the enemy now, and all because we had wanted to survive. Just like they had.

The weight of Carrie's hands was abruptly withdrawn from my shoulders. I bobbed up to the surface of the water, gasping for breath. The chilly air under the dock seemed positively warm when I compared it with the water. That was probably another bad sign...and Carrie was gone.

But the door was open.

I tried to reach for it. My hands fell almost a foot short, and with nothing to grant me leverage or purchase, no matter how much I scrabbled, I couldn't make that distance any shorter. I sank down in the water, staring at the dark hole in the concrete wall. This wasn't how I had expected things to end. It wasn't *fair*. And it was happening, because Carrie was gone, and I was too short to span those last few inches on my own.

"So much for survival," I whispered.

A rope hit the water in front of me, dangling down from the hole like a second chance. I grabbed hold of it without thinking, wrapping my numb hands in its coils and trying to pull myself up. I managed to haul my torso a few more inches out of the water, and hung there shivering, looking for the strength I needed to make the rest of the climb.

The rope moved. Not much—just a few more inches—but

enough to pull me farther out of the water, sliding me up the concrete until I was close enough to the door's lip that I could reach out and slap my hands on the smooth floor beyond. I let go of the rope, trying instead to pull myself up via the stone. I was still scrambling when hands closed over mine, helping me pull.

I raised my head and there was Carrie, her hair a wet tangle covering one side of her face, an intent look in her eyes. "Don't let go," she said.

"I won't," I replied. She pulled, and I scrambled, and together, we were able to get me into the tunnel, where I collapsed against the floor. The stone was cold, but not compared to the water outside; compared to the water, it was as warm as a sunny beach in the middle of July. That probably said something bad about my body's current core temperature. I didn't care. I was no longer in the water: Everything else could wait.

"Are you breathing?" asked Carrie. She didn't sound particularly interested.

I rolled over onto my back so that I could stare at the unseen ceiling. There were no lights down here, and while the light leaking in from outside meant that it wasn't totally black, it was dark enough that I couldn't see more than a few feet directly in front of me. "I'm breathing," I said, and then, "I'm cold."

"Me, too. Can you walk?"

"I don't think I have a choice." I rolled over again, this time so that I could start trying to climb to my feet. My limbs were slow and unresponsive. It took me five tries to get upright, and another two to become fully stable. Even then, I kept a hand against the wall, in case I needed to fall over.

Carrie was close enough that I could see the pale oval of her face through the gloom. That was good. I didn't believe in ghosts, but that didn't mean I wanted to follow someone I couldn't see.

"Where are we?" I asked again.

"Maintenance tunnel. Sometimes dead sea lions or other dead bodies will wash up under the dock. The management company doesn't want them decaying down there, and neither does local law enforcement. So they built a few of these hatches to use in emergencies."

I blinked. "How did you know...?"

"I worked for an Internet news aggregator before everything went to shit. My main beat was local interest—not just things like your accident, Sally 'I survived getting into an argument with a bus' Mitchell, but things like 'Did you know about this secret network of tunnels under your favorite free outdoor concert venue?' Once you said we were heading for Jack London Square, I knew what you were going to tell me to do. I started planning our trajectory so we'd hit the water with a chance in hell of getting out again. Come on." She turned and walked away, heading down the tunnel toward what would hopefully be an unlocked exit.

"Wait," I said, following her. Confusion gave me a burst of unexpected strength, making it easier for me to motivate my frozen legs to carry me in her wake. "You knew about my accident? Why didn't you ever say anything?"

"Everyone knew you were the Colonel's daughter. You didn't need 'medical miracle' on top of that." It was getting darker the deeper we went into the tunnel. I heard Carrie's footsteps stop. "There's just one thing I need to know before we get to the door."

"What's that?"

There was a click. The sound of a safety being thumbed back. I had thought I was cold, but as my blood froze in my veins, I understood that the water had been safer in many ways. It would have killed me, yes. That death would have been impersonal and merciful, taking me down into the dark and not letting me come back up for air. The ocean didn't care.

Carrie was human. Carrie didn't do mercy. And Carrie cared.

"What the hell happened to my husband?"

The cold in my veins and the cold in my bones warred over who would hold dominion while I stood there shivering, trying to figure out where the shot that killed me was going to originate.

"I already told you what happened to Paul."

"You said he turned into one of those *things*. That isn't possible. He was clean. We all were."

I remembered the taste of pheromones in the air, weak but unmistakable, and the moment when the light had gone out of Paul's eyes, replaced by the confused dullness of the cousin that had taken him over. "It may not be possible, but it happened. Colonel Mitchell pulled me in to question me about it. He had a folder. There were pictures. Paul wasn't the first. I'm sorry, Carrie, but I'm not lying to you."

"You just want to save your own skin."

Her accusation was surprising enough that I laughed out loud. The sound echoed off the tunnel walls, becoming alien and strange.

"What's so fucking funny?" she demanded.

"You are. This is *all* about survival. Every bit of it. You and Paul were trying to survive when USAMRIID picked you up. USAMRIID is trying make sure the human race survives— they're not doing a very good job, but they're trying. I was trying to survive when I told the Colonel that you were sick, because I knew I needed a getaway driver. This has been about survival from day one. So yes, I want to save my own skin, but I'm not going to do it by *lying* to you. You're the one with the gun. You'd figure it out, and then you'd shoot me dead."

"So you expect me to believe that one of those worms ate his brain out? He never even had an implant! He was a vegan!"

The urge to laugh again was strong. I fought it back and said, "I know how it sounds, but it's the truth. Now, please, Carrie. I have to get back to my family. My *real* family. Not the Mitchells."

"They didn't want you, did they?"

"Would they have put me in with the general population if they had?" It wasn't really an answer. It was all I had. My situation was too strange and too complicated to be explained here, in the dark and the cold.

"So where are you going?"

"Can we talk about it when we're not freezing to death?"

There was a long pause before Carrie said, "All right." There was another click as she reengaged the safety. "Keep walking forward. Be careful. We're almost to the stairs."

Even with her warning, I stumbled when my foot hit the first step. I felt around in front of me until my hand found the rail. From there, it was a small thing to begin pulling myself up the concrete stairs, my numb feet thudding down on each of them in turn like this was it: I could go no farther.

And then a rectangle of light opened ahead of me, bringing hot tears springing to my eyes, and I found that I could go farther after all.

Carrie grabbed my arm when I reached the top of the stairs, pulling me into the light. We were facing the square, with the ocean at our backs. Nothing moved but a few seagulls, picking listlessly at the pavement in their endless avian search for food. Either the men from USAMRIID had already withdrawn, or they were setting an ambush and waiting for us to walk into the middle of it.

Most jarringly of all, there were no sleepwalkers. I had expected the square to be thronging with the cousins, drawn by the noise of the car chase, but there was no one. I tensed, trying to unobtrusively sniff the air. There were pheromone trails here, old and faded and tattered by the wind. Nothing smelled fresh enough to have been made during the previous twenty-four hours.

"Something's wrong," I muttered.

Carrie laughed. It was a hard, sharp sound. It had teeth. "Really? You think something's wrong? Because I think *everything's* wrong. This is the end of the world, or didn't you notice?"

"It's not the end of the world," I said without thinking, still scanning the area for signs of movement. Apart from the seagulls, there was nothing. "It's just the end of humanity. It's not the same thing."

"Oh, God, you're one of *those*," said Carrie. She sounded more weary than anything else. After the day we'd had, that was sort of to be expected. "So what, you think we did this to ourselves? That we deserve whatever we get, and the tapeworms will inherit the Earth? This is no different from the cars rising up and trying to overthrow us. We made them. They don't get to take the planet away from us."

"I'm cold." It was a nonsensical statement, but it was a true one, and it was better than trying to argue with her about something we could never agree on. I was not the same as a car. Humanity had created me by altering the raw materials nature provided. That didn't make me a machine. It didn't make me property. I was damn tired of people acting like it did. "There's an Old Navy near here. I bet it didn't get looted too hard when things got bad. Nobody ever thinks, 'Society is collapsing, let's go steal tank tops.'"

"That's not a bad idea," admitted Carrie slowly. "But what if there are sleepwalkers inside?"

"You have a gun." There weren't going to be sleepwalkers inside, not with the way the air tasted. There hadn't been sleepwalkers here in at least a day, and possibly much longer. "If there's anything dangerous in the Old Navy, you can shoot it."

Carrie smiled, showing all her teeth. They were even, white, and terrifying. "Let's go shopping," she said.

I somehow managed not to shudder as I turned away from her and started cautiously across the square, watching for signs of an ambush with every step I took. I could detect sleepwalkers before they were on top of us, but that didn't give me any special "know that the Army is about to fall on your head" powers. Where USAMRIID was concerned, I was operating as blind as anyone else.

I knew one thing for sure: It was worth the risk. If I didn't get out of my wet clothes and into something warm and dry soon, then getting out of the water would have been for nothing, because I was going to freeze. My body still felt distant and unconnected after the electrical zaps I'd received from Colonel Mitchell's people, and I wasn't sure I'd know nerve damage even as it was setting in. Better to get into more appropriate clothing, and take one variable off my list of terrible things.

Carrie stuck close to me as we crossed the open spaces between us and the shopping promenade, letting me take the lead. It didn't feel like trust: it felt like letting me be the one who triggered any traps and blundered into any sneak attacks. I didn't protest. My nose was still telling me that there was nothing waiting here to hurt us. Any sleepwalkers that passed through this area were long gone.

She wasn't holding the gun she'd taken from USAMRIID, and while I wanted to ask her where she was hiding it, I wasn't entirely sure I wanted to remind her of its existence. Her hatred for the sleepwalkers was logical, and terrifying. If she found out what I really was…

For her to find out, I would have to tell her, or we would have to make it safely back to Dr. Cale, wherever Dr. Cale was now. The former required me to be a lot less survival-oriented than was likely. The latter would give me a lot of backup.

Only one of the front windows at the Old Navy was smashed in. The lights were out, but the sun was still high enough to illuminate the first ten yards or so of the store. I could see toppled-over displays and windblown racks of shirts and sweaters. Bright signs advertised their post-Thanksgiving sales. The prices were never going to go back up; the Christmas displays were never going to be completed. There was something sad about that, like the essential passage of the year had been disrupted.

As I'd expected, the doors were unlocked. Whoever had smashed the window had done it for their own reasons, and not because it was the only way inside. When things began falling apart, it had happened so quickly and conclusively that there hadn't been time to shut things down and put them away until they'd be needed again. I slipped into the Old Navy with Carrie close behind me, sniffing the air, hoping she'd write it off as a result of water in my nose. There were still no pheromone trails. The temperature inside was at least eight degrees warmer than outside, thanks to the trapped air being unable to circulate. It was still cold, but like the concrete after the water, the difference was enough to make me feel like I might someday thaw out again.

"It would be too much to ask to have a bra shop in this same strip mall, wouldn't it?" asked Carrie.

"I think they were a little too all-ages for lingerie," I said, making a beeline for the nearest rack of sweaters. "If we pass a Target or something, we can go in and raid them for fresh bras."

"I bet guys don't have this sort of problem after the apocalypse."

It was a frothy statement, inviting me to join in and banter with her. I didn't understand. She'd been ready to shoot me ten minutes ago, and now she wanted to talk about gender equality after the fall of mankind? I gave her a blank look through the gloom and stripped to the waist, pulling on a clean, dry camisole and topping it off with the bulkiest sweater I could find.

Both were cotton, absorbent, and not designed to be worn over wet skin, but that didn't matter, because putting them on felt like lifting a huge, freezing burden from myself. I stripped off my wet pants and underwear, leaving them on the floor as I wandered, bare-assed, over to the display of jeans.

Carrie didn't say anything. Either she had no real nudity taboos, or she was distracted by trying to find clothing for herself.

I grabbed the first pair of jeans I found and rubbed them briskly over my lower body, soaking up as much excess water as I could. Then I rooted through the display until I found my size—two down from what I'd worn at the beginning of this crisis—and stepped into them. They fit loosely. I scowled. I had never been particularly interested in weight loss, and apocalypse-as-diet was definitely not a plan I recommended. I wanted to eat a cheesecake without worrying that I was going to be attacked, betrayed, or electrocuted at any moment. When did that become so much to ask?

"Do they carry backpacks? We should find—" Carrie stopped in the middle of her sentence, her words devolving into screams.

I didn't hesitate. I turned and ran back to her, ready to either yank her away from the soldiers or start trying to convince the sleepwalkers to leave her alone. Neither was present. It was just Carrie, pointing into the dark and screaming.

I stopped, squinting in the direction she was indicating. At first, there was nothing. Then, bit by bit, my eyes adjusted, and I saw what had her so upset.

The back of the Old Navy was littered with bodies.

There were at least twenty of them, heaped together and twisted like they had died in excruciating pain. I stepped forward, ignoring Carrie's frantic grabs for my arm, and stared at the sea of corpses. The faint smell of pheromones hung in the air around them, too denuded and pushed down by the wind blowing through the broken window for me to have noticed it before. All these people had been sleepwalkers, and now they were dead.

What was going on? How had they died?

As Carrie grabbed for me, a thin line of fear uncurled in my stomach, bringing a new question with it.

Was this contagious?

There was an escape at the Oakland facility today. Two quarantine subjects managed to trick a squad of men into believing one of them had become ill, and were then able to make their way to the motor pool, where they stole a vehicle and led my men on a high-speed chase that ended at a local waterfront. The escapees drove into the water rather than allow themselves to be recaptured. Both are missing, presumed dead. We do not have the manpower or resources to dredge the Bay at this time.

Neither subject had operational or confidential knowledge relating to the Pleasanton or Oakland facilities. While it would be best if they could be confirmed dead or recaptured, the interests of national security and operational survival do not allow for the devotion of that much time or effort to two frightened civilians. There are more important tasks at hand.

I don't know what you're doing out there in Washington, but we're still fighting a war on the ground here. And we are losing.

—MESSAGE FROM COLONEL ALFRED MITCHELL, USAMRIID, TRANSMITTED TO THE WHITE HOUSE ON DECEMBER 19, 2027

We've been testing the water constantly for the last four days. Water from the local creeks and streams is filthy, polluted,

and crawling with contagions, but it doesn't harbor D. symbogenesis *eggs or hatchlings. If we drank it straight, we'd get
sick, but we wouldn't get new in-body roommates.*

*Seawater shows the same results: lots of local residents, no
tapeworm eggs. Ditto captured and purified rainwater. It's
all the same. But when we look at the tap water...*

*The tap water is so full of tapeworm eggs and infant worms
that it's a miracle more people haven't been seizing and collapsing. We've all switched to bottled water. There's plenty of
the stuff. The Californian instinct to mistrust the water table
after any sort of crisis is serving us well, for now.*

*The power has gone out in all the surrounding neighbor-
hoods. The last remaining cell service died yesterday. Whoever put this in the water knew what they were doing; they're
disabling the last of the human infrastructure, one infection
at a time.*

*I'm terribly afraid that I know who's doing this. I just wish
I knew what Sherman thought he'd have to gain.*

—FROM THE NOTES OF DR. NATHAN KIM, DECEMBER 2027

Chapter 6

DECEMBER 2027

The bodies were relatively fresh, which explained why the smell of decay hadn't slapped us when we stepped into the Old Navy; that, and the fact that all the air was flowing *in*, not flowing *out*. They must have crawled off here to die sometime within the last two days, collapsing in insensate heaps before they finally gave up fighting.

I stepped between the bodies, trying to ignore the whimpering sounds that Carrie was making behind me, and scanned their slack faces for any sign of what had happened to them. It was too dark for me to make out fine details, but I couldn't find even broad strokes to point me in the right direction. Some of them had vomited before they died, while others were clean-faced and even serene-looking. The faint smells of bodily waste and decay drifted up from the floor. They smelled...*clean*, like they were supposed to smell, and not tainted by any outside source.

The pheromones were another story. They were a jumbled mess, some with the complexity I was coming to associate with "old" sleepwalkers, others as fresh and unrefined as the traces I'd gotten off of Paul before he died. It didn't make any sense. Either I was so tired and shocky from my unplanned swim that I could no longer understand what my mind was trying to tell me, or something had caused the cousins inside these hosts to start double-producing the chemical tags that defined them.

"Sal, come *back* here," said Carrie, her voice a harsh whisper through the dark. I knew she was right, that I should be taking care of myself rather than trying to make sense of things, but at the same time, I knew she was wrong. If something was killing the sleepwalkers, I needed to know what it was, and I needed to know *now*... because there was every chance in the world I was vulnerable.

Then something moved up ahead of me, and everything changed.

"There's someone in here," I said, taking another step forward.

Carrie moaned. It was a frustrated, agonized, *human* sound, not a sleepwalker's inchoate hunger, but it still made the hairs on the back of my neck stand up in uneasy horror. "No, no, no," she said. "It's one of those *things*. If something is killing them all off, then you should just let it. Don't go looking for trouble. Don't do this."

It didn't sound like she was coming any closer. That was good. If there was danger in the darkness, I didn't want to pull her into it. I had used her to make my escape, but that didn't mean I wanted her dead. "I have to," I said, and kept walking.

There was a click behind me as she thumbed off the safety on her gun once again. "Don't do this," she repeated.

I stopped, looking back over my shoulder. With the light

behind her, she was nothing but an outline of a woman, a dark shape against the windows. "Is that how this is going to be from now on?" I asked. "Every time I do something you don't like, you're going to draw your gun on me and threaten until I agree to go along with you? Because that's not going to work for me, Carrie. I'm not your slave, and having a gun doesn't put you in charge."

"You're going to get us both killed!"

"I don't think so. But if you're really worried about it, you can go wait for me outside. I need to see what's going on." I turned my back on her and took another step into the dark, heading for the motion I'd seen before. I could hear Carrie moving around behind me. I kept walking. If she wanted to shoot me, I couldn't stop her. She had the gun. All I could do by turning back now was cement her position as "leader" of our little pairing, and I couldn't afford that any more than I could afford a gunshot wound. I needed to find my way home. That meant Carrie wasn't in control.

The shot didn't come. The motion up ahead was repeated, and I picked my way through the bodies and over fallen clothes racks until I saw its source: a thin, huddled figure, probably no older than four or five, packed into a crevice between two of the fallen sleepwalkers. It was too dark for me to tell gender, or anything other than the fact that this was a person, this was someone who was alive and moving and capable of getting out of here.

The pheromones in this little corner of the store smelled subtly different. Not wrong, exactly, but *different*, like something had happened to modify them from within. "Hello?" I said cautiously, hanging back in case my survivor turned out to be a sleepwalker after all. They would eat dead bodies, and the more high-functioning ones wouldn't usually go for targets they couldn't take down, but I didn't feel like taking the chance if I didn't have to.

The thought was almost comical. If I didn't feel like "taking the chance," what the hell was I doing in a dark store, surrounded by corpses, trying to talk to the only person left alive?

The figure scuffed one foot against the tile, lifting its head like it was trying to get a better look at me. It didn't speak, and didn't moan. It just sat there, small and still and frightened.

"My name's Sal," I said. "Do you have a name? Do you remember your name?"

The child—and it *was* a child, short and slim and small, even compacted on itself as it was—hesitated before saying, awkwardly, "Sal." The word had an atonal non-accent, like the speaker had never heard language before. It lacked the moan sleepwalkers always had when they parroted speech.

I risked a small step closer. "That's my name," I said. "What's your name?" Chimera were essentially fully integrated sleepwalkers. Maybe this child had a chimera parent, or a parent who had become a sleepwalker capable of functioning at a previously unknown level. It wasn't impossible to think that a sleepwalker who was well fed could still have protective instincts. They were damaged, but they were still people.

Silence.

"Do you have a name?"

Silence.

I took another step closer. "Are you all right? Are you hurt?" I kept my voice as low and soothing as possible. I didn't want to frighten the child while I was trying to figure out what was going on. "Why are you hiding back here?"

"Sal!" The child moved without warning, pushing itself forward and flinging its arms around my calves. It clung hard, holding on like it was afraid I might cease to exist at any moment. It didn't try to bite. I blinked, bending down to stroke the child's hair... and froze.

Chimera put off pheromone tags just like sleepwalkers, but ours are thinner, subtler, less easily detected. Something about the way we slot into human brains slows production, replacing it with a sort of radar for one another, a strong pull toward unity. It was what had drawn me to Sherman, even before I had known what he was. It was how I had been able to accept Adam as my brother, even as I'd been rejecting the reality of my own origins. Chimera knew each other, and chimera cared for each other.

And the child clinging to my legs like it had just discovered salvation was a chimera. Somehow, it was a chimera. I stroked its hair automatically, staring into the dark, and wondered whether there was any way for me to resist the pull that told me that I had to take care of this new complication.

I had no idea what I was going to do now.

Carrie had retreated outside by the time I emerged carrying the child in my arms like a bundle of rolled laundry. It was a little girl: That had become clear when I carried her into the light, revealing her smooth brown skin and tousled black curls. Her eyes were closed, and had been since we reached the edge of the sunlit zone. I remembered how much trouble I'd had with light when I was first waking up, how strange and painful and unnecessary it had seemed. I wondered whether she was having the same issue, still trying to get her tapeworm brain, which was small but commanded a surprising number of instinctive reactions, to understand that her human brain was correct when it told her the light was never going to go away.

The adjustment wasn't going to be easy. It hadn't been easy for me, and I'd been in a hospital bed, surrounded by people assuring me that I was a human being with a name and an identity I could reclaim, if I worked hard enough. They'd done a lot of damage with those lies, but they'd helped me, too, because they'd given me a clear goal to work toward. I could be Sally Mitchell, if I worked hard enough.

Who was this little girl going to be?

Carrie whirled toward the sound of my footsteps, her expression washing with shock and suspicion when she saw the child in my arms. "What is that?" she demanded.

"It's a little girl," I said. "I mean, I think it's a little girl. I guess she might want to be a little boy once she's had time to think about it. It's a kid. You've seen kids before. We were just living with one, remember?"

Carrie's suspicion didn't fade. "There's no way she's not one of those things," she spat. "Put her down and get away from her."

Technically, Carrie was right. The child was definitely one of "those things." She just wasn't a sleepwalker, and that distinction made all the difference in the world. "She's not," I said. "She didn't try to attack me. She just grabbed my legs and held on, because she's a kid. A terrified kid."

"Why isn't she talking?"

"Trauma? This freaked me out, and I'm a grown-up." I adjusted my hold on the little girl. She wasn't moving, wasn't speaking; was just huddling against me, clearly trusting me to take care of her. In the absence of anything else, she was running off her biological programming, and it said that any other chimera was there to defend her.

It was a good thing Sherman hadn't found her first. He would have taken advantage of that, the same way he took advantage of everything else. Even if I didn't want the responsibility of protecting something other than myself, I knew that I would do better than he would.

Carrie stared at me, clearly fumbling for something else to say, something that would make me understand what a mistake I was making. She couldn't find it, so she threw down the only weapon she had: "You can't bring her with us."

"She'll die if I leave her here. There's no one to take care of her." I was starting to think my guess about the girl's age—somewhere between four and six—was correct: She was small enough for me to carry, but large enough that she was going to become too heavy before much longer. I wondered whether her host's age would make a difference in how fast she learned things like walking and speaking. Her brain was more elastic than mine had been when I first took it over.

Maybe I should have felt guilty about how quickly I was dismissing the personhood of the human girl my newfound chimera had replaced, but I didn't have time for that sort of wasted emotion. All the guilt in the world wasn't going to bring back the lost.

"So let her die," said Carrie. "She's not coming with us."

I blinked before I shrugged, and said, "I guess that means I'm not coming with you. Thanks for helping me get out of the quarantine. Good luck getting wherever you're going from here." I turned away. The sun would be fully down soon. We needed to get somewhere warm and dry, and start figuring out where we were going to go next.

"Wait!"

I looked back over my shoulder at Carrie, who had her hand outstretched, like that would stop me. "What? You said you wouldn't go with the girl. I won't leave her. That means we have to split up."

"You can't do this. You're the one who made me steal that car."

"You could have refused. You did it because you wanted to. You didn't want to stay in a place where you were treated like a prisoner, where your husband had died, and I offered you a way out. You faked a seizure and stole a car because you wanted to."

"I didn't want to do this," she said, and suddenly the gun was in her hand again, pointed at me. "Put her down and get back over here. You're not leaving me."

I sighed as I turned fully back toward her so that she couldn't pretend the child in my arms was anything but that: a *child*, a living being. It wasn't my fault if Carrie would take the girl as a member of her species rather than as a member of mine. "What are you going to do, shoot me? This is the third time you've drawn your gun on me since we got here. It's been less than an hour. I can't travel with you if I can't trust you—and I can't trust you if your response to not getting your way is going to be threatening to shoot me every single time. That makes you worse than USAMRIID. You know that, don't you?"

Carrie's chin wobbled, but her aim remained steady. "I don't care. You're not leaving me alone out here."

"I don't have to leave you alone out here. You could come with us."

"You still haven't told me where you're going!"

"I'm going to find my family. My *real* family, the ones who care about me and want to protect me from people like the Colonel. I know they're out here. I just have to figure out where they've gone." And just like that, I knew where I was going to go next. Dr. Cale would have left a clue in the wreckage of the candy factory. I knew it. Even if it was something so small as to be virtually unfindable, it would be there, and it would be meant for *me*. USAMRIID would never have been able to use it to track her down. I would. I would find them.

All I had to do was get from Oakland to Vallejo, across miles of sleepwalker-controlled territory, evading USAMRIID patrols and gangs of human looters. If Carrie didn't see the necessity of my plan, then I would do it on foot. I had done worse things in my time.

Carrie shook her head. "There's no way. Your family can't have survived this and stayed free. No one's can."

"Mine can." Dr. Cale was smart and tenacious, and she was surrounded by good people. Fang, Fishy... Nathan. They would have been able to get her out of there before USA-MRIID showed up to take her into custody. I *knew* Colonel Mitchell didn't have hands on her. If he had, he wouldn't have been bothering with me. He would have gone straight for the goose that laid the golden eggs, and I could have stayed in the quarantine zone to rot.

At one point he hadn't been taking her in because he thought she did better work when she wasn't under lock and key. Now...I seriously suspected he'd been telling the truth when he said he wasn't bringing her in because he no longer knew how to find her.

Carrie frowned. Then, slowly, she lowered her gun. "What's your deal, Sal? You're the Colonel's daughter, but you live in the mud with the rest of us. You're a total pushover until you start planning escapes that involve driving cars into the water. And you're not nearly as scared of a woman with a gun as you should be."

"My father disowned me when he decided he didn't like the people I was spending time with—my *real* family. They might not be biologically related to me, but they love me, and they respect my choices, and that's all I've ever wanted. His wife hates me for existing, and for not being her daughter." Too late, I realized that I'd just made myself sound like the product of an affair. Well, that wasn't too far off the mark. I decided not to try explaining myself. "I know Dr. Cale will have been trying to figure out how to get me out of quarantine. If she hears that there's been an escape, she—"

"Wait, what?" Carrie's gun was suddenly raised again, aimed at the center mass of my chest. The little girl I was holding didn't react. She was too new to the world of physical things like guns and threatening gestures to understand what was going on, and I was grateful for that. "Who?"

Oops. "Dr. Cale. She's the boss of the lab where I live." I didn't work there. I didn't have the training, the experience, or the high school reading level necessary to observe lab-safety protocols. I helped in hydroponics, and took care of the animals that we kept for both research and food purposes, but actual lab work was beyond me, and attempting it would probably have resulted in somebody getting killed.

"Dr. *Shanti* Cale?" asked Carrie, sounding utterly appalled.

Again, oops. "Look, I know what you're thinking, and this isn't her fault. She wasn't the one who decided to release the implants to the general public. She—"

"She *created* the damned things! How could this be anybody's fault but hers?" Carrie waved her gun in a way that made me want to start moving backward. I knew better. Attempts to get out of range were going to end with me getting shot. "She's the one who made this whole mess. How can you be working with her?"

"I told you, I don't work with her, I just live with her. And she's not the one to blame for everything that's happened. That's Dr. Steven Banks, at SymboGen, and honestly, that's the people at USAMRIID. They knew there was something wrong with the implants years ago, and they didn't do anything." There might have been corporate protections for Dr. Banks to hide behind, but that didn't mean the government had been forced to stay silent. They could have started sounding the alarm bells. Instead, they'd hung back, waiting for the perfect smoking gun, and had allowed the SymboGen implants to become entrenched in all levels of society, all over the world.

How many people would have lived if someone had decided to start telling the truth about the SymboGen implants? How many lives could have been saved if there had been an alternative?

Maybe that was a question I should have been asking Dr. Cale—but then, she'd never been in a position to show her hand. Not with the government playing nicely with Dr. Banks, and Dr. Banks gunning to have her taken out of the picture on a permanent basis. Her hands had been tied the minute the Intestinal Bodyguard went on the open market. It was the people who'd come after her who were to blame for what happened. Dr. Cale had followed the exact same imperative as her children: survival, at all costs. I couldn't blame her for that without blaming myself, or blaming the little girl huddled in my arms, her sweet pheromone tags wafting through the gathering twilight. She had as much right to live as anyone else. It didn't matter whether she'd been created in a womb or in a test tube. She was alive. She got to live.

"She's a monster," spat Carrie, and for a moment I couldn't tell whether she meant Dr. Cale or the child in my arms.

It didn't matter. Maybe it never had. "We're all monsters," I said. "Being a monster is not the same as being a bad person. It just means you're willing to eat the world if that's what you have to do to keep yourself alive. You really want to tell me that you wouldn't eat the world if that was what you had to do? That you wouldn't unhinge your jaw and swallow the sky if it brought Paul back? You're no better than Dr. Cale. Maybe you're even worse. You're not willing to admit that you're a monster too, and you should. You should just let yourself be the monster that you want to be. Maybe then you wouldn't feel the need to hide behind a gun all the time."

Carrie stared at me. "You're insane."

"I hate that word. All it means is 'you don't think like I do,' and by that standard, *everyone* is insane. It's a meaningless idea. If what you mean is 'you're dangerous,' I got you out, Carrie. I made sure they told you about what had happened to Paul. I helped you get out of there before they could start taking samples to figure out why it hadn't happened to you too. I saved you. I didn't have to do that."

"You can't drive. How were you going to get out of there without me?"

I shrugged. "I would have found a way." And I would have. I would have found a way, and if it hadn't worked, I would have tried something else, and something else after that, until I either got out or got myself killed in the process of trying. My patience had already been worn almost to the bone when Paul got sick. I'd only been staying because I was afraid. Maybe part of me had hoped that I could do *something* for Joyce, even if it was nothing more than convincing her father that it was time to let her go. He'd been willing to unplug me once, when he thought that I was gone. I could have convinced him to do the same for her.

"You needed me."

"Yes," I said calmly. "I'm not denying that I needed you. But I don't need you anymore. So you can shoot me, or you can walk away, or you can come with me. I'm not going to stay with you if you're going to insist on drawing a gun every time you want to get your way. I'm not stupid, Carrie."

She narrowed her eyes. "Could've fooled me. You walked into a nest of those things."

"I went to investigate a bunch of corpses. I came out with a little girl who needed my help." I looked up at the darkening sky. "It's going to be night soon. If there are any sleepwalkers left around here, that's when they'll start hunting. We need to get out of the open. Are we doing it together, or are we doing it in opposite directions? I'll let you pick first, if you want to separate. You can have whatever direction you want."

Carrie lowered her gun again, visibly shaken. "You don't mean that."

"I do mean that. You don't need me. I can find a way to get where I'm going without you." Traveling from Oakland to Vallejo on foot, with a newborn chimera who hadn't figured out how to walk, while trying to read maps that might as well have been written in Latin…it wasn't going to be easy. It was going to be the hardest thing I'd ever done, and that included coming to terms with my own biology. I was still going to do it. My survival depended on it.

So did the little girl's, and part of me resented the fact that I had so quickly slaved my survival to hers. This was one quirk of biology that I hadn't been prepared for. It was going to take me some time to get used to it.

Carrie hesitated. Then she shoved the gun back into the waistband of her pants. "I want to stay together."

I looked at her warily. "If you pull that on me one more time, I'm gone. You understand that, right? If you pull it on me, or on her," I indicated the chimera girl with my chin, "I will take her, and I will leave, and I will not come back."

"I understand," she said quietly.

"I need to get to Vallejo. I know you were picked up in San Francisco. Is anyone else waiting for you there?"

This time she shook her head. "No. Paul and I worked for the same company—that's why we were together when the Army picked us up. Everyone else in that building can fend for themselves. I don't owe anything to any of them."

"All right," I said. "We stay together. Now, let's get under cover. It's going to get cold soon."

We wound up taking refuge in a diner that had no broken windows, and smelled only faintly of dust and spoiled food. I wouldn't have wanted to open the refrigerator, which was probably dripping with rot, but the booths were padded in red vinyl, and there was no one else there with us.

Carrie found the diner's earthquake kit behind the counter and set up a pair of lanterns in the back of the dining room, where the light wouldn't be visible from outside. Even then, we wound up bracing cardboard from the supply cupboard next to the bathroom over the windows to prevent leakage. We didn't talk while we worked. We might not be friends, but we were allies, and capture wouldn't do either of us any good.

I settled the chimera girl in one of the overstuffed booths, getting her comfortable while we secured the diner. When I returned, she had pulled herself into a sitting position and was watching me with wary, curious eyes.

"Hello," I said.

"Sal," she said, and opened her mouth like a baby bird, leaving it hanging for a few seconds before she closed it and looked at me expectantly. She was hungry, and the same instinct that told me she was my sister told her that I would take care of her.

I didn't want to leave her with Carrie, but I didn't want to take her with me while I scavenged, either. I bit my lip, trying to decide which would be worse, and finally turned toward Carrie. "She needs to eat, and so do we," I said. "I'm going to go check the kitchen for things that haven't spoiled and don't need to be cooked. Can you stay with her? Make sure she doesn't fall down or hurt herself, or anything?" We hadn't been in the kitchen yet. I didn't know what I was going to find there, or if it would be safe.

Carrie frowned. "You'd trust me with her?"

"I don't want to, but we need to eat, and I think I have more experience with scavenging for what I need." We had scavenged at the candy factory, and I had done more supply runs than Carrie had during our time in the quarantine zone. We'd always known that nothing would really hurt me, not while I was under the Colonel's protection. "Just make sure she doesn't do anything. I'll be right back." With that, I seized one of the lanterns and strode toward the doorway to the kitchen.

The shadows were deeper there, and the smell of decay was stronger. There were no bodies on the floor, which was a relief; I'd been half afraid I would find another group of dead sleepwalkers, like a party favor no one wanted. Most of the stench was coming from the trash cans, which were fuzzed with mold and pulsed with maggots. Flies swarmed overhead, but seemed to give me a wide berth, either because they somehow recognized me as a fellow invertebrate—albeit one in a very fancy suit—or because they were so secure in their resources that didn't see the need to risk getting swatted.

Flies weren't intelligent. I knew that. I also knew that tapeworms weren't capable of rational thought, and yet here I was, skirting the pulsing mounds of maggots with a mixture of professional courtesy and disgust. If Nature had been able to twist science to the point of creating me, who was to say that one day, the houseflies and larvae wouldn't rise up and demand their piece of the sapience pie? It was better to treat them with something like respect, just in case.

Besides, the mindless hunger of the maggots reminded me too much of the sleepwalkers for comfort. It was better if I didn't dwell on it. I kept moving.

The pantry didn't smell of rot: It hadn't been used for the storage of anything that could go bad that quickly. I found jars of prefabricated spaghetti sauce and gravy, and canned vegetables of every description. There was applesauce, and dry pasta, and even potatoes, which were shriveled and sad-looking. There was an attached door leading to the walk-in freezer. I cracked it open, peering cautiously inside.

The short-order cook who had been on duty when things went all the way wrong looked rigidly back, his face frozen in an expression of permanent regret. I blinked. I should probably have screamed, or jumped, or done something else human and visceral, but I couldn't. He looked so sad, like he'd never expected this; like he had been so sure that humanity would find a way to fix things before he was forced to do the unthinkable.

There was no blood, and we'd seen no signs of sleepwalker incursion in the diner. I wondered what had driven him to freeze himself like this. Had his implant started to stir, causing him to realize that soon, he'd lose control of his own body? Had he chosen death before loss of identity, stepping into the cold and allowing hypothermia to steal his breath away? It seemed like the same ending, really, but with the added knowledge that someone else wouldn't be using his body as a weapon after he was gone.

My breath plumed white in front of me, and I realized what else it was: It was proof that the freezer was still working.

I closed the freezer door, barely allowing myself to hope, and turned to scan the pantry wall for the switch I knew must be there. My lantern illuminated it when I had finished half of my turn. I kept going, verifying that there were no windows before I returned to the switch. I reached out, hand shaking slightly, and flicked it.

The light in the pantry came on.

My hands were still shaking as I opened the freezer door again and grabbed a box of premade hamburger patties off the nearest shelf. Maybe they were a sign that the diner had been relatively cheap back in the days when things like that mattered, but right now, they represented the kind of meal I hadn't eaten since I'd left Dr. Cale's. Protein, *real* protein, and as much of it as I wanted to stuff into my face. There was a bag of hamburger rolls on the shelf, and I grabbed that as well. I could thaw them out on the grill, assuming the grill actually worked, and then... and then...

And then we would feast.

Carrie frowned when I returned with my arms full of food that needed to be cooked. "What are you doing?" she asked.

"The freezer works," I said, dropping everything on the counter. I walked over to the windows, double-checking our cardboard coverings to be sure they covered the glass. There were blackout curtains, probably to keep people from looking in during morning setup and late-night cleanup. I pulled them tight before turning and scanning the walls.

The light switches were mostly concealed behind an artificial plant near the door, probably to keep customers from playing with them. I walked over to them, said, "Please cover her eyes," and turned on the lights.

They blazed up white and vivid and impossible, like the last dying gasp of the empire that had built this place, filling it with red vinyl and kitschy 1950s memorabilia. Carrie gasped. The young chimera wailed. I hit the lights again, turning them off, plunging us back down into darkness.

"Hey!" yelped Carrie. "Turn them back on! We need those!"

"I told you to cover her eyes!" I shouted. I was furious. Not just furious: frightened. What if the child never trusted me again? I had allowed the light to hurt her. I should have moved more slowly, should have made sure Carrie was covering her eyes like I'd asked.

That little girl was one of the only members of my own species that I had ever met. Most of the others were already working with Sherman for the downfall of the human race—and he lumped me in with them, since I'd refused to help him when he'd asked. If I didn't want to be alone in the world, I needed to find other chimera who hadn't already signed on with his poisonous philosophy. And apart from my own selfish needs, she was too young and too inexperienced to take care of herself. She *needed* me. She needed me, and I had allowed her to be hurt. I was a terrible person. The fact that my need to keep her safe was at least half biochemical didn't matter. She was my responsibility, by biology and coincidence, and I was damn well going to protect her.

"Forget the kid, turn the lights back on," pleaded Carrie. "Please, please, turn the lights back on."

"If you want me to turn the lights back on, you'll cover her eyes," I said, struggling to keep my words from devolving into a snarl. I couldn't afford to start fighting with Carrie again. Our nascent peace was too delicate, and there were other things that needed our time and energy—things like calming the girl, and cooking the box of frozen hamburger patties that was waiting on the counter.

"Okay, okay," said Carrie. There was a pause, and then, "My hands are over her eyes now, all right? Turn the lights back on. Please."

"You'd better not be lying," I said, and flipped the switches.

This time, when the lights came on, no one gasped or screamed or otherwise overreacted to what used to be such a simple thing. The world used to be defined by light, not by shadows. But we had changed all that, and now light, however fleeting, was a precious thing, to be celebrated whenever it appeared.

I turned back to the booth where Carrie and the young chimera sat. Carrie was staring at me, wide-eyed and slack-jawed. True to her word, she had her hands over the young chimera's face. As for the girl, she sat silent and unmoving, either recovered from her surprise when the lights came on or already resigned to her inability to defend herself against what must have seemed like a huge, endlessly cruel world. If she couldn't save herself, what was the point in trying to fight?

I could understand her resignation, even as I wanted to gather her close and tell her it didn't have to be like this; that the world could be her friend, if she was willing to give it the chance. Giving up had seemed like the right thing to me, more than once. It was sheer luck that had gotten me through some of what I had experienced, and I wasn't to the broken doors yet. I was still trying to figure out the way home.

"How did you...?" Carrie asked.

"The freezer was still on. There's a lot more where these hamburgers came from. Fries, more patties, ice cream." And a dead man, but I didn't see reason to mention that just yet. I wanted her to eat, not repudiate my food as being somehow tainted. The clothes we were wearing had been a lot closer to the dead. "If the freezer was on, I figured there had to be electricity somewhere. If there wasn't, everything would have shut down and thawed out." Probably making the worst stench I had ever encountered in the process. It was a good thing on many levels that the power was working.

"Why does this building have power?"

I shrugged. "Private generator, maybe? I know you can get those, and it's a big freezer. It would make sense for the owners to want to be sure that nothing would rot if the power went out." I walked over to kneel in front of the young chimera, putting one hand on her knee. "You can take your hands away now."

Looking unsure about the idea, Carrie pulled her hands away. The girl looked surprised before screwing her face up tight, wrinkling her nose and lips together until she appeared to have bitten into a lemon. She didn't put her hands over her own eyes. She hadn't figured out that she could do that yet.

If she couldn't figure it out on her own, I would show her. "Here," I said, gingerly taking hold of her hands and raising them to cover her eyes. I pressed on the backs of her wrists, helping to slide her fingers into place until they would block out the majority of the light. "Do it like this, and then the light won't be able to hurt you."

I took my hands away. Hers remained where they were, shielding her eyes from the unexpected brightness. I wondered whether she'd ever seen electric lights before. Depending on when she had taken over her host—which must have been recently, given where I'd found her—she might have spent her entire existence in the comfortable divisions of sunlight and shadow, with nothing like electricity to ever disrupt her understanding of the world. It was a daunting thought.

Slowly, the fingers on her left hand slid open just a crack, and she peered at me through the opening. There was no mistaking the intelligence or the confusion in her dark brown eye. I smiled at her.

"Hi," I said. "I'm sorry the light hurt you before. I didn't

mean for that to happen, and I'm going to be extra-special careful to make sure it doesn't happen again."

"She can't understand you," said Carrie. "There's something
wrong with her."

Only by human standards. By chimera standards, everything about the girl was exactly right. "Do you know how to
work a grill?" I asked. "I can probably cook the burgers, but
I'll ruin a bunch before I get it right."

"I used to work at a McDonald's—that's part of why I
stopped eating meat," said Carrie. She looked relieved as she
moved toward the box of frozen hamburger patties. "I don't
think we want to fire up the grease fryer right now, but I can
manage a couple burgers. I'm hungry enough that I don't give
a crap."

"Just don't go in the freezer if you need more. Send me."

There was a pause, during which Carrie's not asking was
practically audible. Finally, she bowed before the face of common sense, and said, "Got it," before picking up the box and
disappearing into the kitchen.

I turned my attention back to the chimera girl. "Food soon.
There's applesauce, so if you haven't figured out how to chew,
we can still feed you." Chewing came automatically to sleepwalkers, but this was a chimera: Instinct wasn't going to be her
friend, and her body's old muscle memory wasn't going to be
her gentle guide.

It occurred to me that I didn't know anything about who
she used to be. Maybe her host had been a vegetarian, and eating hamburger patty, no matter how well cooked it was, would
make her sick. Maybe she had allergies, and that was what her
implant had been intended to suppress. I didn't know, and I
wasn't going to find a convenient file with her medical history.
She was going to have to muddle through, and so was I. If we
were lucky, neither of us would be hurt in the process.

"I hope you like hamburger," I said, brushing her hair back

with my fingers. It was thick and soft, and needed to be washed. "I wish I knew your name."

"Sal," said the girl, still peeking at me through her fingers.

"No, sweetie, that's my name. We can't all be called 'Sal'; it would get very confusing, very fast, and we try not to make things more confusing than they already are. Do you know any other words? Do you know a word that sounds like your name?"

"Sal," said the girl again.

I sighed. "Okay, so that's not going to work. We'll figure out what your name is when you're farther along in your language skills." I was the one who'd decided my name was "Sal," a nickname that Sally would never have tolerated. It was too short, and too curt, like someone clearing their throat. It hadn't been a big decision—clipping one syllable from the end of a name I got from somebody else—but it had been *my* decision, and I treasured it, because it had taken someone else's name and made it *mine*. I wanted my girl to have the same freedom. Even more, I wanted her to be able to name herself, to begin the process of forging her own identity. People would always be telling her who and what she had to be. At least this way, she could choose one of the things that would define her to the rest of the world.

The scent of seared meat drifted in from the kitchen. The little girl lowered her hands away from her eyes and sniffed the air, looking suddenly excited. I smiled, this time in relief.

"I guess you're a meat eater after all," I said, and squeezed into the booth beside her to wait for Carrie to come out with our dinner.

I became a parent at a relatively young age, only to delay the actual responsibilities of the position for another five years. Nathan was neither planned nor unplanned: His conception was a happy accident, followed immediately by his removal from my womb and storage in a properly certified facility. His father agreed to this because I was the one who would be carrying our son to term, and because, like me, he wanted to finish certain tasks that required an element of disaffected youth before he settled down to become someone else's father.

I did my best to be a good mother for Nathan, who deserved better than me. I was never equipped for the sort of selfless maternity that my mother offered me, and that the media outlets were happy to claim was the only way to be a mother, the only way to love a child. But I did the best I could, and I learned more from him than I had from any other teacher, at any other level.

Those lessons served me well when my second son was cut from my flesh, and I had to start over again. My firstborn son never got the mother he deserved, but he was the one who made me the mother that my second child needed. For that, I will always be grateful.

—FROM *CAN OF WORMS: THE AUTOBIOGRAPHY OF SHANTI CALE, PHD*. AS YET UNPUBLISHED.

I can't reach Shanti. No, that's not quite accurate: That implies I can find Shanti, that she hasn't somehow dropped completely off the grid, taking whatever research she's done, whatever answers she's hiding, with her.

Systems are breaking down. I haven't been able to access the files I hid in the cloud for almost a week. The sysadmins I still have are spending all their time patching things together, struggling to accomplish connections they wouldn't even have needed to think about six weeks ago, and they're not going to be able to hold things together for much longer. But the work goes on, as does the search for Shanti.

She must know something about how this contamination got into the water. She must. *And that means she'll be able to tell us how to fix it. There is no other answer.*

God help me, the survival of the human race is at stake.

—FROM THE PRIVATE NOTES OF DR. STEVEN BANKS,
DECEMBER 18, 2027

Chapter 7

DECEMBER 2027

We glutted ourselves on substandard burgers served on half-frozen rolls. Carrie had found ketchup and mustard and relish in the pantry, and we had applied condiments with abandon, glorying in the taste of spices, crushed tomato, and corn syrup. Everything seemed impossibly rich, impossibly sweet, especially when stacked against these last few weeks. We ate like kings of the world, and for that short time, it didn't matter that the world was ending outside our little stronghold; we had burgers enough for a lifetime, and everything was going to be all right.

The chimera girl knew how to chew, which was a relief. Since burgers were a food that people habitually picked up with their hands, I hadn't needed to worry about Carrie judging the girl's table manners. She'd just stuffed her burger into her mouth with single-minded need, and when her first was gone, we'd given her a second, and the three of us had eaten and kept eating until our bellies were tight as drums and filled with calories.

I had fallen asleep in one of the larger booths, with the chimera girl curled up against my legs like a wayward puppy. All my dreams were of the dark, the hot warm dark, where nothing could hurt me, or reach me, or make me decide what was going to happen next. In the hot warm dark, I could be free.

I woke to find the diner filled with amber sunlight, illuminating the dust motes that danced around me. I sat up, yawning, enjoying the tang of grease still hanging in the air.

Carrie and the girl were gone.

I rocketed instantly from sleepy pleasure into terrified consciousness. "Carrie?" I hit my knee on the edge of the booth as I stood. I ignored it. I had more important things to worry about. "Carrie, where are you?"

There was no answer. I was alone.

The drums pounded in my ears as I looked around the room. It was large enough to easily hold fifty people, but it didn't have that many hiding places. They weren't here. I turned toward the door to the kitchen, my heart beating like it was breaking. Why would Carrie have taken her? Why would she have *gone* with Carrie? It didn't make any sense.

Slowly, I started for the kitchen, forcing myself to move with the sort of calm deliberation that would keep me from doing anything I was going to regret later. My mind—helpful, so-human mind—insisted on presenting suggestions as to what might be happening, ideas about death and dismemberment and bodies shoved into that large walk-in freezer. I did my best to force each of them aside as soon as it reared its head, refusing them the privilege of reality. Thoughts didn't shape the world. I *knew* that. I still couldn't let those thoughts linger. They were dangerous, like snakes, and they would bite me.

I pushed open the kitchen door. Carrie, who was sitting on the counter watching the chimera girl as she calmly, methodically ate pickle relish straight from the jar, raised her head and smiled. It was an easy expression. I didn't trust it.

"There you are," she said. "I was starting to think you were going to sleep the day away."

"I woke up and you were gone," I said.

Carrie nodded. "She," she indicated the chimera girl, who was still eating relish with the single-minded determination of someone who'd learned the hard way that food wasn't reliable, "woke up and got hungry. I figured it was better to let you sleep, and let her eat whatever she wanted that wouldn't kill her. I've never seen a kid suck down relish like that before. It's sort of impressive. Do you think there's some record she's about to beat?"

My hands itched to snatch the girl up and move her away from Carrie, who was being too casual, too easy, for me to believe a word she was saying. Instead, I forced myself to smile, and said, "That was really nice of you. Next time, you can wake me. Are you ready to go?"

Carrie's own smile dropped away, replaced by an expression of confusion. "What do you mean? Why would we be going anywhere?"

"I have to get to Vallejo, remember? I can't stay here. My family is waiting for me." They wouldn't be waiting in Vallejo—they'd be waiting in San Francisco, in Walnut Creek, in some forgotten farmhouse or abandoned animal rehab center, but they *would* be waiting. They were consummate waiters. Dr. Cale could wait out geologic ages, if she thought there was good reason, and she would be enough to keep Nathan in check. I had every faith that they were looking for me, sounding out weaknesses in the systems at USAMRIID and searching for routes into the quarantine zone, and that was why I had to get back to them as soon as possible. If they got captured trying to get me back, I'd just have to go save them, and none of us would be getting anything done.

"But we have food and power here," said Carrie, her voice verging on a whine. The chimera girl was still shoveling relish into her mouth. She was going to make herself sick if she didn't stop soon. Carrie pointed at her and said, "You have the kid to worry about. Don't you want her to be someplace safe? We can defend this place. We can keep the bad things out, and keep ourselves in."

"What happens when the power dies?" I countered. "What happens when whatever made Paul get sick, even though he should have been clean, manages to reach us here? Colonel Mitchell said he was losing soldiers. Why would we be safe just because we found a hole to hide in? Hiding is never the solution. Not forever."

"I don't know what's wrong with you, Sal, and I don't really care." Carrie's face set itself in a mulish scowl. "This place is safe. Nothing you can say is going to change that. And I'm not stupid. I'm not going to run away from safety just because you think it's the right thing to do. I don't know *anyone* who would do that."

The chimera girl looked at her latest handful of relish before dropping it on the kitchen floor with a wet *plop*. Then she tilted her head to look up at me, mouth closed and nose scrunched in an expression of utter contentment. She didn't smile. For us, smiling was something that had to be learned. "Sal," she said.

"Yes, Sal," I agreed, crouching down and offering her my arms. She didn't throw herself into them as much as she leaned until she collapsed, trusting me to catch her. She had inherited a body with the necessary muscle memory for sitting and probably even standing, but she didn't know anything about the way those things were done. She would need to learn the rules for fitting them together before she could really start controlling her movements.

She smelled like pickle relish and sweat. She was going to need a bath soon. I didn't mind. There was something comforting in the way the human odors mingled with her tapeworm pheromones: She was both, and she was more than either.

I stood, holding the girl against my chest, and looked at Carrie. "You can stay here. I told you last night that we could split up if you felt it was necessary. I'll find my own way to Vallejo. But don't think for a minute that you're safe. You can lock the doors, you can board over the windows, and you can die alone. You'll never be safe."

Carrie's scowl faded into an expression of sheer hopelessness. In that moment, I knew I wasn't telling her anything she didn't already know: She was well aware of her situation, and that safety was something she had left behind in another world, in another lifetime. "Why can't you let me pretend?" she asked, voice barely above a whisper.

"Because pretending will get you killed, and I still need you to drive me to Vallejo, if you're willing." There was no point in lying to her. "You're scared. I'm leery. I don't trust you after you drew a gun on me three times and threatened to use it on my little girl." It was amazing how quickly possessiveness had crept in, wasn't it? The child would be nameless until she said otherwise, but in the meantime, she was *mine*. "That doesn't mean I want to leave you here to die, and it doesn't mean we can't help each other. I'll provide companionship and someone who can watch your back. You'll drive me home."

"And if they're not there? What are you going to do then?"

I shrugged. "I'm going to figure out where they *are*, and I'm going to go to them. You can't talk me out of this. You can't make me stay, unless you want to draw your gun again, and if you do that, we're done. I'll climb the walls until I find a way out. All you can do is stay behind or come with me. Those are your choices."

Carrie looked at me, a virtual stranger with a little girl clutched against her chest. She looked at the kitchen around us, with its promise of safety that could never be realized. She seemed to deflate, letting the last of some unspoken tension escape her chest. Then, finally, she nodded.

"I'll drive you to Vallejo," she said. "I think you're crazy. But I don't want to stay here alone. I don't think...I don't think I could take it."

"Good." I nodded. "Let's gather what we can, and let's move."

The diner had apparently done some catering events: We found two large coolers at the back of the kitchen, and packed them full of canned goods, nonperishables, and anything else we could scrounge, including knives and can openers. It seemed silly to be using insulated plastic for warm goods, but cardboard could tear, and we might find a place with a working ice machine a little further down the road, once the ice we'd taken from the freezer melted. It was impossible to really say. Things had changed dramatically while we were in the quarantine zone, and it was no longer clear how much sway, if any, the remnants of the human race held over this part of California.

It was strange to be thinking of humanity as something that could *end*. But the tapering arrivals in the quarantine zone, even during my stay, told a story that was brutal in its simplicity. The implants had started to awaken, and then they had started awakening each other, creating a fractal cascade that first threatened and then overwhelmed the human race. For every sleepwalker who awakened, a human died. If that sleepwalker wasn't stopped before they could go on a rampage, they could kill two, or ten, or twenty more people before they were put down. The first ones who turned were able to do a huge amount of damage, just because no one expected them. The last ones who turned would have found little in the way of resistance. The numbers just weren't there.

How many dead humans—how many dead cousins—for the sake of a handful of chimera? We hadn't even been an intentional side effect. We had just *happened*, one more strange consequence of the complicated genetic engineering that went into the original implants. And now we faced a world where the population was unknown, but so much lower than it should have been.

While Carrie packed the supplies, I took the little girl and went back to the Old Navy to scavenge clean clothes for all of us. The bodies of the dead sleepwalkers were easier to see in the light. They were heaped all over the back of the store, blocking access to the men's department and the clearance racks. The chimera girl looked at them with disinterested eyes, no more invested in their fates than she was in the fates of the racks that had been knocked over since the store was closed. That was a relief. I'd been half afraid that she would start screaming as soon as she saw the dead. But we needed more clothing, and she needed something that didn't smell of bodily waste and neglect, and I didn't want to leave her alone with Carrie. I was willing to travel with the human. I wasn't willing to leave my child with her.

Mine. There it was again. The possessiveness was surprising every time it reared its head, and I wasn't going to let it go. I wasn't going to let *her* go.

The clothes I picked out for her were too large, but they were better than nothing, and she'd need room to grow. I scrubbed her down as best as I could with a bottle of hand sanitizer I'd found hidden behind one of the registers, and stuffed the rest of my scavenged goods into a big cloth shopping bag with the Old Navy logo on the side. Hoisting the girl back onto my hip, I turned toward the exit.

There was a sleepwalker standing in the doorway.

I froze, my grip on the girl tightening. I hadn't heard him approach. I hadn't detected his pheromones either: The wind was blowing the wrong way to have carried them into the store. He seemed to be alone, but he was blocking the exit; if he decided to charge, I was going to have to fight.

Better to fight than to die, especially with the chimera child here, depending on me to save her. Moving slowly, in the hopes that it would keep the sleepwalker from realizing what was happening, I put her down on the counter. "Stay there," I murmured, looking into her bright, bewildered gaze. Did she understand what was going on? Chimera learned fast, but it wasn't like I was taking the time to teach her the way I should. We'd been together for less than a day. There hadn't been time.

She didn't grab for my arm when I pulled away from her. I turned back to the sleepwalker, half expecting to find him standing right behind me. Instead, he was still in the doorway, rocking gently back and forth like he had forgotten what he was doing there.

Hope flooded through me, briefly drowning out the sound of drums with an odd, rosy silence. Maybe he was one of the more high-functioning sleepwalkers, the ones we'd theorized could verge on becoming chimera. They'd always have brain damage to work around, thanks to the way the implants had chewed their way into their host brains, but they might be capable of learning, of reasoning, of analytical thinking. All those things combined could mean they were capable of not killing and eating uninfected people on sight—and according to everything I understood about pheromone communication, those were the sleepwalkers who would be especially susceptible to my instructions.

"Hello." I took a cautious step toward him, reaching behind me to put a hand on the knife I had jammed into my belt.

"My name is Sal. Are you all right? Do you know where you are?"

It was sort of ironic: Sleepwalkers got no or limited higher brain functions, but they understood how to walk, run, and grab from the moment they woke up in their new bodies. Chimera could learn how to do anything their human hosts had been capable of, but in order to get that far, they first had to relearn everything, from sitting up to fine motor control. It would be weeks, if not months, before the girl I'd rescued could stand up like this man, even as he stared at me with empty, uncomprehending eyes.

If he was a high-functioning sleepwalker, it was only barely: There was no understanding on his face, no sign that he knew who I was or what I was doing by approaching him. I took another step toward him and froze as I finally drew close enough to pick his pheromones out of the air. His signature was *wrong*. He should have smelled of mature implant, and he did: he had all the chemical tags and protein twists that my nose had developed to detect. But that wasn't all he had.

The smell of a newborn sleepwalker was heavy in the air all around him, fresh and muddled and new. It shouldn't have been possible. Those two signatures should never have been able to coexist. But in this man, somehow, they were doing just that.

He opened his mouth. I braced myself, expecting the classic sleepwalker moan, which would summon any of his friends who happened to be nearby. All that came out was a squeak, high and tight and quickly strangled as his throat constricted. His eyes flashed alarm—one of the first genuine emotions I'd ever seen from a sleepwalker. Most of the time they functioned on hunger alone, unable to pause long enough to consider anything more complex. They would withdraw to their nests to sleep when they were full, but anything more complicated was supposed to be beyond them.

Maybe he was one of the sleepwalkers who bordered on chimera after all. He squeaked again, the look of alarm deepening until it overwrote everything else about him. Then, without any other warning, he collapsed like his tendons had been cut, rendering his legs incapable of holding him up. He made no effort to catch himself as he fell, and the sound of his face impacting with the floor was wet and red.

I rushed to drop to my knees beside him, grabbing his shoulders and hoisting him onto his back. His nose was mashed, misshapen, and gushing blood. One of his front teeth had been knocked out when he hit the floor. His mouth continued to move soundlessly, and that missing tooth formed a little square of darkness against a field of white washed in blood. His eyes rolled from side to side, trying to focus but failing.

The smell of new sleepwalker was getting stronger with by the second. It had almost overwhelmed the more developed pheromones, making them muddled and difficult to detect. The drums were pounding loudly in my ears as things put themselves together one after another, creating an image that made as little sense as everything else about the situation, while remaining impossible to deny.

Paul had gotten sick despite being certified as clean. So had several of Colonel Mitchell's men—and while I might believe that he wouldn't order as many medical tests as needed on one of the denizens of the quarantine zone, I couldn't believe he'd leave his own people vulnerable in that way. He needed them too much, and there were no reinforcements coming.

There were dead sleepwalkers all over the Old Navy. The only survivor had been the little girl—but sleepwalkers didn't recognize chimera as being the same as them. She should have been eaten long before she was abandoned. Unless they'd all turned at the same time, there was no way for her to have survived...unless.

Unless something was causing sleepwalkers to convert the same way humans did. In the case of the little girl, whose brain was young and elastic and capable of recovering from incredible trauma, it had resulted in a fully integrated chimera. In the case of the adult sleepwalkers...

The man in front of me began to convulse. It wasn't dramatic, not like Carrie's performance back at the Coliseum, but each convulsion was more violent than the one before it, until he was writhing on the floor. The new pheromones rose briefly triumphant, overwhelming the old—and then they, too, were gone, leaving nothing but a broken jumble hanging in the air. The man went slack, the smell of bodily wastes filling the air. I didn't have to check for a pulse to know that he was dead. There was nothing else he could have been.

I stood on legs that seemed almost as shaky as his had been, looking down at his motionless body. I didn't have any proof of what was going on—I would have needed to split his skull open and see for myself if I wanted actual *proof*—but observation was good enough under the circumstances. He'd been a sleepwalker. He had somehow been infected with a second implant. That was the key to everything that had been happening, and it explained all his symptoms. It even explained the little girl, who had, after all, been fine when I found her surrounded by the bodies of the dead.

Paul had been free of infection. Colonel Mitchell's soldiers had been free of infection. And then they hadn't been. Something was allowing new implants to enter already-infected bodies, and once they were there, the origin story that had created the sleepwalkers—that had created *me*—was playing out all over again.

"Oh, no," I moaned, and rushed back to the girl, scooping her into my arms. She held on to me this time: She was learning to cling and be carried, listening to the old primate instincts of the body she now possessed. She had taken it twice, once from the human who bore it at birth, and once from the implant that had chased that human away. Somehow, the second invasion had succeeded where the first had failed. Was that going to be normal? I didn't know what the numbers were supposed to be for how many infections it took to get a chimera.

Suddenly, I wanted Dr. Cale more than I wanted anything else in the world, even Nathan. She would have been able to explain what was going on in a way that made sense and didn't make me feel stupid. She might not *like* dumbing herself down for the nonscientists in her world, but she knew how to do it. So did Nathan. It was just that he hadn't created the implants; he didn't understand them like she did.

No one understood them like she did. That was the problem. People kept *doing* things with and to them, and the only woman in the world who really understood what the consequences might be was largely ignored.

I clutched the little girl and the bag of clothes hard, and ran for the door. I needed to find Carrie. We needed to move.

Carrie was waiting outside the diner, surrounded by a small wall of boxes and coolers and watching the plaza like she was getting ready to bolt. Given that there had been at least one sleepwalker still wandering around as of this morning, I understood the impulse. I decided not to tell her about him if I could help it. What I was about to say was going to freak her out enough.

"I wish this place had a decent shoe store," she said, when I came running up. "There's an Amazon hyperlink ATM near the parking garage, which I guess was supposed to make up for the lack. Who buys shoes off of Amazon? Hell, who *can* anymore? The Internet died, and apparently we have to go barefoot from now on."

She sounded surprisingly unflustered, almost, well, *normal*, like something about having enough to eat and no USAMRIID patrols on the streets outside had hit a reset button somewhere deep inside her. I panted as I stared at her, trying to use my exertion as cover for tasting the air, looking for signs that she was about to fall victim to an implant of her own.

There were no unfamiliar pheromones around her. Either she wasn't infected yet, or her implant—her invader, at this point, since she wouldn't have taken it in willingly—hadn't grown large enough to start causing a problem. I couldn't count on her, no matter which one was true. She was a time bomb waiting to go off.

Maybe I was too.

She finally seemed to notice that something was off. She frowned slowly, putting down the loose paving stone she'd been turning over in her hands, and asked, "Sal? Are you all right?"

Carrie had a history of instability when faced with situations she didn't want to deal with. She'd reacted badly to the dead sleepwalkers in the Old Navy, to my adoption of the chimera girl, even to my insistence that we were going to have to keep moving, because I was going back to my family whether she helped me or not. She'd drawn a gun on me several times. I couldn't count on her, but more, I couldn't *trust* her to act in my best interests if she felt like she was at risk. My survival depended on her cooperation.

I understand now, Sherman, I thought, almost desperately, and I smiled at her as I lied. "I'm fine. I thought I saw a rat back by the store. Probably attracted by all the bodies in there. We should move."

Carrie shuddered. "Oh, gross. You'd think nature could lay off with the vermin for a while, since we're dealing with an honest-to-God apocalypse. Do you think there are more of them around here?"

"Probably." A thought struck me. Everything we'd eaten at the diner had been sealed somehow: wrapped in plastic, or in a closed jug, or even kept in the freezer. If the implants-turned-invaders were coming in through tainted food, Carrie might still be clean. It all depended on whether she had been exposed to the same source as Paul, back in the quarantine zone. "We should probably throw away anything that might have been open. There's no telling what's touched it."

"Ew," said Carrie, with another shudder. "I'll check all the food. I picked up some bottled water from the storeroom, too. Nobody's been maintaining these pipes. When I went to wash my hands this morning, the water that came out of the faucet was all cloudy and gross."

"Avoid the water, check." I didn't like bottled water. It always tasted sterile to me, like all the life had been filtered out of it. Considering that the problem we were facing now was an *excess* of life, maybe that wasn't such a bad thing. And maybe...

Dr. Banks had tried to spin me a story about infection carried through the water supply once. He'd been lying—he had always been lying to me—but maybe there was something to what he'd been saying after all. Avoiding the water might be the only smart thing we could do.

"Sal? You okay?"

"What?" I shook my head, brushing away my morbid train of thought. One thing was for sure: I wasn't going to drink the water. The chimera girl clutched my neck and whimpered. I stroked her hair as best I could without losing my grip on her, and asked, "Are you ready to move?"

Carrie responded with a quick, thin smile, tight-lipped and blessedly free of teeth. "I still wish you were willing to let us stay in that diner. But since you're not, let's go ahead and see the back of this place before USAMRIID comes back and makes us run." She picked up the first of the coolers and started walking toward the parking garage, leaving me with little choice but to follow her.

I followed her.

She had found a large SUV with two-thirds of a tank of gas and the keys still in the ignition, declaring it proof that our luck was changing. I wanted to ask why it was our good luck, and not the bad luck of the original owner—who had clearly either become a sleepwalker or been devoured by them—that mattered here. I thought better of it. Pointing out that we were fighting an uphill battle against a dangerous world was just going to upset her, and upsetting her wasn't going to get me to Vallejo any faster. Especially not when she could begin to show symptoms of sleepwalking sickness at any moment. I was never relaxed when I was riding in a car, but I was starting to think this might be the worst ride of my life. And I still didn't have any better options.

It took us long enough to move the supplies that I was actively worried about someone stumbling over us before we were done. The chimera girl had been happy to sit in the back seat of the SUV, buckled in and chewing on a dill pickle from the diner's supplies. I was reasonably sure she didn't know how the seat belt worked and wouldn't be able to let herself out: That was one small fear removed from my growing supply. If I lost track of her and she got too far away for me to sense her pheromones, I'd never be able to find her again—she didn't have a name I could shout, and she didn't answer any commands yet. I needed to teach her to be safe as soon as I possibly could. She'd been with me less than a day, and I already couldn't imagine a world without her.

Carrie brought her up as we were loading the last of the boxes into the back. "What are you going to call the kid?" she asked. "She has to have a name. We can't just go around calling her 'hey you.'"

"Why not?" I asked. "We don't have the authority to make those sorts of choices for her. She should get to make them for herself."

To my surprise, Carrie actually laughed. "What, like she

won't? My name is 'Carolyn,' not 'Carrie.' I asked people to call me 'Carrie' because it was a name I chose for myself. Your legal name isn't 'Sal,' is it?"

"No," I admitted. "But 'Sal' still sounds a lot like 'Sally.'"

"So you never quite outran the name your parents gave you. So what? That just means you're comfortable with it. I've known people who were named 'Beth' by their parents, and went by 'Belladonna' or 'Chastity' or even 'Susan' as soon as they were old enough to choose. Nothing says she can't *change* her name, and as long as you're willing to respect whatever it is she wants to be called when she's old enough to make up her mind about it, there's no good reason for you not to give her a name to hold on to now. It'll help if you have something you can shout when she makes you mad."

I frowned. "It still seems like I'm making her choices for her, instead of letting her make them herself."

Carrie sighed before slamming the back hatch of the SUV. The sound echoed through the parking garage, making the hairs on my arms stand on end. If there was anything near us, it would be showing up soon. Of that much, I was sure.

"Look, Sal, I get that you don't get along very well with your birth family, and believe me, even if we weren't fugitives from the US Army right now, I wouldn't want to pry. But you're not that kid's birth family. You're the family that found her, and if you're going to keep her, you need to give her a name. You need to show her that you're going to be her home."

I blinked. "I thought you didn't like her."

"I don't," said Carrie bluntly. "I think she's creepy, and I think she's going to slow us down. Maybe even get us killed. That doesn't mean you shouldn't take care of the kid if you're going to keep her. Kids tend to be happier when they have names, and part of being a parent is making some of their choices for them, at least until they're old enough to do it for themselves."

"Oh."

"Think about it, all right? Now, let's get out of here." Carrie turned and walked toward the driver's-side door. I went the opposite way, moving to my own door.

Once we were both in the car, seated and safely buckled in, I twisted around enough to look at the little girl, still gnawing on her pickle. "I know I said I wasn't going to give you a name, but Carrie made a good point: I need something I can call you," I said. "So how about this? I'm going to call you something, and you're going to answer to it, I hope. That doesn't mean you have to use it if you don't want to. Just as soon as you can tell me what you want to be called, we can change it. Does that sound fair?"

The girl looked at me solemnly as Carrie started the car and pulled out of our parking spot. I held my breath, not sure what sort of indication I was waiting for, only sure that I would know it when I saw it.

Finally, without making a sound, the girl nodded. It was a small gesture. It may not even have been an intentional one. It was more than enough for me.

Dr. Cale had created the SymboGen implants in part because her friend Simone had died of allergy-related complications—something that would never happen in a world where genetically engineered tapeworms controlled the body's immune responses. Before she died, Simone wrote a book called *Don't Go Out Alone*, which somehow managed to shape Dr. Cale's approach to life, despite being an incredibly simple collection of words and pictures that even I could manage to read. It was about two children, a boy and a girl, who went into a dark forest following their friend the monster. Their names weren't given in the text, but they were hidden in some of the illustrations, if you looked carefully. Nathan had shown me where to look.

"I'm going to call you Juniper," I said, and turned to settle back in my seat, content in my decision—

—only for Carrie to start screaming as the sleepwalker that had come shambling out of the shadows near the mouth of the parking garage bounced off of our hood, scrabbling for purchase as he fell. Carrie twisted the wheel hard to the side, clipping a concrete pole. It was a near miss, and sent the side view mirror on her side of the car bouncing off into the darkness.

Someone was screaming. It wasn't Carrie: Her mouth was closed now, set in a hard line as she concentrated on getting the SUV back under control. Someone was screaming.

It was probably me.

I reached up and clasped my hands over my mouth, blocking most of the sound. Carrie kept her eyes on the open space in front of us, gunning the engine as she raced for the light outside. The sleepwalker hadn't reappeared. He might be dead; he might be too injured to stand. I knew I should care, but I couldn't quite find it under the screams tearing at my throat and the drums pounding in my ears. Survival was what mattered. That sleepwalker didn't care about our survival, and that meant I couldn't take the time to care about his. No matter how much I wanted to. No matter how much I thought I should.

Then we were out of the shadows and in the light, and Carrie was going as fast as she could while swerving around the wrecked and abandoned cars that clogged the streets. I suddenly saw the next few days stretching out in front of me with perfect clarity: We would be stopping often to move things out of our way. We'd be siphoning gas and scrounging for supplies, and even with all of that, if we were found by the sleepwalkers, or by USAMRIID—or by Sherman, who was still out there somewhere—before we reached Dr. Cale, it was all going to be for nothing. We couldn't guarantee success. All we could guarantee was that wherever we died, it wouldn't be here.

"Knowing the direction doesn't mean you have to go." The

words were muffled by my hands, but they weren't screams: under the circumstances, that was more than I could have hoped for.

"What?" Carrie didn't take her eyes off the road. That was for the best.

"Nothing." I dropped my hands into my lap. My heart was hammering, and the drums were whiting out the world, but that was all right. We were moving. We were facing my fears, and I was going home. "Let's go home."

We drove on.

INTERLUDE I: EXAPTATION

All life is a battleground, and I am the perfect soldier.
I have no other choice.

—SHERMAN LEWIS (SUBJECT VIII, ITERATION III)

I guess I just want to do something amazing with my life.
Isn't that what everyone wants?

—CLAUDIA ANDERSON

December 2027: Sherman

This is not what I intended. This is not what I intended at all.

I forgot that my people are not well schooled in the ways of obedience when I'm not standing over them to enforce the rules: I forgot that so many of them grew up and learned themselves with Kristoph and Ronnie and Maria and Batya standing over them, teaching them the things they'd need to know if they were going to pass unseen amongst the humans. I was a distant god in those days, too wrapped up in my work at SymboGen and my attempts at courting Sal to make myself a constant presence in their lives. They learned to respect me, yes. They learned to fear me, even, and I have been more than happy to exploit that fear when I needed to. But they have never, not for a moment, learned to *listen* to me.

Ronnie made his sacrifice for the sake of our future, and because he was tired of living in a world that would never allow him to conform to his own expectations. I had something to do with that. I was the one who ordered him implanted into a child's body, knowing that his epigenetic memory would gnaw at him like rats, until he hated his own skin more than he hated the humans who would deny us our essential sentience and individuality. I was the one who said it would be too hard for us to move him again, reculturing him in a body that fit better with his self-image. There were times when I thought he would realize what was going on, why I was so firm that he live as a girl even in the company of chimera, who didn't care about human social or gender roles. I'd been priming him to become a weapon since I changed his host, and why shouldn't I have done that? He had threatened my supremacy among the people who were meant to be mine. *I* was going to lead them into the glorious future. Not Ronnie. Not Kristoph. Not anyone else.

Certainly not Sal.

Her name always brought a pang of regret, and a stronger wave of anger. She should have been mine. She should have loved *me*. I played my part so well. I showed her again and again that I was her perfect mate, caring and funny and compassionate and willing to do whatever she needed me to do. And what did she decide? She decided to be *human*. To love a man who had never taken one of us into his body, who would have no immortality—who would inevitably leave her. I could have been with her for lifetimes, moving from host to host as easily as we had once moved through the warm darkness of the prethought. I could have given her *true* children, blending her DNA with mine in sterile tubes until our offspring hatched, and then implanting them in the mewling babes born of her host melding with mine. I could have given her everything, and she would have given me her elasticity, her genes that bent and did not break.

Instead, she'd made me take them from her, harvesting her genes like she was a common human cow. She'd made me into a monster, because she wouldn't let me be a man. But she was the monster now, not me. She was the one whose genetic duplicates were causing everything to go wrong. If she'd been willing to cooperate with me, to give instead of forcing me to take,

I might have known what would happen. I might have found another way.

This is not what I intended. This is all her fault.

"Sherman?" Batya's question was accompanied by a perfunctory knock on the open door, like the touch of her knuckles on the wood would be enough to make her interruption forgivable. I didn't turn. She was not forgiven.

Batya ignored my shunning and pushed gamely on, saying, "The operation was successful. We've removed six cysts from Maria's muscle tissue, and one hatchling from her brain. We think we got everything. Just in case, we took a segment sample from her actual body while we were operating. We'll be able to bring her back if something goes wrong."

Unspoken: We would be able to bring Maria back in a new host, with a new surface personality shored up by her original epigenetic data, if one of the new worms managed to somehow slip past her defenses. Unlike Kristoph, she would not be lost.

"Good," I said curtly, and finally turned. Batya was standing perfectly straight, her hand resting on the doorframe as if for balance, or for strength. More than any of my seconds, she hated to show weakness in my presence, and she was still recovering from her own surgery. They had harvested four invading cysts from her flesh. It would be weeks before we knew whether we'd removed them all.

Perhaps it was petty, but I almost hoped we hadn't. Batya was a threat to my position. It would be…better…if something happened to her that couldn't be traced back to me. We had a sample of her true self. We could always reculture her and try again.

"We're running low on bottled water, and we're still not sure that charcoal filtration gets all the eggs out," she said. "What do you want us to do?"

Curse these fragile hosts, who needed so much water to stay alive—and hence tied us to the same necessity. "Keep testing new filtration systems. Keep scanning for signs of infection. Prep a team. We'll raid the local Costco for more bottled water." The place had locked down early in the sleepwalker outbreak, and the parking lot had been a battleground for weeks. Their stocks had been mostly intact when the blast doors came down.

Now Batya looked alarmed. "There are human survivors holed up in there. We haven't gone in for supplies before this because they're armed."

Survivalists. The thought made my lip curl involuntarily. Why couldn't they roll over and *die* already? "The longer we leave them there, the more of *our* water they're going to drink," I said. "We need to get them out of that supply depot. We can either bring them back here alive as stock and replacement bodies, or we can leave them dead in the parking lot for the crows. Either way, they have what we need. We're taking it."

Batya looked, briefly, disappointed. "I thought we were supposed to be better than them."

I smiled at her, intentionally showing my teeth. She flinched, but didn't recoil. "We're not supposed to be better than them. We're just supposed to be the ones who survive. Don't you have a team to gather?"

"Yes, sir," she said, and turned to walk away. I watched her for a moment before I looked back to the monitors on my office wall. They were showing an endless loop of security footage: Sal, running. Sal, sleeping. Sal, never leaving me.

This isn't what I intended. This isn't what I intended at all.

STAGE I: GENETIC DRIFT

Do not drink unfiltered or tap water. I repeat,
do not drink unfiltered or tap water. Do not allow
water to enter your nose, mouth, or eyes when
showering. Stay dry, stay alive.

—MEMO FROM DR. SHANTI CALE TO HER STAFF

It would be really awesome if I could stop
running away for a little while.

—SAL MITCHELL

Take the bread and take the salt,
Know that this is not your fault;
Take the things you need, for you will not be coming
    back.
Pause before you shut the door,
Look back once, and never more.
Take a breath and take a step, committed to this track.

The broken doors are kept in places ancient and
    unknown.
My darling ones, be careful now, and don't go out
    alone.

—FROM *DON'T GO OUT ALONE*, BY SIMONE KIMBERLEY,
PUBLISHED 2006 BY LIGHTHOUSE PRESS.
CURRENTLY OUT OF PRINT.

We've been testing the worms that Mom isolated from the
water supply, trying to figure out exactly how they got in
there. They all share a strong genetic resemblance to one
subject from her files: an implant she calls "Persephone," as
if that will somehow keep me from realizing that she's talking about Sal. Someone put Sal—or put something tailored
and cultured from her genetic material—in at least one of the

local reservoirs, if not more than one. We know it wasn't any-one here, which leaves two possible candidates: Dr. Banks or Sherman.

Mom wants to think Banks did this. She hates him so much that it clouds her judgment sometimes. She's never been good at feeling things intensely, and the degree of the hate she feels for him doesn't leave room for her to feel anything else. Banks is a bad person, but he's not a fool. Putting tapeworms in the water supply hurts everyone, including him. He wanted Sal to use her as a weapon for *the humans, not* against *them.*

This is Sherman. It has to be. She knows that too.

I just need her to admit it, and act.

—FROM THE NOTES OF DR. NATHAN KIM, DECEMBER 2027

Chapter 8

DECEMBER 2027

The surface streets in Oakland were clogged with abandoned vehicles and debris, but the highways moving out of the city were surprisingly clear. I attributed the cleanup to the proximity of the Coliseum: If USAMRIID was moving through here regularly, they would have taken steps to make it easier. Carrie seemed to have the same thought, because as soon as we hit the interchange into Berkeley, she abandoned the clear highway for the difficult-to-navigate surface streets that would take us to I-4.

"This is going to take forever," she complained, weaving her way through the cars scattered around the intersection near the Telegraph Avenue Whole Foods Market. There were some clear spaces in the parking lot. I considered asking her to stop so we could gather more supplies, and decided against the idea almost instantly. There might be bottled water in there. There were definitely deep shadows, and places for sleepwalkers to hide. We didn't know how far the contamination went. We had gotten lucky in Oakland: If that mob of sleepwalkers had been alive and capable of pursuit, we would have died the second we set foot in the Old Navy. I wouldn't make that mistake again.

"I don't care if it takes forever," I said. The slower speeds were making it easier for me to relax. As for Juniper, she hadn't made a sound since we'd left the garage. I glanced at her in the rearview mirror. She had mostly finished devouring her pickle and was still gnawing methodically, her eyes fixed on the window, watching the world roll past with no signs of distress or dismay. I settled deeper in my seat, feeling the weight of my responsibility to her falling down on me like a collapsing bridge.

My fear of riding in cars wasn't a natural part of being a chimera. It was given to me by people who thought they were serving my best interests when they were actually twisting my mind, trying to turn me into someone I wasn't. If I wasn't careful about how I reacted in front of Juniper, I could wind up passing the fear along, convincing her that something that was essentially safe—and absolutely necessary, given the distances we had to travel—was dangerous. That wasn't right. It wasn't fair. I had to monitor my responses like I never had before.

"Children are complicated," I murmured. I wasn't ready for this, and for a moment, I hated the biological imperative telling me to protect that little girl at all costs.

"Tell me about it," said Carrie. "There's a reason Paul and I decided we were never going to have them." Her face fell a moment after she finished speaking, like Paul's death was hitting her all over again. She focused her gaze back on the road, which spooled out in front of us like an obstacle course of vehicles and debris.

I wanted to tell her I was sorry for her loss, that I understood how much she was hurting, that I would try to keep her safe. I wanted to tell her pretty lies that would act like arnica on her pain, soothing away its edges and releasing its center. I couldn't say anything. The words wouldn't come.

What if I did something wrong, and messed up Juniper the way the Mitchells had damaged me? What if I couldn't love her enough to put her survival above my own? And why *should* I put her survival above my own? She didn't know who she was yet. She would struggle for survival like any living thing, but if she didn't find it, it wasn't like there was anyone but me to miss her. I still wanted her to live, and thrive, and I was already willing to put myself in danger for her sake.

If this was what parenthood was like, it was no wonder Colonel Mitchell had been willing to lie to himself about Sally still being alive. It had been better than picturing a world where his daughter was dead, and was never going to ride in another car, or eat another pickle, or do *anything*. I must have made it even harder on him. Sally didn't intentionally donate her body to science when she allowed her father to give her an implant to control her epilepsy. My takeover had been the ultimate betrayal of his love: The thing that was supposed to protect her, to keep her alive, had been able to save her body, but not her mind.

"*Everything* is complicated," I said this time, and Carrie laughed, short and sharp and bitter, and we drove on.

The streets were deserted, clogged with trash and with gangs of roaming dogs already well on their way to reverting to an older, feral state. They snarled and shied away as we drove by, viewing us as intruders on their territory. They were right, in their way. We didn't belong here anymore. Humans had built this city, and sleepwalkers had destroyed it, and now it belonged to the animals who had managed to keep themselves alive despite the chaos.

It wasn't just dogs. The ubiquitous crows perched on fences and on roofs, cawing raucously as we passed. Cats prowled in the bushes, and fat, lazy squirrels strolled across the road, barely speeding up to avoid our tires. It would take a while for the overgrown yards to begin tearing up the sidewalks and invading the streets, but it would happen; the city would fall, a tiny bit at a time, until it was forgotten. That was, unless humanity somehow managed to win this war, to defeat an enemy that they had created for themselves, and came back to reclaim what had been theirs.

The farther we drove into the ruined city, the less likely that seemed. We hadn't seen a living human since leaving USA-MRIID. They still lived in the world—Carrie was proof of that—but their numbers were declining, at least if the quarantine zone and the dead sleepwalkers in the Old Navy were anything to go by. Too many people had implants, and too many of those implants were waking up. Chimera were functionally humans in a lot of ways, no matter what Sherman wanted to think, but we were too rare, too difficult to create naturally; I had been the only one I knew of for a very long time. Now there was Juniper, and she would have died in that store if I hadn't come along when I did.

Was this whole thing just an elaborate way of giving the world to the dogs? And would it be such a bad thing if it were?

"We'll have to cut through Albany to get to the 4," said Carrie, interrupting my train of thought. "How well do you know this area?"

"I'm pretty familiar with Solano," I said. "I go there once a year for the Solano Stroll." There would be no Stroll this year, I realized with dismay; no huge outdoor craft fair and food festival, no barbecue scenting the air with honey and hickory, no local social clubs trying to recruit new members. I'd manned the Cause for Paws booth there for the past three years, bringing out hopeful dogs and fluffy kittens who were in need of new homes. It was one of my favorite events. It, like the human ownership of Berkeley, was over.

"What kind of traffic are we looking at there?"

Solano was near several schools, and in a fairly heavily developed suburban area. "Lots of cars, but hopefully most people stayed off the main streets when they started getting sick," I said after a moment's thought. "We can take Shattuck all the way, and then it's a straight shot to the freeway."

Carrie nodded. "Okay. Let's do that. I haven't seen any of those things for a while, and I want to get out of here before that changes."

"Do you think we'll make it to Vallejo tonight?" I hated sounding so eager. Even knowing that Dr. Cale and the others weren't going to be at the candy factory anymore, I still wanted to see it. It had been one of the closest things to a real home that I'd ever had, and I wanted to go back there. Not forever. Just long enough to catch my breath.

If I was ever going to breathe again.

"Hard to say," said Carrie. "I'm worried about the freeway. I'm worried about USAMRIID. And I'm worried about the bridge. Vallejo is surrounded by water. Couldn't you decide that we needed to go somewhere else to look for your family? Somewhere more, you know, landlocked?"

"I—" I stopped before I said anything else.

Landlocked.

Dr. Cale had said that she was getting out of Vallejo. USAMRIID knew she was there, and Carrie was right: Staying in a city that was most accessible via bridge wasn't a good idea after the world started coming to an end. She had some incredibly talented scientists and engineers working for her. That didn't mean they were equipped to rebuild a *bridge* if something happened to it. When she moved, she would have moved inland.

Not to San Francisco, because San Francisco was in SymboGen's backyard. Not to Colma, either, for the same reason. Oakland and Alameda were both out for being too close to USAMRIID. Pleasanton being the quarantine zone took out the surrounding cities, San Ramon and Dublin and Fremont. But she wouldn't have gone farther north, either. Even if she'd wanted to, Nathan wouldn't have allowed it—not with Tansy in critical condition and me in Colonel Mitchell's custody. They would have wanted to stay close. Not so close that they got caught, but...close.

"Yes," I said, softly.

"Yes what?"

"Yes, I think there's somewhere else we can look. Keep going. I'll tell you when you need to exit the freeway."

Carrie nodded, and drove on.

Juniper had finished her pickle and gone to sleep in her seat, her head resting against the window and her mouth hanging slack. The sun was sinking lower against the horizon, turning everything orange and rose and making it harder for Carrie to see the road without turning on the headlights. When it got too dark, we were going to have to stop for the night. The chances that we would be spotted were just too high if we were the only thing that was lit up in the entire East Bay.

The idea of waiting in an unmoving car until dawn, with who-knows-what moving through the night outside, was not appealing. The idea of being picked up by USAMRIID when we were so close to what might be our goal was even worse— especially since, if I was right, I would be responsible for leading them to Dr. Cale's doorstep when she'd finally managed to drop completely off their radar. I couldn't do that to her. If we had to sleep in the car, then we had to sleep in the car. Even with the possibility of sleepwalkers prowling the hills, it would still feel safer than the quarantine zone.

"Willow Pass in a mile," said Carrie. "You sure about this?"

"No." I looked out the window at the rolling Contra Costa hills. Cows dotted them here and there, grazing, apparently unaware of the chaos around them. They must have been meat cows, not dairy, or be lucky enough to belong to ranchers who were still alive. Dairy cows who went without being milked for too long could die when their udders became infected, and while cows were good at feeding themselves, they weren't always good about protecting themselves from predators.

Speaking of predators...we hadn't seen any sleepwalkers for long enough that I was starting to worry. Either they were dying off, from the secondary infections or from the many other dangers that the world presented to essentially mindless creatures trapped in fragile human bodies, or they were learning how to hide, becoming more efficient attackers. The higher-functioning sleepwalkers might have had enough time to settle into their bodies that they had figured out how to plan, how to use their resources to best effect, rather than just mobbing and expecting it to get them what they wanted. I didn't know. Not knowing was the worst part.

I-4 was mostly clear, although the sides of the road were lined with the cars of people who had made it this far and no farther. We'd had to go around several accidents. The lack of traffic in the other lanes made it easier than it should have been; when one side was blocked, we could just use the law enforcement cutouts and drive on the other side of the road for a while. It was eerie, and I was glad Juniper was sleeping. She didn't need to see this. Not that it would mean anything to her. She was essentially a newborn, and this was the world she would grow up in: this empty place, filled with deserted shells, and with silence.

The sun was hitting the horizon hard enough to bruise the sky when Carrie reached the Willow Pass exit. We still had a few miles to go before we would be inside the city limits. She looked at me across the gloomy cab, her half-visible expression clearly asking what I wanted to do.

There was only one answer. "Keep going," I said.

"I'd say it was your funeral, but since it's going to be mine too, you'd better pray you're right about this," she said, and kept on driving.

Navigating the hills and tight turns of Willow Pass Road was nerve-racking even when the driver could see. With Carrie essentially driving blind, I felt like my heart was going to burst inside of my chest before we got to where we were going.

"I need to turn on the lights," she said.

"Please, not yet," I said.

She didn't turn on the lights.

We were so close to our destination that I could almost taste it. It tasted like homecoming, like safety, like finding my way back to where I should have been all along. Carrie kept driving, and I kept my eyes glued to the windshield, trying to pick out details through the increasing gloom. There were wrecks shoved up against the side of the road, but there were no cars abandoned in the road itself. That seemed like a good sign. Dr. Cale had been using her people to rearrange the cars in Vallejo to make it look like there was no one living in the area, while also making sure that her teams could move around freely when they needed to. These cars could have ended up where they were by chance, or they could have been placed there.

"How much farther?"

"Not far," I said. I thought of the street in daylight, the area as it had been when I first came looking for the broken doors. It had already been a little run-down, a little decrepit. Berkeley had started showing signs of abandonment fast, because there had been so many things waiting for the chance to fall apart. This place had been crumbling for years. I couldn't see details, but the broad strokes of the streets around me spoke of a place that hadn't noticed yet that it was over.

Something moved in the shadows. I couldn't tell whether it was a coyote, a large dog, or something else, something bipedal and formerly human. I didn't want to roll down the window to check for pheromones. They might wake Juniper, and keeping her from getting upset about what was coming was very important to me. I was taking her to meet her family as well as mine, and I needed her to be ready. Or at least asleep.

"Did you see that?" demanded Carrie.

"Just keep driving. We're almost there." The buildings were becoming denser as we moved from the outskirts of town toward the point of commercial development.

"We need to stop."

"Just keep driving."

Carrie shook her head but kept her foot on the gas and her eyes on the road. Under the circumstances, I couldn't ask for anything more than that.

The bulky shape of the feed store appeared to our left. I pointed to the mouth of the attached parking lot. "Turn in there," I said.

"That doesn't look like a good place to spend the night."

"If they're not here, the facility still will be," I said. "I know how to get us in." That wasn't entirely true. If Dr. Cale had armed her security systems before abandoning the place, the doors might be locked beyond anything I could do to open them. That didn't matter now. I had to get out there. I *had* to.

There was something sweetly anticlimactic about Carrie turning into the parking lot, slowing down as she did, until we were just coasting along. I fiddled with my seat belt, barely realizing that I was doing it, my eyes fixed on the looming shape of the bowling alley. Its windows were dark, but that was nothing new; Dr. Cale had boarded or painted them all over years ago. It was hard to maintain a secret lab when people could see you working.

Tansy had always been a big help with that. I had to wonder how many people had discovered the place, or almost discovered it, only to be turned away by a quirky, homicidal girl in overalls.

Tears sprang unbidden to my eyes. I blinked them away

hard. Tansy wasn't gone. The broken doors weren't closed to her—not forever, anyway. Dr. Cale had been able to create her in the first place, and she was going to find a way to save her. She *had* to.

Carrie rolled to a stop in the bowling-alley parking lot and killed the engine before turning to frown at me across the darkened cab. I could barely see her face. "This is it? This is your other idea? Because it looks like a terrible idea. There's no one here."

"That's just what they want you to think." I wiped my eyes with the back of my hand before unbuckling my seat belt. "Wait here. If anything happens to me, take Juniper and get as far away from here as you can."

"Wait, what? Sal, don't do this. I can't turn on the lights. I can't—"

The door closing behind me cut off her words, reducing them to silence. I stayed where I was, watching the dark parking lot and taking a deep breath, trying to find traces of sleepwalker pheromones on the wind. I failed. If there were sleepwalkers lurking in the shadows, they weren't close enough to pose a problem, or they were downwind and keeping themselves carefully out of sight. I didn't know whether their slow recovery would make that possible, but I had to assume that any sleepwalkers to have survived this long were on the smarter—and luckier—end. I waited.

When nothing came charging out of the dark to devour me, I took another breath, this time to steady myself, and started walking toward the bowling alley. More images flashed across my mind: Tansy laughing, Adam and his shy smile, Nathan seeing his mother for the first time since her "death." Things had already been getting complicated by the time we arrived at the bowling alley, but they had been better then. It had still felt like it was possible for us to win whatever conflicts might be coming, like maybe we were all going to find a way to live happily ever after.

I didn't feel like that anymore. The world was not a fairy tale.

Glass and gravel crunched underfoot as I slowly approached the door. There were no little red lights to betray the presence of security cameras, and none of the cars I could see looked like they'd been driven since things began falling apart. Tansy had always been responsible for a lot of the exterior security. Fang, who had become Dr. Cale's right-hand man after the fall of San Francisco, had taken over a lot of Tansy's responsibilities in the last few months. He wasn't going to do things the way she had. I kept trying to tell myself that, forcing my feet to keep moving, forcing my mind not to dwell on what would happen if they weren't here after all.

It doesn't make sense for them to come back here, warned the small voice of my deepest fears, the voice that always knew Nathan didn't really love me, that he'd stopped loving me the moment he learned I wasn't human; the voice that said I should have let them brainwash me into Sally Mitchell, who could at least have been content with the world, even if she was never quite the same. I hated that voice.

The voice hated me too. That was the only explanation for the way it kept talking, whispering, *This site was compromised. USAMRIID would just come and sweep them up and take them away. You're wrong. You're wrong, and you're going to get yourself killed trying to deny it. You should have stayed in Pleasanton. At least there, you knew where the walls were.*

"I'm not wrong," I murmured, mostly to hear the sound of my own voice, the outside voice that said the things I *wanted* to say, not the things I was most afraid of. USAMRIID never pinpointed the bowling alley. Dr. Cale had spent *years* securing it, as opposed to the weeks she'd had to secure the candy factory. With their resources flagging, Colonel Mitchell's men

weren't going to have time to go looking for a suspected underground lab. Dr. Cale was smart. Smart people didn't go back to
places where they didn't feel safe. She would only have come
back here if she knew, as deeply and as truly as I did, that she
was safe here.

I rapped my knuckles against the door, stepped back, and
waited.

Nothing happened.

I began counting silently, marking time in the only way I
had. I reached three hundred, and still the door was closed, and
still nothing was happening.

The last time I'd been separated from my people, Nathan had
been concerned that I wasn't myself when I finally managed to
get out. Maybe that was happening again. I stepped forward,
resting my forehead against the door. I might get splinters.
That was fine. A few splinters were a small price to pay for the
chance to go home.

"Please, it's me," I said. "It's always been me. Please, let me in."

Nothing happened.

Maybe I wasn't saying the right things. " 'Shadows dancing
all around, some things better lost than found,' " I said halt-
ingly. " 'If you ask the questions, best be sure you want to
know. Some things better left forgot, some dreams better left
unsought. Knowing the direction doesn't mean you have to
go.' " It got easier as the verse went on, each line leading inevitably into the next, until it was like I was trying to keep hold
of a living thing, a snake that turned and twisted in my mouth.

" 'The broken doors can open if you seek them on your
own,' " I said. "Please. *Please.*"

There was a click, like a switch being flipped, or a safety
being disengaged. I straightened, turning wide eyes on the
night behind me. A figure moved in the gloom. For a second—
one beautiful, impossible second—I thought it was Tansy. Then

the moment passed, and it was Fishy standing there, with his riotous curls and his square, practical face. He was holding an assault rifle, the muzzle pointed squarely at my chest.

I almost missed the sound of the door opening. I whirled again, and there was Dr. Cale in her wheelchair, stains on the cuffs of her lab coat, circles etched deep into the skin under her eyes. She looked at me with a hunger that bordered on desperation, hope and fear and anxious need reflected in her eyes.

"My darling girl," she said. " 'Be careful now, and don't go out alone.' "

I threw myself into her arms, and she caught me, and I was home.

Our embrace lasted longer than I would have thought possible. Dr. Cale was my creator and Nathan's mother. She was also the woman who'd once ordered her people to take samples of my true body, the one that slept in the cathedral of my human body's skull, because she thought they might be important for her research. I had thought, after she did that, that I was never going to trust her again. I had thought it wouldn't be *possible* for me to trust her again.

Only it turned out that there were some betrayals that cut deeper than those enacted by people who thought they were saving me and the world at the same time. There were the betrayals by people who had never had my best interests at heart. There were the betrayals by people who *meant* to hurt me. Dr. Cale had acted without my consent. She had also apologized, and I believed her. I was never going to get that from Sherman, or from Dr. Banks...or from Sally's father.

She let me go. I started to straighten, and she lashed out, grabbing the sides of my face in either hand and staring, searchingly, into my eyes. I looked back, trying not to blink, trying to let her see whatever it was that she was looking for.

This time, when she let go, she didn't grab me again. "Sal," she said, and smiled, that sweet, infrequent smile that she shared with her biological son. "You made it. You found us. You came home."

"This is nice and all, but can we get some clear instructions on the lady and the kid?" asked Fishy. "Lady's got a gun. If she shoots somebody, it's going to trigger a cutscene, and nobody's got time for that."

"Oh!" I turned away from Dr. Cale, and then back again, realizing that trying to explain myself to Fishy wasn't going to end well for anyone. "They're with me. Carrie drove me here. I needed her to help me break out of the quarantine zone. Juniper—the little girl—she's special. We need to talk about her."

Dr. Cale raised an eyebrow, looking dubious. "That's how you're going to start our grand reunion? By telling me we need to talk about a kid you picked up somewhere along the way? Children aren't like dogs, Sal. We don't adopt them just because their owners die."

"She's yours as much as she's mine," I said, and then, in case Dr. Cale didn't feel like getting the point, I added, "She's a chimera. And she's the third owner of her current body."

Dr. Cale's eyes widened, dubiousness dropping away. "You mean she's a result of a second implant entering the same body?"

I nodded. "Yeah. She was a sleepwalker, and now she's not. Her name is Juniper. I'm taking care of her. But I knew I needed to bring her to you."

"Yes, you did. How likely is your other friend to shoot someone?"

The sound of a gunshot, breaking glass, and Juniper screaming was our answer. I spun around and ran for the car, past Fishy, who had also turned, and was aiming his rifle at the driver's-side window. That window was intact: Carrie must have shot forward. That was confirmed when I got closer, and saw the shattered safety glass of the windshield gleaming on the hood. There were other shapes in the darkness, people I didn't recognize. I was running into a firefight. I knew it, and I couldn't stop. Juniper was in that car. If Dr. Cale's people started shooting back—

"Carrie, *stop*!" I shouted, waving my arms over my head in an effort to make her focus her attention on me. It was dark enough that I felt the need to make myself as visible as possible. "You're not under attack! We found my family! *Stop shooting!*"

There was a pause, during which the only sounds were Juniper whimpering and me running toward the SUV. Then Carrie fired again, blowing out more of the windshield. Juniper screamed louder.

None of Dr. Cale's people were returning fire. Carrie was essentially shooting blindly into the shadows, and while she was going to hit someone eventually, they had an advantage she didn't: They were capable of moving. Until she got out of the car, she was a known quantity with a small handgun and a limited supply of bullets. There was no reason for them to do anything but evade.

Juniper didn't understand that. Juniper didn't even know how to unfasten a seat belt. She was trapped with a woman who was firing a gun indiscriminately at enemies she couldn't possibly see or comprehend, and she was panicking appropriately.

"Carrie! *Carrie!* This is my family! Stop shooting!" I was close enough now to see Carrie's face through the shattered window. Her eyes darted wildly in my direction, round and white and furious. She was holding her pistol up with both hands, and while it was aimed away from me for the moment, there was no guarantee that would continue.

Juniper was still screaming. It tore at my heart. I would have strangled Carrie with my bare hands in that moment, if I had thought it would make the screaming stop.

"You're not in danger here!" The words felt like lies in my mouth. Carrie very much *was* in danger. If she kept behaving like this, there was no way Dr. Cale would let her stay—and if Dr. Cale didn't let her stay, she was going to die. Not of natural causes, either. Fang took his position as head of security very seriously. Fishy had no normal moral qualms, since he thought that everything that was happening was part of a strange, highly immersive video game. Either one of them would be happy to put a bullet in her skull to keep her from betraying them.

Carrie shook her head wildly. "They're everywhere!"

"Yes! This is where they live! Now, put down the gun and come meet my family." I held my hands up, hoping she could see that they were empty, that I was still unarmed. I hadn't expected this violent response to finding the people we'd come here looking for. It didn't make any sense.

Or maybe it did. She had reacted with violence, or the threat of violence, over and over again while we'd been alone. Now that we were surrounded by other people, maybe she just couldn't help herself.

"Please, put down the gun." I was begging. "They'll shoot you if you don't. Please."

"You asked me to bring you back to your family, and I did it," said Carrie. At least that meant she was hearing me: Even if she didn't fully understand what I was saying, she knew that I was talking. "I brought you back to *her*. She killed my husband. She killed us all, and now I'm going to put a bullet in her head!"

The venom and hatred in her voice was staggering. I stopped where I was, looking over my shoulder to where Dr. Cale sat in her wheelchair, backlit by the soft glow from inside. It wasn't very bright—they must have been keeping the front room of the bowling alley dim, to help them avoid detection—but it was bright enough that I could see her clearly, despite the distance between us. She didn't look angry, or even surprised. She just looked resigned, like this was the only reasonable outcome to my hitching a ride home.

I turned back to Carrie. "That's Dr. Cale. I told you we were coming to her lab, and you agreed, remember? She's my fiancé's mother. She didn't hurt anyone on purpose, and she isn't going to hurt you, I promise." Not unless Carrie kept shooting. If she managed to injure one of Dr. Cale's people, then all bets were going to be off. "Please, put down the gun."

"This is *her* fault!"

And there it was: the factor I'd been missing, the one I should have considered in more depth before asking Carrie to bring me here. The fact that I would never have been able to make it on my own was almost irrelevant; the fact that I had explained the situation, including where we were going, was maybe the only reason she'd come this far. To Carrie—to any human who understood the development of the SymboGen Intestinal Bodyguardor who had been exposed to Dr. Banks's frantic after-the-fact spin—Dr. Cale was public enemy number one, the woman who had singlehandedly engineered the downfall of mankind and the rise of the invertebrate invader. She was the mother of monsters, and I had led Carrie straight to her.

It was understandable that Carrie was out for revenge.

"Oh, no," I whispered, raising one hand to press over my mouth in horror. If Juniper hadn't been in the car, I might have told Carrie to run, to hit the gas and flee. She would never be comfortable here, not with her personal nightmare running the lab. She wouldn't go back to USAMRIID, and who else was there for her to tell? She could run until she died and never give us away...and even as I had the thought, I recognized that I was only allowing it to form because Juniper *was* in the car. Carrie couldn't be allowed to run. Imagining mercy did nothing to endanger me, or the ones I cared about.

Carrie seemed to realize that her little gunshots weren't getting her anything she wanted. She dropped the gun onto the seat beside her and hit the gas, sending the SUV lurching into life. It barreled toward me, moving impossibly fast, from my perspective as a stationary object, and I realized that I wasn't as afraid of being hit by a car as I was of being in one when it hit something else.

The realization was enough to root my feet to the pavement, until a body slammed into mine from the side and knocked me out of the way. The sound of gunshots split the air at the same time, and the SUV spun out of control as the rear tires were shot out. It was dark enough that all I really saw was the vehicle turning, no longer following Carrie's commands. Juniper was still screaming, louder now than ever.

"Are you hurt?" demanded Fang.

"Let me up!" I pushed, and the security chief—who was stronger than I was, by a good measure, even though we were basically the same size—allowed me to move. I scrambled to get my feet back under me and ran for the SUV, which had stopped a few feet from the bowling alley entrance.

The rest of Dr. Cale's security staff had already moved into position around the vehicle, guns drawn and aimed at the front seat, where Carrie slumped motionless against her seat belt, her forehead resting on the steering wheel. Through it all, Dr. Cale hadn't moved once. She was still sitting in the open doorway, her hands folded in her lap, watching the scene in silence.

I wrenched the SUV's back door open, ignoring the armed figures at my back. Juniper's wails redoubled when she saw me, accompanied by her reaching her arms out in my direction, hands making small, unconscious grasping motions. I had only been in her life for a day, but she already knew that I represented comfort: Like all children, she wanted to know that there was something bigger than she was standing between her and the monsters.

My hands were shaking as I undid her seat belt and scooped her into my arms. *I* had been out of the SUV when it was shot to a standstill, but my little girl hadn't. She could have been killed. I think that was the moment when I started hating Carrie. Losing her senses could be forgiven, but endangering Juniper? That was a step too far.

"Good to have you back," said Fishy as I passed him with Juniper in my arms. He blinked at the sight of her. Then he grinned. "Nice mission objective! See you inside." He turned his back on me and began moving toward the SUV. The other figures followed him. I wouldn't have wanted to be Carrie in that moment: If she had survived the accident, she was about to find herself on the receiving end of Dr. Cale's darker brand of hospitality.

Dr. Cale herself gripped the wheels of her chair and rolled backward when I reached the door, looking at me, and at Juniper, who was clinging so tightly to my neck that separating us would have been virtually impossible. "We looked for you," she said.

"I believe you," I replied.

"Welcome home," she said, and then she smiled, and I smiled back, despite everything, because I had done it. I had made it back to where I belonged.

Whatever happened next was going to be easier, because I was going to be with my family.

For me, the remarkable thing is not that things went wrong. Science is a powerful tool, but like any tool, it doesn't care whether it hurts you. Fire warms us, cooks our food, protects us from predators, but it will burn us if we let it. Fire is more than happy to eat us all alive. Science is fire writ large. As soon as we created the prototype for what would become the SymboGen implants, I knew that we were tailoring our own demise. Even if the science hadn't been willing to turn on us, we were entrusting a magic bullet to corporate greed.

Humanity has always been disturbingly happy to sacrifice its future on the altar of right now. Look at the antitrust suits of the early 2000s, or the copyright extensions pushed through again and again by large media companies who feared losing their hold over their greatest moneymakers. We will gladly pay you Tuesday for a hamburger today. So for me, the remarkable thing has never been that things went wrong. It's that it took so long for them to fall apart as badly as they did.

—FROM *CAN OF WORMS: THE AUTOBIOGRAPHY OF SHANTI CALE, PHD.* AS YET UNPUBLISHED.

We lost two more people today. Both had checked out as clean, and then abruptly went into convulsions. They died before we could offer medical help.

It's unclear how this new strain is interfacing with the human brain. We seem to be experiencing more early deaths than we did with the previous strain: It's as if the worm is going so directly for the brain that it skips the "sleepwalker" stage entirely, leading to a quick, violent death. Only two of the impacted personnel have made it from stage 1 (infection) to stage 2 (animation). None have progressed to stage 3 (sapience), although posthumous study has shown that in all cases, the worms had infiltrated the brain to such a degree that stage 3 should have been possible.

I sent men into the city today to round up surviving stage 2 victims of this terrible disease. They came back with thirty-four test subjects. We'll be spraying them down with infected water, to see what happens when someone who has already been infected is infected for a second time.

Still no signs of Shanti. USAMRIID has lost Sal. We may be doomed.

—FROM THE PRIVATE NOTES OF DR. STEVEN BANKS,
DECEMBER 19, 2027

Chapter 9

DECEMBER 2027

Entering the bowling alley was like stepping into a dream. I had never expected to be here again. Dr. Cale was waiting for her people to get Carrie out of the car, so I walked through the familiar, purposefully decrepit antechamber alone, until I reached the door that would take me to the main lab. I hesitated in reaching for the doorknob. Was I ready for what was waiting on the other side? What if we had lost people? What if we had lost *Nathan*? A lot could have changed since I'd been taken into custody by Colonel Mitchell.

There was only one way I was going to find out. I closed my eyes for a moment, taking comfort in the distant sound of drums and the increasingly familiar weight of Juniper clinging to my neck. Then I opened them, and grasped the knob, and turned it.

My first impression of the lab was that nothing had changed.

The workstations were where they had always been; the lights were bright where they needed to be but otherwise dim, keeping the power profile low and the chances of detection even lower. People in lab coats moved like ghosts through the gloom, some carrying clipboards or tablet computers, others transporting biological samples from one place to another. The lab coats were dingier than they used to be, no longer quite so pristinely white, but everyone I saw was wearing one. If you had a lab coat, you were a scientist. More now than ever, these people needed to be scientists.

As I thought that, I blinked, and I realized that *everything* had changed.

The people who moved through the gloom used to do it with calm assurance, like they had all the time in the world. Now they scuttled, moving fast, to the point where two of them nearly collided as I watched. The lights were low in part because some of the bulbs appeared to have burnt out. The charts and diagrams I remembered from the first time we'd been living and working out of the bowling alley were back in place, but they were interspersed with new signs, written in large red letters and often illuminated by pin lights. I stopped in front of one of those signs, squinting as I tried to make the letters stop swimming around the paper. Whatever it was, I needed to understand it if I was going to understand the changes that had happened here in the lab.

Juniper whimpered. I stroked her back with one hand, squinting harder. Bit by bit, the shifting, twisting letters settled down, becoming words.

> WARNING: DO NOT DRINK THE TAP WATER.
> IF EXPOSURE IS SUSPECTED, REPORT IMMEDIATELY.
> DO NOT CONCEAL EXPOSURE.
> SILENCE IS DEATH.

A chill slithered through my stomach. I had been right, and the worms were in the water. It was the only thing that made sense, and it explained everything. I was suddenly glad for the limited water rations back in the quarantine zone, and for the bottled water we'd taken from the diner.

Even sleepwalkers needed to drink. I remembered the desiccated teenage girl I had found dying in her own bedroom. She'd consumed the water from her fish tank before she got really dehydrated. After that was gone, it had only been a matter of time. There had to be faucets that had been left running, accessible toilet bowls still refilled by gravity. The sleepwalkers would have sought out those sources of water, following instincts more powerful than intellect, and then the very thing that had sustained them had killed them all.

"Sal?"

The word was little more than a whisper, familiar and frightened and heartbreakingly near. I was already smiling as I turned to face its source, my hand still stroking Juniper's back, my eyes beginning to fill with slow and welcome tears.

"Hello, Nathan. I came home."

My boyfriend slash maybe fiancé—he had proposed several times, and I'd said yes every time, so I guess that was the better word for him—stared at me like I was a ghost. He hadn't been outside much recently. He was paler than he'd been when he walked away from me in the SymboGen building, although his skin was still several shades darker than mine, going with his black hair and dark eyes, which were wide with pain and hope behind the lenses of his wire-frame glasses. Like the other scientists around him, he was wearing a dingy lab coat over a plain T-shirt and jeans.

Nathan was Dr. Cale's sole biological child, the result of her first and only marriage. He got most of his coloring and his height from his Korean father. He got most of his facial

expressions from his mother, although he was much more emotionally demonstrative than she was: Whatever had been left
out of Dr. Cale when she was being put together was present
in him, in spades. Never did that show more clearly than in
moments like this one as he took a half step forward and raised
his hand, like he was going to reach for me. Then he stopped,
like he wasn't sure he was allowed.

"Nathan—"

"I'm so sorry." The words tumbled out, jumbled together
and barely intelligible. "I should never have left you there. I
should have tried harder to find another way, to find a plan that
let us all leave together, and I'm *so sorry*, can you forgive me?
Please, can you forgive me?"

"Oh, Nathan." Everything was suddenly clear, and there was
only one thing I could do to make it any better. I stepped forward to meet him, putting my free arm around him and pulling
him as close to me as possible. Juniper made a noise of protest
and shifted positions, but she didn't cry or pull away.

"I was never mad at you," I whispered. "I never blamed you.
I stayed behind because it was the right thing to do, to get the
rest of you out of there. It was my choice, not yours, and I
never, ever blamed you for letting me make my own decisions.
That's why I love you. Because you always let me be a person,
no matter how dangerous it is."

Nathan laughed shakily, the sound thick with stress and
unshed tears. "I don't think I could have stopped you if I'd
tried."

"Probably not," I agreed, and buried my face in the crook
of his neck, breathing in the scent of his skin. It was soothing
in more ways than one. This was *Nathan*, the man who'd held
me through my night terrors and told me it didn't matter that
I was a tapeworm in a human skin. He didn't love me any less
because of my origins, and that meant more to me than I could
put into words. But even more importantly, being this close

to him, breathing in the chemicals rising off his skin, I could confirm what I needed to know more than anything else in the world. I could confirm he was still clean: that none of the cousins now swarming in the tainted water had managed to find a way into his body.

Juniper made her small sound of protest again, and Nathan let me go. Now I was the one who wanted to protest. I swallowed the urge, stepping back to let Juniper get a better look at him. She was sitting upright in my arms, her eyes fixed on Nathan. She looked wary. It was a new expression for her, and I wondered how much of it had been born when Carrie started shooting, introducing Juniper to the idea that sometimes the people who fed and held her didn't have her best interests at heart.

"Who's this?" asked Nathan.

"This is Juniper. Juniper, I want you to meet Nathan. He's my boyfriend. We're going to get married someday." Assuming marriages were ever performed again. Maybe Dr. Cale could do it. We could exchange dishes of ringworm, and promise to love, honor, and run like hell before we got captured by the government.

"Hello, Juniper," said Nathan.

"Sal," she said suspiciously.

Nathan blinked. "Sal?"

"She's a chimera," I said, answering the question he hadn't asked. "I found her at Jack London Square, in the middle of a mob of dead sleepwalkers. I think...I think that when she ingested a second implant, it somehow managed to destroy the original and take over the body. It had a better interface. She's a person now." Because the cousins weren't really people, were they? They were my relatives, and they *mattered*, but they weren't people. I wished I could do something to save them, but they didn't think. They didn't understand. All they did was act, and action wasn't enough.

"Wow." Nathan's eyes narrowed as he studied Juniper, now

assessing her as a scientist and not as a surprised boyfriend. "Hello, Juniper. Do you understand what I'm saying?"

"She hasn't had time to pick up much English," I said. "I only found her yesterday. I need to talk to your mom about how she taught Tansy and Adam to talk and write and stuff. I don't think I can do it by myself."

"Fortunately, you won't have to," said Dr. Cale. I turned to see her rolling up behind me. She reached out her hands. "Let me see her."

I didn't want to. Dr. Cale was my ally, and I trusted her more than I probably should have, but she was also the woman who'd cut me open once to serve her own scientific ends. It was impossible to swallow the fear that she'd do the same thing to Juniper. At the same time, she was the one who'd successfully tutored and raised three chimera, and she had never hurt them. I couldn't stay here if I wasn't capable of letting myself relax when she was near Juniper.

"She may not want to stay with you," I cautioned, and unhooked Juniper's arms from around my shoulders. The little girl gave me a reproachful look. "It's okay. Dr. Cale is our friend. She just wants to hold you for a second, and see how healthy and happy you are." *Please let that be true,* I thought, and handed Juniper to Dr. Cale.

"Sal?" said Juniper, looking back toward me as Dr. Cale settled her upon her lap. It was clear that Dr. Cale had substantially more experience with children than I did: She got Juniper settled in a matter of seconds, despite receiving no actual help from Juniper herself.

"Aren't you a strong girl?" asked Dr. Cale, looking at the side of Juniper's face. Juniper turned toward the sound of Dr. Cale's voice, and was rewarded with a bright, close-mouthed smile. "Hello, sweetheart. I'm Dr. Cale. I'm sort of your grandmother, I suppose. It's very nice to meet you."

"Where's Carrie?" I asked.

"You mean the woman who drove you here?" asked Dr. Cale. I nodded confirmation, and she scowled. "She nearly shot Fang in the shoulder. If his reflexes had been a bit worse, we'd be performing emergency surgery right now. What in the world possessed you to choose *her* as your escape route?"

"Her husband checked out clean before he was put in the Pleasanton quarantine zone. Then he drank the water." I jerked a thumb toward the sign behind me. "You know about the water. He got sick. He died. Carrie was the best option I had for getting out of there before the same thing happened to me. I didn't realize how unstable she was until it was too late to find somebody else who might be willing to help me out."

"Fishy and Daisy are bringing her in. We're going to put her in one of the isolation rooms for now, while we figure out how we're going to deal with her being here. You know we can't let her leave."

I'd always known that on some level. Hearing it from Dr. Cale just confirmed what I had already been pretty sure of. "I know. But being here is better than being there. Trust me."

"Wait—you mean they actually put you in the general quarantine?" Nathan sounded horrified. "But the Colonel—"

"His wife didn't want me in the military housing. He may be willing to lie to himself about who I am, but she's not. She knows I'm not her daughter, and she's not going to forgive me for taking Sally's place. Ever." I paused. "Dr. Cale, where's Tansy? And…" Saying the name felt wrong. I forced myself to continue anyway. "Where's Anna?"

"Anna's host body experienced extreme tissue rejection when confronted with the implant," said Dr. Cale. She handed Juniper a pen. The little girl looked at it quizzically before beginning to wave it around, looking fascinated by the existence of material space. "She was already going into organ failure when Dr. Banks brought her to us. Things went quickly after we lost you."

"Oh." Anna hadn't been with us for long, but she had been a chimera, like me, or Juniper. I'd hoped that Dr. Cale would have been able to save her. "And Tansy?"

"You were right: They didn't remove her primary segment from the host's brain," said Nathan. "She's stable."

"What he isn't saying is that Dr. Banks is a butcher," said Dr. Cale, expression darkening. "He sliced my little girl open like a side of meat. She's on life support, and yes she's stable, but if we have to move her again, we're going to lose her. The damage to her host body's brain was so extreme that even patching her back together isn't going to save her—not the Tansy we knew. We can transplant her core segment into another host if we happen to acquire one. She'll lose most of who she is, but she'll survive. That's the best we can hope for at this stage."

Finding another host would mean finding a human being who was willing to donate their entire body to a tapeworm who needed it. It was an oddly abhorrent thought, even knowing that was the way that I'd been made. However involuntary Sally's donation had been. "Aren't there lots of people around? Maybe one of them has been injured enough to qualify."

"I don't have any brain-dead bodies in storage, if that's what you mean, and I'm not Steven. I won't place one of my babies in the mind of someone who's still at home." Dr. Cale stroked Juniper's hair with one hand. "It's also not that simple. Finding Tansy a new host will mean finding someone who's at least a basic tissue match to her original host body. If we don't do that, it'll be Anna all over again. All our hard work will be lost. Tansy may be lost, too."

"Isn't there any other way?" I missed Tansy. I missed her more than I would have thought possible when I first met her. She was my sister. She'd been lost because of me. I wanted her back.

"I could rebuild the human portion of her genetic code from

the ground up. That's what Sherman did when he put the eggs in the water supply: He was aiming for the best broad-spectrum compatibility with the people they might infect, rather than shooting for a specific person's DNA." Dr. Cale gave me an unreadable look. "If I did that, though, I would be wiping her epigenetic data. The parts of her that are Tansy wouldn't carry over—she'd just be another chimera, assuming the procedure was successful."

"So we'd get someone new, and we wouldn't get Tansy back," I said slowly. "I don't want that."

"None of us do," said Dr. Cale. "That's why she's still on life support. We're trying to find another way. Barring a miracle, I don't think that's going to happen."

I worried my lip between my teeth, trying to take some comfort from the drums that were beating in my ears. If there was comfort there to be found, it was well outside my reach. "Oh," I said finally. "Is that why you're back here?"

Dr. Cale nodded. "The basic structure of the lab was still intact. It was a place we could run to quickly, without putting ourselves too squarely in one of the existing danger zones. We couldn't go very far. This was the best option we had."

"Why not?" I asked.

Juniper, apparently tired of Dr. Cale's attentions, turned and held her arms out toward me. "Sal," she said.

"Exactly," said Dr. Cale.

Unlike the candy factory, which had been large enough to contain the lab, provide living quarters for everyone who worked with Dr. Cale, and even allow us to grow our own food, the bowling alley was limited. It was still an enormous space, even subdivided as it had been, but it wasn't enough for everything it would have needed to be if it was going to be our only headquarters.

Shortly after Dr. Cale and her people had returned to the

bowling alley, with chaos reigning in the streets of Clayton and Concord, she had set her people to securing the area. I didn't need to ask what "securing" had meant, or how many bullets they had gone through: The subtext of death and regret was written clearly in the word itself. Clearly, but not cleanly. None of our hands were ever going to be clean again.

"There are almost no sleepwalkers left in Clayton," said Nathan, leading me across the bowling alley parking lot, toward the apartment buildings on the other side. It was dark, but it looked like pieces were missing from the fence between the two places, making it possible to walk straight through. "The ones that weren't killed have been contained in the old Kmart. We're keeping them fed and giving them plenty of sterilized water. Mom wants to see whether they'll eventually start recovering."

"I think it's possible." Juniper was getting heavier and heavier as I carried her. After I'd taken her back from Dr. Cale, she had locked her arms around my neck and refused to let me put her down again. It was almost comforting. No matter what terrible surprises were waiting up ahead, there was someone in this world who needed me more than anything else. She trusted me to take care of her. I was going to do exactly that.

"So does she. She says the neural connections between a sleepwalker's implant and host are damaged, but that they can be repaired or worked around in some cases. Maybe even reach the level of a chimera's connections." Nathan stole glances at me as we walked, like he was reassuring himself that I was actually there. I was doing the same thing in response. I loved Juniper with all my heart—it was almost frightening, how quickly and completely I had come to love that little girl—but part of me wished she had taken to Dr. Cale more, so that my arms would be free. So that I could put them around Nathan.

This is what every parent with a new baby feels like, I thought, and felt laughter bubble in my chest, even as wonder swelled in my heart. I was a parent now. I was a parent like every other parent, ever, regardless of species. Species didn't matter. Only love, and survival, had a place in the game.

"Carrie..."

"Your friend's been sedated, and Mom's got her under observation. When she wakes up, Fang will come and get us. I know you're going to want to be there."

Was I really? Carrie wasn't a "friend," not the way my coworkers at the shelter had been friends, before everything changed. Carrie was an acquaintance that I'd been able to use for a while but who didn't really know anything about me. She already thought I was insane for bringing her to Dr. Cale. How was she going to respond when she found out that I was a monster, like the one that had killed her husband?

But she was here because of me. She was trapped because of me. I owed it to her to be there when she woke up, even if all I could say was that I was sorry things hadn't been different: that I was sorry she had never really had a chance.

"Are you mad at me?"

Nathan's question was so abrupt that I actually stopped walking. He continued for a few feet more, his feet crunching on the gravel, before he realized I was no longer in motion. He stopped, turning back to face me, and what little of his expression I could read through the dark was bleak, all hard lines and self-recrimination.

"What?" I whispered.

"I should have found another way. I *could* have found another way, if I'd stopped and thought about what I was doing. I'm so sorry, Sal. I let them take you because I was scared, and because I thought we'd be able to turn right around and get you back. But they loaded you into that truck, and..." His voice trailed off hopelessly. "You were gone. Before we even had a chance to come up with a plan for breaking you out of there, you were gone."

"Nathan." I started walking again, closing the distance between us, and raised my free hand to touch his cheek. "I was never mad at you. I'm not mad at you now." I had said it before. I would say it again, and again, until he started to believe me. "You left because I *asked* you to. If you hadn't been willing to leave me when it was the only way to save yourself—when I'd traded myself for the chance that you'd get out—then I would have been mad. We're a team. That means we have to trust each other."

Nathan chuckled thickly, and I realized he was crying. "It'd be nice if trusting each other took you away from me less often. Can we try that, please?"

"I think we sort of have to." I nodded toward Juniper, content with her head on my shoulder and her arms around my neck. "Who's going to take care of her if I get captured again?"

"I like the kid already." He offered his hand. This time, I laced my fingers with his, letting him hold me. Let Juniper get heavy and dig into my hip. It was too important that I stay connected to Nathan for me to worry about something so inconsequential.

We walked the rest of the way to the fence hand in hand. Nathan ducked his head as he stepped through, and I did the same, letting him guide me.

The gap led to a dry, dead lawn. The apartments here were built on two levels, with open-air parking underneath. To my surprise, as we got closer, dim lights came on in the carports, concealed by the structures above them. Concrete stairs with rusty iron handrails led to the second-floor balcony. Nathan started for the nearest set.

"This whole block is on generator power, and we have motion sensors on the carports—*all* the carports, not just the inhabited buildings. That way if anyone comes here looking for signs that people are still around, they'll think they've found a wiring error. They exist in this area. Too many architects building too many towns too quickly during the big tech expansions of the naughties and the teens. There are all sorts of redundant systems and channels no one understands."

"Oh," I said.

"Mind the steps. A lot of people have skinned their knees on these things." Nathan shook his head. "I should probably have chosen something on the ground floor, all things considered, but the second-story apartments are more secure. I didn't want us to have to move again until this was over."

All things considered...I swallowed, took a deep breath, and asked the question that had been gnawing at me since we'd started walking across the parking lot. "Nathan, where are the dogs?"

I didn't need to see his face to hear the smile in his voice. "Waiting for you."

He stopped at the first apartment, producing a set of keys from his pocket and unlocking the deadbolt. Silence reigned. He knocked twice on the door, and then pushed it open.

Two things happened in quick succession: The lights came on inside the apartment, revealing a small living room with threadbare brown carpet and an old, stained, comfortable-looking white couch. And we were swarmed by dogs. Beverly and Minnie might not be a whole pack by themselves, but they were more than capable of swarming when excited. Their tails wagged wildly as they tried to shove themselves as close to me as possible. Minnie's stocky bulldog body kept her low to the ground. Beverly, a sleek black Lab, reared up onto her hind legs, planting her forepaws on my upper arms as she shoved her muzzle first at me and then at Juniper.

To her credit, Juniper—who had probably never seen a dog before—merely blinked at Beverly and made a small whimpering noise. It seemed more inquisitive than distressed.

"Hi, sweetie! Hi, my babies!" I said, and ducked my head to let Beverly wash my face with her tongue. Beverly made a whining noise that was not dissimilar to the one Juniper had made. She licked me one more time, and then Nathan was there, gripping her collar and pulling her back.

"Down," he said. "Both of you, down. Guard. Watch."

To my surprise, the dogs quieted immediately, sitting down and turning their eyes on the open door. There was a wary tension in their bodies that hadn't been there a moment before. I turned to stare at Nathan.

"I had to teach them some things while you were away," he said. "Fang has experience with dog training, and there's a Petco near here—we raided the place for all their books on obedience and quick behavioral adjustment. They'd attract too much attention if they barked all the time, and they were incredibly upset when you didn't come home. So was I."

He turned to close the door, locking the deadbolt. He gestured toward the curtains as he turned back to me. "Blackout curtains, triple-thick. We've scanned this whole neighborhood, and we're creating zero light pollution when the doors are closed. It can get stuffy sometimes, but we won't give ourselves away."

Juniper was still watching the dogs, her arms locked around my neck. If the dogs were a danger, she clearly believed I would prevent them from harming her. She was learning who her friends were. That made me feel better about the situation. Chimera were fast learners, all of us, and if Juniper was no different, she might stand a chance at survival.

"Let me show you the rest of the apartment," Nathan said, reaching for my free hand. I let him take it, and he led me onward, to the kitchen.

The apartment was small. Living room, kitchen, bathroom, and two bedrooms at the back, one larger than the other, dominated by a king-sized bed and dresser set. The other room must have belonged to the children of the people who bought that bed: The walls were covered in crayon marks and stickers, and the two beds, one against each wall, were sized for smaller people. The air was musty, but it was nothing compared to the air in the Old Navy, or the diner, or under the dock. In a world that was crumbling into dust and decay, this apartment might as well have been a showroom.

"I picked it because I thought you might want to set the plants up in here when you got home," said Nathan, almost babbling in his nervousness. "I guess it was lucky, since now we have someone who needs the space."

It was clear he didn't want Juniper sleeping with us. Part of me wanted to balk at that—she was my child, she belonged where I was—but the majority of me agreed with him. She wasn't a baby. She didn't need me beside her to get through the night, not here in our safe, well-locked apartment.

Most of all, I needed Nathan. I needed to sleep with his arms around me, knowing that he was never going to let me go again. I needed to know that I was *home*.

"All our clothes and things are in the SUV," I said, stepping into the children's room and flicking on the light. The ubiquitous blackout curtains covered the window, but whoever had hung them hadn't bothered to change anything else. Turning the light on activated a night-light shaped like a pink turtle, and cast a spray of bright stars across the ceiling. They were pink and blue and purple, and visible even with the overhead light turned on.

"That's a Terra Turtle," said Nathan, sounding impressed. "I had one of those when I was a kid. It'll keep making light for about an hour after bedtime, if you leave it connected to the main circuit long enough for it to charge all the way."

"Then that's what we'll do," I said. Juniper was staring in wonder at the lights dancing along the walls and ceiling. I took advantage of her amazement to walk across the room to the nearer bed and set her gently down.

"Sal?" She looked back to me, blinking quizzically, and reached her arms up to be held.

"You figured that one out fast, huh, kiddo?" I pushed her hand gently down. "This is going to be your room. We're going to live here."

"Sal." She pouted. It wasn't a very practiced expression—not yet—but I could tell from the easy way her face fell into it that I was going to be seeing it a lot. Probably more often than I wanted to.

"Yes, Sal. And this is Nathan." I pointed to Nathan. "*Nathan*. Can you say his name, too? You can't have a whole language that's just my name. It won't work."

Beverly and Minnie squeezed through the door and sat down at either side of my feet, leaning up against my legs like they were never going to move again. Nathan was still behind me. The tension in my back and shoulders was continuing to untangle, letting go one microscopic inch at a time. It might never fully release again—I might walk through the rest of my days waiting for the other shoe to fall—but for right now, it was safe for me to relax. Just a little.

"Sal," said Juniper dubiously, looking at the dogs.

"This is Beverly." I put my hand on the Lab's head. She shuddered ecstatically at my touch. Stooping down farther, I set my other hand on Minnie's shoulder. The bulldog was more restrained in her reaction, but looked adoringly up at me, her big pink tongue lolling. "This is Minnie. Beverly and Minnie. They live here with us. They're our friends. Can you say hello, Juniper? Can you say hello to our friends?"

Juniper looked at me, and didn't say anything. I sighed.

"I sure hope she likes your mom," I said, looking back to Nathan. "I don't think I can teach her to be a person all by myself."

"Luckily, you're not going to have to." He stepped forward to put his arms around my waist, pulling me back so that I was resting against him. "We're a family. We take care of our own."

I closed my eyes. Finally, *finally*, I was home.

*   *   *

Juniper seemed to like her new room well enough, but that didn't mean she was willing to stay there alone: as soon as I went to leave, she was reaching out her arms again, demanding to be taken with me. Nathan and I had exchanged a look, and then I'd picked her up and carried her back out to the living room, where we sat together on the couch while Nathan went out to get our things. Beverly and Minnie stayed with me, the bulldog settling at my feet while the Lab leapt up onto the couch and curled up against my hip. Juniper viewed this with wary acceptance, clearly still trying to make up her mind about the dogs.

"They're our friends," I told her. "They'll take care of us, and we'll take care of them. Just like Nathan and I are going to take care of you. That's what families do. We take care of each other."

"Sal," said Juniper, and I took it for acceptance, for understanding, even as I knew that it was probably nothing of the sort. I smiled at her.

"We're going to be happy here," I said, and closed my eyes.

Sleep had been gathering around me, waiting to pounce, and as soon as my guard was down, it took me. I slipped into unconsciousness with Juniper on my lap and the dogs surrounding me, and I didn't wake up even when Nathan came back with the clothes and bottled water from the car. I didn't wake up when he put the blanket over us, or when he sat down beside me, on the side Beverly had left open, and put his head on my shoulder. I was home. I was safe. I didn't need to be afraid anymore. Those things were each of them more precious than anything I could ever have dreamed, and so I let my dreams have me for a while. It was only fair.

I was home, and everything else could wait.

Miracles are apparently still possible, even in this new and alien world that we have made. Sal showed up at the bowling alley last night, following a hunch that told her we might have gone to ground somewhere familiar. She was accompanied by a human who hoped that returning Sal to me would give her the opportunity to avenge her dead. The human is currently in our custody. I am admittedly unsure of the correct course of action. She poses a threat: That much is clear. She has done nothing wrong. If we kill her, we will finally become the monsters Dr. Banks has made us out to be.

The human was not Sal's only companion. She also brought a young chimera, a little girl she's dubbed "Juniper." I have not yet had the opportunity to examine her, but Juniper appears to be fully integrated with her human host, a child of approximately four years of age. According to Sal, Juniper is a second-stage infectee, resulting from exposure to the tainted water.

This could change everything.

—FROM THE NOTES OF DR. SHANTI CALE, DECEMBER 2027

She made it back to me. Sal made it back.

She's asleep in the living room of the apartment I took because Mom said I couldn't live in the lab with the dogs, marking down the hours between losing the love of my life and finding a way to get her back again. She's asleep, holding the strange little girl she brought back with her. She says the girl's name is Juniper. She says the girl is a chimera. Mom nearly wouldn't give her back.

I don't know what they did to her while they had her. She's been saying things about the quarantine zone and how Sally's mother wouldn't let her stay in military housing now that she knows Sal isn't human. I almost hope she doesn't tell me. I'd rather stay here with her than go and kill them all for hurting her.

I think I'd do it, too. I think this war is making monsters out of us all.

—FROM THE NOTES OF DR. NATHAN KIM, DECEMBER 2027

Chapter 10

DECEMBER 2027

Someone was knocking on the door.

I sat bolt upright, instantly awake, every nerve I had screaming that this was it: The patrol had found us, they were going to take me back to the quarantine zone, and they were going to take everything else with us. Beverly, her head dislodged from my knee by my sudden motion, looked at me and whined.

Inch by inch, I became aware of my surroundings. I was in a shabby, clean little apartment, with Juniper in my arms, and my dogs snuggled up to me, and Nathan sleeping, still fully clothed, on the couch beside me. His head was lolling, mouth open as he snored gently. The knock came again.

Now Juniper began to stir, lifting her head with a small noise of protest. I shushed her. From the smell, she had wet herself again while she was sleeping. Dr. Cale had the power on;

I wondered whether she also had working washers and dryers, and whether it would be safe to wash clothes in potentially infected water.

"Shhh, honey, shhh, I just need to see who's at the door," I said. I set Juniper aside, bracing her against Beverly, who began sniffing her curiously. Either Juniper was too sleepy to cling, or she was distracted by the dog, because she let me get up without reaching for me.

I made my way to the door, grateful for having fallen asleep with my clothes on, and peered out the peephole. If it was a team from USAMRIID, I didn't know what I was going to do—although if it had been a team from USAMRIID, wouldn't they have knocked the door down already? They didn't have any reason to be polite. They weren't banging, either. Their knocking was insistent, but it wasn't so loud that it would have woken us if we'd been asleep in the back of the apartment.

The warped glass of the peephole distorted the scene enough that I had to blink several times before I could see who was outside. Then I gasped, and undid the locks so fast that I broke a nail on the deadbolt, leaving it hanging there like a scrap of paper as I wrenched the door open.

Adam didn't wait for me to say hello or invite him inside. As soon as the door was open wide enough for him to wedge his body through, it he was inside, flinging his arms around me and holding me so tight that it felt like he was bending my ribs. My injured rib throbbed with pain. I ignored it as I put my arms around him and held him just as tightly.

He bent to press his head against my chest like a much younger child. I felt the warm wetness of his tears beginning to spread through my grubby, travel-stained shirt. In so many ways, he was the youngest of us. Maybe he always would be.

"You came back," he whispered. "You came back to me, just like you said you would. I missed you. I missed you so much. Don't *do* that again, Sal. You can't do that. You went away."

"I won't," I said, and kissed the top of his head. His hair tasted like salt water and sandalwood. I realized I was crying too. That didn't seem to matter. "I'm here. I'm staying here. I don't ever, ever want to go away again. It's all right, Adam, I'm here."

"I thought you were gone forever." His voice was anguished, filled with the cruel truth of his words. He really had thought that they had lost me.

Nathan was my lover. Dr. Cale was my creator. But Adam was my *brother*, and somehow letting him down hurt me most of all. I held him tighter, and he did the same to me, the two of us crushing against each other until there might as well have been no oxygen between us. We had been two things that became single, hybrid creatures: Now we were trying the same trick again, but with two human bodies that wanted to fuse into one. Adam was the calm one, the sweet one, the rational one, who had never had to run or defend himself. I was...I was me. Together, we might make a whole person.

"Sal?"

There was a depth of confusion, curiosity, and wariness packed into the single syllable of my name that I would have thought impossible. Adam pulled away enough to let me turn around, and we both looked toward the couch. Juniper's head had appeared over the back of it, her hands clutching the cushion for balance, her eyes filled with questions.

"Who...?" Adam paused, and then let me go so that he could take a step toward Juniper without dragging me along. "Hello. Who are you?"

"Sal," said Juniper warily.

Adam looked at me, looking so confused that it was all I could do not to laugh. It wasn't really funny. It was deadly serious, like everything in our lives seemed to be most of the time. But I still wanted to laugh, and that was nice. It was nice to want to be happy.

"Adam, meet Juniper. I found her while I was on my way home. She's—"

"She's a chimera, like us," he said, sounding excited. "A *natural* chimera, like you. Hello, Juniper! I'm Adam. I'm your brother."

"Sal?" said Juniper, looking past him, focusing on me.

"She doesn't talk yet," I said. I stepped past Adam and picked her up, letting her get her arms locked around my shoulders. "She's still learning most things. Like how to use the bathroom. She doesn't get that yet." The smell of her was something else. "How do we manage bathing if the water isn't safe?"

"Chemical showers mostly, but we filter water for the hydroponics. I bet Mom can figure out a way to fill a bathtub." Adam held out his hand toward Juniper, not reaching for her, but putting himself in reach. It was similar to the way that I would approach a skittish or unfamiliar dog, and I realized that it had a similar intent: He was letting her get a feel for his pheromones, which would confirm him as a member of the family, and someone to be trusted.

"I don't want to put her in a chemical shower until I'm sure she'll be able to keep her eyes and mouth shut," I said. "She's still figuring out the things her body already knows. So she sits upright and doesn't fall off things, but it took her a while to start reaching for me. If it weren't for muscle memory, I think we'd be in trouble."

Adam nodded. "Can I hold her?" The question was small, almost meek, and reminded me—not for the first time—that he had gone in quick succession from having two sisters to having none. Not with Tansy on life support and me missing, maybe never to return. It hadn't been fair to him, any more than it had been fair to the rest of us.

"That's up to her, but let's see," I said. I tilted my body, trying to pass Juniper over to Adam. It was amazing how quickly that particular motion had become familiar, almost second nature. Soon, I wouldn't even have to think about it.

Juniper looked at him suspiciously, her arms still locked around my neck. Then, to my surprise and relief, she let me go, and allowed herself to be transferred into the slightly taller man's arms. She leaned back, her butt braced in his elbow, and looked at him gravely. Then, with no further fanfare, she slipped her arms around his neck, put her head against his collarbone, and closed her eyes.

"She's amazing," Adam whispered.

I smiled. "Yeah, she is. She's a lucky little girl, too. If we hadn't come along when we did…" The thought chilled me. How many children like Juniper were out there, chimera created when their second implant fought off the first, suddenly intelligent and aware, but unequipped to take care of themselves? Juniper had gotten lucky beyond belief when I had stumbled across her. A group of human survivors might have taken her confusion and apparent vacancy as a sign of trauma and taken her with them. Or they might have taken her for a sleepwalker, and killed her where she stood. It was impossible to say. Without me and Carrie escaping when we did, she would have starved to death.

The thought of food was a surprising one, and made my stomach, which had previously been silent, give an audible growl. I hadn't eaten in too long. Juniper, leaving her head cradled against Adam's collarbone, opened one eye and gave me a hopeful look.

"We need to eat," I said. "Can you hold her while I go and change into something cleaner?" Getting Juniper herself changed would need to wait until she'd had a bath, or she would just dirty another set of clothes. I was sweaty from the road, but it was nothing I couldn't remove with baby wipes and a dish towel.

Adam beamed like I had just asked him to be responsible for the most precious thing in the universe. "I can," he said. "I'll be right here."

"Thank you. You're the best brother." I paused to kiss the top of Nathan's head—he was still sleeping, the dogs now curled against him like none of them had been able to get any real rest while I'd been away—and then trotted down the short hallway to the bedrooms.

My clothing from the candy factory was in the larger of the master bedroom's two dressers, and the items I'd taken from the Old Navy were piled on top of it. I shimmied out of my dirty things and put on a clean bra and panties, luxuriating in the feeling of having my own clothes next to my body, instead of shabby, boil-washed pieces of cotton handed out by a USAMRIID patrol truck. A shower would have been even better, but that could wait until we were more settled. Smelling like a human being wasn't a problem for me, providing we could teach Juniper to wake people up when she needed to go to the bathroom.

I put on jeans and a clean tank top before returning to the living room, where Nathan was sitting up and rubbing his eyes with the back of his hand. He had placed his glasses on Beverly's head, and the big Lab was practically vibrating with joy at the thought that she was being somehow useful to one of her people. She offered me a doggy grin when I stepped back into the room, her tongue lolling and her ears perked in a "look at me" position.

Adam was still holding Juniper, who seemed content to cling to her newly discovered big brother for as long as he let her. I smiled at the scene. It was everything I had ever wanted. A home: a family. People who would accept me for what I was, and not what they thought they could turn me into.

Now all I had to do was make sure that we could stay

together and that things could be like this forever. "Good morning, Nathan," I said. "Did you sleep well?"

"My back hurts, my knees hurt, my butt hurts, and I haven't slept that well in weeks," he said, reclaiming his glasses and putting them on his face. The look he gave me then wasn't happy or sad or anything so simple: It was pure contentment, tempered with a layer of understanding that we weren't done fighting. This was an anomaly, a moment of happiness before everything inevitably fell apart again. "I always sleep better when you come back to me."

"I hope you never sleep that well again," I said, and he blinked at me and laughed, and everything was wonderful.

It couldn't last. Nathan looked to Adam, and asked, "Did you just come to see Sal?"

"Oh!" Adam's eyes widened, filling with sudden realization. It made my stomach twist. This was it: Our moment of peace was over, and it was time to get back to the business of surviving in a world that wanted nothing more than to destroy us all. "Mom sent me. She said to tell you all that we have a lot of work to do, and that she needs to give Juniper a full physical." His voice changed, becoming soft with wonder. "I thought Sal had brought home another dog or something. I didn't realize she'd managed to find us a *sister*."

"Well, I did," I said. I put a hand on my rumbling stomach, swallowing the urge to sigh. "Let's grab a granola bar or something. Then we can go find out what's going to go wrong next."

Walking back to the bowling alley in daylight gave me the opportunity to look at our new neighborhood. Cars and debris choked the sidewalks, and someone had managed to tip a pickup truck onto its side in the middle of the street, creating cover and the illusion of total abandonment at the same time. If you looked closely at the broken and soaped-over windows, you might notice that a surprising number of the apartments had blackout curtains hanging inside, but that would require getting closer than any casual inspection was going to be.

"We can't prevent heat-signature scans; if someone flies over looking for signs of life, we're screwed," said Nathan. He was walking alongside me, matching his strides to mine. "On the plus side, sleepwalkers show the same heat signatures as humans or chimera, so that isn't really a valid means of finding either survivors or fugitives."

"I don't think they have those kinds of resources left," I said, thinking of the teenagers in fatigues, their assault rifles and cattle prods shaking in their hands. "They're sort of scraping the bottom of the barrel where personnel are concerned."

"That's good to hear," said Nathan. "Fang will want to ask you about what you saw in the quarantine zone. USAMRIID has managed to pick up some of our people while they were out gathering supplies. We don't *think* they know who they have, but Fang's been planning a breakout for weeks. The only reason we hadn't moved is because we didn't have eyes on you, and I wasn't willing to agree to anything that might get you hurt."

A full assault on the quarantine zone would result in a *lot* of people getting hurt. Something stealthy might be able to get the folks they needed in and out without causing too much of a hue and cry, especially now that I was with them. I knew the lay of the land in both Pleasanton and Oakland.

"They don't know," I said. "If they did, they would have told me. Colonel Mitchell wanted me to help my—to help *Sally's* sister, Joyce."

"The one we treated with the antiparasitic drugs?" asked Nathan, sounding surprised. "Did they get the doses wrong? What did they think you could do for her?"

"Dr. Banks convinced them I was Sally. That my implant had somehow been able to keep me—to keep her—alive, just trapped, and that he'd been able to coax her to the surface." I stepped around a large hole in the pavement. Adam and Juniper were about ten feet ahead of us, Beverly sticking to their steps like a big black shadow. She knew that I needed them to be safe, and she was being a good dog. Such a good dog.

"Okay," said Nathan slowly. It was clear that he didn't quite understand, and I couldn't blame him for that, because I wasn't telling the story properly: I was laying it out in puzzle pieces, as if trying to explain the whole thing at once would hurt me somehow. Maybe because it would.

I took a gulping breath, and said, "She's brain-dead. They killed the implant, but not before it had compromised her system so badly that she didn't...they have her on life support. I don't know how long they can keep her that way." The image of my sister—because she *was* my sister; she was the only member of Sally's family who had accepted me without question, without using my differences from the original as a measuring stick that I would always fail to live up to—rose unbidden in my mind. Joyce, laughing. Joyce, insisting I let her take me to the mall, because she needed sister time and I needed to get out of my own head. All the good, glorious things that had made her *herself*, and not just a piece of meat being sustained by computers...all those things were gone.

They weren't coming back. Dr. Banks had peddled false hope to her father when he said that I had somehow been able to preserve Sally in her own mind with my intrusion. Sally was gone, and Joyce was gone, and Colonel Mitchell was a man who didn't have any daughters at all.

"So if he'd known that he had some of Dr. Cale's people, he would have been trying to get them to give her up, and he would have been using that to make me give him what he wanted," I said. "He lost track of her after Vallejo. He wanted to know where she was. I guess the whole 'she does better work when she's free-range' thing stopped looking so appealing when people started getting sick from drinking the water."

"We didn't do that," said Nathan. It was a needless interjection—I had always known that Dr. Cale wouldn't kill her own children that way—but I was still glad to hear it: The denial patched a little hole that had been opening in my heart. "It has to be Sherman's work. He's the only one with the reason *and* the resources."

"What reason could he possibly have for doing something like this?" I asked. "I know he wants to destroy the humans, but this is hurting the sleepwalkers just as badly."

Nathan hesitated. That brief silence was the most frightening thing he could have said. Finally, he spoke: "You need to talk to my mother. She's going to explain everything."

The drums were beating in my ears like warnings. Things weren't better just because I was home. Having people around me that I cared about gave me more to lose.

"Oh," I whispered.

Nathan squeezed my hand, clearly trying to be reassuring, and said, "He lost sight of us because we were smart in the evacuation. Lead-lined trucks to prevent radar penetration, movement underground when possible—the BART tunnels are pretty clear, and they haven't been unmaintained long enough to become safety hazards—and a lot of evasive maneuvers. Fang wanted us to keep going east and get out of California, but he was voted down by the rest of us. We needed to stay where we could get you back, for one. We needed to be where we knew all the players, for another."

"They probably have military of their own in Utah," I said.

Nathan nodded. "And we won't know who's in charge or how they're running their patrols. As long as we can stay out of USAMRIID's sight, we're safer here than we would be anywhere else."

The bowling alley was in front of us now, familiar and decrepit in that carefully maintained way that Dr. Cale had always been so rightly proud of. It was oddly reassuring to know that we were here again, in the place where I'd first learned that I wasn't human and that nothing was ever going to be the same.

The door was open: Adam, Beverly, and Juniper were already inside. Fishy was standing off to one side, an assault rifle in his hands, his eyes scanning the horizon. "I don't mean to disrupt this homey little cutscene and infodump for the players, but if you could pick it up, that would be swell. The longer you're out in the open, the higher your chances of a random encounter get. I, for one, don't feel like wasting ammo today."

"I missed you too, Fishy," I said, walking past him.

"Glad you're still in the game," he called after me. Then he laughed, the high, delighted sound of a man for whom nothing carried any real weight or stakes. All of this was a fiction to him, and he was enjoying it a hell of a lot more than the rest of us were.

"Sometimes I miss lying to myself about the things that make my life complicated," I said conversationally.

Nathan laughed, sounding surprised. "Really?"

"Yeah. But only sometimes." Life had been easier when I thought I was a human being. Not better, necessarily. I missed eating regularly and having access to a hot shower whenever I wanted one; I missed the routines of riding the bus and working at the shelter and generally living like a free person, not like a fugitive. But I didn't miss the uncertainty that had come with it, the nagging feeling that I was somehow failing myself and the people around me by not being better at... well, everything. I was never going to be good enough at being human, because I had never been human in the first place. Having that weight lifted off my shoulders was worth any number of missed showers.

"I'm glad it's only sometimes," said Nathan. "I'm a lot happier having you happy."

I blinked at him, and beamed.

Adam and Juniper were nowhere to be seen when we entered the lab portion of the bowling alley. I considered worrying about them, and decided that it wasn't necessary. I had seen them go inside. I trusted Adam with my life, and that meant that I could trust him with her life, too.

Dr. Cale's staff was everywhere. There seemed to be twice as many people here as there had been the night before, which made sense. Left to their own devices, some scientists will become nocturnal, but they're not the majority: Most of her people had always chosen to work days.

Because these were the technicians and doctors and interns who hadn't been in the bowling alley when I arrived, they all looked surprised to see me. Surprised and pleased, like they hadn't been sure they were ever going to see me again. That was actually reassuring. Everyone here was on my side, not just the people I thought of as my family. We could make it through this crisis, because we would be making it through together.

Dr. Cale was waiting in her office. She looked up when Nathan knocked on the doorframe, then followed his arm down to our joined hands. She smiled, looking obscurely pleased. "Nathan. Sal," she said. "Please, come on in."

"Hi, Dr. Cale." I stepped through the door, pulling Nathan along behind me. The office was small, converted from the old bowling alley manager's space, and barely had room for the three of us and the equipment that it already held. "How have you been?"

"Oh, you know. Same old, same old." She cracked a smile at her own joke, but it seemed to be more a matter of rote response than actual amusement. I have been funny; see, here is my smile; do you feel at ease with me now? Sometimes I felt like Dr. Cale was even worse at being a person than I was. "Did you and Adam have a chance to talk?"

Nothing I did could have suppressed the grin that spread

across my face, or the warm feeling that uncurled in my stomach. "It was really good to see him again. I missed him."

"You were probably experiencing mild withdrawal symptoms," said Dr. Cale.

I blinked. "What?"

"Adam experienced the same thing when we lost Tansy. You didn't, because you hadn't been around her for long enough."

I blinked at her again. "Uh, *what*?"

"I was able to monitor Adam after Tansy left—remember how depressed he got? Well, I monitored him again when we lost you, and watched the changes in his pheromone levels. I think that once chimera have bonded on a familial level, they become, for lack of a better word, addicted to the chemical signatures of their family group. You're so accustomed to Adam's pheromones that when they're taken away, your system overcompensates, which can cause feelings of depression, lethargy, and hopelessness." Dr. Cale shook her head. "It's a complicated chemical system. I'm still trying to fully decode it."

"You can compensate with over-the-counter antidepressants," said Nathan, picking up on my distress where Dr. Cale did not. He gave his mother a sharp look. "I thought we agreed that you'd explain this to Sal after she'd had time to adjust to being back with us."

"No, Nathan, *you* agreed. I said that she'd probably taken this long to escape because she was depressed from the withdrawal, and that on the off chance she was somehow blaming herself for being too slow, it would make her feel better if she knew this was natural for her." Dr. Cale shrugged. "You're the one who told me I couldn't go around withholding information because I thought people weren't ready for it. I'm just following instructions."

"Wow, you know, I've really missed hanging out with science people and listening to them talk about me like I didn't get a say in my own existence." I pulled my hand out of Nathan's and sat down in the chair across from Dr. Cale, doing my best to glare at both of them at the same time. "Is there anything else you thought I didn't need to know? I'm ready to listen."

Dr. Cale took a sharp breath, glancing toward Nathan. He nodded, closing his eyes for a bare moment, like he was trying to brace himself against whatever was going to happen next. That was unnerving.

It was nothing compared to what came next. Dr. Cale turned back to me, and asked, "Do you remember when Sherman took a sample of your primary body?"

Almost involuntarily, I reached up and touched the back of my head. There was a line of scar tissue there, left by Sherman's tools. I hadn't invited him to cut me open. He had done it all the same. "Yes," I said, and I wasn't ashamed when my voice cracked on the single syllable. He had violated me in a way more profound than I'd thought possible. Dr. Cale had also taken samples of my primary body—a violation I was still trying to forgive her for—but she had done it during a necessary and life-saving procedure. Without it, I would have been dead long ago. What Sherman had done…

I might be able to forgive Dr. Cale completely for what she'd done to me. I was never going to be able to forgive Sherman.

"I have analyzed the genetic material of a hundred and seventeen tapeworms cultured from the tap water," said Dr. Cale. She was speaking slowly and clearly, in the way she had when she felt that it was vitally important to be understood. Each word felt like another rock being placed atop my chest, rendering me unable to move away. They were heavy. I was trapped.

Dr. Cale was still speaking. "They are not identical to any existing implant. They have been cultured from a scrubbed source, a sample that was reengineered to be compatible with as wide a range of human subjects as possible. The epigenetic data has been removed. These worms, were they able to successfully bond with a human host, would grow up as individuals, not as reproductions of their parent and original. But they *were* all cultured from a single tapeworm."

"Me." The word sounded distorted. The drums were pounding so hard that they were making everything echo and twist.

Dr. Cale nodded. "You," she agreed. "When Sherman took that sample, he was looking for whatever it was that had made you able to bond with your host without medical intervention. He wanted to give the eggs he was introducing into the water supply the best possible chance."

"The best possible chance at what?" I already knew—she had already told me—but I needed to hear her say it in so many words. I needed to be *sure*.

"At claiming a human host. At maturing into a chimera. People trust the water. It's been filtered and purified for so long that no one questions what comes out of the tap, not even during a situation like this one—not that there's ever *been* a situation like this one." She laughed bitterly. "We are in a unique time. He wanted to infect the remainder of the human race. If he got one chimera out of every hundred warm bodies remaining, that would still be thousands. When he scrubbed the epigenetic data, he also removed the triggers that would prevent maturation in a body already containing a viable implant. He was hoping he might be able to infect a few sleepwalkers. Not many. He always had an overinflated opinion of how well the implants could defend themselves. I genuinely believe that he thought any worm strong enough to have taken over a human body would be able to fight off invaders."

"He thought chimera would be immune," I said.

"I can't be certain, but yes, I do believe he thought that," said Dr. Cale. "When Sherman was with me, he believed chimera were the pinnacle of evolution, that nothing would ever be able to match them for purity and power. I can't imagine his time with Dr. Banks, seeing the worst of what the human race has to offer, would have done much to change his mind."

"So...*I'm* doing this?" The drums had stopped. Everything was silence. "This is me, somehow?"

"No." Dr. Cale's answer was immediate, and left no room for argument. She shook her head, as if in punctuation. "He scrubbed the epigenetic data. Even if he hadn't, he clipped a single segment of your core body. He didn't dig out your core, the piece of you that actually interfaces with the human brain. If he had, you would be dead, and we wouldn't be having this conversation."

"Transplanting a chimera from one human host to another requires the head of the original implant," said Nathan. He seemed to be acting under the impression that his words would help. All they did was turn my stomach. "Mom calls it the 'core segment' most of the time, to differentiate it from the other parts of the implant's body. There's no way Sherman could have accessed your core without killing you."

"Oh," I said faintly.

"He wanted the antiseizure medications coded into your DNA," said Dr. Cale. "Some people will react to them badly— I'd estimate that as much as point five percent of the population will have an allergic response to those medications, leading to convulsions and death. But the rest will have a higher chance of successful sleepwalker integration, and a greatly improved chance of successful chimera integration. It's just that he didn't consider the biggest problem with his little plan."

"You mean apart from all the other problems you're talking about?" I stared at her. This was like something out of a horror movie. It wasn't—it couldn't be—real. At least before, we'd just been dealing with a single, world-destroying issue.

"Yes," said Dr. Cale. She didn't seem to recognize the irony in my question. Then again, when had she ever? "He didn't consider reinfection. Everyone is vulnerable to this. Humans, sleepwalkers, chimera, *everyone*. And it doesn't matter if someone has already been infected by the water. They can be infected again, and again. We've removed up to thirty cysts from a single body after exposure to the water. I don't know if it's going to be possible to fully sterilize the reservoirs in my lifetime—and I intend to live for a very long time. I still have a great deal of work to do."

"Because of me." My lips felt numb.

"It's not your fault." Dr. Cale frowned. "Haven't you been listening? You aren't the one who reengineered the DNA that had been built into you. You're certainly not the one who introduced eggs into the water supply. We're still not sure how Sherman accomplished that so quickly, or on such a wide scale. We've taken samples from three reservoirs, and found them all to have been contaminated."

"I went with him willingly," I said. "When he came to USAMRIID to break me out, I could have screamed. I could have refused to go. I could have *done* something, but I was mad at the humans for treating me the way they had, and I thought I would be able to escape from him more easily than I could escape from them. So I went with him willingly, and now he's using…he's using something that he got from *me*, something that he stole from *my* body, to kill people. This is my fault. If I hadn't gone with Sherman, none of this would be happening."

"And if I had refused Steven when he came to me and asked if I wanted to change the world, there would never have been implants in the first place. You wouldn't exist. Neither would Sherman, or Adam, or Juniper. I might still be a married woman, and the world certainly wouldn't be in the state it's in right now." Dr. Cale sounded calm, but there was a thin vein of agony in her eyes. She had thought about this a lot: She knew what she was taking responsibility for. "Steven is a brilliant man, but he isn't as creative as he thinks he is. He would never have unlocked the genetic code of the worms without me.

So should I take full responsibility for what he did with my work? Should I say, 'Yes, someone else took good science and perverted it in the name of quick profits, but I still did it, so blame me'?"

"No, but—" I began.

She cut me off. "Sherman exists because I was trying to learn how the chimera were able to occupy their hosts. Adam may be the single most ethically questionable thing I've ever done, but I was trying to figure out how bad things could get, and I acted without regrets. Sherman...by the time I introduced him into his human host, I *knew* the process worked. I *knew* what chimera were, and that they could be healthy, stable people. So why did I have to do it again? He was hubris, pure and simple. I wanted another son. I was lonely. Does that mean that I am responsible for everything he's ever done? Are the sins of the son vested on the mother, rather than the sins of the father being vested on the son?"

"No," I said, and shook my head. "You're getting me all confused. I don't understand what you're trying to say."

"If you own a knife, and someone else steals it and uses it to kill a person, you are not at fault. Yes, it was your knife, but you didn't buy it because you wanted to commit a murder. You bought it because sometimes you need a knife. I didn't create the implants because I wanted to destroy the world. My science was sound—my knife was clean. Steven took my work and perverted it in the name of profit. He knew this could happen, and he did it anyway. He doesn't care that the survivors will mistrust science and its gifts for generations. He cared about profits now and stock options later and coming out on top at every possible turn. Sherman did to you what Steven did to me. He stole something precious and turned it into a weapon. That doesn't make you the bad one. It doesn't transform your precious thing into something that is innately evil. Do you understand?" Dr. Cale looked at me, and this time, she was pleading. "You are not at fault here. All of the fault is on him."

Nathan put a hand on my shoulder. "You've never done anything you need to be ashamed of, and that includes going with someone you thought offered you a better shot at survival. You need to take care of yourself. How else are you going to take care of the people you care about?"

I looked at him. I looked at her. And then, very slowly, I nodded.

"All right," I said. "This isn't my fault, but it's still everybody's problem. What are we going to do?"

"That's the real problem," said Dr. Cale. "I have no idea."

Batya has continued to experiment with new water-purification systems. So far, she's had the best luck with gravity filters, and with rainwater reclamation. Even the rainwater isn't safe without processing: We have found eggs there, tiny and captured by the natural interplay of wind and water. They are uncommon. They are common enough that by now, we must assume that all open and standing water sources have become contaminated.

The eggs do not fare well in salt water. Increasing the salinity of freshwater is effective, but not absolutely so. Desalinization may be our next best hope. It will require us to gain access to the coastline. USAMRIID is still functional, and mobs of both sleepwalkers and human survivors remain an issue. We're going to have to figure out a way to deal with them soon. If we don't, we're going to reach a point where water rationing becomes necessary. I can't afford the hit that would represent to our morale.

USAMRIID has to go.

—FROM THE NOTES OF SHERMAN LEWIS
(SUBJECT VIII, ITERATION III), JANUARY 2028

I don't know how I can make this any clearer than I already have: We need help. We are no longer able to afford the luxury of pretending that the situation here on the West Coast is under control. I've heard nothing from Los Angeles for the last ten days. Our team in Salt Lake transmitted a report of contamination in the water supply before they ceased communication.

Attached, please find analysis of the local reservoirs, showing the contamination levels. While the SymboGen implants are unable to mature in other mammals, they are capable of using those other mammals as intermediate hosts, spreading from waterway to waterway in the bellies of deer, raccoons, and feral cats. They will continue to spread until they have contaminated all water sources in North America.

We need to stop this, and we need to stop it now, before it gets too far out of hand.

—MESSAGE FROM COLONEL ALFRED MITCHELL, USAMRIID,
TRANSMITTED TO THE WHITE HOUSE ON JANUARY 6, 2028

Chapter 11

JANUARY 2028

"Adam!" Juniper's gleeful squeal was accompanied by pulling her hand out of mine and taking off at a run for her beloved brother, who stooped to intercept her. She laughed wildly as he slung her over his shoulder, keeping an arm around her waist to brace her. She was a squirmy thing, and getting squirmier by the day, as she figured out the uses and limitations of her body—and as far as Juniper was concerned, there were very few limitations. Whatever she wanted to do, she was going to attempt, and what she didn't accomplish on her first try, she was going to do again, and again, until she got it right.

I followed more sedately, trying to brush the dog hair off my blouse. Getting out of the apartment without a dog in tow had required a thirty-minute brushing session, and a lot of reassurances to both dogs that they were good—excellent, in fact—and that I would be right back. Beverly was generally willing to believe me when I told her things like that. Minnie was less sure, and needed more reassurances before she'd let me walk out the door without at least one canine in tow. Oddly, she was perfectly happy to have Beverly accompany me while she stayed behind. As long as there was a dog with me, she believed I would come back.

"Hi, Sal," said Adam, waving around his armload of frantically giggling Juniper. "I was just coming to get you."

"I know. I tried to hurry." I had been at the bowling alley for almost two weeks, and was still getting used to the idea that sometimes I needed to be places at specific times. I couldn't just dawdle the way I had when I was in the quarantine zone, where nothing but supply runs happened at a specific time, and even those were undependable.

There, I had been a spare part that nobody needed but nobody was willing to throw away, either. As long as Colonel Mitchell hadn't needed me, I'd been left mostly to my own devices. Here, everyone worked. Even Adam, who tended the hydroponics and had taken much of Juniper's education upon himself. After two weeks, she had a vocabulary of more than fifty words, and was adding more every day—people and places and things. Every time she opened her mouth, she astounded me all over again. And she adored him.

I was jealous, but I was grateful, too. Juniper came home with me every night. She slept in her room, and she cried my name when she woke up scared or confused or needing a glass of water. I could share her days with Adam, especially since it freed me to do whatever was needed. Mostly that meant grunt work, unskilled tasks that didn't require me to be able to read or to understand the scientific method. But there were also days like this one, where I had something more important to do.

I was going to talk to Carrie.

Adam walked away with Juniper, heading for the retrofitted supermarket that served as our primary social gathering spot and food preparation space. I kept walking, heading for the bowling alley. The path had become familiar so quickly that I actually didn't trust it to stay the same from day to day: Stability was an alien idea, and much as I wanted to accept it back into my life, I couldn't.

The door opened when I was almost there. Nathan smiled out at me, alerted to my approach by the security cameras. "Hey," he said. "You look nice."

"Thanks." I'd made an effort, putting on black slacks and a nice white blouse, brushing my hair, even putting on a simple necklace and some pearl earrings from the thrift store down the street—all little signs that yes, I was a person, yes, I could be trusted, no, there was no need to react to me as if I was the enemy. Carrie still didn't know that I wasn't human. She thought I was a collaborator, someone who'd thrown her lot in with a monster because it would get me nice things, like a comfortable apartment that I didn't have to share with a bunch of strangers, and dog kibble from the supply room, and the freedom to walk around.

In a way, she was right. I *was* collaborating with Dr. Cale and her team, and I *did* have all those things, from the apartment, where I slept in my own bed with my own boyfriend next to me, all the way down to the privilege of going wherever I wanted within the limited area that Dr. Cale's people had deemed "safe." We might only control a few blocks, but those blocks were free of hostile sleepwalkers, and they offered us a cornucopia of opportunities to improve our little community. Fishy had gotten looting down to a science even before I arrived with stories of scarcity within the quarantine zone. Now that he knew what the bad side of things looked like, he had redoubled his efforts, and he took me with him as often as not. I had a good eye for places where people might have squirreled away their bottled water or their prescription medications. More importantly, I had a good nose for the presence of sleepwalkers, either alive or recently dead. Since I had joined the resource-acquisition crews, we hadn't lost a single person. I was proud of that.

I needed to be proud of something.

Nathan and I walked through the bowling alley, past the scientists working at their stations—which were never turned off or powered down, just switched to their next set of tasks—and the pharmacists compounding at what used to be the snack bar. A few people smiled or waved in our direction, but most kept their heads down and kept working. We could afford to run more power through the bowling alley during the day, when the draw would be largely off the solar arrays in the nearby neighborhoods, and would hence make less of an impression on the local grids. That meant all the really *big* tasks had to happen before the sun went down, and it kept the scientists in a constant state of motion between dawn and dusk.

Beyond the main room was the manager's office, and beyond that was the old storage room, which had been converted into a makeshift jail of sorts. Solar-fed lights covered the ceiling, bathing everything in a soft white glow that was somehow antiseptic, like it was cleansing the room even as it lit it up. There were three cells along the wall, each about ten feet by ten feet. Each contained a small cot that had been bolted to the floor, a chemical toilet, a curtain that could be drawn for privacy, and a particleboard end table stacked with books.

It always made me sad and a little sick to my stomach to look at them, like their existence proved that we had already essentially lost the moral high ground. There was a time when we would never have needed to take prisoners. Now we were prepared to hold them long enough that we had to be concerned about their mental well-being.

Fang was standing near the wall, his rifle slung over his shoulder, working a wooden puzzle in his hands. He looked up at the sound of our footsteps, offering a polite nod when he saw that it was us. "She's awake," he said. "Hasn't opened her curtain, but that doesn't mean much. She doesn't feel social most days."

"Are you sure she's...up?" I asked, giving the closed curtain an uneasy look. There were a lot of ways for the prisoners to hurt themselves. When I'd asked Dr. Cale why she didn't take more steps to keep them safe, she had snorted and replied that if she took someone captive or put them on a medical hold, she wanted them to understand that they had two ways out: her way, or the painful way. If they wanted to commit suicide, that was on them.

It was something I actively worried about with Carrie. She had suffered a lot of losses in a short time, she had just escaped from USAMRIID, and now she was being held, again, against her will. That sort of thing couldn't be good for her psyche.

"She was moving around earlier, and when I asked her if she wanted to trade an open curtain for a nice breakfast, she told me I could go fuck myself," said Fang. "Then she called me a fascist pig, and made a few anatomically unlikely suggestions. So I'm pretty sure she's awake and alive. And awful. Have I told you recently that your friend is awful?"

"Every time we talk about her." There were folding chairs against the opposite wall. I picked one up and carried it in front of Carrie's cell, where I unfolded it and sat down. The drums were hammering ceaselessly in my ears. "You guys can go. I've got it from here."

"She can't break through that Plexiglas without a weapon, which she doesn't have," said Fang, straightening. "You should be totally safe, but just in case, if you need us, yell."

"Like a fire alarm," I promised. Nathan paused long enough to press a kiss against my forehead, and then they were gone, both of them, leaving me alone with the woman who had enabled me to come home, and whose fate was now in my hands.

She had to know I was there. We hadn't been quiet or subtle

when we were talking about her. But the seconds stretched into minutes, and the curtain didn't move, and Carrie didn't speak to me.

I cleared my throat. "Carrie? It's Sal. Could you open the curtain, please? I really need to talk to you."

There was no response.

"Come on, Carrie, please? I know you're upset. I'd be upset too if I'd gone from one prison to another, and I'm really sorry about all this. I tried talking to Dr. Cale, and she said I needed to talk to you before I talked to her." What I didn't say was that Dr. Cale hadn't even been willing to go that far for the first three days, while Carrie was raging and throwing things against the walls of her cell. Or that the first four times I'd tried to get permission to come and talk to her, she had still been considered potentially dangerous, thanks to her ongoing violent outbursts.

Still there was no response. I sighed.

"Do you want me to leave you in here to rot? Because that's what's going to happen to you, you know. Dr. Cale doesn't care how long you sit in that cell, but she's not going to remember you forever. That isn't how she works. And after she forgets about you, somebody's going to realize that you're drinking water and eating food that we could be using for other things. You're not going to like it if that happens. So you should talk to me now, while that's still the future, and not the present."

The curtain finally twitched, and Carrie's voice said sullenly, "If you're trying to convince me that you're on my side, you're doing a seriously shitty job. Most of the time people don't go 'Oh by the way, might have to kill you because you eat too much,' when they're trying to make friends."

"I never said we'd have to kill you." I'd just implied it loudly, and intentionally. It was something she needed to consider. "And I don't expect that we're going to be friends, either. Friends trust each other, and I don't think you're ever going to trust me again. That doesn't mean I need to start lying to you and saying that everything's going to be all hinky-dory."

"Hunky-dory. The phrase is 'hunky-dory.'" The curtain was finally pulled aside, revealing Carrie. She was wearing black yoga pants and a green tank top, both from the supplies that had been removed from the Kmart before it was filled with sleepwalkers. I wondered how they had convinced her to change her clothes, and then realized that was a silly question. Carrie was a survivor. She wasn't going to sit in her own filth just to make a point about being held captive.

"Sorry," I said. "I had to relearn English after my accident." There was still some argument about whether I'd been learning it for the first time or reawakening neural pathways that Sally had used when she was learning the language. Juniper was picking up words faster than any human infant, but was she picking them up faster than a human child with a body as old as hers? Even Dr. Cale didn't know. Some things about the brain were simply determined to be mysteries.

"Your grasp of idiom sucks," said Carrie. She sat down on the edge of her bed, glaring. At least she hadn't closed the curtain again. She was willing to hear me out, however resistant she might be to listening to my actual words. "What do you mean, 'start lying'? You've been lying since we met."

Only about my species, and to be fair, she'd never come out and asked me whether I was human. "No, I haven't. I never lied to you. I asked you to help me get back to my family. This is my family."

"That woman is not your family," snapped Carrie. She pointed to the closed door on the other side of the room. "She's a monster. She's the one who started this whole mess. How can you call her *family*?"

"I'm marrying her son, and that means she's going to be my mother-in-law," I said. "Besides, this isn't her fault. She did the initial design work on the SymboGen implants, but she's not the one who strong-armed them through FDA review or said that they were safe for human use. She had to disappear because she was saying the opposite, and Dr. Banks was the one with all the money, so everybody was listening to him instead of listening to her."

"She's still the one who created them," Carrie spat.

"I don't think we can blame science for the way it gets used," I said. "She did science. She did good science even, not evil science. Understanding genetics better never hurt anybody. It was Dr. Banks who said her science wasn't as important as his profits. And he's the one who said this is all her fault, too. Why do people believe him? Is it just because he has nice hair and white teeth? I don't think teeth tell you anything about whether or not a person is good. They just tell you that the person could afford a really awesome dentist."

Carrie blinked, looking briefly nonplussed. Then she demanded, "If she didn't have anything to hide, why did she disappear?"

"Because Dr. Banks had a *lot* of money, and people listened to him when he talked, at least before all this changed," I said. "And because he was a man. Haven't you ever noticed how when a man says one thing, and the woman says another thing, people will almost always believe the man is the one who's telling the truth? Even if she has more proof than he does. So she ran, because she knew nobody would believe her. You don't believe her. Even after USAMRIID, you don't believe her."

"Colonel Mitchell is your father."

"He didn't act like it." I folded my hands in my lap to keep myself from fiddling, and looked at her gravely. "You know Dr. Cale can't let you leave. I'm sorry I brought you here. I should have asked you to drop me off somewhere on the road, and let you go. That was my fault. I was focused on the idea of surviving—getting home to my people. So I apologize."

Carrie's bark of laughter was almost startled. "You *apolo-*

gize? Like that makes everything better? 'We're going to keep you in a cage until we get tired of feeding you, but hey, I'm really sorry about putting you in this position, let's be friends'? God, Sally, do you know *anything* about friendship?"

"I'm not the one who pulled a gun on my traveling companion," I said. "I'm not the one who brought friendship into this, either. You did both those things. You started shooting at my family. You tried to hit me with your car."

Carrie sat in stony silence, not saying anything.

I sighed. "Look, I never said I wanted to be your friend. I just feel bad for putting you in this position."

Carrie blinked at me.

I continued, "It would probably be easier if we were friends, because it's almost always easier when you're friends with the people you're trying to work with, but I don't care that much. I have plenty of friends. I just don't want you to be miserable for the rest of your life because you helped me. That's why I want to help you."

"Help me how?" asked Carrie warily.

"Dr. Cale needs people, always. If you're willing to talk to her, see what you can do around the lab, she's willing to let you out of your cell." I looked at her as levelly as I could. "She's not going to leave you unmonitored, but it would be better than sitting in that little box, waiting for the world to fall on your head."

"Why would I want to talk to *her*?" demanded Carrie. "She's a monster."

"I feel like we're stuck in a loop here," I said. "What makes her a monster?"

"She created those things. Whether she's the one who let them out or not, they're killing people."

I was starting to get angry. That probably wasn't a good thing. "They're killing people because they weren't tested properly, which wasn't her responsibility. And why should they have less of a right to live than the humans who swallowed them? Nobody forced people to be so lazy that they would rather have a tapeworm living inside them than worry about taking their medication every day."

"Paul didn't have an implant, and look what happened to him!" she shot back. "They're infecting people who never voluntarily consumed them."

"Dr. Cale didn't put the worms in the water, and as for why someone else did, it was because they're scared, too!"

Carrie blinked. "What?"

"The implants didn't ask to be made poorly, but they were, so they started taking people over. And then people got scared, and started killing the implants. So the people who depend on their implants got scared, and now the implants are finding new ways to infect, because it's a race. *Humans* turned it into a race. Who can kill who the faster, and the better, and the cleaner? This is stupid. It never had to be this way."

Carrie's eyes were wide and round in her suddenly pale face. "She's managed to twist you so far around that you've started sympathizing with the worms. Don't you see how sick that is?"

"I *am* one of the worms, Carrie," I said.

She froze.

"The sleepwalkers are what happens when we don't mesh with the human brain right. We're like USB cables. We have to be positioned just right, or we don't make full contact," I continued. "When we do, we have access to all that processing power, and we become people. I'm a *person*, I'm just not a *human* person. I'm one of the worms."

"You're sick," she whispered. "That is a sick, gross lie, and I won't believe it."

I hadn't been intending to tell her about it, either: it had just come out when my frustration with her mulishness became too much to tolerate. I remained seated, looking at her gravely, and said, "Am I sick? Colonel Mitchell said I was his daughter, but his wife wouldn't let me stay in the family housing with the rest of the family. It's not because we fought a lot. It's because she knew I wasn't her child. I'm the invader who took her child's body as my own after Sally had her accident and wasn't there anymore. Fathers may be willing to lie to themselves, but mothers never forgive."

"I don't believe you."

"I guess you don't have to while you're sitting in that cell," I said. "As long as you're in there, you'll be fed and watered and given new things to read, and you won't have to believe anything. But eventually, you're going to want a way out, and then you're going to have two choices. Either you can believe me when I say that Dr. Cale isn't a monster and that not every implant is out to hurt you, or you can try to escape. I don't think you're going to. But I guess it's an option."

I stood, brushing the creases out of my trousers with nervous fingers. I'd tried so hard to look like a human being for her, and she had never even noticed. "I'm really sorry you're stuck here because of me, Carrie. I really, really am."

"Saying 'really' three times doesn't make me believe you," she said. "If you want to show me how sorry you are, you'll open up this door and give me back my gun. You owe me."

"I guess I do, but I don't owe you my life or anybody else's," I said. "It's about survival. It always has been. And if I have to pick a side, I pick the side I'm actually on. Not yours. Sorry, Carrie." I turned and walked back to the door. She didn't call after me. I guess when it came right down to it, she knew as well as I did that we were done.

Fang was waiting outside. He looked at my expression and frowned. "It didn't go well?"

"You still have a prisoner," I replied, and kept walking.

Having Juniper—who was still nailing down the finer points of toilet training—and the dogs meant that I had fallen into the

habit of keeping clean clothes in Dr. Cale's office, since there
was no guarantee I'd be able to make it through the day without getting something spilled on me. I went straight there. Dr.
Cale was out, overseeing some essential piece of science, so I
was alone as I stripped off my human disguise and traded it for
more workaday clothes.

My eyes burned, and when I touched them, my fingers came
away damp with frustrated tears. Carrie wasn't my *friend*. She
had never been my friend. But she was the closest thing I had to
a surrogate for all the humans I'd known in my old life, the life
I had before I chose to seek the broken doors. She was Joyce,
and Colonel Mitchell, and my coworkers from the shelter.
None of them had ever known me for what I really was. I had
lied to them all, whether I intended to or not, and I was sorry.
Carrie was the only one left for me to apologize to. She just
wouldn't accept.

Maybe she never would.

I left my nice clothes in the office, shutting the door behind
me like it could somehow shut away the complicated emotions
of the morning. The bowling alley was still buzzing along,
everyone wrapped up in their own scientific pursuits and
unaware of my inner turmoil. That was…sort of nice, actually. I was one piece in a large and complicated machine, and if I
broke down for a while, it would all keep working without me.

I was halfway to the exit when a tall, well-built woman with
her graying hair cut close to her scalp raised her hand and
waved me over. "Sal! You busy?"

"Not right now," I said, walking to her station. "Adam's
teaching Juniper her ABCs, and he doesn't expect me to come
take over until lunchtime. What's up, Daisy?"

"Can you help me hold this down?" She indicated her work-
space, where a large, dead raccoon had been placed in a metal
tray. She was wearing latex gloves, and a face mask dangled
around her neck. "I know this is a shitty place for a necropsy,

but we need to check this big boy's stomach and make sure he died of natural causes."

I blanched. "You don't think the cousins killed him, do you?"

"It's possible. He's been drinking the water, and that's where they are." She offered me a box of gloves. "Help me out?"

"Okay," I said, and plucked out a pair.

Daisy was one of Dr. Cale's surgical assistants. She had been a parasitologist at SymboGen when the company was still in its infancy, and had left with Dr. Cale when things started going south. She wasn't the most comfortable with chimera—Nathan sometimes called her a "human supremacist," and while he wasn't serious, he wasn't entirely joking—but she was good at her job, and she recognized the skills we brought to the table. Like my ability to stick my hands into a dead raccoon without tossing my cookies, which was surprisingly rare among the geneticists and engineers who flocked around the lab.

I got my gloves on and plucked a face mask from the rack, pulling it over my nose and mouth. Aspirating raccoon was never a good idea. "Where do you want me?" I asked.

Daisy picked up a scalpel. "He's too big to secure to the board with pins. If you hold down his shoulders, I'll be able to open the stomach cavity with minimal trouble."

"Got it," I said, and moved into the spot she'd indicated.

The raccoon hadn't been dead for long, and felt almost like a living thing under my hands. It showed no signs of wasting or decay; if it had taken a breath and opened its eyes, I wouldn't have been entirely surprised. But there was no rush of blood as Daisy opened the abdominal cavity, and the raccoon did not respond when she pinned the flaps to the sides of the board. I remained as a steadying presence, looking with interest at the jumbled puzzle of the raccoon's internal organs. It was always a little surprising, how many colors there were inside a previously living thing. It wasn't just red. It was purple, and green, and yellow, and black. A rainbow written in flesh.

Daisy nimbly moved the raccoon's organs aside as she dug for the intestine, which came into view like a long ribbon of pinkish gray. She sliced into the surface, freeing a thin wash of yellow fluid. Then she set the scalpel aside.

"Adult male raccoon, no signs of internal bleeding or lesions, cause of death unknown," she said. There was no recorder running. I blinked, but didn't say anything. If she needed to talk her way through this, then that was up to her.

Or maybe she was trying to teach me something. This could be Daisy's way of reaching out the hand of friendship, in the form of a lecture about a dead raccoon.

She plunged her hand into the open intestine, feeling around for a moment before she pulled it out into the light. Small white shapes squirmed and twisted in the gunk that covered her palm. She squinted at them for a moment, moving them around with her thumb. Then she scraped the contents of her hand—gunk, worms, and all—into a waiting specimen dish.

"Roundworms," she said. "Endemic in the local raccoon population. They're thriving, too; this bad boy was probably carrying thousands of them with him while he went about his business. That wouldn't be the case if he'd been carrying one of your cousins."

"Because we don't play well with others," I ventured.

Daisy nodded. "That's right. They don't play well with others. One implant and bam, the whole local parasite ecology is thrown off." She plunged her hand back into the raccoon's intestine, pulling out another handful of slime studded with small, squirming things. "I'm going to say this fellow probably died of distemper, or rabies, or something else nasty but not man-made. You can let go now. I'm done with the manual slicing. Thanks."

I pulled my gloved hands away from the raccoon, stepping back and watching Daisy for a moment as she continued to scoop out the contents of the raccoon's digestive system. She was so focused on her work that she didn't even seem to realize I was still there. Maybe that was for the best.

When a minute had passed without her acknowledging me, I peeled off my gloves and mask, dropped them into the trash can, and walked away.

I found Adam and Juniper in the Kmart garden center, which was still filled with green and growing things, despite the time of year. They were safe from the sleepwalkers contained inside the main building: The doors connecting the garden center to the Kmart proper had been sealed off, leaving the plants and potting soil outside in their theft-proof cage. Juniper was sitting on her butt in the middle of a groundcover display, watching avidly as Adam read to her from *Don't Go Out Alone.* I was starting to feel like that was the only book left in the world.

None of this was surprising. Adam was devoted to Juniper, and had been from the moment they met. As for Juniper, she was happy with either one of us. I couldn't tell from a sample size of two whether she liked us in specific, or whether she was attracted to her fellow chimera. Hopefully, when we found out, it wouldn't be because of Sherman.

No, the surprise was sitting a few feet away, next to a display of carefully trimmed and packaged rosebushes. Dr. Cale's wheelchair was sturdy enough to be rolled basically anywhere in the shopping center that didn't involve going up stairs; it probably shouldn't have been so odd to find her sitting there, a small smile on her face, watching as her son read to her first "grandchild." But it was. I stopped, blinking, and just looked at the three of them, trying to make some sense of the scene.

Juniper noticed me first. She raised her head, and smiled her tight-lipped little smile before saying, "Sal. Sal!" Adam also offered me a smile, but didn't say anything. He looked perfectly content, sitting there in his slowly overgrowing artificial Eden, his baby sister nearby and his mother watching on.

My name still seemed to make up half of Juniper's vocabulary. It only meant me about a third of the time, and was slowly being phased out as she learned the words for other things. "Hi, Juniper," I said. I looked to Dr. Cale. "Hi, Dr. Cale."

"Hello, Sal," she said. "How did your little meeting go?"

That seemed enough like an invitation for me. I walked over to her and leaned against a planter as I replied, "Not so well. She still doesn't want to work for you. She thinks you're a monster, and that all of this was your fault."

"Monster," said Juniper contentedly, and turned her attention back to her book.

I stifled a smile. The whole plot of *Don't Go Out Alone* centered on a pair of children trying to find their monster and make their home with it, wherever it was. Given how many times she'd heard that book already—and how many times she would read it once she was reading on her own, if Adam and Nathan were anything to go by—she probably had a very different definition of "monster" than Carrie did. That was a good thing. This wasn't a world that was going to support the old definition for much longer.

"It's interesting, isn't it, how facts fall down in the face of appearances? I've always been fascinated by the way people get their ideas." Dr. Cale didn't sound fascinated. She sounded tired.

The reason was revealed a moment later, when she looked back to Adam and Juniper and said, quietly, "We lost two sleep-walkers yesterday. Convulsions, spasms, and finally death. If it hadn't happened during feeding time, we might have missed it."

"What happened?" I asked, wide-eyed. "Did someone give them contaminated water?"

"Unfortunately, that would be too simple," she said. "We think there was an infected sleepwalker in the group we initially rounded up. The implants are...tricky, for lack of a better word. If conditions aren't ideal, they can form cysts rather than maturing immediately into adult worms. We think the sleep-walker was underfed, and so the intruding eggs didn't mature. Then we fed them up to a point where the cysts felt safe to hatch. If the sleepwalker died when no one was watching..."

"Then the others would have eaten the body," I said slowly. "And they'd have eaten any eggs or remaining cysts at the same time."

"We can't test them all. They'd have to be sedated and removed from the enclosure one at a time. That would frighten and upset them, and it could lead to a stampede. They're mostly calm right now. They eat, they sleep, they copulate." She paused and laughed, seeing my expression. "They still have the instincts of their human hosts, Sal. You didn't know what sex was when you were just a tapeworm. It was your host body that taught you about sexual response and hormonal need. Once a sleepwalker is well fed and no longer needs to search for sustenance, it can move on to other needs. Of course, sometimes they get hungry in the middle of the act and begin attacking one another, but they manage to get by. They've been observed masturbating and engaging in group sex, as well. It's fascinating, from a purely biological standpoint."

"I never thought about that," I said honestly. Adam continued to read to Juniper, ignoring us and our topic of conversation completely. It didn't matter to him if we wanted to talk about sex. It wouldn't matter to her either, once she was old enough to understand it. Of all the chimera, I was the one with the most human-esque ideas about things like sex and nudity and bodily functions. One more side effect of having been raised as a member of a species that wasn't my own.

Dr. Cale wasn't finished. "A few of the women are pregnant. They're early along yet, but we're working on separating them from the rest of the mob. We want to start adding prenatal vitamins to their food, and monitor their health in general until the babies are born."

Now I stared. "*Pregnant*?"

"Yes." Dr. Cale looked at me levelly. "Do I need to explain how that works before you and Nathan decide to declare yourselves married? I'm happy to become a biological grandmother, but not for a while. I have things to do, and a world to save. All that gets complicated when I'm being tapped for babysitting."

"I'd be happy to babysit," said Adam, looking up from his book. Juniper was patting the pages, and seemed content to keep doing that for a while. "I like kids."

"Kids and babies aren't the same, sweetie, and besides, we'll have plenty of babies around here when the sleepwalker women begin delivering," said Dr. Cale. "Don't make promises you'll be unhappy about keeping."

"I like kids," said Adam again, and turned back to his book.

I worried my lip between my teeth for a moment, listening to the drums beating in the distance, before I asked the most important question of all: "Dr. Cale, will the babies be…you know, will the babies be *human*?"

"I don't know," she said. "It depends on whether the original implant lays eggs, and how those eggs react to the fetus. They may be sleepwalkers. They may be chimera. The implants weren't supposed to cross the placental barrier, but as the three of you will attest, the implants have learned to do a great many things that they weren't supposed to do. If the children are human, we'll take care of them, and find a way to deliver them to the quarantine zone for care. If the children are chimera, or God forbid, sleepwalkers, then we'll care for them here. It's the least we can do, considering that their parents will never be able to raise them."

I shook my head. "It seems like we spend a lot of time looking for people to take care of kids whose parents couldn't do it."

"That's not a part of the current crisis, I'm afraid," said Dr. Cale. "It's always been that way. All we can do is struggle to build structures around the chaos, and hope that they will hold."

"Yeah," I said. There was a momentary silence, both of us looking toward Adam and Juniper, before I asked, "How's Tansy?"

"Holding in there. Her primary segment is still intact, and it isn't losing viability. I'd always assumed that an implant could live indefinitely in a healthy growth medium, and she's got that." Upon seeing my bewildered look, Dr. Cale sighed and said, "When you lived in Sally Mitchell's digestive system, you fed on whatever she ate. Since most people got more cavalier about their diets after their implants were in place, you probably had a high-fat, high-protein diet. Once you migrated to her brain, you switched over to a blood-based meal plan."

"Blood's not that nutritious," I said.

"No, but it's nutritious enough to keep you healthy, happy, and physically connected to your host's brain, without ever letting you get so hungry that you start eating the tissue around you—not that there's ever been a case of a chimera doing that," Dr. Cale hastened to add. "You would have to be starving, and the blood supply to the brain would have to be interrupted for long enough to cause a second brain death. Right now, Tansy still has access to the veins that provide the bulk of her nutrition. When she starts looking distressed, we've been adding fluids via IV to the brain itself. That isn't normally a good idea—tissue damage and the like—but that butcher did so much damage to the host when he cracked its skull open that it isn't going to make any difference. Not to Tansy. Not now."

It was interesting the way she insisted on gendering Tansy—who was technically genderless in her original form, as were all tapeworms—while reducing the host to something neutral and undefined. It was a way of distancing herself from the non-person in this equation...and I didn't have to be a genius to know that the non-person was the human being. Tansy was all that mattered to her. Tansy was all that ever *would* matter, at least where those two lives were concerned.

The host body had been broken by Dr. Banks. There was still a chance that Tansy could be saved.

"How hard is it going to be to find another host for Tansy? How long can the current one hold out on life support?"

Dr. Cale looked at me wearily. "It took me years, with access to the entire hospital system and a working Internet, to find the subjects I used for my work. Only three of them were able to successfully integrate with their implants and become chimera: Adam, Tansy, and Sherman. Tissue type matters, as do a whole host of other factors. Given the dysphoria you described in your friend Ronnie, we need to hold out until we can find a female host, which is just going to take longer."

I worried my lip between my teeth again before asking, "What about the sleepwalkers?" It felt like a betrayal. I was suggesting taking perfectly good bodies away from the cousins who had them and giving them to Tansy, all because she was my sister. Why did she deserve a body any more than they did? She wasn't even a natural chimera like Juniper or me: She had acquired her first body through surgical means, when Dr. Cale had implanted her directly into an unoccupied brain.

I didn't want to feel like I was somehow "better" than Adam or Tansy just because I'd managed to accomplish what they'd never had the chance to do. At the same time, it was hard to reconcile the desire to take care of the cousins with the suggestion that we crack out of them open and scrape it out of its original host so that Tansy could come back to us.

It was all about survival. Sometimes, when I thought about the survival of the people I cared about versus the survival of the rest of the world, it was hard not to wonder just how different we really were from the humans.

To my relief and shame, Dr. Cale shook her head. "It would

take more effort than it's worth to round up all the possible candidates, do tissue typing, and then attempt to flush their systems of any protein fragments, eggs, or other traces of infection. Even then, there'd be no guarantee. We need a clean host body if we're going to transplant her safely."

I paused again. The answer was obvious. Terrible, but obvious. "Have you ever done tissue typing on me?"

"Of course I have. I had your full workup before we ever met, thanks to Chave."

Chave had been one of my handlers at SymboGen, an icy, professional woman who just happened to have been a double agent the whole time I'd known her. She had been reporting back to Dr. Cale about the things Dr. Banks was doing, and that had included full details on my care.

Too bad she hadn't realized how much human DNA he was putting into his newest generation of implants. Too bad she hadn't known that Sherman was a tapeworm.

Too bad she had died.

"Am I compatible with Tansy?"

Dr. Cale went very still. Then, in a tight voice, she said, "I don't think Nathan would be very happy if I extracted you from your host so I could try to bring Tansy back, Sal, and you know as well as I do that the two of you can't coexist."

"That's not what I meant," I said. "If Tansy is compatible with my tissue type, then isn't there a good chance she'd also be compatible with my *sister's* tissue type? Joyce's body is on life support back at USAMRIID, but Joyce is gone. She's never coming back." Just like Sally was never coming back. The Mitchells had sacrificed both their daughters on the altar of this war, and they had never even known that they were signing up to fight.

Dr. Cale blinked slowly. Then she gripped the wheels of her chair and started rolling toward the door. "I'll get back to you," she said.

Adam looked up as she rolled past him. "Bye, Mom."

"Bye," said Juniper.

"I'll see you soon," said Dr. Cale, and then she was gone, rolling away across the parking lot with the sort of speed that came from long familiarity with the places where the pavement dipped, the spots she could use to her advantage. She rarely needed anyone to help her get around when she was on familiar ground, and the bicycle gloves she wore to keep her palms from getting shredded were so familiar that I barely even registered them anymore. They were just a part of her hands, as ineluctable as her fingernails, which were always cropped short and buffed clean, like part of her remembered that manicures were essential, to be taken seriously in a male-dominated workplace.

I'd never had a manicure in my life. The thought of sitting still for an hour while a stranger played with my hands was disturbing, and I had no interest in finding out whether the reality would be any different.

Sally had probably gone for a lot of manicures. We were never going to be the same person.

A hand tugged on my shirt. I looked down, and there was Juniper, eyes bright, mouth curved downward in the dour semi-scowl that was her neutral expression. She only smiled in response to other people, or when she was too excited to fight the muscle memory of her inherited face. Smiling was a human trait, and while it was one that we were able to learn, it was never going to be one that came completely naturally.

"Up," she said.

"Up what?" I asked.

"Up now," she said. Then she paused, clearly reviewing her sentence for missing pieces, and amended, "Up now, *Sal.*"

"She's managing to remember that she needs to specify parts of her request," said Adam, walking over as I boosted Juniper into my arms. "She hasn't quite grasped the purpose of 'please' and 'thank you' yet, but Mom says those took me a while, too."

"Why should she?" I asked. "She knows we'll do anything she asks." I looked over my shoulder toward the Kmart. It seemed like a fortress, impermeable and safe. The Oakland Coliseum had seemed like a fortress too, but I'd been able to escape from it twice, and only once had I had outside help.

Things were delicately balanced, but they were good. They were...they were *functional*. Even with the sick sleepwalkers and Carrie in her cell, they were *working*. I stood there, Juniper on my hip and Adam by my side, and wished that there were any way in hell I could believe that this was going to last. It felt like the calm before the storm, and we were not prepared.

INTERLUDE II: CO-OPTION

I don't think anybody asks to be born.
I don't see why that should be a factor.

—ADAM CALE (SUBJECT I, ITERATION I)

You are all monsters. I don't care what you do to
each other, but keep your hands off of me.

—CARRIE BLACK

January 2028: Sherman

The assault on the Costco had gone better than expected: We'd come away with no losses, but had gained a decent stock of bottled water and nonperishable foodstuffs. Between the supplies from the Costco stockrooms and the food we'd been growing ourselves, we were well positioned to move into the coming year. As long as our chickens continued to lay and our hydroponics continued to yield good fruit, we'd have no issues with our nutritional needs, and would even be able to continue feeding our stock.

That was the greatest victory of our raid on the Costco: the *humans*. We had captured twenty-nine of them, all implant-free and defiantly alive, filled with the burning anger of an apex species that could see its hold on the world eroding from beneath its feet. They were healthy, alert, and presented an excellent cross-section of races, genders, and ages, making them perfect for our purposes.

One of them—a Latina woman in her early twenties, who had fought and screamed like a banshee when we came for her—was stretched out on my operating table, tubes running from her arms to the IVs that kept her sedated. This worked better if the subject wasn't awake and fighting the whole time.

My mother—what a loaded word that was, even if it was accurate in all the ways that mattered—used to insist on using subjects who had experienced clinical brain death, "vacating the premises" as it were. I understood the reasons for her squeamishness. She was human, after all, and could be forgiven for not wanting to evict her own kind from their bodies. But Maria needed this body more than the woman on my table ever would…and I needed Maria.

With Ronnie sacrificed to bring about our glorious future, and Kristoph killed by the unexpected side effects of the same act, I needed Maria. My people respected her as one of their leaders. They would listen when she spoke. True, she wouldn't be saying much for a while—even epigenetic data couldn't save her the long, slow process of learning how to be a person again, after she had been so abruptly reduced back to her original state—but having her by my side would change things. It would make my people more willing to listen to me, and more willing to believe me when I said that I was working for the good of all.

Batya moved around the body, a shallow dish in her hands. She was looking at it with something like reverence, her eyes shining so brightly with unshed tears that I could see the gleam even through the goggles she wore. The dish was filled with jellied growth medium, engineered from human brain tissue, and in its center writhed an off-white worm, segmented and capped with a mouth like a beautiful flower.

There are those who would call us "ugly" outside the human shells we wear. I think it's only when the lumps and imperfections of the human body are stripped away that our true beauty is revealed. Symmetrical; simple. A perfect form, unchanged by centuries upon this Earth. Even when my mother and her research team split us open and reworked our DNA in a thousand new directions, our form remained essentially the same, because it was already, unquestionably, perfect.

"Bone saw," I said, and one of the assistants handed it to me, pressing it carefully into my hands. I started the machine, listening to the reassuring whir for a moment before lowering it to the sleeping woman's scalp.

She probably had a name once, I thought, apropos of nothing, as I began to cut. I batted the thought away like the meaningless noise it was. Her name didn't matter: Whatever it had been, that was done. She was Maria now, and would be Maria forevermore.

I was just glad we'd been able to find a Latina woman in such excellent condition. As Ronnie had demonstrated, putting one of my people into a body that was too radically different from their epigenetic self-image could have negative repercussions, and I didn't feel like dealing with that again. It might make for an interesting study somewhere along the line, and it would definitely be a topic to keep in mind as we began setting up the breeding camps for the surviving humans, but for now, it was best that each transplant involve a new host as similar to the old host as possible.

The woman's scalp peeled away under the clever fingers of my assistants, and I finished removing the piece of bone that we would be replacing in a few minutes, after Maria had been properly introduced to her new home.

It took my first forays into neurosurgery to really understand what a feat of scientific engineering my mother had accomplished when she made me. The brain was well supplied by veins and concealed arteries, and was contained by the rigid dome of the skull. Even opening a panel large enough to grant access ran the risk of compromising the entire delicate structure.

Cut in the wrong place and the whole thing would become useless, compromised, and unable to support the developing tapeworm's needs. Place Maria against the wrong vein and she would be unable to connect herself to her host, leaving her trapped in a living corpse until we reopened the skull and pulled her back out into the unforgiving light. Truly, whatever hand engineered the human mind was more interested in laying traps for whoever might come along than they were in making the system efficient and safe to use.

It was no surprise that most of the sleepwalkers were profoundly damaged. The worms, driven by instinct to seek control, had chewed their way through the brains of their hosts without concern for the system as a whole. If anything, it was a surprise that so many of the sleepwalkers lived.

Bit by bit, I worked my way through the tissue, peeling back layers and clamping off veins when necessary, until I reached the spot we had identified as optimal for the integration process. "Batya, the dish," I said.

Solemnly, my last remaining lieutenant handed me the dish containing her sister. I removed Maria with a pair of sterile tongs, lifting her as gently as I could. She writhed and squirmed against the metal, twisting fiercely. She was still a fighter. Even here, stripped of her body and her agency, she was a fighter.

The assistants held the tissue aside as I introduced Maria to her new host, tucking her between the folds of the brain. She continued to writhe as I withdrew the tongs, beating her soft, fragile body against the soft, fragile tissue that surrounded her. She wasn't chewing; she couldn't hurt anything as she was. We all held our breaths, waiting to see what she was going to do. Would she settle? Or would she begin to chew at her surroundings, tearing through the brain and ruining it for all future purposes?

The writhing slowed; stopped. Maria pressed her head against the vein, which pulsed, blue and tender, in the tissue. Then, with a small wiggle, she latched on and began to feed. She was integrating.

"Close her up," I said, amazed by the strength of the relief that washed over me. We had navigated this small thing safely.

We had so much ahead of us.

STAGE II: MACROEVOLUTION

Where a person comes from doesn't matter as much as what they do once they're here.

—DR. NATHAN KIM

Having a home means having somewhere to go back to. Having a family means having something to defend. Having a life means knowing you'll do anything to keep it.

—SAL MITCHELL

The girl Sal found in Oakland is a revelation. Sal named her "Juniper," after the character from Don't Go Out Alone. *I couldn't think of a more fitting name for a child who found her own way to the broken doors, and more, found her own way through them.*

I have done multiple MRIs. It appears that her original implant did minimal damage to the brain when it attempted to integrate, and that it was integrated long enough for her tissue to have begun repairing itself, unmaking the damage. Once that was done, it was an easy thing for a second worm to slide along the path of scar tissue and claim the mind as its own.

Surgery may be necessary at a later date, to remove any traces of the original implant. There do not appear to be any. The new implant—the one we now call "Juniper"—consumed its rival before moving on to the brain. It's a miracle of science. It's a triumph of genetic engineering. It's the end of mankind.

—FROM THE NOTES OF DR. SHANTI CALE, JANUARY 2028

Colonel Mitchell—
Please understand that the President sees and respects the difficulties you have faced in attempting to secure the West Coast. The contamination in the waterways has spread as far

inland as Iowa, and does not show any signs of stopping. At this time, we cannot provide you with any support beyond what you already have.

I'll be frank, Alfred: if there were any way for us to pull some of those men out of your command and bring them closer to D.C., we'd do it. We may have delayed the impact of the SymboGen problem here on the East Coast, but we didn't stop it. A large number of civilians did not come forward when asked to report for extraction of their Symbo-Gen implants, and we're facing mobs as big or bigger than the ones you described. We can't afford to help you. We can barely afford to help ourselves.

The end of days is upon us. Make your peace with God.

Sorry about your little girls.

—MESSAGE FROM MICHAEL PETERMAN, UNITED STATES
SECRETARY OF DEFENSE, TRANSMITTED TO
USAMRIID ON JANUARY 6, 2028

Chapter 12

JANUARY 2028

Our lack of preparation came to a head three days later, in the middle of the afternoon.

Adam and Juniper were in the garden supply center, where they spent most of their days—if it wasn't raining, they were happy to sit in the rich, mulch-based mud with their books and their flash cards, Adam coaxing his youngest sister out of her initial isolation and into the world of human understanding. Math and language were things we had stolen from our hosts, and now that we had them, we weren't giving them up.

Fishy and Fang were outside the lab, going through the motions of their daily patrol. They spent a lot of time checking the edges of our small settlement, which became larger every day as everyone relaxed into what felt increasingly like a permanent home. The sleepwalkers in the area were either dead of the secondary contamination or safely locked in the Kmart, where they couldn't hurt us. The suburbs had been under-inhabited and largely ignored for years; none of the remaining uninfected humans were going to come running to us for shelter. USAMRIID was far away, and had problems of their own. Sherman's people hadn't been seen since the water contamination began. We might not have been safe, but we had the illusion of safety, and under the circumstances, that felt as if it might be just as good.

I was helping Daisy with another necropsy—a goat this time—when everything started. She still didn't like me much, compared to some of the other residents of the lab, but she said I had steady hands, and she appreciated the way I never threw up on her specimens, no matter how decayed they were when she found them. She had sliced up just about every species of mammal and bird that the area had to offer. Most mammals were infected. Of the birds, the only ones that had been carrying viable tapeworm eggs were the big predatory ones, the hawks and falcons. They couldn't be infected, but they appeared to make a viable secondary host, which meant the eggs would continue to spread through the local waterways, until all the groundwater was contaminated, forever.

The alarm above the necropsy station began ringing. Daisy glanced up, unconcerned, before she went back to her cutting. "Ignore it," she said. "There's a short in that thing, it goes off for no good reason all the damn time."

I was opening my mouth to answer when another alarm rang, and another, until the entire lab was filled with strident bells and flashing lights. Daisy looked up again, this time meeting my eyes with evident dismay.

"Is this a short?" I asked.

She shook her head. "No. This is all-hands." Then she dropped her scalpel, right into the dead goat's abdomen, and ran for the front of the bowling alley.

I stayed frozen where I was for a count of five before my

eyes widened and the drums began pounding in my ears, so loud that they almost drowned out the sound of sirens. If Dr. Cale hadn't already repaired the veins in the back of my skull, I would probably have lost consciousness as the blood drained toward my feet.

Adam and Juniper were outside. They wouldn't hear the alarm. I ran.

Most of the security personnel ran with me, or more accurately, ran *past* me, heading for the door. The rest of the workers were running deeper into the bowling alley, toward places of known safety. Part of me wanted to follow them—the part of me that prioritized my own survival above everything else, the part of me that had decided to move through my host's body and take it as my own. Another part wanted to find Nathan, to let him protect me from whatever was about to happen. That was the point of having someone who wanted to protect you, wasn't it? Let them go first. Let them keep you safe, for as long as they could.

But the rest of me—the greater part of me—knew that what I needed to do was get to Adam and Juniper. Adam was older than I was, in chimera terms, but he was also more sheltered, and wouldn't know what to do if USAMRIID or Sherman took him. He wouldn't be able to lie and convince Colonel Mitchell that he was human; he wouldn't know where to begin. As for Sherman, he'd been willing to cut me open, all while professing to care for me. What would he do to Adam? What would he do to *Juniper*?

I ran. The guards had propped the door open to keep it from hampering them, and so I was able to charge straight through to the outside, where I stopped and stared in horror at the parking lot.

The Kmart doors were open. The sleepwalkers, well fed and healthy as they were, were shambling out into the parking lot. They weren't running or rushing anywhere; they seemed almost curious about their surroundings, and hadn't started attacking anyone. Yet. As soon as the sleepwalkers were startled, or alarmed, or just hungry, everything was going to change.

I was too far from the storefront to see into the garden center, but I could see that the little metal gate that was usually kept open to allow for access had been closed. Adam and Juniper were almost certainly still there.

"Sal, get back inside." The command came from Fang. He was holding his rifle braced against his shoulder, his eyes flicking back and forth as he marked the paths taken by the sleepwalkers. They were still pouring out of the store, and showed no signs of stopping any time soon. How many had Dr. Cale been able to capture? How could she say it was humane to keep that *many* of them in there? They must have been living virtually on top of one another.

No wonder they all came out as soon as they had the opportunity. They'd been confined for a long time, and like all living things, they wanted a better situation. I could sympathize with that, even as my heart hammered wildly against my ribs and the drums pounded in my ears.

"I can't," I said. "Adam and Juniper are out there."

Fang shot me a quick glance before he shook his head. "It doesn't matter," he said. "Get back inside. We'll take care of everything."

The sleepwalkers had been rounded up one and two at a time. There must have been nearly two hundred of them in the parking lot, with more emerging from the store. They weren't moaning or grabbing at each other. They were just *walking*, as calm and unhurried as anyone who was heading out for a stroll.

That gave me an idea. It might have been a terrible idea, but it was mine, and it was the only one I had. "No," I said, and took a deep breath, trying to still the frantic beating of my heart. I didn't have conscious control over my pheromones, but I'd been able to summon them a few times before, or at least it had felt that way. So I reached as deep as I could, trying to command the body I had stolen for my own to obey me.

Tell them I'm a friend, I thought, and started walking.

Behind me, Fang swore, but he didn't run after me or start shooting into the crowd. I kept on going, pressing forward until I reached the leading edge of the sleepwalkers. They turned their blank, dirty faces in my direction, eyes tracking my movement. Some of them looked almost curious. I couldn't know how much of that was muscle memory and how much of it was actual emotion, but none of them grabbed me, and none of them bit me, and I kept walking.

The sleepwalkers parted just enough to let me through. Then they closed around me, and I was surrounded.

They smelled of human waste and sweat, of long-dried blood and occasional whiffs of infection. I wondered whether their implants were still delivering their medications, pumping them straight into the bloodstream despite their new locations in the body. I realized distantly that I'd never asked about that. Was I still producing medication for my host? Sally Mitchell was an epileptic. I had never experienced a seizure—the last one she'd had was the one that had led, indirectly, to her death. So I must have been putting medication into her bloodstream. Any diabetics among the crowd would still be cared for.

A sleepwalker caught my arm. I stopped walking. She leaned close, sniffing at my face, the smell of her breath rolling over me like a rancid wave. She had been pretty, once, with dark-brown skin and curly black hair. Now she was a walking shell, like the rest of them, a home for the parasitic hermit crab that had needed a place to call its own. There was no comprehension in her eyes. Just a bottomless emptiness, brightened by the faintest flickers of curiosity.

Moving slowly and carefully, I removed her hand from my arm. "No," I said, hoping my voice would carry my pheromones closer to her, bathing her in them. "No, I'm not food.

But I'll take you back where the food is." Still holding her hand, I resumed walking, tugging her along with me as I moved toward the Kmart.

The sleepwalkers parted to let us through. Some turned to walk with us, their mobbing instincts motivating them to keep pace. The urge to drop her hand and run like hell was unspeakably strong. All I was going to do was get myself killed, at least according to the small, screaming voice at the back of my head. It was my survivor-voice, my pre-primate-voice, the voice of self-interest above all else. But while I was willing to live my life by the principles of survival, I wasn't willing to let that turn me into someone I couldn't face in the mirror. I kept walking.

We were almost to the Kmart now. I glanced toward the closed garden-center fence, and there was Adam, holding Juniper in his arms with her face buried against his chest, watching me with wide and terrified eyes. He understood what I was doing better than anyone; maybe even better than I did. He just couldn't help me.

Dr. Cale's people had to be securing the lab by now, moving into place and waiting for the sleepwalkers to turn aggressive. I didn't know how many of the cousins were following my pheromone trail, but I hoped it was lots of them; I hoped I was showing them the way home.

The woman whose hand I held made a querulous sound as we approached the Kmart doors. I didn't let her go. "I'll talk to Dr. Cale about improving your living conditions," I said, keeping my tone as light and pleasant as possible. "Maybe we can open up the garden center for you, so you can go outside." Adam would have to find a new place to hold Juniper's lessons. I didn't feel too bad about that. He had the whole world open to him, and it was just going to get wider when this war was over. Giving up one little spot for the sake of those who had essentially nothing was no big deal.

The smell inside the Kmart was terrible, a roiling mix of human waste, spoiled food, and other, less pleasant things that I couldn't identify and didn't want to. The stench was practically visible. The sleepwalkers who entered with me didn't seem to notice it. They just kept shuffling along, sometimes making small noises, but otherwise keeping whatever thoughts they were capable of having to themselves.

There were more sleepwalkers in here, lying on display beds or in nests of clothing yanked down from hangers in the clearance section. They watched with dead, disinterested eyes as we walked past.

The store was bigger than it had looked from the outside, and it had looked plenty big. I kept walking, not sure how to stop. If I let go of my unwitting companion, was she just going to wander back toward the open doors? More sleepwalkers were following me, and the exodus seemed to have stopped, but how could I keep them from bolting in the other direction?

Gunfire in the distance. Dr. Cale's people were winning. That was the only explanation. If it had been USAMRIID, if they had seen this many sleepwalkers, they would have just set the whole damn place on fire.

The sleepwalkers around me started to stir, waking from their walking stupor. Their faces sharpened, eyes darkening from simple blankness into a state of wary apprehension. A few turned, walking back toward the exit—toward the sound of gunfire. Their shoulders were suddenly tight and their motions were precise, indicating that they somehow understood the sound as representative of a threat. I couldn't understand why that would draw them *toward* it.

I kept my grasp on my first companion and breathed out as long as I could, filling the air with the smell of my pheromones. The sleepwalkers that had turned away turned back, suddenly more interested in me than they were in the gunfire. It couldn't last. They were more restless now than they'd been before, and some of them were starting to moan, the thin, half-strangled sound that they usually made before they attacked.

I was surrounded, and I was so deep inside the Kmart that there was no way I could get away if they decided to attack. They'd tear me to pieces in seconds. I suppose that was better than a slow, lingering death would have been, but I would have preferred not dying at all. I had become very fond of staying alive since I had first opened my eyes in the hospital. Dying like this…

Dying like this would be worth it if it meant that Adam and Juniper got away. That realization seemed to tint everything in a rosy glow, like the redness of the hot warm dark had come flowing up my body to make whatever happened next easier to bear. My survival was important. The survival of the people I loved and had promised to protect would always matter just as much. It always had. As long as I kept hold of that, I could endure anything. Whether or not I survived. No matter how much it hurt me.

The sleepwalkers around me were becoming a more tight-pressed mass, making movement hard. The drums in my ears had virtually stopped, and I realized my heart was no longer pounding like it was going to break out of my chest. I was calm. It seemed silly, like calm should have been impossible in this place, but it was true. Whatever happened next wasn't entirely out of my control, but I'd accomplished what I had set out to do. I'd drawn the sleepwalkers away. It was all on Dr. Cale and her people now.

There was more gunfire outside. The sleepwalkers around me mumbled and shifted again, becoming restless. I breathed out, trying to keep them under my control. I was blindingly thankful to Dr. Cale for keeping the sleepwalkers so well fed that they hadn't thought of eating me yet. That would come with time, I was sure.

A woman shambled into the crowd next to me, nearly bumping into my first companion, who hissed and clicked her teeth in warning. The newcomer looked down at the floor, her view blocked by the swell of her belly. She was at least six months along, and the skin of her stomach was stretched tight as a drum where it was visible through the tears in her clothing. She wasn't cradling or protecting it the way I'd seen pregnant humans do; she bullied her way through the crowd with her belly as just one more weapon to be swung. It didn't seem to have troubled the developing fetus any; she looked like any pregnant host woman, save for the filth on her face and the rags on her body.

I watched her move past, wanting to grab her wrist as well, to keep her safe from the scene around her. Dr. Cale needed to examine her. She needed to know what was going on with that baby—the baby the woman would probably eat as soon as it was outside of her body, because what else was she supposed to do with a tiny, helpless thing? Even if it was a sleepwalker, it would smell more like food than family. Babies arrived covered in blood, didn't they? Maybe dropping something tiny and helpless into the world with its own gravy was a terrible decision on the part of evolution.

We had almost reached the back of the store. Moans rose from the darkness, wavering at the end before they broke. These were the most damaged, least functional of the sleepwalkers, I realized, the ones that would have been devoured by their fellows if they'd been in a less curated environment. They seemed to understand that, in their way, because when the doors had been opened, they hadn't tried for their freedom. Where else were they supposed to go? Here they had food, they had comfort, such as it was, they had the safety to eat and sleep without fearing attack. Outside, there would be only pain.

Sleepwalkers might not be intelligent compared to humans or chimera, but they had their own type of brilliance. They were all about survival, unmitigated by emotion or intellect. No sleepwalker would walk into danger to save someone else. It would be alien to them. ·

For the first time, it occurred to me that maybe in the end, neither humans nor chimera would inherit the Earth. We were focused on survival, but we weren't *good* at it. Not the way the sleepwalkers were. They could sleepwalk their way to the top of the food pyramid, and all they had to do was wait for us to betray ourselves.

"Sal!" The shout came from the front of the store. I looked over my shoulder, but I couldn't see anything. There was a dim light in the distance, sliced by shelves and diluted by the bodies of the sleepwalkers between me and its source. It might as well have been on the moon, for all the good it was going to do me. I didn't even know who was yelling. The shape of the store—cluttered and cavernous at the same time—distorted the voice, twisting it and bouncing it off the walls until all I could know for sure was that it belonged to a man.

There was no more gunfire. Either Dr. Cale's people had stopped the sleepwalkers from escaping, or they'd been over-run. I looked at the crowd around me, standing agitated but docile, and hoped it was the first. I hoped they'd fired their guns into the air and driven the sleepwalkers back, rather than killing creatures that intended them no harm, because they weren't capable of "intending" anything. They just existed. They just survived. That was all they wanted to do. I would still fight if they tried to eat me, because my survival mattered too, but if they weren't hurting anything, they deserved the chance to live.

There was a clang. The light from the front of the store suddenly dimmed, and I knew the doors had been closed. The windows were still allowing a certain amount of illumination into the store, and I wondered briefly whether that might not explain the slow shamble of the sleepwalkers across the parking lot. If their eyes weren't accustomed to bright lights anymore, they would have been blinded by the sun. Of course they would have moved slowly. They wouldn't have known what else to do.

"Sal!" This time, the voice was closer. The sleepwalkers around me moaned and grumbled, making little wordless noises of discontent. They looked around themselves, their eyes more adjusted to the gloom than mine were. When they didn't find the source of the voice, they stilled.

I breathed out again, trying to put as many reassuring pheromones into the air as possible, and looked the one place they hadn't: I looked up.

A figure was crouched atop the nearest shelf, keeping low to reduce its profile and avoid knocking over the dusty merchandise still piled there. He must have crossed the store at high speed, unimpeded by crowds of sleepwalkers, but knowing all along that a misstep would send him crashing to the floor.

"Come on," he whispered. "Get up here, and we can head for the roof."

"Fishy, get out," I whispered back. The sleepwalkers around me were getting more upset by the second. I didn't know how long I would have before my pheromones were no longer enough to keep them calm. I was running blind here, and the consequences of failure were going to be dire. "You're *upsetting* them."

"We can't leave you in here," he replied. He thrust his hand down, fingers moving palely into my line of sight. "Grab hold. I'm here to get you out."

The fact that only the person who didn't believe any of this was real had been willing to follow me into the store said something about how bad the situation was. I didn't know how many sleepwalkers were crammed in behind me, but judging by the smell and the crush of bodies, it was more than enough. We could both die in an instant if we made a misstep.

Not making a misstep was going to be virtually impossible. I breathed out again. Every time I did that, it seemed to work less well. Either the sleepwalkers were getting accustomed to my pheromones, or they were becoming agitated enough that they didn't care anymore. Neither option was going to end well for me.

I let go of the sleepwalker woman's wrist and took a step toward the shelf where Fishy crouched. She hissed and began moaning, but she didn't grab for me or otherwise try to stop me from moving away. That would come next, I was sure: Once she figured out that whatever purpose I'd been serving for her was no longer being served, she would lunge. Then it would be strong fingers hauling me back, and teeth biting into my flesh, and everything would have been for nothing.

I could see my own death as clear as day, played out in blood and screaming and the rainbow splatter of my internal organs. That motivated me to take another step, moving closer to the shelf, and to the point where I could get a decent grip on Fishy's waiting hand. If he could just haul me up…

One of the sleepwalkers made a querulous noise, like it had just realized that maybe I didn't belong there. Then it moaned, deep and low in its chest, and lunged for me.

The sleepwalkers might be tapeworms in human suits, but that didn't give them special powers: Their reflexes weren't enhanced, and their eyesight was no better than it had been before they took over their hosts. They moved fast. That was all. When I was frightened, I was faster. He lunged, and I jerked away, grabbing Fishy's hand with my own even as I began scrabbling my way up the shelf. While the sleepwalkers had been fed and left to linger in their own filth, which had to confuse their senses of smell at least a little, I had been running and jumping and working to become stronger than I had ever been in my life. He was fast.

I was faster.

Fishy's hand closed tight around my wrist, hauling me upward as I scrambled for footholds on the loose shelving unit. The sleepwalker grabbed for me again, but it was too late: I was already out of his reach.

"Are you okay?" Fishy boosted me onto the top of the shelf, putting a hand on my waist to steady me until I could balance on my own. "Did they hurt you? Are you bleeding?"

He was talking too loudly. The sleepwalkers were becoming more active with every word, twitching and moaning and shambling to surround the shelf where we crouched. We were outside their reach, but that didn't mean they couldn't knock the shelving unit over. While they didn't seem to make plans— not really—they were good at feeding themselves. It was maybe the thing they were best at in the world.

"Shhh," I said, shaking my head fiercely. In a whisper I continued, "They didn't hurt me, but you've got to be quiet. You're *upsetting* them."

"I'm upsetting them? Sal, we're stuck in a cutscene-level battle here, and I didn't find a single power-up on my way to get you. I don't think we're the player characters in this situation."

I paused in the act of shaking my head to stare at him, open-mouthed and stunned into silence. I had always known that Fishy's grasp on reality was shaky at best. I hadn't realized it was this bad.

"No," I said finally. "No. You can pretend you don't believe in anything when you're out there, but right now, in here, I need you to take this seriously. This is *real*. If you're here to get me out, then you need to be *here*. With me." In this darkened, abandoned Kmart, with the sleepwalkers all around us, moaning their agitation to the gloom.

Maybe it wasn't a surprise that he'd decided to divorce himself from the real world. The shock was that he had taken it so far.

"I'm not pretending, Sal," said Fishy. He sounded unusually serious. Part of me pointed out that this was a ridiculous place to have this conversation. The sleepwalkers were pressing closer and closer, until it felt like we were perched on the last island in the world, waiting for the sea to carry us away. The rest of me ordered that part to be silent. This, too, was survival. Survival of the mind, not just survival of the body. "Sometimes when I close my eyes, I see the pixels bleeding off the edges of the world. This is a game. It has to be a game. If it's not a game, then everything I've ever loved is gone, and I'm not getting any of it back. So let it be a game. I'll play to win, until the day I don't. It's the least I can do. But I refuse to let this be real. I refuse to let her be gone."

Fishy's wife had been killed when her SymboGen implant decided it would be a better driver for her body than she was. According to Dr. Cale, his disassociation from reality had accompanied her conversion. His wife tried to eat him, he decided the world was actually a complicated video game. It wasn't the worst coping mechanism I'd ever heard. It was just, under the circumstances, pretty inconvenient.

"So what do we do?" I asked. "We can't climb down, and we can't stay here."

Fishy's teeth were a flash of white through the darkness. "Can you jump?"

The shelves were firmly affixed to the floor, thanks to California's earthquake regulations. The magnetic clamps that held them were old, and some of them were misaligned, but they were holding fast, doing their duty even after the people who had installed them were long gone. Maybe some of those same people were here with us, mindless meat-cars being driven by my cousins, no longer able to understand their own technology. The thought should probably have been unsettling. I didn't have the time to waste on feeling bad for them.

Fishy, who apparently spent his free time training for video-game survival situations, went first. He leapt across the space between shelves without hesitation, as if some unseen controller was guiding his actions. He didn't need to be afraid of falling: He knew that none of this was real, and that if he toppled into the waiting hands of the sleepwalkers below, he would simply wake from the terrible dream that had redefined his reality.

My own fate was much less assured. I didn't have a comforting delusion to wrap around my shoulders and keep me safe: The only thing I'd ever had to lie to myself about was my own humanity, and while I had held on to that lie for as long as possible, I had also willingly set it aside when it became clear that it was no longer doing me any good. I knew this was the real world. I knew that I couldn't fly. And I knew I was scared out of my mind, which didn't help.

The sleepwalkers were becoming more agitated, and the hands that were reaching up to grab and drag us down were becoming more plentiful, clustering around the shelves until even the magnetic clamps weren't enough to keep us from rocking slightly.

That was the motivation I had been waiting for. The shelf rocked, and I leapt, flailing wildly until I felt Fishy's arms lock around my waist and pull me safely away from the edge of our new perch. He was grinning again, his teeth gleaming in the faint light that was capable of reaching this deep into the old Kmart. It should have turned my stomach—I hate the sight of human teeth, the violent, hard reality of them—but given the circumstances, his obvious joy was more of an anchor than anything else. I could hold on to that joy, using it to keep me from toppling into the waiting hands below.

"You okay?" he asked.

"No," I said. "I am *not* okay. What's happening? How did they get out? Why did you come in?"

"Uh, well, I came in because you decided to play Saint Patrick and the Snakes with our shambling buddies here, and Dr. Cale freaked out, and Nate freaked out, and everybody freaked out, and nobody was willing to, like, burn the place to the ground while you were still inside it, even though that would have been the most reasonable reaction under the circumstances," said Fishy. "So I said I'd do it, since hell, what are they going to do to me? Eat me? Game over is something I'm really looking forward to." There was a faint wistfulness to his tone, like he spent his nights dreaming about the day this game would end.

I didn't know what to say to that. I pulled away, getting my feet under me, and looked down at the crush of moving bodies around us. I couldn't see more than sketchy outlines and shadows, but that was more than enough, all things considered. "How did they get out?" I asked again.

Fishy sighed. "You're like a dog with a bone sometimes, Sal. Anybody ever tell you that? Like a dog with a bone."

Maybe I was like a dog. People had spent enough of my short life telling me to sit and stay, telling me when to speak, and ordering me to be quiet. This wasn't a time for that sort of command. "I'll follow you out of here, but I need to know."

"All right," said Fishy. "Come with me." And he turned, and jumped for the next shelf, leaving me no choice but to follow.

As soon as I landed on our new perch, the reason for both the pause and the leap became clear. By lingering on the first shelf as long as we had, we'd lured sleepwalkers over to it, and were now above a relatively clear stretch of aisle. He leapt a second time, and I followed, trying not to think about what would happen if I missed my landing and fell to the floor below. I was Sal Mitchell. I had survived worse things than an obstacle course in a darkened store, and this was not going to be the thing that took me down.

Fishy stopped after the second jump, taking a few breaths, before he said, "The doors were tied shut from the outside. We couldn't chain them—it would have been too obvious that we were using the place for permanent storage, instead of closing the place off like terrified suburbanites. Aside from that, it would have made the place a death trap if anything had ever gone wrong. Start a fire, watch everybody die when no one could get close enough to deal with a padlock."

"Did someone cut the rope?" I asked, following his words to their obvious and horrifying conclusion. Sherman had been a part of Dr. Cale's family, once. He probably knew where the bowling alley was, and it wasn't like he would be above that sort of treachery, if he thought that he had something to gain from it.

To my surprise, Fishy laughed. It was a low, rueful sound, packed with regrets. "Oh, man, that would almost be better, you know? We could have some DLC about spies and traitors and maybe get some pew-pew going. But no. Something chewed through the rope. Probably a squirrel."

"What's DLC?" I asked blankly.

"Downloadable content," he said, and tensed, and jumped again. I followed him. There were no other alternatives.

The shelves had been positioned so they were never more than about four feet apart, creating aisles that could hold a shopping cart but were still narrow enough to force consumers to fully engage with the material goods around them. Most physical stores had changed their designs as Internet retailing took over an increasing share of the market. Not places like Kmart. They had a working formula, one that was built on low prices, impulse buys, and narrow aisles.

I was starting to feel like we might actually reach our destination when Fishy stopped jumping, his shoulders suddenly going limp. I crept closer, squinting to see through the darkness, and realized what had happened.

We were on the edge of the women's clothing section, a vast, open space broken only by the silver skeletons of the racks that had once held discount scrubs and polyester trousers. There were no shelves here for us to use as higher ground. There weren't that many sleepwalkers, either—the main concentration was still a half-dozen shelves back, trying to figure out where we had gone—but that would change soon.

Soon didn't mean immediately. "I can get us through this, but you have to trust me," I said. "Can you trust me?"

"I guess it's my turn," said Fishy. "What do I have to do?"

I told him.

Climbing down from the shelf without making any noise would have been impossible without the metal clamps to lend stability to the enterprise. As it was, I held my breath until my feet were back on the dirty linoleum floor, and only started breathing easy when Fishy was beside me, looking tense and unhappy in the gloom. I couldn't fault him for that. He'd seen me walk among the sleepwalkers without being devoured, but he knew that I was half one of them, while he was just a human, heir to all the sins of his forefathers, including the mad, brutal science that had put him into this situation.

Silently, I slipped my hand into Fishy's, tangling my fingers with his, and began walking toward the back wall. There were a few sleepwalkers here, full-bellied and too lazy to have joined the exodus when the doors were first opened. I breathed slowly in through my nose and out through my mouth, trying to fill as much of the air as possible with the taste of my pheromones. *Friend,* I thought fiercely. *Friend, friend, do not eat us, for I am your friend, and he is mine.* It was a complicated thought—too complicated for my primitive chemical messengers to convey— but I hoped it might seep through, at least a little. At least enough to let us get away.

There was a soft, fleshy sound as Fishy opened his mouth like he was going to say something. I turned to him and shook my head fiercely. *No.* No, do not speak, do not remind the cousins that you're something they aren't; do not give them cause to notice you, to fall upon you in a living wave and take you for their own. Anything "other" would be seen as food, and as a threat to their survival. I was not "other": I had my pheromones to protect me. If I could keep Fishy as an extension of myself, and not a being in his own right, he might have a chance.

I couldn't see his expression, but I heard his teeth click together, and I was content. We continued walking.

The sleepwalkers around us were stirring, rustling in the dark as they turned toward us and the disruption we represented. I kept my breathing slow and even, filling the air around me with pheromones. The wall was a gray ghost in the distance, a haven that might offer no salvation at all, but was at least something for us to strive toward. I felt better about the idea of dying while I was *doing* something than I did about the idea of dying while holding perfectly still, frozen in my own failure.

Fishy's breathing was starting to get unsteady. The stress of the moment was getting to him. That was fascinating, in an objective sort of way: Normally, Fishy was the one who never got upset about anything, cocooned in the soft unreality of his delusion. But here, he was being forced to live through something slow and terrible, knowing that the end could come crashing out of the dark at any moment, and that there would be nothing he could do about it. He was as captive in the real world as I was, and he didn't like it.

One of the sleepwalkers moaned. The sound was small and inquisitive, and was answered by another moan, from the other side of us. They knew we were there. Whether they were holding off because my pheromones were working or because they weren't hungry yet was anybody's guess. I kept breathing slowly in and out, but I picked up my pace, and was relieved when Fishy did the same. If we could just get to the wall...

What? If we could get to the wall, then what? I was leading

us there because Fishy had been leading us there, but he'd never told me why, and I'd been so wrapped up in the moment that I hadn't asked. It felt foolish now, not to know where I was going or what I was going to do when I got there, but foolishness was a luxury for hindsight. Foresight was all too often based on instinct and on fear, and those were things that left very little room for introspection.

As we got closer to the wall, I saw something wonderful: a door, a slice of darker gray cut out of the haze around it. Better yet, it was a *real* door, with a doorknob, not one of the swinging doors that connected to the stockrooms. Sleepwalkers didn't understand doorknobs. The odds were good that whatever was on the other side, it was a form of safety.

Unless it was locked.

Fear knotted and unknotted in my stomach, making it difficult to continue my slow, rhythmic breathing. What if we had come this far, only to find the door was locked? We'd never be able to make it back to the relative safety of the shelves. The sleepwalkers were becoming too agitated, and even breaking into a run wouldn't get us out of their reach before they could lunge. This was our one way out, and I had no way of knowing whether it would work.

Fishy squeezed my hand. I glanced to the side. He was holding something up; something that gleamed in the faint light.

A key. He had a key.

I swallowed the urge to laugh in relief, and just kept breathing in and out until we reached the wall. The sleepwalkers were getting more active, shuffling and shambling and making those little inquisitive moaning noises, but they weren't rushing us yet. That was all going to change when Fishy turned the knob. My pheromones were confusing the issue, making it difficult for them to tell whether he was an uninfected human—and hence easy, uncomplicated prey—or another sleepwalker. They didn't understand concepts like "loyalty" on a rational level, but I had to think they ate humans before they ate their own kind because they knew, in some deep way, that eating your own kind was bad. They still turned to cannibalism when it was convenient or when supplies were low, but it wasn't a preference the way it could have been without the pheromones and the vague understanding of the swarm versus the individual.

When Fishy turned the knob, however, he would be doing something no sleepwalker understood well enough to do spontaneously. After that, we would be "other," and things that were "other" were subject to attack. So we moved slowly toward the door, knowing that as soon as we reached it, we would have to start moving very quickly indeed.

Something brushed my ankle. I kept breathing in and out, not allowing myself to look down or back. It could have been a piece of forgotten clothing, still dangling on its rack. It could have been a sleepwalker's fingers, inquisitive and questing through the gloom for a better sense of the intruders. As long as it didn't grab me, as long as I could keep moving forward, it could be ignored—could even be forgotten.

That was my life. I moved through dangerous places, among dangerous things, and as long as they didn't grab me and force me to stay with them, I did my best to ignore, to forget, because anything else would be the end of me.

We had reached the wall. Fishy let go of my hand and stepped forward, feeling for the knob, for the little indentation of the keyhole. It seemed almost quaintly old-fashioned, this door that locked with a key and not a magnetic swipe card or a fingerprint scanner. But if it had been something more modern, we would have had no way of getting out of here: We would have been trapped, and in even more trouble than we already were. Quaintness had its advantages.

Fishy found the keyhole. The key slid in with a click, and he turned it, and then the door was swinging inward, a dark hole in an already dark space, revealing absolutely nothing. Whatever was on the other side was too far from the front of the store for even the watery light that we had been enjoying so far. Fishy looked back at me, visible more in contrast with that utter blackness than anything else.

The sleepwalkers were moaning louder now. They knew we weren't their kind, that we were enjoying the fruits of a civilization that wasn't theirs to claim. We were out of time. I nodded, once, and followed Fishy into the dark.

Sal's latest MRIs show that her integration with her host remains complete and undamaged by the things she's been through, including Sherman's clumsy attempts to extract her genetic material. At this point, I'm not sure she could be removed from her host's brain without killing both of them. Contrast this with Tansy, who was introduced to her host well before Sal met Sally Mitchell, yet never accomplished so thorough an integration. It's like looking at a masterpiece in comparison to a child's paint-by-numbers kit.

The main difference between the two of them seems to lie in the host itself. Tansy's original host had suffered some physical damage to the brain before she moved in: She could never have fully bonded with those neural pathways, because they were already scarred from the accident. This gives me hope. Maybe we can bring Tansy back to us, only better, by finding her a body that has suffered less damage.

—FROM THE NOTES OF DR. NATHAN KIM, JANUARY 2028

We have sufficient supplies to continue our work for another year. We have sufficient "clean" humans to serve as breeding stock and replacement hosts. Some of them seem to think the former will carry more weight than the latter: Most of us seem healthy, after all, and will be keeping our current hosts for some time. They haven't considered that we can make our own replacement hosts. We have all the tools that they have, and why shouldn't we have children of our own? A human child is a blank slate, ready and waiting to have the soft bones of the growing skulls opened and used as perfect doorways for the next generation of chimera. They can be ours in every sense of the word.

We'll still need the humans, of course—replacement parts will always be necessary—but they're not as essential as they think they are. They never were.

All that remains now is to secure the future. It was always meant to be ours.

—FROM THE NOTES OF SHERMAN LEWIS
(SUBJECT VIII, ITERATION III), JANUARY 2028

Chapter 13

JANUARY 2028

The door slammed behind us. Fishy put a hand on my shoulder, like he was verifying my location, and then pulled it away as he turned to feel for the door and make sure it was locked. There was always the chance that we'd encounter a sleepwalker that was particularly high-functioning and capable of mimicking what it had witnessed, even if they hadn't thought to try the door before we opened it. Their unexpected flashes of intellect were part of what made them so dangerous. There was no one way that they behaved.

There was a click, and Fishy said, voice dripping with relief, "Okay. That's got it. We're locked in."

"Okay," I said, and inhaled, checking the air for any signs of pheromone trails or traces. I wasn't a perfect sleepwalker detector—I would have needed more opportunities to hone my skills, and since those were also opportunities to get disemboweled, I was mostly content not to seek them out. It was still better than nothing.

All I smelled was dust, and gently decaying cardboard, and the curious stillness of a room that had been sealed off for so long that it might as well never have existed.

"I think we're alone," I said. Then: "Where *are* we?"

"The loading dock," said Fishy. "It connects to the storerooms, but those doors were locked when the store was closed down. There shouldn't be any direct route for the sleepwalkers to take from where they are to where we are."

"That's good," I said. The darkness was absolute, which was starting to soothe my jangled nerves. Being born an eyeless creature that was never meant to see the light of day had left me with a strange affinity for the dark, one that was shared by my sleepwalker cousins. It was rare for me to find pure darkness that wasn't also dangerous. "Do you know how we're supposed to get out of here?"

"There's a door to the outside on the other side of the dock," said Fishy. "If we walk slowly and watch our steps, we should be able to get there without twisting our ankles or anything."

I blinked into the darkness. Then, almost reluctantly, I started to laugh. Fishy joined in, and for a minute or so it was just the two of us, alone in the dark, laughing at the sheer relief that accompanied our survival.

Finally, we calmed and quieted. Fishy's hand sought mine in the darkness and clasped it tight. Then, together, we began walking away from the door.

It was soothing, moving through the dark like that, trusting my feet to carry me and my outstretched hand to warn me before I walked into anything dangerous. I had a human's body and a tapeworm's world, and it was a beautiful reversal of the way I usually had to live. Fishy kept hold of my hand, allowing me to lead. He recognized that I was more confident in the dark than he was, even if he didn't fully understand the reasons why.

Bit by bit, we crossed the cavernous span of the loading docks, stopping when my fingers found the opposing wall. "We're here," I said, and my voice was very small in the vastness of space, and very loud in the silence, all at the same time. "Fishy?"

"Just a second. Stay where you are." Fishy let go of my hand. I felt immediately adrift, unmoored from the anchor that had been keeping me from floating away into the darkness. I pressed my palm against the wall, using that as a touchstone, something that meant the world had limits and was thus still real.

Fishy's footsteps moved away from me, but not very far. Then there was a click, and a rectangle of blinding light opened in the wall of the world. I moved toward it, squinting, my eyes filling with hot, aggravated tears. But I wanted that world, I *needed* that world, brightly lit and painful as it was.

Fishy waited for me, his own eyes as stunned and tear-filled as my own, and we stepped together into the light.

It was a dramatic transition for a mundane place: We stepped out of the loading dock and onto a short metal staircase so drenched in rust that it was probably a health hazard. The railing was barely bolted on, and wobbled under my questing hand like it was going to give way at any moment. The pavement back here was in worse shape than the parking lot: It was basically potholes and gravel, stitched together by the jaunty, jutting shapes of weeds, forcing their way through cracks and up into the sun.

Carefully, moving slowly while our eyes adjusted, we descended the stairs and started toward the front of the building, our feet crunching with every step. We were maybe halfway there when another sound caught my attention. I stopped dead. Fishy, thankfully, followed my lead, and I listened as hard as I could, trying to figure out what was wrong.

Tires, moving on gravel. Moving slowly, like whoever was driving didn't want to attract unnecessary attention. But we didn't use any of the vehicles during the day. It would have been too big of a risk, given USAMRIID's presence in the Bay Area. If we needed to get out one of the cars, we did it at night, when we'd be harder to spot via a simple visual inspection. So who was driving around in our lot?

The sound was getting closer. I had an instant to decide what I was going to do. I turned, grabbing Fishy's hand, and ran back toward the back of the Kmart. The door to the loading dock was ajar. I hauled Fishy up the metal steps and swung it open, diving through into the safety of the dark. Then I let him go and spun around to push the door most of the way shut, leaving it just slightly cracked, like it had been left that way by the people who had abandoned the store in the first place.

"What—" began Fishy.

"Shhh," I said, and pressed my eye to the crack, and waited.

Only a few seconds had passed when the Jeep came around the corner. It was moving slowly, so that its occupants could scan the area without coming to a stop. I didn't recognize the woman in the passenger seat. She was wearing a snood of some sort over her hair and holding an assault rifle; her eyes were cold. She didn't scare me half as much as the driver. He was familiar. He was my darkest fear, come back to haunt me.

Sherman kept his hands on the wheel, head moving slightly from side to side as he looked for stragglers. For a terrible moment I was afraid he was going to notice the open door to the Kmart and stop the Jeep, but he rolled on by, still searching the open areas. I pulled back and scrambled away from the light, pulling Fishy with me, until we were safely cocooned in the darkness. If Sherman came back to look for us, he'd have very little trouble finding our hiding spot…but there was no place left for us to go. Not unless we wanted to flee back into the Kmart, where the sleepwalkers were waiting.

Fishy squeezed my hand. His fingers were shaking. Whether he believed any of this was real or not, he understood that some things were worth being afraid of. That just made me feel worse. If the man who didn't believe the world existed was scared, I should probably have been vomiting with fear. As it was, I just felt numb. Utterly, perfectly numb.

The sound of Sherman's Jeep driving back the other way drifted through the open door. I didn't move. We had no weapons—*I* had no weapons; Fishy might have had a gun in his holster, I hadn't asked or checked—and we couldn't just release the sleepwalkers, not without putting ourselves and our friends in even more danger.

I don't think it was squirrels that cut the rope, I thought, almost frantically, and clapped a hand over my mouth to keep my terrified giggles inside. My guts were churning, filled with hot terror and cold anger, until everything was warm and nauseating. I forced myself to keep breathing in through my nose and out through my mouth, blowing softly against my fingers, until I realized that Sherman might be able to pick up on my pheromones. Then I moved to breathing purely through my nose, trying to pretend it was enough, and that the narrower airways weren't leaving my skin feeling tight and ill-fitting, stretched too harshly against my bones.

What was Sherman *doing* here? How had he known to look for us at the bowling alley? What was he hoping to accomplish by letting the sleepwalkers out of their comfortable prison? At least my third question was answered easily enough: He'd been looking for a distraction, and had probably been counting on a bigger one than he actually got. He couldn't have anticipated my interference with his plan.

That should have made me feel good. It just made me feel more afraid. Sherman was out there, and we were hiding in here, and neither of us was brave enough to go and see what was really going on. Either he would lose, and we would emerge to find our friends relieved and delighted by our survival, or he would win, and we would need to stay free in order to save them. The only thing we could do now was wait.

Waiting burned.

The seconds ticked by, stretching like taffy, and everything was silence, except for the endless pounding of the drums in my ears. It would have been easier to wait if I'd dropped down into the hot warm dark, where time had no meaning and nothing could touch me, but I would also be unaware of my surroundings, and unable to defend myself or run if Sherman's people found our hiding place. My choices were either sitting in terrified darkness or sinking into comforting oblivion, and while they were both terrible, my current position seemed a little bit less bad.

Fishy was still shaking slightly behind me, the tremors passing from his hands into mine, and then all the way down to my bones. I was listening as hard as I could for footsteps crunching on gravel, but the more upset I became, the louder the drums pounded, until it felt like they were the only things in the world. Normally, I loved the drums, loved the comforting mortality that they represented. Now, I would have done anything to make them stop, just long enough to let me *hear*.

I started counting silently, trying to give myself something to do, something that would distract me from the unknown dangers outside. When I reached a hundred, I paused, trying to decide whether that had been enough, and then resumed counting. I needed more. I needed to *know* that the danger was past, and that we hadn't been hiding in here for nothing.

When I reached five hundred, I paused again, trying to shunt the drums to the back of my awareness and listen to the world outside. There was nothing: only silence. Slowly, cautiously, I uncurled my legs, noting the pins and needles that shot through them in protest. It hurt to move. That was a good sign, under the circumstances. I wouldn't be able to run as fast, but if I had to run, I had already lost. I needed to hurt like this. I needed to know that I had been still long enough to save myself.

"Are you sure?" Fishy's voice was a whisper that seemed loud enough to shake the world.

I nodded, and then realized that he wouldn't be able to see the gesture through the dark. "I think so," I whispered back. "We can't stay hidden here forever." And there was the truth of the matter. Hopefully we had stayed hidden long enough… but nothing living thrives concealed for more than a short time, even during a crisis. We had to move.

Inch by inch, we moved toward the door. My heart was pounding so hard I could feel it, and the answering drums echoed in my ears, making it difficult to hear anything else. Fishy was right behind me, and I couldn't tell whether he was allowing me to take the lead, or whether he was too frightened to step in front of me. It could have gone either way. His comfortable delusion was wearing thin, and whatever he did to sustain it for himself, he needed to do it soon, or risk losing his veneer of unreality completely.

When we reached the door, I pressed my eye to the opening, squinting against the light, and scanned the lot for signs of movement. There was nothing, not even a breeze. Everything was still.

Pockets were wonderful things. Even in this new world, where money and cell phones were useless affectations, we found things to keep in them. I fumbled in my left hip pocket until my fingers found a smooth stone that I had picked up to show Juniper. Slowly, I pushed the door farther open and tossed the stone out into the parking lot. It slid across the gravel, rolling and clattering, before coming to a stop some ten feet away. I held my breath.

No one came.

Still moving slowly, I straightened up and pushed the door open wider, increasing both my frame of view and the amount of light flooding my abused retinas. Everything took on a teary, blurry halo. I squinted through the pain, still looking for motion, and found nothing. We might not be alone, but this lot, at least, had been checked and abandoned by our attackers.

"Come on," I said to Fishy, and stepped outside.

Together, we crept around the edge of the building, stopping every five feet or so to listen for footsteps or tires, anything that would indicate that the danger was returning. A crow called somewhere in the distance; another crow answered, shriller and farther away. Leaves rustled. But nothing had the distinct sound of a human or a human's machines. We were alone.

Fishy took a deep breath. I stopped and looked back, waiting to see what he was going to say. The pause was almost a relief. We were less than five yards from the corner of the building; even at our current glacial pace, we would be there soon, and we would have to face whatever had happened to our friends.

"I think you should wait here," he said.

I blinked at him.

"You're a playable character, and I'm NPC support," he said. "It's obvious that we've just been through a major cutscene, and this is probably kicking off a pretty big quest for you. We don't need you to go first and get killed when it would just mean playing through the whole Kmart jumping sequence again. Although I guess there could have been an autosave somewhere in there."

I had never been a video game player. I blinked at him again before saying, hesitantly, "Okay."

Fishy looked relieved, some of the old cockiness coming back into his eyes. He was reasserting his video game reality now that we were moving again. He needed this to make it all the way real, and keep the edges from slipping out of his grasp. "Wait here," he said, and walked past me, still slowly, but faster now, like he had made an important decision and no longer wanted to wait around to see what the consequences would be.

When he reached the corner he stopped, and for a moment, he was perfectly still, just looking. Then his shoulders slumped, and he called back to me—making no effort to keep his voice from carrying—"Sal. Come on."

His tone was dead, devoid of any real emotion or life. I think I knew then. I think I *understood*. I came anyway.

The bowling alley doors had been torn off their hinges and reduced to splinters. The windows, always boarded or soaped over, were so much shattered glass on the pavement. There were bodies. Some had obviously been sleepwalkers who hadn't fallen for my lure and returned to the building. Others...

A tall woman with short-cropped hair lay facedown on the ground near the entrance to the bowling alley. The back of her lab coat was the dark red-brown of dried blood, and she wasn't moving. Daisy was never going to move again. A few more technicians were on the ground near her, all of them motionless, even the young man with his face turned toward the sky, his eyes open and filled with unforgiving sunlight. Their wounds were almost abstract from this distance, but that didn't make them any less real.

Someone moaned, low and strained. I realized it was me.

"Sherman's people must have released the sleepwalkers to keep us from seeing them coming," said Fishy. He still sounded dead, like someone had snapped all the circuits connecting his emotions to his voice. That might have been a mercy. "We weren't expecting something like this. We had security. We were watching for USAMRIID. But we weren't expecting this sort of frontal assault. How could we have?"

I tried to speak. No words would come, just another low, pained moan. Then, almost without realizing that I was going to do it, I started to run.

It wasn't graceful. It was a loping, scrabbling thing. I nearly

fell twice, catching myself on my palms both times and pushing away from the ground, heedless of the gravel and glass that
bit into my skin. I was still moaning, as frantic as any sleepwalker. I couldn't make the sounds stop. Making the sounds
stop would have left my panic with no place to go, and then
things would have really started to fall apart.

I was halfway between the Kmart and the bowling alley
when I remembered what had caused me to step between the
sleepwalkers and my people in the first place. I stopped running, feeling suddenly numb, and turned to look at the garden
center.

The door was on the ground. The door was on the ground,
and most of the plants were on their sides, and Adam and Juniper were gone.

My knees went suddenly weak, and it was all I could do to
stay standing. I swayed from side to side like a tree in a strong
wind, moaning, until Fishy's hands closed on my shoulders,
pulling me upright.

"They can't have killed everyone," he said. "We have to move."

We moved.

The smell of gunpowder, blood, and emptied bowels hung in
the air around the bowling alley, a thick miasma of fragility and
loss. I breathed in and out through my mouth, shallowly, and
grimaced every time I tasted the lingering pheromones of another chimera. Sherman had been here. Sherman had probably
pulled the trigger, more than once. He hadn't been content vio-
lating my body. He had to come here and violate my home.

Daisy's body was the closest to the door. I had to assume that
she'd been defending the bowling alley when she was gunned
down. I stepped around the bloodstains, feeling strangely
squeamish, and then stepped inside, barely three feet ahead of
Fishy.

Something slammed into the back of my neck, hard enough

to send a bolt of pain jolting through my entire body, and I collapsed, unconscious before I hit the floor.

"—have been killed! Are you stupid, or just high?" Fishy sounded furious. "What if the last save point was before we left the Kmart, huh?" Furious, and delusional. At least one of us was getting back to normal.

My head hurt. No: That was insufficient. My head *throbbed* with every breath I took, and even the distant pounding of the drums was enough to make my skull feel like it was coming apart, like I had lost all structural integrity and was going to fall to pieces at any moment. I considered opening my eyes, and realized that adding light to the pain I was already experiencing would do nothing to make things better, but could make things substantially worse.

"I didn't know you weren't Sherman's men," snapped Fang. Relief swept through me, almost strong enough to distract temporarily from the pain. "The bastard missed some things. I thought someone might have talked."

"Our people wouldn't talk!"

"Spoken like someone who's never met the wrong end of a pair of pliers," said Fang calmly. He still sounded shaken. I realized that I'd never heard him sounding that unsure of himself, even when they were rushing me to the hospital for emergency brain surgery. Why shouldn't he be unsure? Everything we'd built, everything we'd worked for... it was just gone, and I didn't know whether there was going to be any way of getting it back. "Put enough pressure on a body, and they'll talk. *Everybody* talks. I'd talk, you'd talk, even our sweet, sleeping Sal there would talk, if only to make the hurting stop. Well. Maybe not Sal. She could do that trick of hers, the one where she takes herself away from pain."

The words were casual, but they seemed aimed at me in a

way the rest hadn't been, and I realized something. He wanted me to go down into the hot warm dark. Dr. Cale must have told him about it, told him how I could enter that state at will, when none of the other chimera could, and now he was trying to get me to take myself down. If I wasn't awake, I wouldn't have heard him say that, and he could speak freely. If I *was* awake, and I went into the dark, I wouldn't hear anything else he said, and he could speak freely.

I focused on my breathing, making sure it was slow and level, mimicking the breathing of a sleeping person. But I didn't go down into the hot warm dark. Whatever he didn't want me to hear, I very much wanted to hear it.

Fang's silence stretched out for long enough that I thought he knew I was awake. Then he sighed, and said, "I didn't mean to hurt her. I'd do it again, under the circumstances. They took Dr. Cale, Fishy. They took Nathan. They took all the lab techs that they didn't kill. God help us, they took Adam and Juniper, and Juniper represents a leap forward in chimera evolution that we're still trying to comprehend."

"Sherman used Sal's genetic material," said Fishy. "How is that a leap?"

"He used Sal's genetic material, but he scrubbed her epigenetics," said Fang. "He couldn't prevent tissue rejection, but he was able to minimize it, almost like he had made the tapeworm DNA more dominant in the recognition phase. The important part, though, is the brain of Juniper's host. It should have been much more damaged than it was by the initial take-over. MRIs show light scarring, and areas of tissue improvement. It's like she's spurring the brain to recover around her, and that means that eventually, she may be the only chimera with a fully functional, undamaged human brain for a host. If Sherman can figure out how she's accomplishing that, and increase that tendency in the next generation, he may be able to coax even badly damaged sleepwalkers fully back to sentience."

"That's some DLC bullshit," said Fishy. He sounded shaken. "I don't need smart grunts attacking me every time we go into a combat situation."

"There are times when I question whether or not you actually know how to speak English," said Fang. He sounded exasperated, and his accent—which I had never been able to quite identify—got stronger, like a reminder that he, as a man of Chinese descent, had probably been asked about his grasp of the language a great deal more often than Fishy had. "If Sherman can isolate what has allowed Juniper to heal her host, he can use it to increase the size of his army tenfold."

"He doesn't have the skills for that," said Fishy.

"Dr. Cale does," replied Fang. "More, and more terrifyingly, Dr. Cale's allegiances have always been…negotiable. She stands in the middle, because she sees both sides as valid, and since neither side has held her, she has done her work to benefit both of them as much as she can. With Sherman holding her prisoner, and holding the lives of her sons in his hands, I think it very likely that she is about to become in earnest the enemy of the human race that some people have taken her to be. Even if Juniper's life is the cost of theirs."

There was a pause before Fishy said, "You mean she's going to go all boss level because she's working for the bad guys now?"

Fang sighed. "It's a distinct possibility, yes."

"You don't have to use so many fancy words, you know. You could just say what you mean."

They were verbally sparring, something I had come across members of the lab staff doing when they were nervous and needed to do something to make themselves feel better. It was an understandable and very human reaction. It was something that we didn't have time for.

The pain in my head was still bad enough to make me yearn for the safety and weightlessness of the hot warm dark. I opened my eyes anyway, forcing them to stay open even as the light lanced through them and involuntary reactions filled them with tears. Then, with a force of will that I wasn't sure I possessed until I had to use it, I sat up.

My head rang like a bell at the motion, creating a wave of pain so intense that it converted itself into sound that nearly deafened me. I didn't lie back down. Instead, I turned, seeking the source of the voices. Fang and Fishy were standing only a few feet away, staring at me, Fishy in clear shock, Fang in resignation. He *had* suspected I was awake, then, and simply hoped that I would take his cue to drop down into the dark.

How I wished I could. But Juniper was in danger, and I couldn't afford to let myself rest. I swallowed to try and force the pain away, and asked, "What did Sherman's men miss that you were afraid they'd be coming back for? Is there anyone left here besides you?"

Fang looked at me, discomfort written plainly across his face. "When Sherman's people arrived, I wanted to defend the doors," he said finally. "I thought it was important. But Dr. Cale ordered me back. She told me to defend...something else. God forgive me, I followed orders."

I frowned. "What did you defend?"

"Tansy. She and I are the only ones who remain, aside from the two of you."

My mouth was suddenly dry. "Oh," I whispered.

Tansy's condition was delicate enough that she'd been put in a private room at the back of the bowling alley, one that had originally been a pantry, and was hence designed to be as unobtrusive as possible. If Fang had gone inside, closed the door, and turned off the lights, it was reasonable for Sherman's people to have missed it. Leaving one security officer and one comatose, badly damaged chimera alone in the bowling alley.

Bracing my hands against the cot they had placed me on, I took a better look around. All the equipment that could be easily lifted and taken was gone. The workstations, the computer towers, even most of the paper printouts, they had all been carried away by the people who had taken Dr. Cale and her staff.

Her staff, and your brother, and your daughter, and your fiancé, whispered the voice of my anxieties. *You've lost. It's over.*

"It's not over," I said aloud. Fang and Fishy frowned at me. I reached up to touch the back of my head with my fingers, gingerly prodding the lump I found there. Nothing shifted under my touch. I'd been hit hard, but not hard enough to actually break my skull. "It can't be over. We're not letting Sherman win. That isn't how this ends."

"That's, uh, really heroic of you to say and all, but I think it's also sort of misguided," said Fishy. "There's three of us. Four if you count the popsicle. We're not coming out of this on top, unless you've been hiding a bunch of nukes in your underwear drawer."

"Sherman took our people: We need to get them back," I said, sliding off the cot. My legs wobbled, but held me up. That was good enough, for now. "Sherman put the eggs in the water supply: We need to get them out, or everyone's in danger, regardless of species. Dr. Cale was working on that. She's not going to be working on it anymore if Sherman has her. There are two real sides in this fight, and we've been standing in the middle, waiting to see which one would win. Isn't it obvious? The one we decide to help is going to be the winner."

"Meaning what?" asked Fang warily.

I sighed. The words burned even before they left my lips. I had to say them anyway. "Meaning we can't help Sherman, or give Dr. Cale the chance to help him either. Meaning we need to go to USAMRIID. On our terms. Because things are just going to get worse from here."

They're never going to let me out of here. I am going to die here. I am never going to see the sun again. I am never going to walk free again. I am never going to feel the wind on my face again. They are monsters, and they have taken me to be their toy, and I am not afraid, I am not afraid, I AM NOT AFRAID.

When they kill me, I will see my husband again. I will see my home again. I will go back where I belong, finally, and I will be so glad to be there.

How did it get this bad? How did we hand the world over to the monsters? How were we so willing to believe in miracles that made our lives easier, even when we knew that they couldn't be true?

How?

—WRITTEN ON A SCRAP OF PAPER FOUND IN
CARRIE BLACK'S CELL, JANUARY 2028

The results are in, and they point to one, inescapable conclusion: We've lost. Oh, we can continue to thrash and posture and fight, and pretend that we can do something to change what's already happened, but it will be just that: pretense. We'll be lying to ourselves, even as our numbers fall and our walls fail to hold.

I wonder if this is how the Neanderthals felt, seeing whatever works they had managed to create being swept away by the tide of modern man. And then I realize that the comparison does not hold, because the Neanderthals didn't create us, their successors: They didn't feed us on their flesh and nurture us inside their bodies, only to see us turn on them. We are the engineers of our own destruction, and when all is burning, we will have no one but ourselves to blame.

Maybe it's a mercy that both of my daughters are dead. They didn't need to see this.

No one needed to see this.

—FROM THE DIARY OF COLONEL ALFRED MITCHELL,
USAMRIID, JANUARY 2028

Chapter 14

JANUARY 2028

Fang had gone to recover the largest of our trucks from the garage where it was concealed, far enough from the bowling alley that it wouldn't lead USAMRIID to us if they found its heat signature after it had been used—and ironically, far enough from the bowling alley that Sherman and his men wouldn't have seen it during their sweep for assets. Fishy, who understood weapons better than I did, had gone to see what we had left, leaving me to the unpleasant task of sweeping the apartments for people who had not been at work when the raid occurred.

Sherman had been created in the bowling alley. He must have been acting on what he remembered about the lab and its environs when he planned the raid, because none of his people had gone anywhere near the apartment buildings we had repurposed for our use. If I had only encouraged Adam to hold Juniper's lessons at home, with the dogs, they might still be with us. I could have saved them. I could have—

No. Following that rabbit wouldn't lead me to Wonderland: It would take me down an increasingly dark series of tunnels, until there was no way for me to find the light again. I couldn't live my entire life waiting for the darkness to come and claim me. Adam had enjoyed holding Juniper's lessons at the garden center. Everything we'd had access to had told us it was safe, and since both of them were happy, what was the harm? It didn't matter that the harm had shown its face, and proven itself more dangerous than we could have ever guessed. We'd allowed them to make choices. We'd allowed them to *live*.

That was all that any of us could ask.

I knocked on doors, waited for a count of ten, and then moved on to the next apartment, both glad that I didn't have to explain what had happened, and aching from each successive bout with silence. Had Sherman and his men really taken everyone? Were Fishy, Fang, and I all that remained? It seemed impossible. I'd known Dr. Cale for less than a year, but she had already become one of the fixed points around which the universe revolved, untouchable and unimpeachable and indestructible. But here we were.

I was halfway through the neighborhood when a door opened in answer to my knocking. The technician on the other side—a slim, dark-skinned woman with black hair and long-boned hands that were currently occupied in clutching a sheet around her body—blinked at me. I blinked back.

"Er, Sal, yeah?" she said. "Please don't tell me there's another chemical fire. I just got the smell of the last one out of my hair."

"It's not a chemical fire," I said. I hadn't been expecting to find anyone, even though I probably should have been: The night shift would have had no reason to be in the building. I just didn't know how big the night shift *was*. "Um, Heina, right?"

"You remembered," she said, sounding pleasantly surprised. Her smile was quick, bright, and filled with teeth. "Wasn't sure you would. We've met a few times, but I get up around the time you're going to bed, and you always look like you're dead on your feet."

"Sorry about that," I said. I tried to keep talking, to tell her what had happened to our friends and colleagues. My lips refused to move. "I guess I'm sort of a morning person most of the time. I. Just. I…" I took a deep breath, and then spilled it all out in one great, indigestible chunk: "Sherman and his people raided the bowling alley, they took Dr. Cale and Adam and all the equipment and all her research, they're probably planning to use it to make the worms in the water even better at doing what they do, and then we're all going to be in big, big trouble, no matter what we are, so Fishy, Fang, and I are going to USAMRIID to tell Colonel Mitchell what's going on and try to convince him to join forces with us and make Sherman stop. Only I came here to see if anyone from the night shift had managed to miss the whole thing, and it seems like you did, so now I guess I have to ask you whether you want to come with us or stay here and hold down the fort."

Heina blinked. Slowly, once, twice, and then a third time, the animation draining from her face more with each small motion. By the time she was done, she looked like a brown wax figure of a woman, perfectly still, filled with waiting.

"They got everything?" she asked.

I nodded.

"There's a transmitter just under the roofline. Did they take it? Do you remember seeing it after they came through?"

"I…where would it have been?"

"Near the front door." Heina took a step forward, eyes suddenly intense. "It would have been tucked next to the sign, where it wouldn't have been super obvious to someone who didn't know the place. Taking it down would have probably required breaking the sign away from the wall. Was the sign broken?"

That question I could answer with confidence. "No. The door was off its hinges, but the sign was still intact."

"Did they cut the power?"

Tansy's life support had continued to operate throughout the entire fight. "No," I said again.

Then, to my surprise, Heina smiled. It was nothing like her quick, easy expression when I'd remembered her name. This smile was slow, and dark, and filled with the simple joy of a techie who had managed to get one over on the world. I'd seen a similar smile on Fishy, usually right before he did something irresponsibly dangerous. "Then I'll stay here. I'll get the rest of my team on it."

"On what?" I asked.

"Sal, please don't take this the wrong way, but you've never struck me as the most tech-savvy person around. Is that accurate?" Heina waited for me to nod before she continued: "That antenna was feeding everything from the servers in the bowling alley into the cloud, which is local and sustained by machines in the spare room of this apartment and in the entire floor space of the apartment underneath me. If the local network was disrupted, then those machines I just mentioned? They sucked everything *out* of the cloud, and turned it into solid, stored, salvageable data. And if Sherman's men were unplugging things all willy-nilly? Oh, poor them."

"Why?" I asked blankly.

"Because they just carted off a bunch of empty hard drives with nothing interesting for them to look at." Heina's smile was virtually feral, and seemed to contain more teeth than a single human head could hold. "As soon as those machines were uncoupled from the network without appropriate protocols, they started wiping themselves. It was a counterespionage measure we decided to put in place when it became clear that Dr. Cale didn't know jack about computer security. As long as everything turned on when she told it to, she was perfectly happy to carry on with minimal backups and no off-site. Love her to death, but that woman is lucky she made it this far."

"I don't understand."

Heina's smile grew broader still. "I'm saying we have all her data—everything—and that Sherman may have our people, but he only has the research they bothered to print out."

I blinked again. "Oh," I breathed. Then: "Can you come with me? We need to tell Fang about this."

"Can I put some clothes on first?" asked Heina.

I nodded.

Fang was back with the truck by the time I returned to the bowling alley with Heina. It would have taken longer, but she had promised to finish going through the apartments, since she knew which ones were supposed to be occupied. "Besides, Princess," she'd said, once she was clothed and willing to step outside. "We're all fun-and-frisky folks, and you don't know us well enough to be walking in on some of those scenes."

Modesty about nudity and sexual situations was a human trait, one I had learned how to mimic reasonably well, but had never quite managed to internalize. Still, it seemed somehow important to Heina that she be shocking me, so I did my best to look embarrassed. Mostly, I think I just managed to look anxious, which nicely matched my actual mood.

Fang turned at the sound of footsteps, his shoulders locked in the way that usually meant someone was about to get punched. When he saw me, he relaxed. When he saw Heina, he actually brightened. "You found someone!" he said, jumping down from the truck's rear bumper. "Heina, you old goat. I should have realized you'd still be asleep at this unreasonable hour of the afternoon."

"I was getting my beauty rest while you were all getting shot." Heina scanned the front of the bowling alley, looking sad when her eyes skated over the bodies lying in the gravel. She brightened at something, and I assumed that meant her transmitter was still in place, doing whatever it was that hidden transmitters were supposed to do. "I'm sorry I wasn't here."

"I'm not," said Fang firmly. "If you had been, you'd have been shot along with everyone else, and I'd have missed your smiling face."

I was starting to wonder whether there might be something more than workplace friendliness between the two of them. That would have been nice. Fang needed more people he actually liked well enough to relax around. Still, this wasn't the time to deal with that. "Heina says she has cloud backups of all the data from the bowling alley."

"They didn't knock out my transmitters," she said in a tone that implied confirmation of what I had just said. "Amateurs. Evil amateurs, which is the worst kind. Couldn't we have had the villains we deserved?"

"You'll forgive me if I don't sit around wishing for more competence on the part of the people who killed Daisy," said Fang. "Can you prepare a quick sampler platter of data? Not enough to give our location away to someone who doesn't already have it, but enough to make it clear that we have some valuable information to barter with?"

"Sure, but why?" asked Heina.

"Because we're going to USAMRIID," said Fang.

"Even if all those computers wiped themselves, Sherman still has Dr. Cale, and Nathan, and *everybody*," I said. *Juniper, he has Juniper, he's going to see what she means for everything, and then he's going to take her apart.* The thought was a constant chant at the back of my mind, almost dismissible when it wasn't allowing myself to focus on it. "He's going to be able to re-create their work, and do work of his own, until he figures out how to make the DNA do what he wants it to do. We have to get Colonel Mitchell's people on our side."

And then there was Tansy. I didn't want to look in the back of the truck and see whether Fang had already transferred her over. I couldn't hear the beep of the heart monitor or the whistling hiss of the intubation, so I supposed that she was probably still inside. Without a full team to monitor her around the clock, she wasn't going to be able to stay alive for much longer.

Without someone to drive the bus, neither would Joyce. They would both die, both of them broken beyond repair by bad people and bad science. But together, they might stand a chance. If we could get Tansy to Oakland before she gave up. If I could convince Sally's father that my life honored hers, and didn't shame her death. It was a lot of "if." It was all that we really had left.

Fishy came trotting out of the bowling alley with his arms full of small firearms and large pieces of metal rebar. He stopped when he saw Heina. Then he brightened, and called, "Hey, Bonus Player! You didn't die! That's awesome."

"Hello, Fishy," Heina replied. "Fang tells me you're heading for USAMRIID? You sure that's a good idea?"

I wanted to rankle over how quickly she had dismissed me from the decision-making process, but I couldn't: not really. These three were coworkers, and I was someone who just happened to live there, and more, had accidentally become a miracle of science. That didn't mean I'd let her undermine me—if she started really trying to convince them that we shouldn't go, I'd step in—but it meant that she would take this better if she heard it from one of the people whose work she actually respected.

"Nope, but Sal's the main PC of this run, so I'm going along with her," said Fishy. Then he paused, and straightened, his posture shifting so completely that for a moment, it was almost like I was looking at an entirely different person. "It's a bad situation, Heina, and it's going to get worse from here. USA-MRIID has men, they have resources, and they have the sort of firepower we can only dream of. So we go to them, because it's the last good option we have. Maybe we're all going to get gunned down. Maybe we're going to be arrested for crimes against the US government. I don't know. But it's better than sitting here and waiting for the world to fall down."

"You get the network stable, and shift everything over into the apartments," said Fang. "Have your people feed the sleep-walkers, but don't do anything else around this shopping center. If Sherman sends a crew back to check for stragglers, I want them to think that they killed us all."

"That means we can't bury the dead," I said quietly. The other three turned to look at me. Fishy and Heina both looked shocked. Fang looked almost relieved, like he had been hoping someone else would come to that conclusion before he had to be the one to say it. I wanted to be angry at him for that, but I couldn't. These had been his friends and colleagues long before they had been mine. He could seem stoic sometimes, but his situation was just as bad as everyone else's.

"What do you mean?" demanded Heina. "We can't leave them out here to rot."

"They won't," I said. "There are coyotes around here, and raccoons, and feral cats. The bodies won't last very long once night falls."

That didn't seem to help much. Heina scowled, and even Fishy looked faintly nauseated. Only Fang's face remained neutral. I was saying things he'd already considered, and while that didn't mean he had to like them, it did mean there were no surprises hiding in my words.

"That's disrespectful and unhygienic," said Heina. "How are we supposed to work with a bunch of bodies rotting outside the door?"

"You're not supposed to be working in the bowling alley at all, remember?" I was so tired. I needed to be moving, running, racing against time to get my people back, and instead I was standing here arguing about the dead. How much time were we going to spend arguing about the dead before we started to understand how unimportant they were compared to the living? The dead were *nothing*. They were food for worms that had never been uplifted by science. The living, the survivors... that was what we needed to be concerned about. "You're going to shift everything to the apartments, and you're going to leave the bodies here."

"I don't take orders from you," said Heina.

"Why not?" I asked. "I'm the last chimera standing. I'm the boss's genetically engineered daughter, and I'm the one who's marrying her biological son. No matter how you slice it, I'm technically in charge now that she's gone, and I say we're wasting time."

"Cat's got claws," said Fishy. He sounded surprised and pleased, like this was the best possible outcome.

"Sal is correct," said Fang, not giving the argument a chance to continue. "We need to leave if we're going to reach USAMRIID before the sun goes down. Heina, you have to get the equipment transferred over, and more importantly, you have to leave the bodies where they are. They're essential camouflage."

"But they're our friends," she said softly.

"I know," said Fang, his tone echoing hers. "I am going to miss them forever. But they wouldn't want us to die because we were unwilling to let them protect us one last time. Leave their bodies where they fell. They'll keep you safe by keeping the wolves away."

"How did it come to this?" asked Heina.

Fang shook his head. "I'll be honest with you," he said. "I really don't know."

*   *   *

Working together, the four of us had been able to transfer Tansy and her life-support equipment into the back of the truck without jostling her more than was absolutely necessary. Her heart monitor beeped once, signaling an increase in her resting vitals, before calming again.

Fishy had managed to secure a generator in the corner of the truck, small enough to be unobtrusive, large enough to power the machines that were keeping Tansy's host—and hence Tansy herself—alive. One by one, he plugged in her life-support components, swapping them from the lab extension cord with a speed and grace that spoke to a lifetime spent doing similar work, albeit with less potentially fatal consequences.

We had food for a day, in case we got held up on the way to USAMRIID; small weapons enough to get us through whatever dangers we encountered; and all the medical supplies Fishy and Fang had been able to scrounge from the bowling alley. If anything went wrong during transport, we'd be in the best possible position to try to put Tansy back together. Not that it was ever going to work completely. Until she got a new host, this persistent vegetative state was the most that we would have to hope for.

Heina was going to take care of my dogs until we got back. I didn't like the idea of leaving them with a virtual stranger, but I liked the idea of taking them with us even less. There were no animals inside the quarantine zone, save for the ones that had been there before USAMRIID moved in and hadn't been hunted down and euthanized yet. Beverly might have been okay with the trip. Minnie wouldn't have been. And I wouldn't have been okay with the stress of looking out for either one of them. Better to leave them here, where they would be safe, even if they would also be lonely. It wasn't like I needed them to detect sleepwalkers for me anymore. My pheromones had evolved. I could detect the sleepwalkers for myself.

I sat on the truck's back bumper, watching the sky and wishing we were already in motion. The waiting was killing me. Sherman wasn't waiting. Whatever he was going to do to our people, he had probably already started. Maybe he hadn't realized yet how special Juniper was; maybe he thought Dr. Cale had just decided to implant one of her babies in an actual baby and see what happened. But Sherman was smart, and if he didn't know already, he was going to figure it out. He *had* to figure it out. Once that happened…

The clock was ticking, and we needed to move.

There was just one problem: We were the good guys. We were the ones who were still trying to hold on to empathy and compassion—things that it would be easier to call "humanity," but I had them too, and I wasn't human. Sherman could roll in and roll out like a hurricane, destroying whatever happened to be standing in his way. Colonel Mitchell could run the world like it was an extension of his army, letting everything be sacrificed in the name of a "greater good" that many would never live to see. Even Dr. Banks had his excuses. He'd never cared about anyone but himself, so why should he start now?

We couldn't do that. If we wanted to hold on to the only things that made us better than they were, we *had* to take the time to say good-bye to our people, no matter how much I wanted to be moving. We *had* to remember that everyone mattered. That was going to keep us from losing sight of ourselves.

But oh, how I wanted to move.

Fishy walked into my frame of view, boosting himself up onto the truck's bumper next to me. "Fang and Heina are almost done," he said. "I'm driving. Will you ride up front with me? I know you're not super big into cars and all that, but you're the only one who's actually been to USAMRIID before. I figure you can give me directions."

"They might also be less likely to shoot first and ask questions later if they see me in the front seat with you," I said.

"So very, very true," said Fishy amiably. "Fang can monitor all the beeping things in the back. He's good at that. Way better than I am. I'm an engineer, not a neurosurgeon."

"Yeah," I said. I hesitated and then asked, "Fishy? Do you think we're doing the right thing?"

"Honestly, Sal, I think 'the right thing' sort of fell by the wayside when the cities started burning," said Fishy. He looked morosely out over the parking lot. His eyes fell on one of the corpses, and he flinched, looking away. "At this point, we're doing the best that we can. USAMRIID has bigger guns and better resources. If we get them on our side, we'll be in a much better position to take on Sherman. If we can't, we'll figure something out."

"It's not that easy," I said.

Fishy smiled and nudged me with his elbow. "Sure it is. You managed to get away from them twice, right? Three times, if we count that horrifying story Dr. Cale tells about you and your sister and the Colonel back before shit got real. We'll just follow you, and you'll know what to do."

I wasn't so sure. I didn't want to disillusion him when we were already getting ready to march into danger. So I just smiled thinly and didn't say anything.

Fang came walking around the corner of the truck. "Heina has gone to wake the others and start her work. We should go, if we don't want to be stuck here while we explain everything again."

I slid down off the bumper. "Let's get moving."

"Yes," said Fang, swinging himself up into the truck and moving toward the back to check on Tansy. "Let's."

He was bending over her cot when Fishy pulled the truck's door down, and cut Fang off from view. Together, Fishy and I walked around to the cab, and climbed in. I fastened my seat belt. Fishy didn't. Maybe believing that life was a video game made personal safety seem less important.

I watched out the window as we drove out of the parking lot and back onto Willow Pass Road. No one watched us go.

No one but the dead.

Sherman and his people had taken advantage of the relatively clear road outside the bowling alley to make their approach. They would have needed to move very little aside in the way of blockages: While Dr. Cale's people had worked to keep the area looking realistically deserted, they had also needed to rearrange the crashes and abandoned vehicles to make it possible for supply runs and scavenging parties to move freely. We were using those same streets now, following them back to 1-4. We didn't dare clear a new route. Like the bodies outside the bowling alley, the unmoved vehicles littering the streets would make it seem like we had never passed through here.

Fishy took it slow, moving around the blockages and swerving to avoid spills, all while trying to keep the ride steady enough that it wouldn't jostle Tansy and Fang more than absolutely necessary. I admired the artistry of it all, even as I tried to focus on the drums pounding in my ears, forbidding myself to listen to the small, gnawing voice of my own panic. I had no reason to be afraid of riding in cars. There was no traffic to contend with. There was no way Fishy was going to lose control of the truck. All I had to fear was fear itself, and honestly, I didn't have time for that.

"I miss the radio," said Fishy after taking a quick scan through the available frequencies and confirming that everything was off the air. "I used to have this old junker I inherited from my dad. It was a piece of rust that drove like a car, you know? Actual ferrous frame, weighted like a personal tank. It had a CD player instead of a proper satellite radio hookup. Man, I hated that thing. If I wanted music, I either had to play it through my phone or remember to grab a bunch of actual discs before I got in the car. I guess the joke's on me, though. I'd kill for a CD player now."

I didn't even know what a CD player was. I stayed quiet.

"It's weird how technology changes everything, isn't it?" Fishy drove around an overturned semi. "Once, there were CD players everywhere. Before that it was tape decks, and before that it was these weird things called eight-tracks that looked like video game cartridges from the eighties and only held like two songs. But every time, it was a revolution. More control, more content, more choices. And now here we are, back to silence, because we got rid of all the physical media and then we lost the radio."

"I don't know what you're talking about," I admitted.

"That's cool," said Fishy. He smiled, and there was something terribly sad about the expression, like he had always known that he was speaking into the void. "Sometimes I just talk so I'll know I still exist, you know?"

"That, I know," I said quietly.

The landscape outside the truck windows was oddly blasted. It had been a low-rain year—normal enough, although according to the Mitchells, California used to experience heavy rains during December and January, back when we were the greatest produce supplier in the United States. The climate had shifted since then, enough that rain was rare and fires were common. Enough that the brown, dry hills around us didn't seem so unusual, although they were more overgrown than they used to be, thanks to the relative absence of cows. Oh, there were a few here and there, dotted around the hills like bruises on a banana. Horses were more plentiful. They were smarter, and didn't have the same milking requirements. Even more important, they were better at getting out of their stalls.

In a similar vein, goats were more common than sheep, and cats were more common than dogs. Birds of prey roosted atop telephone poles, watching us pass with their cold avian eyes.

They wouldn't care if we never managed to resolve this conflict. Sherman could kill us all, and the hawks and falcons and crows would inherit everything.

"Sorry, birdie, but we're not ready for that," I muttered as we rolled under yet another red-tailed hawk. Fishy shot me a faintly confused look, but didn't say anything. I suppose he was so accustomed to being the one who didn't make sense that he was willing to let me take a turn.

"The freeways are open this way, you said?" he asked.

"They should be, unless things have changed since Carrie and I got out of the Coliseum," I said. "Did anyone see which direction Sherman's people came from? I wouldn't put it past them to have collapsed some wrecks over their path, just for cover." In this context, "anyone" could only mean Fang, since Fishy and I had both been inside the Kmart when everything went wrong.

Fishy shook his head. "Not enough survivors, and there wasn't time to check the security footage. You think we're going to catch up to them?"

"No. They'd have to be holed up in Albany or Emeryville if they drove down this road to reach us, and neither of those has anything like the big abandoned mall Sherman was using as his headquarters. I'm almost positive." Almost wasn't good enough—had stopped being good enough before I was engineered in the SymboGen lab that made me—but it was all we had left, and I was clinging to it as tightly as I could.

Besides, Sherman was *smart*. Smart enough to know that Dr. Cale, when driven out of Vallejo, would have gone back to familiar ground; smart enough to check the bowling alley. He had been smart enough to build an army of chimera under everyone's noses. He must have hid the disappearances in an untold number of counties, burying the Missing Person alerts in a dozen local news reports. He wouldn't have stayed in a hideout that was equidistant between his creator and his enemies at USAMRIID. There was too much chance that one day Dr. Cale would go too far and bring the Army down on her head, and he wouldn't have wanted to be in the path of that.

We drove amongst untouched hills, under the watchful eyes of hawks. For maybe the first time since this freeway was built, there was no roadkill anywhere; the pavement was free of blood. Cars sat on the shoulder, and glass glittered on the blacktop, but as far as the natural world was concerned, the age of man was over. It had come to an end when the last raccoon was struck by a car's bumper, when the last deer was left to rot on the median.

Speaking of deer…a whole family raised their heads from cropping the grass by the side of the road, watching us go by. I had seen deer before, but never so many of them, and never so bold. I pressed my face against the glass and watched them until they were out of sight. None of them jumped into the road. We killed nothing, destroyed nothing, as we sailed down the black ribbon of the highway and into the devouring distance.

Clayton dropped far behind us, a forgotten dream of a place where we'd been happy, for a time; where we'd allowed ourselves to feel like we were safe. Other cities followed, until we were moving through the thicker traffic on the approach to Oakland. It wasn't quite gridlock: There was space between the abandoned cars for Fishy to maneuver the truck, as long as he took it slow and didn't worry about scratching the paint. We had just squeezed through an opening between two electric cars when I realized that I hadn't felt the need to drop down into the hot warm dark once during this drive. I was getting better, or at least I was learning to swallow my fear more efficiently, leaving myself capable of riding in a motor vehicle without hyperventilating.

I guess after you've been in a car that was intentionally

driven into the ocean, and raced the sunset to find your way home, normal vehicular transportation loses some of its sting.

The shape of the Oakland Coliseum loomed up ahead and to our left. Fishy looked toward me, eyebrows raised.

"Well?" he asked. "How do you want to play this?"

I took a deep breath. "Follow my lead," I said.

We pulled up to the gate that blocked the Coliseum parking lots from the road. It was manned by four men in fatigues, each of them holding an assault rifle. My stomach unclenched when I realized that none of them had a cattle prod. This was going to be much easier if I wasn't living in fear of being separated from myself.

One of them walked to Fishy's window and rapped on it with his knuckles. Fishy obligingly rolled the window down, smiling his customary, toothy smile at the officer.

"Afternoon," he said. "I guess maybe it's technically evening? Sun looks like it should be going down any minute. How strict are we being with the day divisions now that most of the clocks are toast?"

"Sir, this is a restricted area," said the officer. "We're going to have to ask you to turn around."

"Sorry, no can do. I'm here on a mission of medical mercy, and turning around would sort of go against the whole purpose of driving here. Besides, aren't you supposed to be rounding up survivors like me and making sure that we're comfortable in quarantine, not being snacked on by tapeworm-zombies all the damn time?"

The officer looked uneasy. That was the first inkling I had that things had gotten worse in Pleasanton after Paul's death: that we might, in fact, have lost the entire quarantine zone.

I leaned forward, tucking my hair back behind my ears so that the officer who was talking to Fishy could see my face. Sally had always taken after her father: Her features were Colonel Mitchell's, softened by genetics and estrogen into the face of a reasonably pretty woman. Now they were my features, and I was going to put them to good use.

"Hi," I said. The officer went very still. "Can you tell my father that I'm back?"

Sherman has finally proven himself to be my son in truth as well as by circumstance of birth: He has taken us all. His people killed several of mine, and I will not forget that fact, no matter how hard he may try to convince me that it was an accident, no matter how much effort he may be willing to put into the idea that somehow, he can convince me to become a convert to his cause. He would have me become the monster that they have made of me, and he doesn't understand why I wouldn't want that.

I know you're going to read this, Sherman. I know I have no hope of privacy, and that you'll kill me before you let me go free. I also know that you will read what I have written in hopes of uncovering my secrets, while you would never listen as I said these things to you. My beautiful, clever, flawed boy.

You are my son, in every way that matters. I bought the body you now wear from its human wife, who couldn't afford the medical bills. I cultivated the core of you in petri dish and agar, choosing the best genes, the best chances for survival. And maybe, in the end, I put too much of myself in you.

Sherman, my weakness has always been a lack of empathy. Whatever guides the mentality and emotions of normal humans was left out in making me, and I have had to live my entire life measuring myself against the people around me, which is why I have striven to be surrounded by those of high empathy and higher morals.

If I am surrounded only by you, what horrors will I unleash? Please, son, if you don't care about the human world, care about me. Don't make me into what you need me to be.

Let me go. Let your brothers go.

Live.

—FROM THE NOTES OF DR. SHANTI CALE, JANUARY 2028

I did nothing to deserve this. I was a good wife. I was a better mother. I raised my girls with a sense of right and wrong, and if Sally was a little wild and Joyce was a daddy's girl, well, that was all right. They were still my children, and I loved them more than anything. Loving them was all that I was meant to do. Being a mother was everything I had ever wanted in my life. I could have been a mother forever.

I am still a mother. My body remembers the little girls it made, shaping them one bone at a time in the safe haven of my womb. My arms remember the babies that they held. I will always, always be a mother. But now my babies are dead, and I don't know what I'm going to do without them. Alfred tries to tell me that there's a chance for Joyce, but I'm too smart for that lie. I wish I weren't. It would be easier on both of us if I could make myself believe him. But I can't.

What is a mother who has buried both her daughters? What, if not alive too long?

—FROM THE DIARY OF GAIL MITCHELL, JANUARY 2028

Chapter 15

JANUARY 2028

The soldiers at the gate had walked with the truck as they led us to the front of the Coliseum. They had looked surprised and only a little confused when Fishy led them to the back and opened the door to reveal Fang, bent over Tansy's unmoving form and checking the connections on her ventilator. It must have been an odd sight, from their perspective: an unmoving woman with a shaven head, lying unconscious on a gurney, while a man in a white coat worked to make sure that she was still breathing.

Then Fang had straightened, and turned, and said—in his most polite, most congenial tone—"I suppose you'd like me to move away from the equipment now. Is one of you a trained medical professional? If not, is there any way I could convince you to let me keep working until we have my patient inside and stable? It's not that I don't trust you, it's just that we've brought her this far, and we'd rather not lose her now."

The soldiers hadn't known what to say. Dr. Cale's people tended to have that effect.

Their leader had taken custody of me. I wasn't making any effort to run away. I hadn't strayed from his side since he'd pulled me out of the cab, wrapping his vast hand around my upper arm so that I felt small next to him, reduced to the child I had never been. We stood some feet away, watching as his men—still puzzled, and somehow taking orders from Fang, however temporarily—helped Fishy and Fang get Tansy's gurney down from the back of the truck.

"I never thought we'd be seeing you again," said the soldier who was watching me.

I shrugged as best I could with my right arm effectively locked into position. "I wasn't planning on coming back. But we need your help, and I'm pretty sure you need ours too."

"There's nothing you could offer us."

"How long ago did you lose the quarantine zone?"

His hand tightened on my arm, clamping down almost hard enough to become painful, and I knew that I was right. "That's classified."

"It was almost a war zone in there while I was confined. It wouldn't have taken many of those unexpected conversions for things to get really ugly. Did everyone die, or were there riots? Were you able to get anyone out?" I tried not to think about the people I'd known by name while I was there, the ones who'd shared the house with me and Carrie and Paul. The teenage mother, the little girl who'd never had a name...was my desire to let Juniper be nameless until she could name herself partially an attempt to honor that child? I sort of thought it might have been.

The rest of the soldiers walked past, pushing the gurney, Fishy and Fang among them. My companions had been disarmed but not restrained. I wondered how long it would be before anyone noticed that. I wondered whether this was some sort of silent challenge. Let them try to run: They'd just be taken again.

My captor pulled on my arm and started after his companions. We left the truck and walked across what remained of the parking lot, heading for the loading-bay door in the side of the Coliseum wall. It wasn't the door I'd escaped through twice before, thankfully: a building this size had multiple entrances and exits. Four more soldiers flanked the door, guarding it from interlopers. Each of them was holding a cattle prod.

My mouth went dry, and my feet stopped listening to my commands, instead digging into the gravel and trying to bring me to a halt. My captor ignored my stumbling as he dragged me forward, into range of those men.

One of them was my old "friend," Private Larsen. He looked utterly surprised to see me, eyes going wide as the end of his cattle prod dipped toward the ground. I reached down deep and managed to muster a strained smile.

"Hi," I said. "Long time no see."

"What are *you* doing here?" he asked—less a demand and more an exclamation of sheer, confused surprise. "You stole a car! You escaped!"

"And now I'm back," I said. "My friend needs medical assistance, and I need to see your boss."

"Colonel Mitchell is not taking visitors," snapped another of the door guards.

Private Larsen looked toward him, and said, "Don't you know who this *is*? That's Sally Mitchell, man. That's the Colonel's daughter."

"The Colonel's daughter is on life support, you goon."

"That's my little sister, Joyce," I said. My voice was surprisingly steady. I felt like I was channeling my Sally-mode again, but not as a lie: as a way of getting what I needed. It was surprisingly easy, and even more surprisingly comfortable. I didn't have to pretend to be her to use the lessons I'd learned from my time in her shadow. "I'm the older daughter. The bad daughter, the runaway daughter, the one people blame for killing a bunch of soldiers, even though I didn't do that. And right now, I'm the daughter who needs to see her father. So if someone could go and tell him that we're here, that would be awesome."

The three guards who weren't Private Larsen readied their cattle prods, apparently prepared to zap the insolence right out of me. Private Larsen looked to the leader of the group of soldiers who had accompanied us from the gate.

"Sir?" he asked.

The man nodded. "If you would."

"Yes, sir." Private Larsen snapped a quick salute before he turned, cattle prod still lowered, and trotted away down the hall.

The officer in charge snapped, "At ease, men," and the other three guards lowered their weapons. I let out a slow breath, relaxing marginally, only to tense again as he turned to me and said, "You realize you're not escaping for a third time. Once Colonel Mitchell sees you, it's over."

There was a warning in his tone that I couldn't quite make sense of—at least not until I looked over to Fang and Fishy, and saw how open the route back to our truck was behind them. We could still run. For whatever reason, this officer was willing to leave us with an escape route, even as he held on to my arm...but his grip wasn't as tight as it had been, was it? I could probably pull away, if I really tried.

Chave had been one of Dr. Cale's people, embedded in SymboGen and kept in place by a combination of loyalty and the need to know what was coming. She had never been able to let me know who she was. And she had died without breaking cover. I looked harder at the officer, trying to remember whether I'd ever seen him before, either there or in the bowling alley, before things got bad. His face seemed familiar, but I had been a captive here twice already: I could have seen him through a fence, or passing in the hall. There was no way for me to know for sure.

But he was willing to let us run, and somehow, that made me feel all the more certain that we were making the right decision. "It'll be okay," I said, and touched his arm. He didn't pull away. My conviction that he might be one of Dr. Cale's people grew. "I just need to talk to the Colonel."

"Soon would be good," called Fishy. "Tansy's not doing so well."

"What?" My head snapped around. Fang was bending over one of the machines, his expression suddenly much more serious than it had been only a few minutes before. "What's happening?"

"I'll need to run some tests to be sure, but I believe her kidneys have started to fail," said Fang. "This was always going to happen before too much longer. The body is not meant to survive indefinitely under these conditions."

"But she can't die."

Fang looked up. The expression on his face was infinitely sad, and infinitely patient at the same time, like he was trying to convey a lesson he knew I wasn't ready to learn. "We can all die, Sal. The last few months should have taught you that, even if they've taught you nothing else. We can all, no matter how clever, no matter how beloved, die."

Private Larsen reappeared before I could answer. "The Colonel says we're to escort them in," he said stiffly.

"You heard the man," said the officer. "Move."

Fang and Fishy pushed Tansy on her gurney, and I stayed close to the commanding officer—as far away as I could be from those menacing cattle prods—and we moved onward, back into the belly of the beast.

*   *   *

Our escort saw us to one of the larger interrogation rooms and left us there, locking the door behind themselves. Under the circumstances, it was something of a relief. Fang and Fishy connected Tansy's monitors to the wall outlets, sparing the portable generator from a little of the drain, and got to work stabilizing her.

There was a table, and chairs, but I didn't feel like sitting—not after the day we'd had, and not with the specter of my father hovering over us like a knife about to fall. I stalked back and forth in front of the shoddily installed two-way mirror, wondering whether there was anyone on the other side, wondering equally whether the joints with the wall would stand up to a little battering. I knew how hard the glass was to break, but I was willing to bet the wood would give way if I hit it hard enough with a folding chair. Then I could see the people who were no doubt on the other side, monitoring us.

Of course, then they would *know* that I was dangerous, and would be able to justify anything they did to me—to us—as self-defense. I couldn't risk it. I left the chairs where they were and continued to pace, shooting sour looks at the glass and waiting for the door to open.

Colonel Mitchell's sense of dramatic timing hadn't gotten any worse while I'd been away. As soon as Tansy's monitors were all beeping steadily and without alarms, the door opened, and he stepped into the room. I stopped pacing, turning to face him.

He was still a mountain of a man, broad-shouldered and thick-armed and built like a monument to the idea of humanity overcoming the world. His hair was grayer than it had been before my escape, like he had managed to age years in just a few weeks. Soon, there wouldn't be anything left *but* the gray. There were deep lines around his eyes. Those, too, had spread since my departure. He stopped in the doorway and just looked at me. That was all. That was all he needed to do. There was a depth of loss and longing and betrayal in his eyes that said more than words could ever manage.

This was it: This was the moment where we had to choose whether we were telling him the truth or continuing to lie, continuing the petty fiction that Dr. Banks had created to save his own skin. I took a step forward.

"I'm not Sally," I said quietly. "I never was. I'm sorry I lied to you about that: I did it to save some people who were very important to me, and I would probably do it again if I had to, but that doesn't make it right. I do think it makes us even, don't you? You lied to me about who I was, and then I lied to you about who I was, and now the scales are balanced. We can start from equal ground."

Colonel Mitchell didn't say anything. He just dipped his chin, very slightly. That was all the acknowledgment I was going to get.

I took a breath. "You understand why I ran before."

"I do." His voice was, if anything, even more revealing than his eyes. He sounded exhausted, beaten down almost to the point of breaking. This was a man who'd seen every inch of protection he thought he possessed pulled away, and was doing his best to hold the line despite it all. He was a good man, who'd been forced to make some bad decisions, first to protect his family and then to protect what he saw as the world. He had just been put into the position of so many good men before him: the place where there were no good options left, only the ones that did a little less damage than the rest.

"These are my colleagues—my *friends*. Fishy and Fang." I realized I didn't know their last names. I also realized that it didn't matter anymore. They had their dingy, tattered lab coats and their willingness to work: Everything else was secondary. "The girl on the gurney is my sister, Tansy Cale."

Was it my imagination, or did he flinch at the word "sister"?

"I don't understand why you brought her here," he said. "Surely the medical care wherever you were hiding was sufficient to keep her alive."

"It was, before some dick-wad decided to come in and trash the place and shoot a bunch of our people," said Fishy, looking up from Tansy's monitors. "That's why we're here."

Right: It was time to stop beating around the bush. "Sherman Lewis, who was responsible for my first escape, and for the deaths of your people, found Dr. Cale's lab. He raided it this morning. He got away with basically everything. All our people, all our research. Nathan. He took Nathan, and we have to get him back, because Nathan doesn't have an implant, and Sherman doesn't think humans have any place left in this world."

Sherman would see Nathan as just one more host body waiting for a new owner. I loved my fellow chimera, I *loved* them, but could I ever forgive the worm that took Nathan away from me? Would I ever be able to make the jump from loathing to love? I didn't think so...and just like that, I forgave Sally's mother for rejecting me. It was all well and good to think of a chimera as just a new occupant in an abandoned home, and in my case, that was true: I had taken over when Sally left. But she didn't really know that, did she? That was never going to be something she could accept, just like I was never going to be able to accept someone else driving Nathan around like his body's original owner didn't matter.

It made what I had to ask next even more difficult. I took a deep breath, and forced myself to continue anyway. Tansy's life depended on it. "Sherman is responsible for the contamination of the water supply. I have some ideas about how we could maybe fix that, but we're going to need to work together. We brought copies of the data we were able to salvage. Fang is one of the best neurosurgeons I've ever met, and he's been with Dr. Cale for years. He can explain things to your scientists."

"That doesn't explain why you brought the girl," said Colonel Mitchell.

No, it didn't. I took another breath. Then I paused, and looked at him. "I would have been your daughter, if you'd allowed me to be myself," I said. "Adoption is as important as biology. I tried so hard to be who you wanted me to be. I broke myself trying to become your little girl. All you ever had to do was say, 'You are a stranger, and I love you,' and I would have been yours forever. You know that, don't you? I never wanted us to be on opposite sides."

Colonel Mitchell glanced at the mirror. We were definitely being watched, then, and if the people on the other side of the glass hadn't known about what I was before, they knew now.

Too late to take it back. "Your friend, Dr. Banks? He captured Tansy when she came to get me out of SymboGen. He took her apart. He pulled out parts of her brain, and I think you knew, because he was trying to make a chimera to show you. One of those 'perfect soldiers' he talked about. He broke my sister. He thought she'd be more useful in pieces, and he broke her. He broke both my sisters. He was the one who designed my implant, wasn't he? He designed *me*. That's why there's no record in their systems. You paid him to delete all the traces that I was anything other than the standard, to keep your secrets, and he did it. He wanted something he could hold over you."

Silence.

"He designed Joyce's implant too, didn't he? There's no way he'd want a hold over one Mitchell girl when he could have a hold over both of them. He could have told you to yank her implant the day I opened my eyes in Sally's body, but he didn't. He killed her. He took one sister apart, and he killed the other one, and you still kept working with him, because he had the better PR."

"What do you want from me, Sal?" asked Colonel Mitchell.

Any joy I might have felt at hearing him use the proper name for me, hearing him use *my* name, died when I processed the weariness in his tone. His shoulders were even more bowed now than they had been when he first came into the room. I didn't know how much more he could take before he broke, but wherever that line was, we were approaching it more rapidly than I cared to consider. "I can't undo what's already been done."

"No, but you can help us set at least one piece of this right. You can undo a little of the damage you've enabled." I looked him squarely in the eye. "Is Joyce's body still on life support?"

Colonel Mitchell went perfectly still.

He must have known what I was working up to—I hadn't been exactly subtle, and I'd conflated Joyce and Tansy several times in the lead-up to my question—but actually hearing the words seemed to cause him physical pain. He closed his eyes. Everything was silence, save for the beeping of the machines that were keeping Tansy alive.

Then he opened them again. "Yes, she is still on life support, and no, I will not hear what you are going to ask me next. This conversation is over."

"Joyce's life is over," I said. I tried to make the words as gentle as possible, but they still fell into the space between us like stones. "She's dead. She died. And I know she was an organ donor. We talked about it, when we talked about my...about Sally's accident. How afraid she'd been that you'd keep Sally on life support until her organs failed. How much she'd loved her sister, and how much she'd wanted her sister's death to *mean* something. I know she had the same conversations with you."

Colonel Mitchell didn't say anything. But he didn't leave the room, and he didn't close his eyes again, and under the circumstances, that was about as much as I could have hoped for.

"We don't need a kidney or a lobe of her liver. We need *her*, intact and breathing, because Tansy is dying. Please. Let us save Tansy. Let us give Joyce the meaning she wanted. She used to say that the accident was the best thing that had ever happened to me—and she was working with you that whole time." I paused. The words made sense. I had said them to myself before, but now, hearing them aloud…almost wonderingly, I asked, "She knew, didn't she? She knew I wasn't Sally, and she loved me anyway."

"Sally was always cruel to her little sister." The words were halting, pulled from Colonel Mitchell's mouth one at a time. "She didn't understand why we'd want a second child when we had *her*, and she couldn't forgive Joyce for taking up space that should have been hers. Joyce loved her, wanted to be friends, but Sally wouldn't have anything to do with her unless it was because she was planning to cut Joyce down somehow. Joyce knew even before I told her. There was no way any version of Sally could have learnt how to be kind."

"She loved me anyway," I said. "She said the accident was a good thing. You know she would have agreed to this, if she'd been here."

"If she were here, we wouldn't have to *do* this," said Colonel Mitchell.

I nodded. "True. If she were here, we would have stayed away, because there was no way we'd ask this if there were any way to save her. She's gone. She left her body behind. Please. Please, let us save my sister."

"You think her mother—you think *your* mother—will forgive me if I turn another of her daughters into a monster?" Colonel Mitchell's head swung from side to side. It seemed to have become an impossible burden, too heavy for him to lift without an effort. "She gave birth to that body you wear so familiarly. Whether you like it or not, she is your parent."

"I want to like it," I said. "I remember loving her. I remember loving *you*. Before you both started treating me like an invader, like I'd done something wrong. I didn't hurt your daughter,

Colonel. I didn't take her body until she left it behind, and I always did my best to be a good girl for you. I loved you. I loved my whole family. You rejected me first."

"You were never ours," he said.

I didn't say anything. I just looked at him, and waited for him to pass judgment on whether my sister—both my sisters— would live or die.

"We never let you be ours," he said, after a long pause. "What will you give me for my daughter's body?"

"Fishy, I need the hard drive," I said.

"On it." He moved away from Tansy and Fang, pulling up his shirt to reveal a block of synthetic skin. He peeled it away. There was a small black rectangle taped to his side. The guards had missed it when they searched him; the synth-skin had confused the issue. Pulling the rectangle loose, he held it up for Colonel Mitchell to see before pressing it into my hand. "Nice to finally meet you, Colonel. I've heard a lot about you. Sure, most of it was pretty awful, but it's still nice to put a face with a name."

"I've heard absolutely nothing about you, Mr.…?"

"Fishy," said Fishy, with evident delight. "If you'd heard of me, you'd be proof of bad AI. So hey, score one for the dev team." Then he turned and walked back to Tansy's side, leaving Colonel Mitchell staring after him.

"Fishy has that effect on people," I said, pulling the Colonel's attention back to me. I held up the hard drive. His eyes locked on it. "Sherman's people took most of the research, but we managed to save enough. Enough to get started. When he took me from your holding cells, it was so he could extract my DNA and use it to make a worm that would be able to interface with the human brain without surgical assistance. He was trying to destroy the human race. He's managed to destroy a lot of the sleepwalkers in the process. But it means that all the worms currently in the water share a single genetic source. We can tailor antiparasitic drugs to kill them without poisoning the water for everybody else. We can fix this."

I paused, taking a breath and gauging his reaction. It hurt to admit that Sherman had used me to make his perfect weapon, even though I had nothing to do with the creation of those tiny, uncaring clones. My epigenetic data was not included; they would never mature into me. But still, I should have found a way to stop him.

Colonel Mitchell frowned. "Are you telling us everything?"

"All the data's here," I said, giving the hard drive a shake. "Everything we were able to save. Dr. Banks and your people should be able to start work on a counter almost immediately. All we're asking is that you let us take something you don't need anymore, so that we can save one of our own."

"Well, that, and we were rather hoping you would help us track down and destroy Sherman's encampment," said Fang, looking up from the monitors. "He's a danger. He needs to be stopped. We're not going to accomplish this on our own."

"Joyce is not 'something we don't even need anymore,'" said Colonel Mitchell, and there was no mistaking the bitterness in his tone. "She is my *daughter*."

"She's gone," I said. "If she's still your daughter, then so am I. Don't you think we'll be happier together? There's this thing Dr. Cale calls 'epigenetic data.' It's sort of like…genetic memory. Maybe I am who I am because Sally's DNA told me who to be. So I'm still a little bit her, even if I mostly never could have been. We put Tansy in Joyce's head…maybe we get a Tansy who's a little bit Joyce. Isn't that better than losing her completely? Forever?"

"I could take your data and lock you up for treason," he said. "You say you didn't kill anyone. You have no proof."

"You know me," I said. "That's your proof. The only lies I ever told were the ones you taught to me."

He looked at me for a moment, eyes running over my face

like he was trying to unlock something he couldn't quite define. Then he turned and walked away, moving toward Tansy.

She hadn't opened her eyes since we'd recovered her from Dr. Banks. A cloth covered her skull, concealing the ugly sutures and missing skin. She looked like a coma patient, which was a reasonably accurate impression: She was never going to wake up again, not in that body. She also looked frail, and defenseless—two things I'd never associated with Tansy before Dr. Banks took her away from us.

"Will she be kind to my little girl's body?" he asked, directing his question to Fang. "Is she a good person?"

Fang smiled at the word "person," like he hadn't been sure he would ever hear it in conjunction with Tansy—at least not from this source. "She's a spitfire and a half," he said. "Always running for the hills and shouting when they don't come to meet her. She loves her mother, and her brother, and her sister. She was the one who wanted us to contact Sal long before we did, because she didn't think it was right for family to live apart. She can be passionate about the things she believes. She's not perfect, not by a long shot, but she's ours, and we love her."

"Will she be kind?"

"If you'll forgive me for saying so, sir, she'll be kinder than you're being right now. She'll let your daughter's body live again. Maybe not in the same way. Maybe not as the same girl. But *alive*." Fang's expression turned grave. "Isn't that what a father wants?"

"Have you ever been a father?" asked the Colonel, voice hard.

"Once. But that was a long time ago, on the other side of the world, and all my restless dead have been mercifully buried."

Colonel Mitchell looked at Fang for a moment longer. Then he reached over and gently touched Tansy's cheek. She must have been cold. She looked so cold.

"Private Larsen," said the Colonel without raising his voice.

"Contact Dr. Caldwell. Tell her to prepare an operating room. We're going to be performing surgery today."

They wheeled in Joyce's body on a gurney so much like the one Tansy was on that it hurt a little: the symmetry, and the knowledge that the symmetry was about to become even stronger.

The Coliseum hadn't been designed to serve as a hospital. It was meant for sporting events and concerts, not sterile procedures and surgical interventions. Everything USAMRIID had done to it since moving in had been makeshift, retrofit on top of retrofit, as they tried to twist it to suit their needs. That was why our "observation window" was tight-stretched clear plastic, of the same material as the quarantine bubbles. That was why the operating room walls were white sheets, and why the air flow was controlled by plastic sheeting. But somehow none of that seemed terribly important anymore, because there was my sister.

Joyce looked better than Tansy. She looked like she was just sleeping, with a respirator in her nose and tubes running from her arms to the IVs that the keepers rolled in with her. Tansy was already in place, already scrubbed down and sterilized.

Then one of the white coated men took the kerchief off Joyce's head, revealing her freshly shaven skull, and I knew that Joyce wasn't sleeping. Joyce had been gone for a long time. If there had been anything left of her, she would have woken up as soon as they started to cut her hair.

I started to cover my eyes and turn away. Colonel Mitchell's hand clamped down over my wrist, startling me. I lowered my hand, looking at him in confusion.

"You have to watch," he said. "This is on you as much as it is on me, and you have to watch."

"I don't want to," I whispered.

"It doesn't matter. We pay our debts in this family, Sal. We look at the things we have built, and we acknowledge them for what they are. That means you look. That means you watch. That means you understand."

"I don't want to," I repeated.

"Neither do I," he said, and we both turned to the window.

Transplanting an implant into a human host was a fairly straightforward procedure, according to Fang. If the implant was tissue-compatible with the host body, then rejection and infection were both extremely unlikely. There was some necessary movement of brain tissue, but nothing needed to be removed save for a small piece of skull. The rest was easy, if anything about neurosurgery could ever be considered "easy."

I knew more about medicine than I'd ever believed possible, thanks to the time I'd spent with Dr. Cale and her people, but even that wasn't enough to make the scene on the other side of the window make sense to me. The first thing they did was the tissue typing: They had explained in detail how that would work. First they took a sample from Joyce, and then they took a sample from Tansy's host body. When they confirmed that the bodies had similar blood types and antigen responses, they moved on to opening the back of Tansy's skull and exposing the shattered remains of her implant. I looked away at that, and Colonel Mitchell didn't stop me. He had already seen what I had seen: brain tissue that looked like it had been churned up with a heavy hand, and pale loops of tapeworm poking through it in disarray, nothing like the symmetry I saw when I looked at my own MRIs, or Juniper's.

We were supposed to live comfortably within our hosts, not be used to destroy them once harmony had been achieved. I shuddered, forcing my panicked nerves back under control, and turned in time to see the response panels testing Joyce's genetic compatibility with Tansy—the *real* Tansy, not the lost, lamented host—turn from neutral red to compatible yellow. My sisters were compatible with each other. They could coexist.

They could share space, and they could both live, in their way, although each would have lost something precious forever.

One of the USAMRIID scientists held up a hand, signaling the rest of the room to stop what they were doing. They all did, even Fishy and Fang, as he turned to face the window. He looked at the Colonel, eyes grave behind his goggles, and waited.

"Please," I whispered.

The Colonel closed his eyes and raised his hand in a thumbs-up. The procedure was approved.

They did not pull a curtain across their makeshift surgical theater: They left everything open and exposed for the world to see. I had already looked away once. I would not look away again. Colonel Mitchell was right. I owed them that.

Bit by bit, Fang extracted Tansy from the brainpan of her host, picking her free of the jumbled brain tissue an inch at a time, until the entire damaged length of her was visible. He sliced a piece of the host's original brain loose along with her head, allowing her to keep her floral mouth clamped down on what she mindlessly believed to be a source of nutrition. The gender label was inaccurate at that point, I suppose—Tansy was no longer a "she," not without the shell of her host to give her definition. But Ronnie had always been male, even when he was moved into a female body. I couldn't make myself stop thinking of her as my sister, my *sister*, and to be honest, I didn't want to. Only the labels were allowing me to look at the slick, pinkish-gray length of her with anything other than pity. She was so damaged. Dr. Banks had used her so cruelly.

That's what you are too, I thought, and my stomach churned acid-hot and nauseous. I was a length of boneless tissue, somehow enhanced by science to the point where it could hijack an entire human body and make it my own. I was not a human being.

But the brain tissue left behind when Tansy was removed

from her host's brain didn't look so different from Tansy herself, did it? It was soft and boneless and pinkish gray, without structure or form. She had fit into it so well because she was virtually the same thing. Maybe we had never been that different. Science hadn't created monsters. It had just given brains the capacity to move from one body to another, to feed without dependence on the host, to masticate and chew, to *live*. We were made to live. We were survivors.

"Come on, Tansy," I whispered. Colonel Mitchell shot me a surprised look, but all my attention was on the delicate surgery being performed on the counter behind Joyce's comatose form. Fishy had covered Tansy's host with a sheet; life support was ongoing, but that was more a matter of their not wanting to share the room with a corpse before they had to than it was anything else. Tansy was no longer a resident in that hollow shell, and the original owner, whoever she had been, had moved out years before.

Fang had stretched Tansy out in a Pyrex baking dish filled with agar solution, and was now carefully, delicately excising her segments from each other, bisecting them one at a time and moving them to different quadrants of the comforting jelly. Most would be frozen, assuming we could find a freezer that we were allowed to use; only the primary segment, that beautiful, terrible flower, would be placed inside Joyce's unused brain. The rest were backups at best, and egg factories at worst—if we lost Tansy completely, Fang could culture a new head segment from her eggs, effectively cloning her. But I didn't know how much of Tansy would carry over into that second generation, how much epigenetic data would be passed down, parent unto child, so that she could live again.

I was almost sure, watching him work, watching how much care he took and how deep the furrows in his forehead had grown, that it wouldn't be enough.

Then he finished his work on Tansy, and turned away from the agar, and picked up the bone saw.

Colonel Mitchell's hand clamped down on my shoulder, pressing so hard that I winced, although I didn't pull away. He was allowing us to do this. He had granted us access to his daughter, against all better judgment, against all reason, because he wanted his daughters to be together, even if we had to be together as new people. His marriage was probably over. Mom—Gail—was going to leave him when she realized what he'd done. Slow understanding wormed through me, replacing the acid in my belly with wonder.

He'd given up any chance of saving his marriage because he wanted to make up for his actions toward me. He was giving me back my sister, both my sisters, because I mattered that much to him. I turned, looking up at his face as the bone saw bit into Joyce's skull. He was watching Fang work, and while there were tears in his eyes, they weren't falling. Not yet. Because he wasn't watching his daughter die: he was watching the world give her another chance at survival.

"Thank you, Daddy," I whispered, turning back toward the window. Fang had removed a small square of bone from the back of Joyce's head. I couldn't see her exposed brain from where we were standing, but I didn't need to. Brains, as a rule, look basically the same from person to person—incredibly unique and utterly individual in the eyes of a neurosurgeon maybe, but to me still just slabs of pink-gray fatty matter, shot through with veins and furrowed with deep canals.

Fang reached into Joyce's brain with forceps and scalpel. He worked in silence for almost a minute before he called, "Fishy, the sample."

Fishy picked up Tansy's primary segment with a pair of forceps and carried it gently over to place them in Fang's waiting hand. I thought I saw Tansy thrash, once, and I clung to that motion, because it meant she was still alive. Then Fang was lowering her into the opening at the back of Joyce's skull, and if Colonel Mitchell was going to call this procedure off, he was going to do it now, he would have to do it now, he wouldn't have another chance—

His hand remained clamped hard on my shoulder, hard enough that it was going to leave a bruise, but he didn't say a word. He didn't ask Fang to stop. He just let it happen.

Colonel Mitchell was crying, big, wet tears that rolled silently down his face, as he watched Fang close up the surgical site and suture Joyce's skin back down. There would be some scarring, unfortunately; the facility just wasn't equipped with the sort of stimulating lasers he would have needed to close her wounds without leaving any sign that they'd been there. But maybe that was for the best. Maybe this was the sort of thing that had to be remembered, just so you could believe that it was real.

I was crying, too, but unlike the Colonel, there was no grief in my tears. I had cried myself dry over Joyce enough: I knew that she was gone. Until this moment, I hadn't allowed myself to really believe that Tansy could still be saved, that *Tansy* might make it back to the broken doors, and hence back home to us.

There was still hope in the world, and the proof of it was on the stretcher in front of me, being hooked back up to the machines that would keep her breathing until the integration was complete. Tansy was going to live again.

Now we just had to find a way to say the same about the world.

INTERLUDE III: SPANDREL

*I am proud of all my children. I just feel I did a better
job with some than others.*

—DR. SHANTI CALE

*There are some things you can't forgive.
No matter how much you want to.*

—GAIL MITCHELL

January 2028: Sherman

Sherman? Your mother is asking for you."
  I turned toward Batya, irritation gathering in my chest, and opened my mouth to chastise her. Then I paused, catching myself. She was right. Dr. Cale was my mother, no matter how long we had been estranged, or how much it sometimes pained me to consider that I, Sherman Lewis, conqueror of the known world, existed only because of her dedication to science and her insistence on following her experiments to their logical conclusion. I might not have been the result of a sweaty night of bodies rubbing against bodies, but I was her child all the same. It was, perhaps, time for me to acknowledge that, to even embrace it—because if I accepted her as she had already accepted me, things might go easier for all of us.

  "How is she?" I asked. The question came easy, because the question was honest. If she was hunger-striking or ill, I would have more difficulty dealing with her. I had never been able to handle it well when she was sick.

  "She's amazing," said Batya, and her voice was filled with shy, starstruck wonder. Of the chimera in my camp, I was the only one who'd worked directly with our creator. She made me with her own two hands, and I had taken the knowledge of my creation and used it to create children of my own. But it was hard for them not to look at Dr. Cale like she was some sort of fallen god. She was our creator. How could they not love her?

If they had known her as I had known her, it would have been easy. She had never been a loving mother, not to me: not when she had her precious Adam right there, so apparently flawless, and born of her body in a way that none of the rest of us could ever match. He had broken her, *crippled* her, and she doted on him for his innocent crimes, because how could he have known?

I shook myself out of the memory and plastered a smile across my face, trying to look reassuring, for Batya's sake. She didn't know Dr. Cale as I did, and Mother had always responded better to worship than she did to insolence. Let Batya have her delusions. Maybe they would find a way to serve us.

"I'll be right there," I said. "I just need to finish setting up this simulation."

Batya nodded, but she didn't leave, lingering in my doorway like a moth clinging to a light. I frowned.

"Was there something else?" I asked.

"We did as you told us, and sorted the people we took from the lab into 'useful skills' and 'potential hosts.' Most of her staff are willing to work with us as long as she is. I guess pragmatism is a human trait."

"It is indeed," I agreed. If it hadn't been, we would never have been created. How a species that was so blissfully willing to betray itself had managed to remain dominant for so long was beyond me. Well, soon enough, they would be gone, and we, their successors, would not make the same mistakes.

"You had some names you wanted us to watch for."

"Yes."

"Um. Nathan Kim was present—"

"I know that, Batya; I handcuffed his smug little hands behind his back myself."

"—and you have him listed as a potential host, not as a resource. But he's a parasitologist, Sherman. He understands how we work almost better than we do. More importantly, he's Dr. Cale's biological child. She's not going to forgive us if we cut his head open and put an implant inside."

"And why not?" I demanded. "We're her children. He's her child. Shouldn't she be delighted to combine her two greatest creations? If I didn't need to remember all the things I've learned, I would take him for myself." Sal already loved him. She would learn to love him again, with someone else living behind his eyes. She was adaptable, my beloved little traitor, and she would do whatever she felt was necessary.

Maybe putting him into the general pool of host bodies was a bad idea. "Wait," I said, raising a hand. "I think I *will* save him for myself. Do his blood work, make sure we're genetically compatible, and then allow him to work with his former colleagues. I'll need him eventually, I'm sure. This body can't last forever."

"Dr. Cale—"

"Mother has chosen us over them every time the decision has been put in front of her. Her recent recalcitrance to commit to our cause is more a matter of lingering loyalty to her species than any misguided belief that humanity deserves this planet. So we let her keep the boy she birthed for right now, until her loyalties are swayed, and then we make it clear what his purpose is. By the time we get that far, she'll rejoice at the idea that his body can serve our cause."

Batya still looked unconvinced. I sighed and reached out to rest my fingertips against her cheek, focusing on bringing her heartbeat into rhythm with mine. She gasped at the touch, her eyes going half-lidded with the shock of the stimulus.

I hated to do this to her, but sometimes she needed to remember who was in charge here. Sometimes she needed to remember that it was not—would never be—her.

"Listen to me, little Bat," I murmured. "My mother is a forgiving soul as long as you keep dangling the promise of new scientific discovery in front of her. I left her because I knew that in order to earn her love, I would have to bring her something greater than Adam ever could. All he brought was newness. I am bringing her the world. You are not going to interfere with that because you have somehow managed to pick up a dose of human sentimentality. Do you understand me? We're going to remake the world in our image, and Mother is going to help us, but that can only happen if we make her understand why our way is the *only* way."

"I understand," said Batya, eyelashes still fluttering against her cheeks like the wings of captive birds. She was beautiful, when she wasn't wrapped up in her own righteousness. It was truly a pity that she spent so much time in that state.

I wished, not for the first time, that I had time enough to work on her properly, to condition her to the point where her interests and mine would more perfectly align. Alas, that sort of time was a luxury we would not have for a while yet, if ever. Conquering a world was so much more work than I had ever anticipated.

"Tell my mother that I will be coming to her soon," I murmured, and brushed my lips across Batya's brow. She shivered at the touch. I let her go, smiling beatifically as she stepped back, out of my grasp, but never out of my reach.

"Don't worry," I said. "Everything is going to be fine."

STAGE III: MICROEVOLUTION

I categorically deny the accusations that I have betrayed the human race.

—DR. STEVEN BANKS

Children grow up. You have to let them, even if you don't like the people they become. That's what life is about.

—SAL MITCHELL

My "brother" has ordered us to start unstitching the genetic code of his waterborne creations, looking for the switches allowing them to thrive in a body that already has an implant. We're supposed to turn them off, so his precious cousins will stop infecting his people. I've tried pointing out that this won't clean the waterways that are already contaminated—adding a new strain of tapeworm to the water not only won't remove the old one, it will double the number of infectious agents in any given sample. As there is no outward method of distinguishing tapeworm eggs from two different strains, this will just result in the water being more dangerous for everyone.

Sherman doesn't care. Sherman is planning to become King of the World, even if he has to destroy everything to accomplish it. According to Mom, Sherman is reading these notes. I wouldn't expect anything else. I know he's only keeping me alive for as long as he thinks it helps him keep Mom under control; I know that as soon as she comes fully over to his side, I'm finished.

He never did forgive me for being the son that came before him. I am afraid for myself. I am afraid for Sal, and for my mother, and for everyone I love. But most of all, I am afraid for Adam.

—FROM THE NOTES OF DR. NATHAN CALE, JANUARY 2028

Sally—she likes to be called "Sal" now, I have to remember that—is awake. She's starting to talk again, and her physical therapists say she's not going to have any motor deficiencies. If she doesn't have permanent brain damage (and how are they supposed to measure that? I know there was scarring, there's always scarring when the accident is that bad), then she'll probably be able to resume a normal life. She won't even have a limp.

That's all great. I mean, I'm really, really happy to know that she's going to be okay. I never wished for her to die, although I guess if I'm being honest, I wished for her to get hurt a few times. Just so she'd understand what it was like to not get everything you wanted. Just so she'd learn to be kinder. But.

But this woman, Sal, she isn't Sally. She looks like Sally, she has Sally's face and Sally's smile and sometimes she moves like Sally used to…and I think that's all muscle memory, because those flashes of similarity are fading as Sal figures out how she wants to move. It's like my sister suddenly has a twin.

I don't think Sally woke up. I think…I think someone else did.

—FROM THE DIARY OF JOYCE MITCHELL, JUNE 2022

Chapter 16

JANUARY 2028

We weren't prisoners, and we weren't guests: we were enemy combatants facing the concept of an uneasy alliance, and that discomfort wrapped around all three of us like a rough blanket as we paced around the small room where we'd been asked to wait. "For our safety," according to Colonel Mitchell, whose people were overseeing the transfer of Joyce's body—Joyce, who would be Tansy when she woke up, please, please, she would wake up, and please, please, she would be Tansy—to a room where she could recuperate. I wasn't happy knowing that she would wake up without us.

Fang was even less happy. "They had best give me access to my patient," he muttered darkly, pacing back and forth across the room. At least he had stopped kicking the chairs. "If she experiences any medical distress, I'm her best chance. She needs to make a successful integration. If she doesn't, we could lose them both."

I bit my lip and didn't say anything. Fang was worried about his patients. I was worried about my *sisters*. I wanted them to live. I wanted them to *thrive*, as much as they could with half of themselves missing. Colonel Mitchell wanted his daughters back, and would probably always want that, no matter how much he came to accept that it was never going to happen. Fang wanted Tansy back—whether it was because he missed her or because he was trying to make Dr. Cale happy didn't really matter so much. I was the only one who wanted them both, combined and perfect and capable of being happy.

Fishy was sitting atop the table that had been in the middle of the room when we arrived. He had promptly shoved it into the corner, creating more room for Fang to pace and making the whole space seem less like an interrogation room and more like a lobby. I was leaning in the corner, out of the way but still ready to move if I had to. I was never going to be comfortable here. Not even now, when we were present voluntarily. This was where I had been held against my will, and I was not going to forget that, or allow myself to trust them any more than I had to.

The doorknob turned. Fang stopped pacing. All three of us turned to watch, with varying degrees of nervousness. I shrank back into my corner, letting the smallness of it reassure me. Fishy leaned back on his hands, seeming utterly relaxed.

Colonel Mitchell stepped into the room.

Fang stepped forward. "I need to see my patient," he said, without giving the colonel a chance to catch his breath. "Her condition will be very delicate at this stage; any disruption could prevent proper integration, and then we risk losing both of them. It's essential that she undergo the correct monitoring, and that—"

"She's asleep, and her vital signs are stable," said Colonel

Mitchell, speaking calmly over him. "Three of my people are with her, adjusting her life support and hooking up the IVs you requested. I needed you here, because I need to talk to you. Once we're done, you can go back to Joyce."

"Tansy," I said.

Colonel Mitchell turned to look at me. He didn't say anything. He didn't need to.

But I did. "Her name is Tansy now." I pushed away from the wall, moving into the middle of the floor. "Joyce was an organ donor. I'm going to miss her a lot. She shouldn't have died. That doesn't change the fact that she *did* die, and now we're using the parts she left behind to save my sister."

He winced at the word "sister." "I think you're being a little too literal."

"No, I think I'm protecting both of them," I said. "I'm protecting Tansy, because she needs to not have you confuse her into thinking she's Joyce—the way you confused me into thinking I was Sally. You made me think I didn't know how to be myself, when the problem was that I didn't know how to be somebody I'd never met. I'm protecting Joyce, too, because she deserves better than to have you dress a stranger up in her clothes and pretend that nothing has changed. Didn't I teach you that? Love your daughter. Mourn your daughter. Let your daughter go."

"Sally…"

"That's not my name, and you know it."

Colonel Mitchell went very still. So did I. It was possible that I'd gone too far, pushing him past the point where we could converse like normal people. But it was important that we start this conversation from a place of equality, or as close to equality as we were going to be able to get. He needed to remember that he was not my father, and that while he might have more power than I did, that didn't mean that he was in charge—and more, he needed to remember that he had ceded his claim on

Joyce as soon as he'd allowed us to place Tansy in her head. She was my sister now, and she was going with us when we were done here, if we had to fight every uninfected human in the place to set her free.

Finally, he nodded. "My apologies, Sal. Old habits can be difficult to break."

"I know," I said, offering him the thinnest scraping of a smile. "I'm just getting to the point where I can ride in a car without hyperventilating. I have to remember that the fear doesn't belong to me." It had been a gift from Dr. Banks, in the interest of keeping me convinced that I was Sally. I couldn't give it back to him, but I could take everything else he had away. That was enough.

"I'm glad to hear that." He looked back to Fang. "I promise that you will have full access to your patient. I don't want to do anything that might hinder her recovery. I just wanted to speak to you before things went any farther. Your arrival here was... dramatic, to say the least, and it didn't leave us much time to really set terms."

"And now you have a hostage to fortune, in the form of our colleague, slumbering in your daughter's body," said Fang coolly. "The last time this situation arose, things didn't go so well for us."

"No, but I'm hoping it can be different now," said Colonel Mitchell. "Forgive me for asking this so bluntly, but are you a human?"

"My body is," said Fang. "Does it matter what's inside my skull? I'm a thinking individual regardless of my origins, and I deserve to be treated as such."

Fang wasn't a chimera. He worked for Dr. Cale because he believed in what she was doing, not because he viewed her as his creator. Even as I thought that, I realized what he was doing. He was making it easier for us to separate the Colonel from

Dr. Banks, whose promise of chimera for military and cleanup use depended on us being so "other" that we didn't have to be treated as the people that we were. It was easier to abuse things that weren't your equal. I knew that from my time at the animal shelter.

"I'm human," volunteered Fishy. I glanced at him, startled by his apparent failure to realize what Fang was doing, and had to swallow a smile as he continued, "I'm also suffering from severe disassociation and can't tell fiction from reality most of the time. Of the people in this room—one a tapeworm in a human body, one not saying, and me—I'm the last one you should listen to. Humanity isn't the final deciding factor in whether or not a person is worth trusting. There's so much more that you're just not looking at, and all of it matters."

Colonel Mitchell looked nonplussed. Then he turned back to Fang, and said, "I need to know what I'm dealing with, son. My superiors are going to want to know."

"I'm a scientist," said Fang. "Moreover, I'm the scientist who currently stands the best chance of saving the human race, if you decide to listen to us and do what we ask of you. Does anything else matter at this stage?"

"Sherman's going to kill *everyone*," I said. "You, the rest of the uninfected humans, even me, because I didn't go with him. He's the worst of what the world has left to offer, and we can help you stop him. But you can't act like you're better than me just because you were born in your body, and you can't pretend that what Dr. Banks wants to do with the chimera is right. We're people too."

"You're thieves," said Colonel Mitchell. "You stole the bodies you're standing in, and now you act like you have some divine right to them. Sally—Sal—I love you. I wish I didn't. It would have been so much easier to get the help we needed here if my superiors hadn't been asking whether I'd been compromised—whether my love for you had compromised me. But that doesn't make you my daughter. You took what you needed, and you never considered what it would do to the rest of us."

"I wasn't a person then," I protested. "That's like saying that when a baby is conceived, it's stealing the womb from all the other babies that could have grown there. I didn't *make* Sally swallow the implant. I didn't make her have the accident, either. And what about Tansy? She didn't *steal* Joyce's body. We put her inside it to save her life, because otherwise they were both going to die. She's not a bad person just because of where she comes from. Saying that she is isn't fair. Sherman is a bad person. He got access to a human brain, and all the wonderful things it can do, and he decided that the appropriate thing to do would be to act against the species that had created him. The rest of us just want a chance to survive. You *made* us, and then as soon as we started wanting more than you were happy to provide, you started hating us."

"The sleepwalkers are a problem," said Fang. "But we don't want to round them up and slaughter them any more than you do—and the fact that they still exist in the Bay Area tells me that you don't want to go in for wholesale slaughter."

"It's hard to get people to sign on for shooting their own kind," said Colonel Mitchell. "Whatever's happened to those poor souls, they still look like human beings."

"There was a huge upswing in zombie media in the teens," said Fishy abruptly. "Lots of really classic movies and books and video games came out of like a ten-year span. Defined the genre. And the government looked at that as an excuse. They generated a bunch of hokey 'zombie-preparedness plans' that everybody laughed at, but that were actually blueprints for mowing down mobs of unarmed American citizens if it ever became necessary. Pretty good smokescreening, if you stop and think about it. Which most people didn't. They just laughed at the idea that the government knew about zombies, even as a fictional device."

"It's weird when you say things that make sense," I said.

Fishy beamed. "I am the living incarnation of the Konami Code."

"And the making sense is over." I turned back to Colonel Mitchell. "We're people. You have to understand that by now. I've caused you too much trouble to *not* be a person, and when Tansy wakes up, both your daughters are going to be walking around being different people. Being *us*."

"Why is this so important to you?" asked Colonel Mitchell. "I let you into my facility. I allowed you to have what you… what you asked me for, even knowing what it would cost. Sal, you lived with me. You know what Joyce's mother is going to do when she finds out. But I did it anyway, because you were right, and because I am trying to treat you fairly."

I knew what I wanted to say. I didn't know how to begin. The words were too big, and the stakes were too high. I looked toward Fang, silently pleading.

He cleared his throat, and said, "Because we're about to give you the keys to the kingdom, and we need to believe that you're not going to try to use them against us."

"What do you mean?" asked Colonel Mitchell.

"The tapeworm eggs in the water were derived from a sample taken from my original, tapeworm body," I said. "Sherman Lewis, an early experiment of Dr. Cale's who has turned against us all—he infiltrated SymboGen, he infiltrated *you*—cultured them, and scrubbed the epigenetic data that might have enabled them to retain some sense of humanity." Better not to go into that in detail: better to keep moving on, and hope he wouldn't put too much value on that statement. "He used those eggs, and my genetic material, because of the antiseizure medication I was created to secrete. They have a higher chance of successfully bonding with a human host, because they can prevent seizures that would disrupt the bonding process."

"Still mostly fatal," said Fishy. "I mean, we're monkeys, and monkeys don't like to share. Especially not with squishy brain worms that want to drive us all around like happy meat-cars. No offense, Sal."

"Some offense taken," I said. I kept my eyes on the Colonel, watching to see how he would react to all this.

He was frowning. Slowly, he asked, "Why is this relevant? The worms are still in the water, and from what you're saying, we have to worry about more of you people cropping up because of them. That doesn't seem like the kind of good news that would drive you into the arms of the enemy."

"We have a full copy of the invasive eggs' genetic code," said Fang. "We can create a tailored antiparasitic drug that, once introduced into the waterways, will kill off a large percentage of the eggs."

"We may never be able to completely scrub the water, because water is complicated," added Fishy. "It's hard to reliably model, and it's a pretty common spawn point for new enemies. But we can make it so a glass of water isn't an automatic death sentence."

Now, for the first time, Colonel Mitchell was starting to look genuinely interested. "You can do this."

"Yes," said Fishy.

"We could be putting antiparasitics in the water without hurting people—human people."

I could see where this was going. I put my hand out, shaking my head, and said, "Stop. This is going to be a *tailored* antiparasitic. The only reason it'll be safe for people to drink is because it's going to be targeting a specific genetic line. Even then, drinking too much water without filtering it could make your precious 'human people' sick. Putting something more broad spectrum into the water would mean killing everyone. I know you're upset about all the deaths. So am I. But are humans really so petty that you'd wipe out *everyone* in order to say that you died as the dominant species on the planet?"

I wasn't as confident about the science as I was trying to sound. I was still a layman in a world of specialists, and I was always going to be, since that wasn't where my head was. I glanced to Fang, who nodded very slightly, confirming that I had the right shape, if not the right details. That was a relief. I didn't want to lie to the man who had been the only father I'd ever known. It would have been one betrayal too far.

Colonel Mitchell seemed to wilt. "You seem awfully confident that humanity is going to lose," he said. "It isn't as bad everywhere as it is here in America. We're the only ones who've had the water contamination, at least so far. There have been outbreaks in Europe, Africa, South America—even Asia and Australia—but they're holding up better than we are here. If the tapeworms take the North American continent, we'll be avenged."

"That's a fight for another day," I said. "Right now, we just want to clean up the water and stop Sherman before he does any more damage."

"Don't forget our personal Frankenstein," said Fishy. "You can't work with Banks. He'll promise you the moon and stars, and then he'll cut every corner in the galaxy. Fuck the black holes that follow him to your doorstep. He just cares about making delivery and getting paid."

"We're people," I said. It was starting to feel like a mantra. "You can't let him turn us into slaves because you need to rebuild and you're convinced that we're not real. That leads us right back here in another generation—and next time, you won't have people like us showing up to try to find a way we can all live together. Next time, the center doesn't hold."

"She's right," said Fang. "This is your chance to save your

people and protect your future. Are you going to take it? Or are you going to risk everything because you need to be the dominant species?"

"One-time offer," said Fishy. "No refunds or returns."

"Please?" I whispered.

Colonel Mitchell closed his eyes. "All right," he said. "What is it that you want us to do?"

The lab facilities at USAMRIID had always been top of the line, filled with gleaming equipment I didn't understand and packed with some of the nation's best and brightest. That wasn't the case anymore. Just like Dr. Cale—just like all of us—the military scientists had been forced out of their comfortable, familiar surroundings when everything started to fall apart, and were living in a world of makeshift facilities and jury-rigged systems. They had been able to move most of their gleaming equipment, and it looked out of place in the middle of the Coliseum lobby, like they were preparing for a play. But the scientists who moved around that gleaming equipment were all deadly serious. Their lab coats were still pristine, thanks to having access to industrial-strength laundry facilities, and their hands were occupied with tablet computers instead of clipboards and pencils.

Fang moved among them like he belonged there. It was sometimes difficult to remember that he had spent a significant amount of time working for Dr. Banks at Dr. Cale's request, trying to learn what her rival was doing to the genetically engineered tapeworms she had created. Looking at him now, calm, confident, and utterly undisturbed by the complexity of the setup around him, belief became easy again. This was his element, more than the bowling alley or the candy factory had ever been. He was supposed to be in labs like this one, doing great work, changing the world.

Fishy stepped up next to me and said, in his usual calm, amiable tone, "Three exits, all guarded. They only have two guards on the one behind the men's bathroom, though, so I figure we could punch our way out if we needed to."

I glanced at him, startled. He smiled. There was more understanding in that smile than I had ever seen from him before.

"They held you prisoner here, right? Twice. So I figured you might be more comfortable if you knew how to get away. Not that we're going to need to. Captain Protocol over there," he gestured toward Fang, "has them all eating out of his hand. It's amazing what a little confidence and a lot of scientific bullshit will get you, isn't it? Things are going to be okay."

"This isn't going to fix anything except what Sherman did." And even that wouldn't bring back the dead. Not the dead humans, and not the dead sleepwalkers. How many had he killed, between the quarantine zone and the pockets of survivors hiding around the state? How many of his own cousins had he driven out of their stolen bodies? The death toll had to be in the thousands, if not the millions. Everyone needed water. It was the best weapon he could have used against us.

"I know." Fishy looked at me soberly. "A human created your kind. Another human released you into the world without checking to make sure that it was safe. But this time, you attacked the humans. Not you in specific—I know you're not that kind of person—but your species. It was the first time you intentionally raised a hand against your creators. Colonel Mitchell and his big brains may work with us now, because they want a solution more than they want to hold a grudge, but you need to be careful. You need to watch for exits. Because once this is done, they're going to want someone to blame."

"You think it's going to be me?" The thought was appalling. All I had ever done was stay alive. That wasn't supposed to be a crime.

"I think you're a perfect figurehead for either a revolution or a war crimes tribunal," said Fishy. "I know you, okay? I've watched you walk your dogs and burn your toast. I know you're not some evil mastermind of a conqueror race. But look at you from the outside. You're the first natural chimera. You just *happened* to take over the body of the daughter of the senior officer of our local USAMRIID branch, and you just *happened* to start dating the son of the woman who created you in the first place, all while visiting the man who released you into the wild. You got hands on all three sides of this conflict, all without seeming to do anything but smile and walk blithely on. So do I think some people are going to look at you and see an evil mastermind? Yeah, I do. If I were programming this game, you'd be either the protagonist or the villain, and at this stage, I'm still not sure which way I'd go with you."

"Um," I said. "I'm not a bad guy."

"Which is exactly what a bad guy would say," said Fishy.

My dismay must have been easy to read on my face, because his own face fell.

"Aw, Sal, no," he said. "I don't think you're a bad guy. I'm just saying what other people might think, once they get their feet under themselves and need to start looking for someone they can blame. You know how humans are. We love having people we can blame. Maybe that's the real reason we made you. We got tired of blaming ourselves."

"Don't you blame us?" A tapeworm very much like me had been responsible for the death of Fishy's wife. Even if her body was still out there somewhere—and it might have been; no one had ever told me differently—the woman who'd originally owned it was gone, wiped away by the invader that had taken her body. It would have been easy for him to blame us.

"Nope," said Fishy. He somehow managed to sound cheerful and sad at the same time, like the two emotions weren't contradictory. Maybe for him, they weren't. "You never asked Sally Mitchell to swallow you and give you access to her tempting brain. She did that all on her own, and then you did what came naturally. Blaming you would be like...like blaming a baby when its mother dies in childbirth. The baby didn't do anything wrong. No one gets to do anything wrong until after they've been born, you know? That's where morality and culpability begin. With birth. You just wanted to live, like anybody else, and I can't fault you for that."

I noticed that he hadn't addressed the question of his wife at all, and I decided not to push it. He deserved to have whatever peace he'd been able to hold on to through all of this.

As I watched Fang walk Colonel Mitchell's people through the process of making a poison that was tailored to kill me and my tiny, involuntary clones, I wished that I could find a little distance. It might have made things easier.

"They're going to turn on us," I said. "We're teaching them how to be better killers of our kind, and they're going to use it against us."

"Maybe," said Fishy. "You're sort of lucky that you got to be human for a while. Not because being human is better than being what you really are—it's always best to be what you really are, when you can manage it—but because it meant you got to see the world when it wasn't at war. Your brother Adam and this Sherman dude, they've always been at war. They never saw the world when it wasn't through oppressed eyes. But you're sort of unlucky, too. You're going to understand what it means that you're never going to live in another time of peace."

I understood what he was saying. The war against the implants—and the subsequent war against the chimera—was going to last beyond my lifetime. Even if we could somehow convince Colonel Mitchell and his people that we *meant* no harm, we had still *done* a lot of harm. That was what most people would see. They wouldn't be able to forgive us. They would never be able to forgive us. But we couldn't survive without them. Take away our human hosts and we would become nothing more than mindless parasites, eating and existing, but never really *living*.

The thought of going back to what I didn't truly remember being was a terrifying one. It would be so *easy* to disconnect me from my host. Sherman and Fang—working under orders from Dr. Cale—had both had the opportunity to do exactly that. It was the genetic sampling Fang had done that was now allowing him to show Colonel Mitchell how to kill me more efficiently. It was targeted at my cousin-clones, but it would still work on me; poisons didn't have morality or compassion, they just had chemical structures and a job to do. A merciless, fatal job.

No one was ever going to get inside my skull again. Not unless they had come to kill me, and I was sure they would succeed. I wasn't going back. I *couldn't*.

"We'll find a way," I said, and my voice was a useless protest against a world founded on the principles of unfairness and survival above all else. The humans wanted to survive. Maybe they wanted it even more than we did.

Maybe there was only room for one.

Colonel Mitchell turned away from Fang and walked toward us, moving with the slow, unhurried stride that had always meant his work was going well. I swallowed and stood straighter, watching him approach.

"Sal," he said once he was close enough that he didn't need to raise his voice. "Dr. Dockrey." This was directed at Fishy, and I realized with a start that I had never learnt his real name: I had never even asked. He was always just "Fishy," and if that was enough for the people he worked with, it was enough for me. Asking for more would have seemed unfair.

"Evening, military man," said Fishy cheerfully. "How go the WMDs?" He sounded less rational than he had only a moment before. I wondered how much of that was a routine, him using the public fact of his neurological atypicality to keep people from taking him too seriously. It was...useful, the way people looked right through him sometimes.

"The antiparasitics are coming along nicely, and once we have a batch that works, we'll be able to synthesize enough to start treating the local waterways and reservoirs," said Colonel Mitchell. "We're expecting some die-off in smaller organisms, and we may disrupt the local food chain past repairing, but we'll be able to drink the water again. That matters more than a few small snails and worms."

The snails and worms would probably have thought differently. Telling him that wasn't going to make a difference, so I swallowed the thought and asked, "Will it hurt people?" People. Not humans, not chimera: people.

Colonel Mitchell looked at me, and I knew from the lines around his eyes that he understood my meaning. He had raised me, after all. No one knew me better than he did. "It will hurt the invading parasites," he said. "In the case of fully infected humans, it may damage them when the parasites are killed. We've had very little luck with surgical intervention after a certain point."

"You mean it's going to kill all the sleepwalkers who have worms genetically close to me," I said. "They're going to seize and die when they drink the water."

For a moment, I thought Colonel Mitchell was going to lie to me. Then he nodded, and said, "Yes. They are."

"But humans who haven't been fully infected yet, they'll be okay," I said. "It'll just clean out the eggs and cysts."

"Yes."

"What about chimera who are within the genetic target zone? Do you have a way of putting up signs to warn them?"

Colonel Mitchell sighed. "There are people—even now, there are people—who would see a warning and think that the government was trying to poison them. They believed Big Pharma was such a threat that they advocated for moving a living drug delivery system through FDA approval, all to avoid pills and vaccinations. If USAMRIID puts up a sign saying 'if you are a fully integrated tapeworm-human hybrid, do not drink the water,' then *they* won't drink the water either. They'll think the water is a trap. We won't be able to save them."

Losing a few humans who couldn't put down their paranoia long enough to save their own lives seemed less important than saving what might be half or more of the world's chimera community. I didn't say it. I couldn't say it. Here and now, I needed these people to stay on my side. "And it's staying narrow spectrum, right? You're not going to try to poison us all?"

"What do you want me to say, Sal? That humanity is going to be best friends with you now? You walked in and stole our bodies. You've killed millions. Do you understand how bad this problem is?"

"No," I said flatly. "The news stopped airing, and the Internet went down, so I know it's pretty bad, but I wasn't exactly invited to come and sit at the table and talk it over with the big boys. All I know is what people tell me."

"Well, then, I'm telling you, it's bad. The SymboGen implants were shipped all over the world. No one has been left unscathed."

"You said North America was hit worst."

"There's a difference between 'not hit as badly' and 'not hit at all,'" he said. "If the American government agrees to offer your people sanctuary, there are those who will view it as us consorting with terrorists. So no, Sal, we're not using a broad-spectrum antiparasitic in the water, because it would kill things we need to keep alive. It would disrupt California's ability to recover, and more, the rest of the country's ability to do the same, since the water contamination has spread. But that doesn't mean we're prepared to work with your people, or that we're going to come to some sort of peaceful accord."

"You're working with us," I said.

"I am not the United States government. We can have a temporary truce without my actually committing the President to anything."

This was an aspect that hadn't occurred to me. I glanced at Fishy, who nodded marginally. He had been aware that this might come up, which meant Fang had been aware as well. Hopefully, the knowledge that coexistence was not going to be possible extended all the way up the line to Dr. Cale. She would have a plan, if we could get her back.

"We've traded you a service for a service at this point," said Colonel Mitchell. "We provided you with a new home for your colleague, and you provided us with a means of clearing the waterways. I appreciate that you were willing to put the survival of the human race ahead of your own agenda. I'm afraid that we don't have anything else to offer each other."

"Uh, hold up, big guy," said Fishy, sounding suddenly concerned. "We *can't* move Tansy. She's just had brain surgery. I don't know if you know this, being a big bad virologist and not a neurosurgeon and all, but people who've just had brain surgery aren't the most mobile. Also, Tansy's going to need full reeducation now that she's in a new host. She'll catch on quick, but quick isn't the same as 'snap your fingers, there's our girl.'"

"If you would like to remain here in our custody, I'm sure something could be worked out," said Colonel Mitchell politely. "Please understand, I could have you seized and imprisoned for crimes against the human race right now."

Treason on a genealogical scale. The drums were hammering hard in my ears now, providing an ominous backbeat to everything around me. I breathed in through my nose and out through my mouth before saying, "We still need your help."

"Sal, I am already breaking every rule I know just to give you the option to walk out that door," said Colonel Mitchell.

"You may have been my daughter for a time, but that doesn't mean the rules don't apply to you. My career is going to be over for giving you as much as I have."

"You're worried about your career?" I asked. "What about the world?"

He looked at me levelly. "I have lost my children and will soon lose my wife. My career is all that I have left."

"Oh, come off it," snapped Fishy. "You kick us out now, you get to keep Tansy, because *she can't be moved*. So you wind up with a functional, properly integrated chimera, no real risk of rejection, to study and take apart at your leisure. Add that to having a solution for the water contamination, and your career isn't over. Hell, you've just become a hero of the revolution. Of the institution? Hero of the institution. We're the heroes of the revolution, and we're doing a piss-poor job of choosing our allies."

"Sherman dropped those worms in the water, and he *has our people*," I said heatedly. "We told you that when we got here. You said you'd help. Was that just a way to get us to tell you what you needed to know? We didn't bring you all that research because we needed a body. We could have found a body somewhere else."

"But it wouldn't have had Joyce's face," snapped Colonel Mitchell. "There's more of Sally in you than you want to think there is, Sal, and there's more in you that's human than I care to contemplate. You're not impassive plants from space or quiet, passionless invaders. You're *us*. We made you to be *us*, and you want your sister with you. Tansy is your sister in biology, and Joyce is your sister in paternity, and you saw the chance to combine those two things. What I gave you was worth more than you want to admit."

"And now you're trying to take it back!" I glared at him. He glared at me.

"Alfred?"

We both froze before turning to face the pale, hollow-cheeked woman who had given birth to my host body. She was standing in the doorway, holding a knitted wrap around her shoulders, and staring at the two of us like we were some sort of impossible mirage, something that couldn't exist outside of fiction.

"I went to check on Joyce," she said, not moving. "You know she sleeps better when I tuck her in and tell her we're still here waiting for her. But she wasn't there, Alfred. The room she was supposed to be in was empty. And when I asked the guards where she was, they said I had to talk to you if I wanted to know what was going on. They said I wasn't cleared to know where she was. Where's my daughter, Alfred? Where's Joyce?" Her eyes flicked to me, and then back to him. "What is that monster doing here?"

I looked at the face of the woman who had called herself my mother, who had kissed my forehead and laughed with me over plates of scrambled eggs and bacon, and I saw nothing there but loathing. She didn't love me. She had never loved me. She had loved the girl whose face I wore, and that love had died the day she admitted that her daughter was gone.

Humanity was never going to be able to accept us. We would always wear the faces of their dead, and we would never be those people, not really, not in any of the ways that mattered. I had asked once whether amnesia was a form of dying, and I had been assured that no, no, it was just a second chance at figuring out who you really were. If that was true, then why couldn't they love us? Our bodies were the same. Only our minds had changed, and while I couldn't say for sure that the change was for the better, it was no different than the change that came from a blow to the head and a loss of previous self. But it seemed to make all the difference in the world to them, our parents and creators. It made more difference than anything else could have.

"Gail, darling, you know you're not supposed to be in this part of the facility," said Colonel Mitchell, stepping forward to play the peacekeeper and prevent his wife from getting too close to me. She'd swung at me before. There was no question whether she'd do it again, and I couldn't defend myself—not with this many armed humans standing by and waiting to see what I would do.

"Where's Joyce?" she demanded. "Why is that thing here? If you recaptured her, you should have pulled her out of our baby's brain. She doesn't deserve to live."

I winced. If she wanted me extracted from Sally's brain, she was *definitely* going to be unhappy about Tansy setting up shop inside of Joyce. Even if Joyce wasn't there anymore, Gail Mitchell wasn't the most forgiving of mothers.

But then, how many would be? Juniper had been mine for only a short time, and I would have killed anyone who had opened her skull and pulled her out of the safe space she had found for herself. Maybe forgiveness wasn't a parental skill because it wasn't supposed to be. Forgiveness was for people who didn't have as much to lose.

"Joyce…Gail, I'm so sorry, I don't know how to tell you this, but Joyce didn't make it." Colonel Mitchell swung his head slowly, like the motion pained him.

Gail stared at him, her eyes going round and impossibly wide in her suddenly pale face. She made a sound, guttural and low in her throat, like she was trying to decide between speech and vomiting, and couldn't settle on either.

Colonel Mitchell reached for her. She all but danced away.

"No-no-no," she said, scolding like a treed squirrel. Then: "No-no-no," again, followed by, "I don't believe you *I don't believe you* where is she? If she's dead, where is she? I want to see my daughter I want to see my baby I want to see my *little girl*." Her voice rose steadily as she spoke, although she never shouted. She just got louder and louder, until everyone was looking at us, and all the technicians and clever scientists who had been working with Fang to develop the antiparasitic drugs for the water had stopped working in order to turn and stare. None of them said a word. They were smart people. They recognized an unwinnable situation when they saw one.

"Gail, please. Not in front of my command." Colonel Mitchell used the tone he might have used to say "not in front of the children," and the way his eyes darted to me made it clear that he was saying exactly that.

Unfortunately for both of us, it made his meaning clear to his wife as well. "You!" She whirled on me. "You did this somehow, you killed her, you weren't content killing just one of my daughters, you had to have them *both*, you had to have *both* my babies, you monster."

"Wow," said Fishy. "I don't think I heard a single full stop in there. You know, when you start talking entirely in comma splices, you're probably ready for a time-out and a tranquilizer."

Normally, his mild, slightly off-kilter observations helped to defuse bad situations. It was hard to stay angry or upset when someone was standing there treating everything like a comedy in the process of winding down. Gail Mitchell seemed to be one of the few people who was immune to his charms. Her lips drew back from her teeth, and I flinched. Primates showed their teeth. Tapeworms didn't.

"You did this," she repeated, and reached behind her, producing a service pistol much like the ones worn by the guards around us. Colonel Mitchell reacted with alarm, putting his hands up. Most of the guards reached for their own weapons. Gail ignored them. All her focus was on me.

"You did this," she said, for the third time, as she trained the muzzle of her gun on the center of my chest. "You killed Sally, and then you came back and you killed Joyce. My husband may look at you and see his little girl, but he was always blind where she was concerned, and you can't fool me anymore, you monster. I'm going to stop this. I'm going to get revenge for my babies."

"Gail, please," said Colonel Mitchell.

"Please," I echoed. I didn't raise my hands. I was afraid to move. I could barely even look at her face. It was a wall of teeth and hatred, and part of me would always think of her as my mother; would always look to her for comfort, and be startled by the now-inevitable rejection. "I didn't hurt your daughter on purpose. I would never have decided that my life mattered more than hers. Things just happened, that's all. Please. I have a family."

"I had a family," she said. "Before you barged in and started killing them, I had a family too. If I can't have mine, you can't have yours." She unhooked the safety with her thumb, her aim never wavering—

—and collapsed to the floor in a twitching heap, revealing Private Larsen standing behind her with an electric prod in his hand. His face was pale, and his eyes were filled with the horrified realization that he had just electrocuted his commander's wife.

"Sir, I..." he began, and stopped, clearly unsure what he should say next.

"Stand down, son," said Colonel Mitchell. There was pain and sorrow and a surprising amount of sympathy in his voice. "You did the right thing." He knelt and gathered his fallen wife into his arms, lifting her off the floor. She jittered, but was otherwise still.

"I'm sorry," said Private Larsen, and fled back to his post, an unlikely savior setting the mantle aside as quickly as he possibly could.

Colonel Mitchell looked to me. "Do you understand now why we can't be allies?" he asked.

I nodded, because I did. Gail Mitchell was a microcosm of the human race, of the thousands of people who would look at us and see their children, friends, and lovers turned into monsters and turned against them. We were the invaders, and we would never be accepted. Even people like Fishy, who claimed not to resent us for killing his wife, probably wouldn't have been accepting if she had opened her eyes and started talking with someone else's voice. Sleepwalkers were an easy enemy. You could see them coming, and you could mow them down without considering the people they had been. Chimera...chimera were hard.

"We can't be allies," I said. "I understand that. I...I wish it were different."

"So do I," said Colonel Mitchell.

But I wasn't finished. "Not being allies doesn't mean we can't work together for a while. Long enough to make sure that there's a future for all of us."

Colonel Mitchell frowned. "What did you have in mind?"

"It's simple." I looked at Gail Mitchell, still collapsed bonelessly in his arms, and then up to his face. "You're going to help us save the world, and then we're going to disappear."

Attached please find the formula for a new antiparasitic treatment now being deployed in the Californian waterways. We have provided this formula to outposts in Oregon, Utah, and Nevada, and are hoping to have all publicly used water in the western United States undergoing treatment by the end of the week. Our manpower is sketchy at best, but the faster we are able to treat the contaminated water, the more we will be able to reduce the speed of spread and prevent further infections. This antiparasitic is tailored to the specific strain of tapeworm that has been used to contaminate our water supplies, and should be safe for the majority of people and animals who will ingest it. Adverse reactions are of course possible—there is someone who is allergic to virtually anything you can produce—but the casualties that may arise from this treatment are far less than the casualties that will arise from withholding it.

I understand that I have acted without authorization, and that I will be repudiated by environmental groups for the rest of time. As there will be environmental groups partially due to my actions, I am willing to accept the consequences of what I have done. I will not stand aside and let judgment fall on my men, who have only ever followed orders.

History will decide how great my crimes were, one way or the other.

—MESSAGE FROM COLONEL ALFRED MITCHELL, USAMRIID,
TRANSMITTED TO THE WHITE HOUSE ON JANUARY 15, 2028

I'm starting to lose my grip on my delusions. Which sounds like I'm getting better, I guess—"Hey, it's getting harder for me to hallucinate my way through the afternoon! Score one for neurotypicality!"—but it's not that simple, and it's not that positive. I think things have gotten too bearable around here. That's part of it. Humans are novel animals: We need constant variety if we don't want to get used to things. I'm getting used to things.

Every morning I wake up and you're not there, and somehow that's becoming normal. Every day I work with people who are really worms inhabiting human skins, but are still perfectly nice people, *and somehow that's becoming normal. Every night I brush my teeth and go to bed alone, and somehow the fact that* that's *becoming normal is the worst part of all.*

I'm starting to accept this world as the real one, and I'm starting to forget what your shampoo smelled like, and I don't know how long I can do this before I go sane, and I can't cope anymore.

—FROM THE DIARY OF MATTHEW "FISHY" DOCKREY,
JANUARY 2028

Chapter 17

JANUARY 2028

Colonel Mitchell had the most detailed maps of the Bay Area I had ever seen. They covered the entire table in the conference room, and more spilled over onto the walls and floor. We had been able to reject a great many of them as clearly not being suitable: They showed neighborhoods that didn't have indoor malls of the sort Sherman had been using for his base, or that weren't close enough to the house where I'd been found to be a reasonable journey from the nearest such shopping center. Ronnie wouldn't have wanted to be caught sneaking me off the property. He'd knocked me out before he took me out of the mall, but that didn't mean he'd been able to take forever moving me.

"Do you remember anything else about this place, Sal?" asked Colonel Mitchell.

"There was a fountain," I said. "Inside."

"That's not helpful," said Private Larsen, who had somehow been drafted into this little planning session. I guess once you electrocute the boss's wife, you become a lot more interesting to him. "A lot of malls built in the seventies and eighties had fountains, and that covers most of the indoor shopping malls in the Bay Area."

"Didn't you say you got up on the roof?" asked Fishy.

"Yes." I had had to crawl through a series of air-conditioning ducts. It had been a surprisingly soothing way to make an escape—I like tight spaces—except for the part where I had been constantly afraid of falling.

"Were there mountains?"

I blinked. "What?"

"When you looked off the edge of the roof, were there mountains?"

I blinked again, more slowly this time. I had only been able to see the landscape for a few moments before Ronnie had been there to subdue me and take me away. Had there been mountains? I thought maybe there had been. "Y-yes," I said hesitantly. "Off to the left. In front of me there was just parking lot, and a street, and the freeway."

"So that means we have dedicated parking, visible from the rooftop, mountains, and no nearby residential housing." Fishy pushed another three maps off the table. "Was it warm?"

"No. It was the middle of winter."

To my surprise, he pushed another map off the table. "Means you weren't in San Jose. Which wouldn't make sense anyway—we picked you up in Pleasant Hill. Do you remember seeing a movie theater?"

"No," I said. "I would have remembered that."

"Good, because that was a trick question." He pulled a map closer to himself. "So here's a fun fact for you. Malls used to be a much bigger deal than they are now, and sometimes you'd get multiple malls built in the same city. Pleasant Hill, California, for example, had two major malls for a long time. Sun Valley, which is here"—he tapped the map—"thrived. It was near a major freeway on-ramp, there was a nearby community college, a high school, lots of residential housing—basically perfect growing conditions for a mall. It never closed its doors."

"So it's not our mall," I said gloomily, and reached for another map.

Fishy held up his hand. "Ah-ah-ah, my young student, you haven't let me get to the cool part. I don't get many awesome cutscenes. Give me this one, okay?"

"Okay," I said.

Colonel Mitchell scowled. "I don't know what a cutscene is, but get to the point, son. We don't have all day."

"We owe it to the people Sherman is holding captive to get this right; give me my moment," said Fishy. He tapped another section of the map. "The Monument Mall. It was never as big as Sun Valley, the stores were never as diverse, and the population was never as interested. It originally grew up around a big theater called 'the Dome' that got driven out by the local multiplexes and torn down in the teens. Even that wasn't enough to save the place. It shuttered its doors about eight years ago. Total bankruptcy. They didn't even clean out most of the stores."

"And you know this how?" asked Colonel Mitchell.

"The maker group I was involved with used to do a lot of scavenging for materials. We broke in there a couple of times before somebody went and installed a better security system on the place. I sort of figured that was because they were going to reopen it, but that never happened."

"How long ago was that?" I asked.

"Four years," said Fishy.

I thought back to the level of . . . well, entrenchedness I had witnessed from Sherman's people. They hadn't been squatting on the surface of the mall: They had been fully integrated with the spaces they were planning to use, having long since converted them to their purposes. Four years would have been sufficient time for the changes I'd seen, and more, for Sherman to have surgically induced all of the chimera I had seen there. If he'd started with one or two, and then trained them to assist him with the medical procedures necessary to make more...

"That's it," I said. "At least, I think that's it. Are there pictures?"

"No, but look." Fishy tapped the map again. "Here's Sun Valley. And here"—he moved his finger less than an inch, into the nearby residential zone—"is where we found you. He dumped you next to a different mall. That way, if you insisted that Sherman was in '*the* mall' instead of '*a* mall,' we'd be looking in the wrong place."

His explanation worked, except for one small part. "It wasn't Sherman who dumped me, it was Ronnie."

Fishy shrugged. "Makes no difference."

"Makes all the difference. Ronnie was trying to cover for his boss, even while he was letting me go. Sherman doesn't know I had help getting away, unless this was some really complicated double cross that I still don't understand. So as far as Sherman knows, I figured out where he was hiding forever ago, and then I didn't bring people to his doorstep."

"So?" asked Colonel Mitchell.

I took a deep breath. Sometimes it felt like I only had one plan, a plan that predated my existence as a thinking creature: infiltrate; invade; enter without permission. "If we can't sneak up on him without risking our people, I think I know how we can get inside. It's not going to be fun. But we can do it."

Fishy looked at me with stunned approval. Colonel Mitchell, who didn't understand yet what I was suggesting, just frowned.

"All right," I began. "This is how we get in..."

Fishy liked my plan: He said it was the sort of stealth mission that would be included in the downloadable content, and probably win some sort of award for clever use of the game mechanics.

Colonel Mitchell didn't like my plan. He said it was an unnecessary risk, and that it smacked of martyrdom, like I had decided that the only way to prove my loyalty to the human race was to get myself killed trying to defend them. I considered telling him that I had no interest in dying for the human race, but that I'd be willing to die for certain humans. I decided against it. He wasn't seeing nuance. The fact that he was willing to sit in a room and talk with the monster who had stolen his daughter's face was nuance enough. He was *trying*.

Fang didn't look up from Joyce-turning-Tansy's chart as I explained that we had found what we believed to be Sherman's hideout, and what I wanted to do. He just kept making notes and adjusting documentation, until I stopped talking. The silence stretched out for almost half a minute before he looked up, and asked, "Are you quite done telling me what I missed?"

"Yes," I said, almost meekly.

"Are you here to ask for my permission? Or for my approval?"

"Not really." Hearing the word "permission" made the drums beat harder and my stomach turn a little more to stone. I didn't need anyone's permission to save the people I loved. I might need help, but it was never about *permission*. "I wanted to know what you thought of the plan."

"I think it's dangerous," said Fang. "Sherman cut your head open once before, and you didn't run away from him until after he did that. He had to know when he seized Nathan rather than shooting him, that you'd be inclined to follow. This whole thing could be a trap, and you could easily be its intended target."

"If it's a trap, it's a trap that serves two purposes," I countered. It was hard to keep looking at him, rather than at Joyce/Tansy. She was still asleep, sustained by machinery while Tansy got herself integrated. When would the changes start?

When would her face stop being slack, and become tense with a new personality's expressions? I wanted to see that moment. I wanted to avoid it at all costs. "He wanted Dr. Cale and her research. He's always wanted her to be on his side, and maybe he thinks he can accomplish it now that the water isn't safe for human consumption."

"Or chimera consumption," said Fang. "You have to consider that he may also have lost people, and is looking for a way to prevent that from happening again. There's a very real chance that you'll walk in and he'll be waiting for you, because he knew this might happen, but doesn't have the time to waste on making you want to be with him."

"I know." I shook my head. "But if we want to get in without killing the people we're trying to save, we need to know what the internal layout is. Will they be holding their prisoners in the old department store where they kept me, or are they counting on us focusing on that as a goal, and putting our people in the area they figure we'll attack first? We need *information*. This is a way for us to get it."

"You think Sherman won't realize that you're wearing a wire?"

"I think it's the best chance we have." He wouldn't be able to resist me. Anyone else, maybe, but not me: not if I walked up to his doors and said I had been wrong. Sherman suffered from the same problem I did, the same problem all the chimera except for Tansy and maybe Juniper did: He had been raised by humans, and he *was* human in many ways, heir to the hopes and dreams and vanities of his parent species. He wasn't content with the sense of family that all chimera felt for each other. He wanted something that was his, and only his; he wanted me to belong to him. He might be suspicious if I suddenly walked up to his door with open hands—he *would* be suspicious, because he'd never been stupid—but he would want to believe that I was there for him. Colonel Mitchell had tried to believe it, and he'd had far less reason to do so.

"It's a terrible plan," said Fang. "You're putting yourself in unnecessary danger, and since this isn't the first time you've gone with a plan like this, I have to wonder if you might benefit from some therapy. Putting yourself in harm's way over and over again is not the most effective means of committing suicide."

"I don't want to die, but I don't want to be the reason the people I care about die, either," I said. "I want them back. I want them all back." My eyes darted again to Tansy.

Fang followed my gaze and smiled. "You never want to let anybody go, do you? I suppose that isn't part of your genetic makeup."

"I think it's part of my emotional makeup," I said. "Those aren't the same thing. You know Sherman, Fang. You worked with him at SymboGen. You've read Dr. Cale's notes. Is this going to work? Will he fall for it?"

"He might," said Fang. His voice turned solemn, all traces of his smile fading away. "He's an arrogant man. A brilliant man, who picks things up far too quickly—I sometimes think he might have been a bit less quick to embrace the myth of chimera superiority if he hadn't been so damn *smart*—but still, an arrogant man. He'll want to believe that you've come groveling to his door. That's part of what worries me. If he's been keeping Nathan alive to lure you back, there's every chance that having you there might make Nathan's continued survival seem, well, unnecessary. Do you really want to risk hearing the gun go off while you're standing in the doorway?"

"Every minute we're not there is another minute where Sherman might get bored and pull the trigger anyway," I said. "I don't see a better choice. Do you?"

Fang hesitated. Then he sighed. "No," he admitted. "But you

know I can't come with you. I have to stay here with Tansy, to monitor her integration, and—" He glanced at the door, which was open just a crack, and went quiet.

"And to get ready to run if you have to," I said, finishing the sentence for him. "I don't think Colonel Mitchell is going to double-cross us, but he says we can't be allies, and I think he's right. There's too much bad blood between my species and yours, and people like you are going to be looked at as traitors when the dust settles and the humans start looking for people to blame. I just hope Dr. Banks gets to be a traitor too. I don't want him finding a way to land on his feet."

"He always does," said Fang. "Regardless of what the future holds, I'm stuck here until Tansy is stable enough to move, unless things change dramatically."

"So we're doing this without you." I took a step forward, looking down at my sister's sleeping face. Then I leaned forward and pressed a kiss against her forehead. Her scent was already changing as chimera pheromones bubbled through the mammalian sweetness of her skin. She was becoming one of us.

I blinked back sudden tears. Tansy was going to live, and that meant Joyce was really gone, forever. It was a wonderful, terrible thing, and I couldn't stop feeling conflicted about it. I didn't *want* to stop feeling conflicted about it. It was important that we never stop remembering that our actions had consequences, and that we were a species that existed in symbiosis with our creators, no matter how much we might want to be free.

Straightening, I flashed Fang the most reassuring smile I could muster, and said, "She's integrating. She's starting to generate mature pheromones. I think she's going to be all right."

"Good," he said. "Now get to where you can say that about the rest of us, and we'll be in pretty good shape." He turned back to his machines. I had clearly been dismissed, and that was all right by me. He had work to do.

So did I.

Private Larsen was waiting for me in the hall, trying to look like he hadn't been listening in on our conversation. I closed the door behind me and met his eyes squarely, waiting for him to begin squirming. It didn't take long.

"Yes, Miss?" he said.

"If you were us—if you were a community of sapient tapeworms inhabiting human bodies that you didn't mean to steal but can't exist without—what would you do?" I asked. "If you didn't have to be loyal to the human race, but you wanted to stay alive."

"I would run," he said without hesitation. "I'd do whatever I had to in order to convince the humans that I wasn't a threat, and then I'd take my people, and I would run for the hills. I would go where no one would ever find me. I would never come back."

"There aren't many places like that in the world," I said.

"Gonna be more, since so many people died," he said, and shrugged. "I'd find a place that hadn't been very popular before the outbreak, and I'd go there. Build myself a community. Get a reputation for not liking strangers. And never come back."

"That's the second time you've said that," I said.

Private Larsen looked at me sadly. "That's because I really mean it."

I cocked my head to the side. "You don't have to mince words with me, you know."

"I know," he said. "I watched my superior officer beat the shit out of you, remember? I felt bad about it then, and I feel bad about it now. You're not an enemy combatant, and you didn't kill all those people. You're just someone who wound up in the wrong place, at the wrong time, in the wrong body."

"And yet, if I hadn't been Sally Mitchell, I might never have been able to make it this far," I said.

"True," he said. "Or maybe you would've made it even farther, since you wouldn't have been dealing with all this military bullshit. It's pretty much impossible to say. Hindsight is always twenty-twenty."

"I hate hindsight," I muttered, and held out my hand. "We've never had real introductions. Hi. I'm Sal Mitchell. I'm a sapient tapeworm in a girl-suit, and I didn't kill anybody who wasn't trying to kill me."

"Private Sonny Larsen," he said. "Nice to meet you."

"I thought you didn't like me," I said, shaking his hand once before letting go. "You seemed pretty happy when I was bruised and wilting."

"People talk," he said. "People said a lot of crap about you when they heard you were back on base. Things like 'she slit a bunch of throats last time she was here, let's make sure she doesn't do it again.' But there was never any evidence of that, you know? And you're nice and all, but you're not a criminal genius. You wouldn't have known how to commit that kind of crime without leaving *some* sign that it was you."

"Thanks," I said with a small smile. "That's kind of you to say."

"I didn't say anything kind," said Private Larsen, looking surprised. "I just stated the facts."

"In a situation like the one we've been in, the facts are sometimes the first thing to go," I said, and started walking back toward the room where Colonel Mitchell and Fishy were waiting for me. "Everyone gets wrapped up in what they *think* is going on, or what they've *decided* is going on, and they don't look at what's *actually* going on. The fact of the matter is, Dr. Cale designed something that could have been useful, but that needed more testing, and Dr. Banks released it anyway, because a decade of human trials was more trouble than he wanted to put up with. Colonel Mitchell knew Dr. Banks was moving a product that could hurt people—he had me in his house, as proof and collateral damage—and he didn't do anything about it, because he was trying to study the phenomenon and protect his career at the same time. Dr. Banks knew Sally was epileptic, after all. Meanwhile, Dr. Banks didn't check the credentials of his employees well enough, because Dr. Cale had at least two spies on his staff, plus Sherman, who snuck in all by himself. This whole situation is a big snarl of people ignoring facts. If Banks had responded to 'We're not ready' with 'Okay,' I wouldn't be here now, and you wouldn't be worrying about whether or not you'll have a species at the end of the day."

Private Larsen blinked. "But you wouldn't exist."

"So? I wouldn't miss existing, since I would never have started. Now that I'm here, I plan to survive: Survival is the main drive of any living organism. But I wouldn't know to want survival if I hadn't been made." I considered telling him what Fishy had said, about not blaming babies for the things they did before they were born. Babies didn't ask to exist, but once they did, they wanted to keep going.

I decided against it. The situation was complicated enough as it was.

At the end of the hall was a door. On the other side of the door there were people, talking. I stopped when a familiar voice drifted through the conversational din, caressing my ears in that old, paternal way.

"Sal? You all right?" Private Larsen sounded concerned. That made a certain amount of sense. I had gone pale, and the drums were hammering harder than ever, making me wobble slightly where I stood. "Should I go get a doctor?"

"No," I managed to say. "No, that's the problem." And then I was moving forward, gathering speed with each step, until I slammed my palms into the slightly ajar door and sent it crashing against the far wall. Colonel Mitchell and Dr. Banks, who had been bent over the map of the Bay Area, looked up in surprise. Fishy, who was sitting on the counter with his shoulders slumped against the room's rear wall, raised his head and gave me a feral grin. *He* wasn't surprised by my reaction. Gauging solely from the look on his face, he had been counting the minutes until it came.

"What is *he* doing here?" I demanded, pointing at Dr. Banks. "This is his fault. He shouldn't be standing here looking at the maps, he should be locked up."

"Hello to you, too, Sally," said Dr. Banks. "It's good to see that all that poison Shanti poured into your ears has had a permanent effect on how you think of me."

"Sal, please," said Colonel Mitchell. "Dr. Banks has agreed to assist in this process, in exchange for certain considerations."

"Money, or freedom? Because those are the only things he cares about, and only when they belong to him." I narrowed my eyes. "He cut my sister open and dug around in her brain because he was curious about how she worked. He put her into the living brain of a *conscious* human."

"Your so-called sister was an enemy combatant who attacked my property, and the subject I implanted her in was a volunteer who knew what was going to happen to her," said Dr. Banks. "We were pushing forward the bounds of science."

"You're the monster here," I said. "Not me. Not any of my kind. Not even Sherman. You. You're the one who couldn't leave the broken doors alone."

"It's adorable how your kind has imprinted on a second-rate children's book as your Bible, but it's just like any other holy book: It doesn't actually change the world," said Dr. Banks. "USAMRIID needs someone who understands these monsters if they're going to succeed in taking them out. Since Dr. Jablonsky is not available, and Dr. Cale is not impartial, it's going to be me."

"Dr. Jablonsky shot himself because you let us out into the world without proper testing, and you're not impartial either," I snapped. "You're on your own side. We can't trust you."

"It's a good thing for me that you don't have a choice," said Dr. Banks. He turned back to Colonel Mitchell and said, as if I had never interrupted, "Aerosol grenades would be an excellent approach. We can load them with a wide-spectrum antiparasitic gas and throw them through the mall skylights. There's no way they'll be able to kill or even incapacitate all the tapeworms in the building, but the degree of confusion they'll create will be enough to let us enter without resistance. After that—"

I'd been listening with growing horror. Now I interrupted, putting out my hands as I said, "You can't do that! Adam's in there! And not all of Sherman's people are evil, they're just confused and following their creator! You can't do this, you'll *hurt* them."

"Hurting them was the idea, Sally." Now Dr. Banks sounded annoyed, like I was intentionally missing the point he was trying to make. "They're enemy combatants."

"They're *people*." I turned on Colonel Mitchell. "I don't believe I'm having to tell you this again. I thought we had this conversation. I thought you *understood*. They're people, and we're going there to save them, not to kill them for the crime of being in the wrong place at the wrong time."

"Sal, I don't know what you expect me to do," said Colonel Mitchell. "I have a responsibility to the American public, and to the human race above all. History is going to see me as a traitor and an ecological terrorist for what I've already done. I refuse to let history see me as a coward."

I stared at him. "What about me?"

He frowned. "What do you mean?"

"Is the plan still to send me in first, so that Sherman will open the doors? Because any antiparasitic broad enough to hurt Sherman's people is going to affect me, and I can't walk in there with a gas mask around my neck and expect not to raise some questions. There's no way I'm going to be in and out fast enough for this plan."

"You'll know it's coming," said Colonel Mitchell. "You can cover your mouth and nose when you hear the glass break."

"That's not good enough."

"It's going to have to be good enough. I know you want everything to go your way, and I respect it: It's one of the only traits you share with the real Sally. She didn't like to be told what to do either. But I am not a father speaking to his daughter. I am a colonel in the United States Army, speaking to a representative of an opposing force, and I am telling you that no, you don't get your own way this time. Your own way is off the table. You can go in knowing the attack is coming, or you can refuse to go in at all. At this point, we're the only chance you have—and while you may not want to hear this, we don't need you anymore. We know where the enemy is located. We know how to kill them. We're offering to let you help us because you want your people back, and because we appreciate the service you provided by bringing us this information. But that doesn't mean you're running this operation. If anything, it means the opposite. Do I make myself perfectly clear?"

Colonel Mitchell folded his arms as he stopped speaking, and looked down his nose at me like he was passing judgment on the entire world. I couldn't breathe. My lungs had locked up: Like having my own way, oxygen was suddenly off the table. I was going to die here, shocked into suffocation by one betrayal too many, one act of treason beyond what I could bear. I...

I saw Fishy. Fishy was winking so hard that it looked like he'd developed a nervous tic. When he saw me looking, he stopped winking and flashed a quick, secretive smile before returning to his previous, sullen pose. I was missing something. I was missing something, and for whatever reason, he wasn't in a position to tell me what it was.

Suddenly, breathing was possible again. "I go in first," I said. "You have to give me thirty minutes."

"Fifteen," countered Colonel Mitchell.

"Twenty," I said. "Sherman's going to want to have me searched before he does anything else, and I refuse to be naked and surrounded by armed guards when you decide to attack the place."

"Done," said Colonel Mitchell. "We roll out in an hour."

"I'll go tell Fang," I said, and turned, and left them all—even Private Larsen—behind.

The formulas provided to USAMRIID by Dr. Cale's people produce a very narrow spectrum antiparasitic, intended to target only those implants created by cloning the implant provided to Sally Mitchell. Adding this chemical to the waterways may result in some die-offs among amphibian and snail species, but the ecological impact should be relatively minor, and should be over within a three-year span. Additional water treatments may be necessary in the future, as eggs may have settled in the silt at the bottoms of ponds and streams. If this silt is stirred up for any reason, it's possible that the infections could reoccur.

Modifying these formulas to target other strains of parasite should be difficult, but not impossible. Given the damage that has already been done to the western United States, I don't see why we shouldn't seize this opportunity to kill off more of the rogue implants, thus creating a "clean slate" on which we can build a better, brighter, human future.

—FROM THE PRIVATE NOTES OF DR. STEVEN BANKS,
JANUARY 15, 2028

I went to see my mother this afternoon.

She's adapting surprisingly well to captivity. She asked if she could have her wheelchair back; I told her I would consider it, once I'd seen that she could continue to behave herself. I feel like we've achieved a good balance between us, where she understands her place and doesn't push for more than she deserves, and I respect her human autonomy. It hurts me to see her stuck in one place, unable to move, but I can't give her the chair unless she promises not to run over more of my people. She can be quite aggressive when she feels thwarted, and she feels thwarted a surprising amount of the time. She has a lot of anger in her.

I get that from her side of the family, I suppose.

I think that she will come to see my side of things, given time and sufficient incentive. She has never been foolish, and I know she still loves me. I'm her son, after all. On some level, she has to realize that I'll be her only son sooner rather than later: She should be transferring all her love to me, where it will be safe, and still have someone to receive it.

We're so very near the end of things. I can feel it in my bones.

—FROM THE NOTES OF SHERMAN LEWIS
(SUBJECT VIII, ITERATION III), JANUARY 2028

Chapter 18

JANUARY 2028

Getting to the mall where Sherman and his people were holed up wasn't an issue. It was near a major freeway, and accessible from several major and minor surface streets. We could easily roll up and knock on the front door, if that had been what we wanted to do. But that approach—that direct, aggressive approach—would have made it impossible for me to pretend to be alone. We had to do something else.

"Odds are good that he has eyes on the surrounding buildings, and on the freeway overpass," said Fishy, with the manic good cheer of a man who had spent his entire life figuring out how to lay siege to ridiculous video game locations. "But if we take I-4 through Concord, and then approach up Monument Boulevard, we can probably get to the Oak Grove intersection without being close enough to attract attention. At that distance, movement is going to get ascribed to sleepwalkers or carrion birds, not an army convoy."

"Okay," I said. "What then?"

Fishy smiled brightly, lips barely staying closed over his teeth. "Can you ride a bicycle?"

I looked at him, aghast.

Twenty minutes later, I was riding a bright pink bicycle with tassels on the handlebars down the middle of Monument Boulevard. I was wobbling but I wasn't falling over, thanks to the training wheels Fishy had attached to the base. He'd scavenged the whole thing from the Big Lots near where the convoy was waiting, producing it with the sort of flourish that told me he'd been dreaming of this moment for years. I wasn't sure what that said about him.

One thing that could definitely be said about me: I had never learned how to ride a bicycle. It hadn't seemed like a major priority, and even if it had, there was no way the Mitchells and SymboGen would have ever signed off on the idea, back when I was living by their rules and following their ideas of what my world should be. Buses were safer than bicycles. Bicycles got hit by cars, and stolen by bored teenagers looking for something to do with their time. They definitely didn't belong with mentally unstable amnesiacs who had panic attacks when they tried to ride in private vehicles.

Still, the principle was simple, and even I could work a set of pedals. I wobbled down the street, trying to avoid potholes and abandoned cars, and watched the businesses and buses to either side as I went. Nothing moved but birds and one bored orange cat, which looked so much like Tumbleweeds—a cat I used to know in San Francisco—that I almost stopped. Only the knowledge that no domestic cat could have made the trip across the Bay on foot kept me from checking to see if it was Marya's old pet.

Marya hadn't survived the first wave of sleepwalker attacks.

I was almost sure of that. But Tumbleweeds had always been allowed to roam freely, and I hoped he was all right. Maybe someday we'd be able to go back to San Francisco and find out.

Getting to that someday started now. I pedaled faster, and tried not to think about the fact that I was riding on a rickety assortment of bolts and pink tubes. It was faster than walking. That was the only good thing about it.

The mall appeared in front of me, set off to the left and surrounded by some rather impressive traffic jams. I was close enough now that I was sure I'd make it, whether or not I had a vehicle. I got off the bike, walking it through the snarl of cars, and propped it up against a defunct traffic light, where anyone watching from the mall would be able to see and identify it, but wouldn't necessarily see the training wheels. I wanted them to think I'd pedaled much farther than I actually had. I wanted them as confused as possible—and hence as focused on me as possible—for as long as I could manage it.

Walking across the parking lot felt like walking to my own execution. Every part of me strained to turn around and go back, to run for the promise of my own safety, my own survival. I kept going anyway. Survival would be meaningless if it came at the expense of everyone I'd ever cared about. That wasn't the point of staying alive. I wanted my friends, and my family, and I wanted to get the hell out of here before things fell apart again.

"You can't reach the broken doors without going through a bunch of trials, remember? You can do this," I whispered, and squared my shoulders, and kept on going.

Like most malls, which were sort of pitcher plants for people, sucking them in and spitting them out again without the contents of their wallets, the mall on Monument had multiple entrances. Some of them were built into specific stores, including the old Kohl's that had been my prison when I was here before. Others were built into the side of the mall proper.

Those seemed like the best bet for getting inside. I angled for a door set between a health food store and a Hawaiian Barbecue. The glass was soapy and opaque, making it impossible to see more than the vaguest shadows filtering through from inside.

Had something just moved in there? I thought it might have. Sherman's people had to know that I was here. They had to be watching their surroundings, because there were no sleepwalkers in the immediate vicinity. Riding a bicycle down the middle of Mission or Market would have triggered a swarm.

Unless the water had killed them all. For the first time since we'd arrived in Pleasant Hill, a trickle of doubt worked its way through my heart, twisting through the ventricles until it felt like it was going to block the blood flow altogether. What if we were wrong? What if Fishy's careful logic and Colonel Mitchell's detailed maps had led us to the wrong conclusion, and Sherman was somewhere else entirely?

What if we hadn't found them after all?

I walked up to the door and knocked, quick and light. Then I stepped back, waiting for something to happen. Seconds ticked by. If I *had* seen motion from inside, it wasn't repeated. I crossed my arms, trying to look annoyed, rather than anxious. *Don't make me wait, Sherman*, I thought, projecting the concept into my face with every ounce of acting skill I possessed. It wasn't much. I hoped it would be enough. *You've made me wait long enough.*

There was a sound from behind me, like a shoe scuffing ever so briefly against the pavement. I relaxed slightly. It wasn't a sleepwalker. Sleepwalkers didn't sneak. That meant that it had to be someone who wanted to come up behind me without being seen, and *that* meant...

"I guess you've probably been waiting for me," I said, dropping my arms. "I missed you."

There was a pause, long enough that I started to wonder if

I'd guessed incorrectly. Then, sounding slightly bemused, Sherman said, "I think you may be in the wrong place. There's no one here for you to miss." His incongruously British accent was as strong as ever, the result of some neurological tic triggered by his integration. I got dyslexia, he got an accent, Tansy got a misplaced sense of whether or not she was allowed to hurt people. I still didn't know what Adam got. Or Juniper. If I wanted to find out, I had to play this precisely right.

I turned around. I didn't smile. "I missed *you*," I repeated, this time stressing the last word as I looked him in the eye. "I thought you'd come after me. But I knew that if I came back, you'd be here."

Sherman blinked. His bewilderment was even clearer now that I could see his face, and it gave me hope: hope that this would work, hope that I could bluff my way through the encounter that all my other bluffs had been leading up to. Pretending to be Sally, pretending to be dutiful, pretending to be brave, they were nothing—*nothing*—compared to pretending to be the girl who could have missed this man.

But I had been her once, hadn't I? Before everything had gotten so strange, back when I was human and Sherman was my favorite SymboGen escort, I had been that girl. All I had to do was remember what it felt like in her skin, and pull it over me.

"You must be kidding," he said. "Do you think I'm that stupid? We capture a bunch of your people and suddenly you're on my doorstep claiming to miss me?"

"You mean you captured the *human* who put his hands on me and told me I should feel lucky that I'd taken over a body he liked? Or do you mean you captured the *human* who designed me and then told me I was a flawed experiment that was never supposed to get out of the lab? I'm sure you're talking about one of them. Just tell me which one is supposedly 'my' people, and I'll be happy to tell you how wrong you are."

Sherman blinked again. Then, slowly, he reached out and cupped his hand against my cheek. I felt a jolt, like his fingers were buzzing with static electricity. The drums changed their tempo. Slowly at first, and then faster, until they were beating to an entirely different song.

I forced myself to keep breathing. This was what Sherman did. He manipulated the bioelectric fields of other chimera, bending us to his will. But he couldn't do what I did: He couldn't wrap the hot warm dark and the peace it brought around himself like a cloak, insulating himself from the world. I reached deep and pulled it as far up as I could, letting it engulf me.

"Do you mean what you're saying?" he asked.

The word "no" struggled to form on my lips. He wanted to hear the truth; the rhythm of the drums that were my heartbeat told me that. He wanted to hear the truth, and I wanted to give it to him, because it would make him happy. But he would be happier with the lie, wouldn't he? I pulled the hot warm dark closer. Yes, yes, he would be happier with the lie; the lie would give him everything he'd ever wanted, the lie would make him *complete*, while the truth would only make him empty.

"Yes," I sighed, and my voice was the ghost of empty labs and abandoned buildings, places that were in the process of being forgotten by the world. There was no coming back from this lie. The course was set.

Sherman's eyes widened, suddenly alive with hope. "Yes?" he echoed.

"I came here for you." Not a lie, not quite. I was leaving a lot of things out, but I wasn't *lying*. That was easier to do, with the hot warm dark to bolster me and his hand on my face, compelling me to tell the truth. Editing was so much simpler than outright falsehood. "I wanted to see you." Also true. "I thought you'd come for me by now." Also true: the stuff of nightmares, but true. I had lain awake waiting for him to come for me. I had woken up convinced that his hands were on my skin. But I didn't have to tell him those things. No matter what he did, he couldn't make me tell him.

His left hand came up to cup the other side of my face, so that he was holding me captive. I couldn't have gotten away without stepping forcefully back and pulling my face out of his hands, and then he would have known something was wrong. I didn't pull away.

Slowly, Sherman lowered his mouth to mine and kissed me.

He had only kissed me once before, when he was breaking me out of USAMRIID. Then, he had been doing it to rewire my bioelectrics. This time he was kissing me because he wanted to be kissing me, and I knew that my survival, and the survival of the people I loved, depended on my kissing him back. So I did. I kissed him like I was still that confused, desperate-to-please girl who wanted so badly to be normal, to be human, to be *loved*. I kissed him like she was still inside me, and like I wanted to be with him forever. I kissed him until I started to feel like it was a betrayal of everything I had ever wanted to be, and just as I was about to pull away, he pulled back and let me go, eyes wide and bright.

"Sal," he breathed. "You really did come back for me. You little fool." He made the words sound like "I love you." He made them painful to hear.

I shrugged, managing somehow to muster a smile, and said, "I didn't know where else to go."

"So you came to me. You came to *me*." He turned to the mall door, and called, "Stand down the snipers, open the doors. She came to *me*."

The door swung open. There was a short, gently rounded woman standing just inside, wearing a snood over her hair and a scowl on her face. "Of course she came to you. Where else would she have gone? We stole her pet humans, and the military would cut her up as soon as look at her."

"Batya, be nice," said Sherman. "She is our guest."

"She is a traitor to her species, and she's already run away from you once before, or have you forgotten?" The woman—Batya—looked me up and down. Then she turned back to Sherman, shook her head, and said, "You can't do this. We're not stable enough for you to do this. Put her back where you found her."

"I found her right here," said Sherman. "Right here, because she came to *me*. She's going to be our guest for a little while, aren't you, Sal?"

"Forever, maybe," I said, trying to keep my voice from shaking. "Hi, Batya. I'm Sal. It's nice to meet you."

"Oh my God give me strength," muttered Batya. "I know who you are, Sal. I've been looking at your genetic material through a microscope for weeks, and I've watched your clones explode the brains of several of my friends. You've been a busy girl, haven't you?"

I considered pointing out that it had been *Sherman* who extracted my genetic material and turned it into a weapon, not me, but realized it would be futile to even try. Batya was on Sherman's side. All I could do was convince her that I was a backstabbing loser, and endanger my tenuous grasp on his goodwill. I needed that goodwill. I needed to get inside.

"I ran because you people were slicing my skull open without my consent, and I get a little squirrely about bodily autonomy and my right to not have my skull sliced open when I don't want it to be," I said. I didn't try to moderate my tone. Batya might be a useful ally, but I wasn't planning to be here long enough to need useful allies: I just needed Sherman on my side, as much as was possible during the time that I was in his custody. "Only then I got taken back by the humans, and you know what? There are worse things than a few cell samples. There's being locked in a box and treated like a lab specimen. There's people looking at you like you're worse than dirt because you dared to pick up something they'd already thrown away. You people might have acted like I had fewer rights than you did, but you never acted like I wasn't a person."

I hesitated. This was the hard part. This was the part that needed to get me inside. I glanced at Sherman, trying to project shyness through my eyes, and added, "And I missed Sherman. He was the only one who ever really *knew* me and was kind to me anyway. Everybody else either saw a lab specimen or a confused human girl. He saw a chimera. I didn't realize how important that was until it stopped."

Sherman put an arm possessively around my waist. "You see? She's here for the right reasons, and I'm going to keep her. You know you can't stop me, Bat. You might as well just step aside and let us in."

"You're going to get us all killed," said Batya. She looked at me for a moment, and there was no warmth or welcome in her expression. I fought the urge to shiver. I'd been worried about running into Ronnie, who might not forgive me for coming back after he'd helped me escape. Maybe I should have been worrying about the people I didn't know yet. They had less reason to trust me.

Then she stepped aside. Sherman's hand went from my waist to the small of my back, and he propelled me into the mall.

The tracking device Fishy had installed in the heel of my shoe would be showing Fishy and the others that I was moving again: It would be flashing on their monitor with every step I took, keeping them apprised of my status. We hadn't been able to find a way to wire me for sound without the risk that I'd be found out, but the tracker was small and virtually undetectable, unless Sherman decided to take my shoes apart. When I found the place where our people were being held, I was supposed to pace back and forth—five steps one way, five steps back the other way, and repeat twice to show that it wasn't an accidental pattern. Then they'd be able to come in without killing our people.

Not that it would help Adam or Juniper very much once the gas grenades started flying. I needed to find them and somehow tell them to get a filter over their mouths and noses, or I was going to watch them die. I didn't think I could survive that.

The interior of the mall had changed since I'd been there last. There were more stacks of boxes pushed up against the walls. I couldn't stop long enough to let my eyes focus on the letters, but some of them had helpful pictograms of their contents— pineapples and tomatoes and fish. They were stockpiling canned food. Water, too, and soft drinks, and juices—anything that wouldn't spoil within the next year. We walked down the hallway to the main concourse. The small, buzzing sensation that always told me I was near another chimera was stronger than it had ever been before. I had a better hold on it than I'd had the last time I'd been in Sherman's custody.

Sherman's... I glanced at him, suddenly startled. "I can't feel you," I said, trying to make my voice a little petulant, like him hiding himself from me was rude but not terrifying. "Why can't I feel you?"

"So you *are* one of the radar children!" Sherman beamed, first at me and then across me at Batya. "I told you she'd have interesting skills to bring to the table. Only one in four chimera is lucky enough to be so connected, Sal. I should have guessed that you could be one of them, if you bothered to work with your own abilities long enough to figure out what those feelings meant."

"I was always drawn to y—I mean, to other chimera," I said, and ducked my head, hoping he would assume that the redness in my cheeks was a blush, and not anger. "I can feel them when they're near me. This building is *full* of us. I can even feel her"—I gestured toward Batya—"and we only just met for the first time. But I can't feel you. Why can't I feel you, Sherman?"

"Because, my poppet, I can turn off that part of my broadcast when I need to. I find that I generally need to. It helps me do important things, like intercepting visitors in my parking lot."

That explained how Sherman had been able to sneak up behind me without setting off any alarm bells: He'd been somehow suppressing that part of his pheromone signature. He really was the ultimate infiltrator. The thought came with a thin, jagged line of fear that raked its claws across my heart. Sherman was *built* to lie and cheat and work his way into places he didn't belong. Even as a chimera, he was a parasite. I didn't have those advantages. All I had was a lifetime of trying to play along and play by the rules, and that didn't guarantee me anything. I was going to get caught. I was *going* to get caught, and the only question was whether they'd have time to start taking me apart before Fishy and the cavalry arrived to save whatever remained.

"That's amazing," I said. "Why?"

"I don't know!" Sherman's whole face lit up when he confessed his ignorance, like this was the most exciting thing that had ever happened. It was...sweet. It made me remember the days when he'd been one of my best friends, and I'd thought that we would be friends forever. Too bad he'd turned out to be a murderous asshole. That really put a damper on our hanging out. "It's something to do with the tailoring that my creators did. I've asked Mother to explain it to me, when she's done reworking your children—you did find out about that, didn't you? The children?"

"You mean the clones you cultured from my body? Yeah, I found out." Juniper, he had Juniper, and I couldn't let him know about her. I forced my face to stay neutral, but allowed a sliver of disapproval to seep into my voice as I said, "You could have asked me, you know. That's why I left the last time. I really don't like it when people cut into my head without permission."

"I'm sorry about that; it won't happen again," he said. I didn't believe him, of course. I was willing to risk myself for my family. That didn't make me a fool.

We had entered the main concourse while we spoke. The fountain was still going, the water trickling down in an endless shower of droplets. I wondered whether *that* water had been contaminated, or whether they had somehow managed to keep it clean. If it was connected to the taps somehow, it would eventually fill with antiparasitics from the general water supply. The thought was oddly entertaining, and quietly terrible.

People I didn't recognize sat on the edge of the fountain or moved between the open shops, talking to each other, carrying things from place to place, doing the normal things that normal people did when they didn't have anything more pressing at hand. Something about seeing them made my heart hurt. This was a civilization of chimera. It was small, yes, and it had done some terrible things, but as Colonel Mitchell had made clear, we were at war. Only one side of this conflict was going to walk away triumphant. Was I siding with the humans over my own species because of how I'd been raised, or because the humans were actually right about who deserved to inherit the Earth? I didn't know. I wasn't sure that anybody did.

These people could have been my friends, if things had gone differently, if Sherman had actually been able to win me over to his side. He could have convinced me to make this place my home, and I would have been fighting with him all this time. The thought turned my stomach. We walk on the graves of our unborn selves, the futures we never got to live, and some of those people wouldn't get along very well with the ones we actually decided to be.

"What brings you here *now*, Sal?" asked Batya. Her question had knives tucked inside, like terrible prizes.

"Someone decided to raid Dr. Cale's lab while I was asleep in my quarters," I said calmly, meeting her gaze without flinching. Next to Sherman, and Dr. Banks, and Gail Mitchell, she was nothing scary. She was just another chimera, and I knew how to deal with them. "I woke up and everyone was gone. So I realized that no one was going to be in a position to stop me. I stole a bike from the Kmart, and I got moving."

"The Kmart," said Batya. "Really. You mean the Kmart that was swarming with throwbacks?"

It took me a moment to realize that "throwbacks" was her way of saying "sleepwalkers." It made sense, in a backward sort of manner. For a human, a sleepwalker was a person who had suddenly taken leave of their senses and fallen into a violent fugue state. For a chimera, a throwback was an implant that had failed to properly integrate with its human host and was thus unable to participate in a fully intelligent world. It was all in which direction you chose to look at the thing from.

I liked "throwback" better. It implied that they could someday find a way to stumble forward, and join the rest of us in the light.

"Yes, I do," I said. "You mean you can't communicate with them? I thought it was like the chimera-detection trick. I thought everyone could do it."

Sherman frowned. "What are you saying?"

"They say my name a lot. The throwbacks. I think I have really good pheromones, because most of the time, they listen to me, as long as they're not too hungry. When they're hungry, they don't really listen to anybody."

"They say your *name*?" Batya sounded frankly disbelieving.

"Yeah," I said. "I don't know why. No one's ever been able to tell why. Don't you remember, Sherman? You've heard it. You were there when Chave got sick. She started saying my name right before she tried to kill me."

"She knew your name because she was responsible for you," he said, but there was doubt in his tone, like he was suddenly questioning a lot of things he had previously taken entirely for granted. "You can control the throwbacks. Really."

"As long as they're not hungry." I could see the abandoned department store that had been my prison up ahead of us. I shivered. I couldn't help myself. "Dr. Cale always made sure the throwbacks in the Kmart were well fed, since otherwise, she couldn't keep them from trying to get out."

"Fascinating," said Sherman. "I hope you won't mind if we test this. It could be useful in the months to come." His hand was still nestled at the small of my back, keeping me from moving away from him. I wanted to shrug it off. I didn't dare. If he needed me to stay in place, then I was going to stay, at least until he decided that he was willing to let me move.

"As long as you feed them first, I'm game for pretty much anything," I said. "I want to understand myself better. I want to understand all of us better. I like the humans. Some of them have been kind to me. But they're never going to know what it is to *be* me, and I need that. I need people who know."

It wasn't hard to make those words sound sincere. They came from the heart of me, from the place that died a little every time one of Dr. Cale's lab techs looked at me like I was less than they were, the part that was still bleeding from the look on Gail Mitchell's face. I needed my own kind to remind me that I wasn't an aberration, I wasn't a mistake: I was as worthy of existence as anyone else. I just didn't need Sherman, or his assemblage of would-be monsters. I needed Adam, and Juniper, and Tansy. I needed *my* people, and I was going to get them back, whatever it took.

"You realize we can't trust you right away," said Sherman. He sounded genuinely apologetic. "You can't waltz in here, say 'I'm on your side now,' and expect us to be all right with that."

Batya snorted. I got the feeling she was never going to be all right with that. I wasn't clear what her job was, but she seemed to be filling the same bodyguard-slash-security-expert position that Ronnie held. Under the circumstances, it made sense that she wouldn't be in a hurry to put her faith in me.

"I understand," I said, and smiled, trying to look hopeful. "I figure we have time for everyone here to get used to me. But... where's Ronnie? I expected to see him."

"She sacrificed herself to contaminate the humans' water supply," said Sherman.

Hearing him misgender Ronnie so casually made me want to glower. I forced my face to remain smooth, betraying only my honest shock as I said, "He did what?"

"We had to get the eggs and infant worms into the water somehow, and they only mature properly in human flesh," said Sherman. "It's why the humans are so foolish to believe that we would wipe them out entirely. That has never been, will never be, the goal. Without humans, we'd have no place to properly incubate our young. Ronnie swallowed an entire test tube of eggs cultured from your DNA, and she went to the reservoir, and she let herself go for the greater cause."

"Not just Ronnie," said Batya. There was a heat in her tone that had nothing to do with me. I had stumbled across some ongoing argument between the two of them, and it was all I could do not to duck my head to get away from the force of her glare. "We lost five people in that action, and since it turns out that your babies aren't selective about where they hang their hats, we've lost more people since."

"They're not my babies," I said. "I didn't volunteer."

"You're not still mad about that, are you, Sal?" asked Sherman. "It was for the greater good. You should appreciate that sometimes choices must be made that feel less than optimal for the individual. Or did Tansy manage to make a miracle return when you ran off and left her at SymboGen?"

He didn't know about Tansy. *He didn't know.* His spies, if

he had any remaining, had not managed to infiltrate the new, smaller SymboGen, and my sister's survival was still a mystery to him. I managed to suppress my gasp of delight, transforming it instead into the glower I had been holding back for so long.

"Yeah, I'm still mad about that," I said. "I'm not as 'burn it down' resentful, but you shouldn't have cut me open. Not without my permission. You know it was wrong. You knew that it was wrong when you did it. It's going to take me a while before I can trust you again, because you did that."

"The needs of the many must outweigh the needs of the few." We were almost to the department store. Was that where they were being kept? It only made sense if Ronnie had closed the avenue I used for my escape before he committed suicide for the cause. Otherwise, Sherman would have been locking people up in a box with a hole in the side. Not a good way to hang on to your prisoners. "You have to understand, Sal: It doesn't matter how much I care for you, and it never will. I will always put the needs of our species ahead of what you may personally desire. If you can't handle that, this is not the place for you."

"But we're not going to let you leave," interjected Batya. "You know where we are now. There's being generous with other members of our species, and then there's being a fool. Only a fool would let someone with loyalties as fluid as yours step out that door knowing where we were."

I blinked at her. My "loyalties"? "Fluid"? My loyalties had never wavered. I had always been loyal to my family—and while my definition of "family" had shifted from the Mitchells to Nathan, Dr. Cale, and my fellow chimera once I discovered what I was, it had been a natural transition. I hadn't been fickle or fluid.

But then, I only knew that because I lived with myself every day. To someone on the outside, it could easily appear that I was just going from easy answer to easy answer. The Mitchells to Dr. Cale; Dr. Cale to USAMRIID; USAMRIID to Sherman, and then back to Dr. Cale, at least according to the story I was feeding to Sherman. That story ended with my choosing to come back to Sherman—choosing the apparent winning side, just like I had all along.

The thought was sobering. How many people's motives didn't match up with what I'd taken for their actions? How many villains were the heroes of their own stories? I didn't know, and I was terribly afraid that I was never going to find out.

"I don't have anywhere else to go," I said. "I'm staying here. Whatever I have to do to prove my loyalty, I'll do it."

"Good. I was hoping you'd say that." Sherman stopped. We were standing in front of a shoe store, with metal sheeting pulled down to block it from view. He nodded to Batya, who moved to open the store's first layer of protection from shoplifters. The second layer, a metal grate that served as surprisingly effective prison bars, remained in place.

It shouldn't have been such a surprise to see Nathan and Dr. Cale inside, bent over workstations, their attention mostly focused on the tasks at hand. Nathan glanced toward the front of the store when the shield began to retract, whining and scraping all the while. His eyes went wide. He stood so fast he knocked over his stool.

"Sal!" he exclaimed. From the sound of his voice, he couldn't decide whether to be relieved that I was in one piece or upset to see me in this place. I shared the sentiment. "You're here!"

Nathan's eyes flicked to Sherman, and to the hand still resting against the small of my back. His face changed then, becoming a mask of fury. Hands clenching into fists, he stalked toward us.

"Get your hands off her, you bastard," he spat. "You don't have the right to lay hands on my fiancé."

"She came here of her own free will, Brother," said Sherman.

"I told you she'd make the right choice if she had the opportunity to do it all over again. All she has to do now is earn the right to stay."

"How do I do that?" I asked. I lifted my chin slightly as I spoke, hoping Nathan would remember me doing the same as I spoke to Dr. Banks, back when I had pretended to be Sally. *If I can pretend to be one kind of loyalist, I can pretend to be another,* I thought. *Don't give up on me yet. Don't let him convince you that I'm lost.*

"Easy," said Sherman. He took his hand away from my back and pressed a gun into my hand. I hadn't even seen him draw it. "You kill him."

Oh.

The surgery was performed perfectly. Subject VII-B, code name "Asphodel," was alert and mobile when introduced to the brain tissue of the host. Subject immediately began to display normal burrowing activity and established a preliminary connection with the host tissue before the incision was closed and stitched. At this point, all ability to monitor the subject's vital signs was lost, as they were masked by the stronger vital signs of the host.

After six hours, Subject IX-A, "Persephone," confirmed the presence of chimera pheromones rising from the host body, signaling that initial neural integration had begun.

The host began to demonstrate the muscular twitches characteristic of a body undergoing final integration fifteen minutes ago. I have been monitoring constantly, and she has thus far not done anything to indicate that the integration is not proceeding as planned. Barring unforeseen complications, I believe we have succeeded. We have saved her life.

—FROM THE NOTES OF DR. FANG HSIANG, JANUARY 15, 2028

Colonel Mitchell:

The water contamination has spread as far as the Mississippi River, and there have been unconfirmed reports that the river itself has been contaminated. In light of this development, you are authorized to do whatever is necessary to reclaim the waterways of the United States. You will be forgiven for whatever ecological damage is done, as failure to move would constitute a form of treason against the human race.

I was sorry to hear that Joyce passed. Our thoughts and prayers are with you in this time as you continue to fight for the survival of humanity.

We will endure. We are stronger than our adversaries, and this will not be the way we die.

—MESSAGE FROM ANGELA WILLIAMSON, SECRETARY OF DEFENSE, TRANSMITTED TO USAMRIID ON JANUARY 15, 2028

Chapter 19

JANUARY 2028

What?" I looked at Sherman. "I don't—"

"I'm not a jealous sort," he said, folding my hands around the handle of his gun. There was probably a name for it, something technical and deadly, but it was hard to think of it as anything other than the handle, the part I was supposed to hold while I pulled the trigger. "I don't mind that you've had another lover. If anything, it'll cast me in a better light. No human could ever love you like I will. But I refuse to let your loyalties be divided. You've already shown that you can be swayed, like a reed in the wind. That's a good thing! Reeds don't break. I just don't see why I should make it easier for you to bend."

"I've never killed anyone," I said. My voice squeaked, breaking. And that wasn't true, was it? I had killed before, but they had always been sleepwalker-throwbacks, people who were never going to remember themselves and come back into the world. How was that any more forgivable? I was already a murderer. No amount of pretty dancing around the subject would change that.

"So you can start," said Sherman. "Oh, and in case this was some sort of trick, and you're thinking about shooting me? You should be aware that two things will happen immediately if you try that. Batya will shoot you."

"Happily," said Batya.

"And then my people will take your precious boy there and crack him open and place me inside his skull, where I will make myself at home." Sherman smirked. "I'll miss this body. I like the things it lets me do. But I can get used to something a little more...scholarly."

"Sherman, please stop trying to kill my biological son," said Dr. Cale. She hadn't looked away from her microscope. "I'm not going to love you any more than I do right now if you take away the other objects of my affection. I'm just going to be angry with you for taking my best lab technician away from me."

"Thanks for the sentimentality, Mom," said Nathan. He was staring at me and the gun in my hand, looking faintly ill.

"I don't have time for sentiment," said Dr. Cale. "Besides, your brother isn't the sentimental sort. But he won't like what happens if I get mad at him."

"I..." I tried to make myself raise the gun, to at least pretend to be playing along, but this was it: We had found the limits of my pretense. I shook my head harshly, and started to pace.

Batya twitched like she was going to stop me. Sherman gestured for her to be still, and she held her position.

"I'm so tired of all of us trying to kill each other all the time." Five steps and turn. "Why do we have to lower ourselves to their level? Why can't we be better than they are?" Five steps and turn. "They made us, and that means we have to be better than them, or they might as well never have made us at all."

Five steps and turn. Five more steps, back to the place where I had started, and stop. I resisted the urge to look up at the skylights overhead. If the cavalry was coming, I didn't want to give them away. Instead, I looked at Sherman, pleading. "We have to be better than they are. They made us. We have to prove that we're not a mistake."

"Oh, Sal." Sherman reached over and plucked the gun from my hands. For a moment—just a moment—my fingers tightened, trying to keep him from taking it away. But I couldn't defend myself from all his people. More and more of them were taking notice of us, stopping whatever they'd been doing to turn and look quizzically in our direction.

"I told you," said Batya. "Didn't I tell you? She's never going to be on your side. She's never going to be on *our* side. She's just here because she wants her human fuck-toy back."

"Don't swear, Batya: The woman I got your body from wouldn't approve. As for my Sal…" Sherman reached out and ran his fingertips down my cheek. His touch tingled like a mild electric shock. "You wouldn't lie to me, would you, darling? I'll be honest with you. I don't think that you can."

"Get your hands off her," snarled Nathan. He grabbed the metal grate keeping him inside the store, pulling it inward until the whole thing rattled without effectively budging. "Sal, get the hell away from him!"

"He's not the boss of you, is he, dear?" Sherman's eyes narrowed. "*Is* he?"

I could feel the drums thrumming through his skin, trying to force my heart to beat in time with his. I reached for the dark, holding it close, and allowed my face to go slack. "He's not the boss of me," I said dreamily. "Also, that's not grammatically correct. He should be grammatically correct if he wants people to listen to him."

"My little pedant," said Sherman, stroking my cheek again. "You can't lie to me, can you, darling?"

"No," I said.

"Are you lying to me?"

"No."

"Are you here because you want your human lover back?"

"No." I glanced to Nathan. I couldn't stop myself. The stricken look on his face would follow me to my grave. He'd really believed that I was there to rescue him. *I am here to rescue you*, I thought—but of course, he couldn't hear me. All he could hear were the lies I was telling to Sherman. And I couldn't stop. If I stopped, we were all doomed, and then I would never be able to make it up to him. Everything depended on how good of a liar I had learnt to be.

Sherman wasn't done. "Are you going to betray me?"

"No." I already had. As soon as I'd triggered the tracking device in my shoe, I'd betrayed him.

Sherman leaned closer, until I could see the stretched-tissue pattern of his irises. Human poetry always compared eyes to flowers, but to me, they looked more like the blossoming mouths of tapeworms, brightly colored and filled with secret teeth. The eyes were the window to the soul. Maybe what you saw there said more about you than it did about the person you were looking at. "Are you going to stay with me this time?"

"Yes," I whispered. He leaned in and kissed me fiercely, as much to make the claim in front of Nathan as to possess me for his own. I didn't pull back or resist. I stood there, and I kissed him, and I knew that Nathan was watching, and I couldn't do a damn thing about it, because I was trying to save our lives.

Sherman pushed me away. He looked at me sadly, and shook his head. "I don't believe you."

Hands grabbed my upper arms. I twisted, and saw that Batya had me in a surprisingly strong grip. She was snarling at me without opening her lips, turning her face into a mask of malice. "What are you doing?" I demanded, trying to squirm away. "Stop it!"

"I'm sorry, Sal, but you've betrayed me one time too many," said Sherman. "I still love you. You're still my miracle girl. But that's why we're going to be together. Don't you see? For us, there's always a second chance to make a first impression."

Just like that, his plan became clear. I screamed, high and shrill and angry, before redoubling my efforts to get away from Batya. "You bastard! I came to you because I wanted to *be* with you! You can't do this to me! You can't cut me open again!"

"When next we speak, you won't remember any of this," said Sherman, still perfectly calm. "We'll open you up and slide you into a new host—a better host, I think, one that's been through less trauma. You were already planning on using her, I'm sure. Otherwise, why would you have kept her so neatly isolated from the rest of your stock?"

Carrie. He was going to slice my skull open and pull me out of it like a prize in a box of cereal, and then he was going to put me inside of *Carrie*, who hated what I was more than anyone else I'd ever met. It was a horrible thing to do to her. It was a horrible thing to do to *me*. I screamed again, thrashing harder. Batya was shorter than I was, but she was also stronger, and her grip on my arms wasn't wavering. Nathan was shaking the bars of his cage and yelling. Sherman rolled his eyes.

"You are so dramatic. It's from all that humanism you absorbed while you were living with them. We'll strip it right out of you, sweetheart, and then we'll be together, and you'll be the good, obedient helper you should always have been. There was never any need for things to be like this." He reached out and grabbed my chin, forcing my head to be still. I stopped thrashing rather than risk wrenching my neck. "Never. Any. Need."

The pounding of his heartbeat in my veins was almost irresistible, drowning out the drums that had been my anchor and absolute for so long. I took a breath, pulling the hot warm dark around me as much as I dared. The temptation to drop down into it was so strong. I could make all this go away. I could remove myself from the situation, and then when I woke up, I would be someone else, and all the hard choices and difficult situations would be over.

I would be dead.

I would be as dead as Sally Mitchell, as lost as Joyce; I would no longer exist. Epigenetic data might carry my essential core into the new body—hence Sherman's insistence that he would still have me, that we could be in love despite my change of skins—but *I* would be gone forever. *I* would never come back.

I had worked too hard and fought too long to give up that easily. Holding the hot warm dark around myself like a shield, I whipped my head to the side and bit his hand.

Sherman yelped as he jumped back, eyes wide and wounded. He looked offended, like I had somehow violated the laws of the universe by daring to stand up for myself. "You can't—" he sputtered.

"Fuck you," I snapped. "I was *never* here for you Sherman, do you hear me? *Never.* I came for my lover and my friends and my family, and you are none of those things to me, you are nothing but the man who betrayed me, who told his goons to kill my sister, who tried to kill the entire world. You're a murderer and a bastard and the only proof I ever needed that we're no better than the humans! We may as well *be* humans for all the difference it's made to us. I will never love you. You can cut me open a thousand times, you can slam me into a million different bodies, and I will never, never love you. I am not yours to control."

"Now can I shoot her?" demanded Batya.

"You little bitch," said Sherman wonderingly.

"Get your hands off her!" shouted Nathan.

The sound of glass breaking was almost obscured by the noise. My eyes widened. The assault had begun, and I still didn't know where Juniper was.

I couldn't save her if I couldn't save myself. I took a deep breath of the hopefully untainted air, and held it, squinting my eyes closed as tightly as I could. The antiparasitics would be aerosolized and could potentially enter my body through my mucus membranes.

"What the fuck is she doing?" demanded Sherman.

There was a clattering noise, as if metal objects were falling from the sky and landing on the mall floor. Someone shouted. Someone else screamed. The sound of hissing filled the air. I held my breath and kept my eyes closed, trying to keep the caustic medicines from entering my body.

"Sherman?" Batya sounded distressed. Her grip on my arms had weakened, ever so slightly, as she was overcome with surprise. That was my opening. I kicked back, slamming the heel of my shoe into her knee. She yelped and let go. Eyes still closed, I ran in the one direction I was sure was safe: toward the storefront where Nathan and Dr. Cale were confined.

My hands slammed into the metal grating. I latched on, holding tight. If I could just keep myself from needing to breathe; if I could just hold on…

"Sal, the gas!" Nathan's voice, so close to my ear that I could have wept. I'd been so afraid that I would never see him again. Now I was going to die only a few feet away from him, and he wasn't going to be able to save me. "Is it poison?"

I shook my head desperately, eyes still closed. He was safe. He needed to know he was safe. Humans might get sick from inhaling too much of this stuff—we had human DNA in us, anything designed to target us was by its very nature going to affect our creators—but they wouldn't die. He was safe. Everyone who mattered to me was safe, except for Adam, and Juniper. And me. I wasn't safe at all.

Maybe that was only fair. If I couldn't save the people I loved, why should I be allowed to save myself?

"Is it something that's going to hurt you but not us?"

This time I nodded vigorously, still clinging to the grate. Someone behind me was coughing, a steady, harsh sound. I hoped it was Sherman. I hoped he was going to cough his guts out before he died. Maybe then he'd realize that he had committed crimes that could never be forgiven.

"Sherman, come on!" Batya again. Her command was followed by the sound of stumbling footsteps, as if someone was running away. Oh, how I wanted to follow them, to cut them down and make them breathe deep of the consequences of their actions. Things had never needed to go this far. Sherman had forced the situation, and now there was no taking it back.

"Here." Dr. Cale's voice was surprisingly close. Something wet was shoved up against my face. "Nathan, hold this in place. Sal, go ahead and breathe. You're turning red, and if you pass out, you're not going to be able to help yourself. This should make things a little better."

Cautiously, I took a breath. The cloth had a sharp, antiseptic taste to it. My lungs didn't start burning. I hoped that was a good sign.

"You should be able to work it between the bars. Careful now. You don't want to drop it."

Bit by bit, pausing only to steal a little more air through the sodden cloth, I worked it through the grate and held it over my nose and mouth.

"Put out your hand again," said Dr. Cale. I did as I was told. A sheet of what felt like cling film was pressed on my fingers. "Put this over your eyes. It's supposed to protect us from splatter when we can't wear goggles. It should keep you from going blind."

Again, I did as I was told, opening my eyes at the last possible second. The thin, flexible film clung to the skin around them, making the world look a little distorted but clear. Nathan was right in front of me, pressed up against the grate. Dr. Cale was next to him, seated in her chair, a wan look on her face.

"Get us out of here," she said. "We have to find my children."

I nodded, not daring to speak through the cloth, and rushed to the lever that controlled the gate. I yanked it as hard as I could, putting all my weight into the action. It creaked. It wobbled. And finally, it dropped into place, triggering the mechanism that opened the store. I stepped back and watched as the grate retracted upward.

Nathan was the first out, ducking under the rising grate as soon as it was high enough. He rushed to me, embraced me, whispered, "I knew you would find us," in my ear, and then he was gone, running away down the mall concourse, heading for the distant doors to the old department store.

"Go, go, follow him!" shouted Dr. Cale. The grate was still rising, but slowly: She was trapped until it was high enough to let her wheel her chair out. She looked frustrated, and almost anguished. It was the first time I'd ever seen her really limited by her circumstances, and it made me hate Sherman even more. How dare he put her in this position? How dare he put *us* in this position? "He's trying to find Adam and the others! Here!"

She lobbed a stack of white towels soaked with whatever solution she'd mixed up to shield me out onto the concourse floor. It hit with a wet smacking sound. I grabbed the towels and ran after Nathan. He had a head start, but I was faster, and I had as much to lose as he did. In very little time, we were running side by side. Then I was pulling ahead, scanning the wall for the same lever setup that had allowed me to access the store where he'd been kept. If I could get the grate open…

The lever was almost ten feet away when I heard the gun go off. I staggered, almost dropping the towel I was breathing through, and looked back over my shoulder. Sherman was standing some twenty feet away, wearing a mask over the lower half of his face. Where had he been able to find a mask? Was he expecting this sort of attack?

No, no, he couldn't have been. There was a sporting goods

store in the mall, and he'd been stockpiling medical supplies for who knew how long. He must have had it already, and come back for his revenge when he realized that he'd been set up. He shook his head as he looked at me, the gun in his hand still raised. I stumbled onward, trying to put more distance between us. He'd missed me once. He could miss me again.

Then the men broke through the skylights, and the sound of machine gun fire filled the air. Sherman's attention was instantly wrenched away from me. He turned to fire on them, and they shot back, and he fell, he fell, his body bloomed red, like the hot warm dark was finally coming up into the light, and he *fell*, and I turned, and I ran for the lever.

Nathan was already rolling up the metal shielding when I hit the lever to retract the grate. As soon as he had enough of an opening, he slid inside, and I realized—with dawning hope—that if USAMRIID hadn't thrown any grenades into the department store itself, they might still be safe. There were no skylights in the store. There would have been no way for the gas to get inside.

The men in their black armor were on the ground now, unclipping themselves from the cords they'd used to jump down. I wondered how many of them I knew. I wondered how many were men like Private Larsen, who had been able to accept me as a person, if not a human being; I wondered how many were women like his sergeant, who had been so happy to bury her fists in my stomach. There was no way of knowing. They were faceless behind their helmets, and their hands were full of rifle barrels and electric prods.

I ducked and followed Nathan under the grate. The towels were soaking my clothing, making everything wet and warm. I kept running. We had passed the point where there were any other choices left for me.

"Sal!"

The shout came from the direction of the stairs. I turned, and there was Nathan, standing above the level of the creeping gas, with the terrified faces of our friends and colleagues behind him. Adam was there, and he was holding Juniper in his arms. She squealed when she saw me, a screeching, inhuman, beautiful sound, reaching out her hands like she could somehow seize the distance between us and throw it away.

"Coming!" It was hard to yell through the towel; my voice came out muffled and strange. I ran for them. I seemed to be slowing down for some reason, but still, I ran, and pressed the extra towels into Nathan's hands. "Your mom sent these."

He looked at me, and his eyes went wide even as his face went pale. He turned, handing the towels to Adam. "Put one of these over your face, and one over Juniper's. They'll protect you from the gas. Close your eyes. Everyone else, take a towel if it makes you feel better, but you don't need to worry as much. The gas is an antiparasitic, it shouldn't hurt you if you're human."

Towels were passed around. Juniper reached for me and made that high keening noise again, her hands starfishing in the air as Adam pressed a towel over her mouth and nose.

Nathan reached for me, taking my arm. "Sal, focus on me."

"What?" I blinked at him. He was getting fuzzy around the edges. Maybe I'd breathed in more of the gas than I had thought. "Nathan. We did it. We got you back."

"Stay with me, Sal. You can't go now, I'm not ready for you to go now. Close the broken doors. Just don't look at them."

"What? I'm not... I'm not going anywhere."

He sounded more anxious than I had ever heard him before. I blinked again, more slowly this time, before looking down at myself, and at the large red stain that was spreading across my abdomen as the blood soaked my shirt.

"Oh," I said, suddenly understanding. "I've been shot."

Saying the words seemed to unlock a whole world of displaced pain and weakness. My knees buckled. Nathan was there to catch me, and I smiled at him before I closed my eyes and let him hold me up. Juniper was keening, Adam and the others were shouting, and the broken doors were there. The broken doors were open, and I entered, and I was home.

I floated in the hot warm dark, where I had begun, where I had gone whenever I needed safety or comfort during my brief, confusing human life, and where I was apparently going to die. Everything was formless and safe, holding me in the warm embrace of weightless perfection. I moved with a thought, and there were no clumsy, unnecessary limbs to get in my way: I was evolution's darling, a ribbon of flesh capable of reproducing without aid, of regrowing from even the smallest segment.

I wonder if they're growing a new me, I thought. They could do it. One little snip and they'd have a whole new Sal, epigenetic data and core personality intact, but ready to learn and grow and have a second chance at everything. I'd thought of it as dying before, when Sherman was threatening me with a transplant. Now, in the hot warm dark, it seemed like a beautiful rebirth, as long as *I* didn't have to leave. If they wanted to take a little piece and grow themselves a new friend and lover and companion, I was all right with that. But here…

I was finally home.

I was going to miss my friends and loved ones, but not forever. Their names were already fading around the edges, going soft as trauma worked on my brain. I would be down in the hot warm dark until the mind that sustained me shut down, and then I would be gone. My body would live, my epigenetics would live, but the memories and experiences and ideas I had stored in the tissue of Sally Mitchell's mind would be lost.

I don't want to go, I thought, and *I am already gone*, I thought, and both things were true at the same time, and I made my peace with that.

The hot warm dark that surrounded me was part real, part

memory: I knew that. I couldn't move weightlessly when I was tangled in Sally's brain, but part of me remembered moving like a delicate ribbon through her digestive tract and then through her major arteries, tracing a pathway from her intestines to her brain. The human body was a miracle. Teeth always felt so big when you touched them with a tongue, and so small when you touched them with a finger. Everything was like that, a shifting scale of outside and in. As Sally—as Sal—my body had been the sum of the universe, so small and so fragile and so brutally defined. But before I had a name, Sally's body had *been* the universe, so enormous that I could have wandered it until I died and never have seen all that it had to offer. Everything was a matter of scale.

"—me? Sal, can you hear me?"

There was no sound in the hot warm dark: even the distant, constant pounding of drums was more vibration than noise, echoing through everything without ever making itself heard. For a moment, I didn't understand. I had no concept of sound, and thus had no concept of spoken words, or the meanings they were intended to convey.

"Don't give up, honey, just hold on for me. Hold on. It's going to be all right, you'll see. You'll see. We're going to get you out of here."

The words continued, and began to carry meanings, little packets of information that burst like fireworks across the night sky of my mind. They were for *me*. I was Sal, and someone was telling me to hold on. Hold on to what? You needed hands to hold on, and I had no hands, not here, not down in the dark where the monsters lived.

You don't have to stay here.

The thought was more interesting than the words were. I turned my full attention on it. I didn't have to stay here? But here was where I existed: Here was where I had settled after running for so long. How could I not stay? Here was where I belonged.

You could belong somewhere else. You could belong with your family. We could belong with your family.

I recoiled from the thought. *Sally?*

No. Sally's dead. Sally's been dead since before we existed, but we'll be dead too soon if we don't do something about it.

Who are you?

I'm you, and you're me. You're the me that yearns for the hot warm dark, for vastness with limits. I'm the you that dreams of hands and fingers, of smallness that goes on forever. I'm your connection to the human brain where you store the person you have become, and I am that person, and we don't have to let go yet. They're trying so hard to save us. They're fighting so hard to save us, and Sal, it's up to you. You're the part that endures. What do we do? What do we do? What do we—

"Just please, do something!"

The voice sliced through the thought, breaking it into a thousand pieces. I couldn't forget sound now, and with that memory came the memory of sight: The hot warm dark went red around me, filling with the movement of blood through veins and bile through the stomach. I couldn't be seeing any of this—I had no eyes—but I could see it all the same. My memory was good. I had looked inside so many animals when I helped Daisy with her necropsies. I had looked inside so many people when the sleepwalkers ripped them apart. I knew what I should be seeing.

"—to stop the bleeding. I need more cloths!" This voice belonged to Dr. Cale, which meant the other voice belonged to Nathan.

Nathan.

I didn't want to leave him. He was so important to me, and it had been so long since we'd been able to just be together, existing together, figuring out the future together. He was all I wanted. He was sweet and kind and stable, and he would hold my hand while I decided what was going to happen next. I couldn't leave him. Not like this.

Help me, I thought.

Breathe, I replied.

I breathed. A great, sucking breath that required a mouth to take, and lungs to hold, and so I had both of those things. Pain crashed into me like a wave, and I let it fill me, because pain was better than serenity in this moment: Pain was more important than floating in the hot warm dark until everything ended.

With pain came gravity, and I was suddenly anchored to a body, pinned down to the surface I was lying on. I tried to force my eyes to open, but that was one thing too many; I couldn't make my eyelids do more than twitch.

"I've got a pulse," someone shouted.

Everything was jittering. I was in the back of a truck, I realized: We were driving away from the mall. Where were we going? Who was behind the wheel? Was I heading for safety, or for another disaster?

"Keep her head steady, Nathan, we don't want her jostling around more than she has to."

Nathan. The hands on the side of my face belonged to Nathan. Had I even realized that there were hands on the side of my face? It didn't matter now. I tried again to open my eyes, and this time I succeeded, looking up into the wan, worried face of my boyfriend.

"Sal," he said. The relief in his voice was painful. "You're okay. You're going to be okay. Sherman shot you, but we have some of the best doctors left in the world, and you're going to be *fine.*"

"Juniper? Adam?" I whispered.

"They're okay, too." He bent to kiss me. I closed my eyes again.

We were going to be fine.

STAGE IV: SPECIATION

*The broken doors are closed now; there is
nothing left unknown.
You are my dearest darling ones.
Please don't go out alone.*

—SIMONE KIMBERLEY

*This isn't who I thought I was going to be.
This is someone better.*

—SAL MITCHELL

*I am pleased to confirm that Sherman Lewis, the mastermind
behind the contamination of the western American waterways, has been killed. We were able to take out most of his
terror cell, and the survivors are unlikely to get far. Treatment of the waterways is ongoing.*

*I regret to say that there were more casualties than antici-
pated. Dr. Shanti Cale and her son, Dr. Nathan Kim, were
both killed during the raid on Lewis's headquarters, as was
the transgenic infiltrator that had taken over the body of my
eldest daughter, Sally Mitchell. Sally died long ago. I have
mourned her. Her body died saving the United States of
America, and possibly the human race.*

*I know we will never be able to regard these monstrosities
of science as anything other than the invaders and abomina-
tions that they are. But I hope that someday, when this crisis has faded behind us, we will be able to acknowledge my
daughter as a hero.*

—MESSAGE FROM COLONEL ALFRED MITCHELL, USAMRIID,
TRANSMITTED TO THE WHITE HOUSE ON JANUARY 22, 2028

*Someday, I hope this can be published. I look at it sometimes,
its sprawling scope, half confession and half manifesto, and
think that no, it should be allowed to molder in a drawer*

somewhere. But then I realize that allowing it to go unread would be to give in to my greatest flaw.

I am proud. I am arrogant. I am a manifestation of hubris in this modern world. I have played God. I have remade the world in my own image, because I thought I could do it better. Maybe I was right and maybe I was wrong, but I cannot be allowed to pretend that I didn't do the things I did.

This is your world now. It's not the same as it was when it belonged to me and my kind; it's better in some ways, worse in others. It must be shared, always, between the humans and the chimera. It will not go back to what it was. I did this, and I am sorry, and I have no regrets.

The broken doors are open, children. Now show me what you can do.

—FROM *CAN OF WORMS: THE AUTOBIOGRAPHY OF SHANTI CALE, PHD.* AS YET UNPUBLISHED.

Chapter 20

MAY 2028

Sherman's bullet had been what they called "through and through": It had passed through the skin of my back and through the skin of my stomach, and through a few other things on the way. It had taken Fang and Nathan working together almost two days to stabilize me, while Dr. Cale had taken over monitoring Tansy.

Nathan had never left my side. Not once. Every time I'd woken up, he was there, watching me, waiting for me to get better. Sometimes Adam and Juniper were there too. Neither of them had been seriously hurt in the attack on the old mall. Sometimes the world was fair. Not often, but…

Sometimes.

After two days, I had been stable enough to no longer be considered critical. After three days, I had been sitting up. And after a week, I had been ready to be moved. That was a good thing. A week was all that the Colonel had been able to buy us. He'd lied and he'd called in favors and he'd isolated the part of the facility where I was kept, claiming that it was being cleaned after a biocontamination incident. He had done everything he could, as Sally's father, as a man who regretted the way the world had fallen apart, and when the clock had run out, he'd been the one to cut the power long enough for our ragged little group of survivors to make it to the motor pool, which had been conveniently deserted.

The last time I'd seen him, he'd been standing in the loading bay, wearing his uniform, saluting silently. He'd also been crying. I still wished I had been able to run back, to hug him and tell him I was grateful. Sometimes, there isn't enough time. Even when you have all the time in the world.

The sound of the bedroom door opening pulled me out of my recollections. I rolled over, knocking Beverly's head off my hip, and smiled at the two figures peeking around the doorframe. Juniper was getting taller all the time, and Heina had been showing me how to do her hair. Her braids from the previous day were frayed but still intact. She was wearing one of her handmade jumpers, stitched from fabric scavenged from a Jo-Ann's, and she was smiling, closed-lipped and bright.

Tansy towered over her. Joyce had never been tall, but somehow the way my living sister carried my lost sister's donated body made her seem longer, leaner, made less for study and more for motion. Her hair was several inches long now, coming in thick and brown. She still kept her scalp covered by scarves most of the time, for warmth.

"Mama," said Juniper, and launched herself at the bed. The dogs watched indulgently as the little girl flopped against the mattress and climbed toward me. Nathan stirred, a warm lump under the covers.

"You couldn't distract her for another hour?" I asked, looking at Tansy.

She shrugged and flashed me a sheepish smile, but said nothing.

Tansy was adapting quickly. After five months in Joyce's body, she could walk and feed herself, and had toilet-trained in record time. She *could* talk, just not well, and mostly chose to stay quiet unless she was having a speech therapy lesson. Hopefully that would change as she became more confident with language. Her fine motor control was improving daily. Dr. Cale had been teaching her basic sign language, and that seemed to be helping with her frustration. Anything that got her communicating was important.

She looked more like herself every day, like she was growing secure inside her skin. The day before, I'd found her wallowing in a mud puddle with Juniper, both of them laughing their heads off. She was still Tansy. Another iteration, yes, with so much left to learn but…still Tansy.

"Mama," said Juniper, finally reaching me and flinging her arms around my waist. I stroked her hair with one hand, and poked Nathan with the other.

"Up," I said. "The alarm clock has arrived, and that means it's time for breakfast."

He made a small mumbling noise, but sat up and reached for his glasses. "Is it morning *again*?" he asked.

"Daddy!" squealed Juniper, and switched her attentions to him, allowing me to slide out of the bed and stand.

The scar on my stomach pulled as I stretched. The soft-tissue damage had been bad enough that Fang hadn't been able to repair it all. I would always have that little reminder of Sherman. I was all right with that. Remembering things would keep us from making the same mistakes twice. That was important.

Dr. Banks was still with USAMRIID, more under supervision than as a consultant now. He had managed to land on his feet. He always did. Maybe it would be a few years before he convinced the government that he could be trusted again, but he would. I knew he would. If I had any regrets about the way we'd left things, it was that we'd left him alive. I didn't like to think of myself as a killer, but for Dr. Banks, I would have been happy to make an exception.

At least he'd be busy for a while. Dr. Cale had called Colonel Mitchell from the bowling alley after we had finished collecting our surviving people and the last of our supplies. USAMRIID had the remaining sleepwalkers from the Kmart. It wasn't ideal. We had no way of knowing how many of the sleepwalkers would survive being in human custody. But they would have access to purified water that hadn't been treated in a way that would kill them, and maybe the next generation would have a chance. There was work to be done. We just weren't going to be the ones who did it for a while.

Sherman was dead. I had gone to see his body before I left USAMRIID; I had asked to see his brain. There was no sign of life in the slick, limbless length of him. I had cried. How could I not? He had been my friend and he had been my enemy, and he had been with us from the beginning. It was always appropriate to mourn when someone like that left you.

Tansy handed me my robe. I smiled at her, and walked over to the window, looking out.

When Colonel Mitchell had agreed to look the other way as we "stole" a truck and supplies, we hadn't been sure where we were going: just that we couldn't stay where we were. The world had changed, but not enough to allow humans and chimera to coexist. Not without building a whole new society. We had fled north, clinging to the coast, looking for a place where there were no survivors to ask what we were doing there. We needed to dig in and create our new normal before the humans started coming back.

We had found our safe harbor on a small island in Puget Sound. There were only nine houses there, and all of them had been empty when we arrived. So we had moved in, and begun the process of making ourselves a home where we'd be safe. Fang and Heina were monitoring the recovering Internet; according to them, the President was granting squatter's rights to anyone who'd survived in the areas that had been hit particularly hard. We were going to be able to keep our island, if we could get our roots in deep enough.

And people *had* survived. Sleepwalker outbreaks were still happening—would maybe always be happening—but humanity was difficult to kill. Cities had burned, whole industries had been destroyed, and still the human race went on. Heina and Fishy argued at night about how much recovery was possible, and how long the United States would hold together with its reduced population and decimated centers of commerce, and they both seemed so happy about the problem that I didn't try to stop them. This, too, was part of the recovery.

Nathan rolled out of bed, holding Juniper on his hip, and joined me at the window. "Sleep well?"

"Yes," I said, and craned my neck to kiss his cheek. "You?"

"Mostly."

It was Nathan's turn to have bad dreams, to wake up thrashing in the middle of the night because he was convinced the world was ending. I was doing my best to stand by him and be as good a wife as I could. He had stood by me when I needed him.

Yes, wife. There had been no wedding, no priest from a religion neither of us believed in or representative of a government that didn't currently exist where we were. There had just been Fishy, ducking into an abandoned mall en route to Puget Sound and stealing us an assortment of rings from the only jewelry store that hadn't been looted. There had just been Dr. Cale, saying that science had ordained her.

There had just been us, kissing and making a promise. There had always been us. We just needed to be willing to stop long enough to see it.

"Story?" Juniper pulled on my arm. "Story?"

Most families did bedtime stories. Ours did good-morning stories. Dessert first, in the most practical way possible. "All right," I said, and took her from Nathan, walking back over to the bed. Tansy was already there, sitting on the edge of the mattress with a hopeful look on her face.

I took the book from the bedside table as I sat. The world was putting itself back together. Juniper and I had to avoid all groundwater. We'd decided that it was best if Adam and Tansy do the same; they hadn't been created from my specific genetic strain, but there was still a chance the antiparasitics in the water could hurt them. Dr. Cale was working to find ways to help the sleepwalker population, and to keep the human survivors near us from being endangered, all without revealing her identity to anyone outside our island. Fishy and Fang were rebuilding three boats for us to use, just in case. Everything we did, forever, was going to take "just in case" into account. You can't survive the end of the world and not carry a few scars.

The drums were pounding gently in my ears as I settled Juniper beside me, where she snuggled close. Nathan sat down on my other side.

"You can come in," I said as I opened the cover.

Adam laughed as he ran into the room, and sat down at Nathan's feet, where he could lean over and see the pictures.

This was my family. This was my home.

" 'The two children had been next-door neighbors all their lives…' " I read.

The broken doors were closed.

We had so far left to go.

ACKNOWLEDGMENTS

The broken doors are closed.

Thank you all for coming with me to the end. I don't get to finish a series every day, and it's always emotional for me. Like closing a door that may never open again. I am so honored that you spend your time letting me tell you stories, and now I need to thank a few people.

Michelle Dockrey is my best friend and puts up with basically everything. She is all that is good and right in the world, and the reason I do not view Dr. Cale as a role model. Brooke Abbey and Dr. Wesley Crowell answer my medical questions with a minimum of grimacing, while Diana Fox makes sure that I can keep telling stories without needing to worry about whether or not my audience exists. These are the people I would be lost without.

The Parasitology trilogy was originally acquired as a duology, by DongWon Song, who moved on to other opportunities before the first volume was ready to be edited. *Parasite* was edited by Tom Bowman, who moved on as well (I swear it wasn't my fault) before Will Hinton arrived and saved the day, editing the second and third volumes of the trilogy. Will is awesome, and I am lucky to get to work with him. Lauren Panepinto, who has provided all three covers for this trilogy, has hit it out of the park every time. Really, everyone at Orbit is fantastic, and I adore them.

Great and lasting thanks to Patty Pace, Sarah Kuhn, Amber

Benson, Margaret Dunlap, Dr. Mary Crowell, Nikki Purvis, Amy Mebberson, and everyone who had to share a dinner table with me during my "let's talk enthusiastically about parasitic infections" phase (which isn't actually over). As always, acknowledgment for forbearance goes to Amy McNally, Shawn Connolly, and Cat Valente, who keep me on an even keel; to my agent, Diana Fox, who remains my favorite superhero; to the cats, for not eating me when I got too wrapped up in work to feed them; and to Chris Mangum, the incredible technical mind behind www.MiraGrant.com. This book might have been written without them. It would not have been the same.

If you're curious about parasites, check out your local library. There's a lot to learn, and some of it will really amaze you. And disgust you. And make it hard to sleep at night.

Once more, from the bottom of my heart, thank you. All of you. Thank you for reading, for being here, and for following me when I asked you to come into the dark. When I said you could trust me. You did, and that means the world.

See you soon.

The broken doors are closed now; there is nothing left unknown.

You are my dearest darling ones. Please don't go out alone.

ABOUT THE AUTHOR

Born and raised in California, Mira Grant has made a lifelong study of horror movies, horrible viruses, and the inevitable threat of the living dead. In college, she was voted Most Likely to Summon Something Horrible in the Cornfield, and was a founding member of the Horror Movie Sleep-away Survival Camp, where her record for time survived in the Swamp Cannibals scenario remains unchallenged.

Mira lives in a crumbling farmhouse with an assortment of cats, horror movies, comics, and books about horrible diseases. When not writing, she splits her time between travel, auditing college virology courses, and watching more horror movies than is strictly good for you. Favorite vacation spots include Seattle, London, and a large haunted corn maze just outside of Huntsville, Alabama.

Mira sleeps with a machete under her bed, and highly suggests that you do the same. Find out more about the author at www.miragrant.com.

Find out more about Mira Grant and other Orbit authors by registering for the free monthly newsletter at www.orbitbooks.net.

SYMBIONT

By Mira Grant

The Newsflesh Trilogy
Feed
Deadline
Blackout

Countdown (e-only novella)
San Diego 2014: The Last Stand of the California Bureaucrats
(e-only novella)
How Green This Land; How Blue This Sea (e-only novella)
The Day the Dead Came to Show and Tell (e-only novella)

Parasitology
Parasite
Symbiont

SYMBIONT

PARASITOLOGY VOLUME 2

MIRA GRANT

www.orbitbooks.net

ORBIT

First published in Great Britain in 2014 by Orbit

Copyright © 2014 by Seanan McGuire

The moral right of the author has been asserted.

A CIP catalogue record for this book
is available from the British Library.

ISBN 978-0-356-50193-2

Printed and bound by CPI Group (UK) Ltd, Croydon, CR0 4YY

Papers used by Orbit are from well-managed forests
and other responsible sources.

MIX
Paper from
responsible sources
FSC® C104740

Orbit
An imprint of
Little, Brown Book Group
100 Victoria Embankment
London EC4Y 0DY

An Hachette UK Company
www.hachette.co.uk

www.orbitbooks.net

*This book is dedicated to Aislinn Suzanne Ellis,
who had the excellent sense to be born
while it was being written.*

Welcome to the world, my dearest skeleton girl.